Sharon,
The threat
is real. Enjoy
The read. Scary

HARM'S
WAY

GARY COCHRAN

HARM'S WAY

a CPID
book

Published by CPID Books

      3686 N. Littlerock Ter
      Provo, UT 84604
Web   http://www.galaxymall.com/stores/harm.html
e-mail cpidbook@itsnet.com

First Printing, January, 1997
10   9   8   7   6   5   4   3   2   1

Library of Congress Cataloging-in-publication Data
Cochran, Gary G.
    Harm's Way / Gary Cochran
    p.   cm.
    ISBN 0-9655609-0-2

Printed in the United States of America
Designed by Cochran Studios

Publishers Note
This is a work of fiction. Names, characters, places and incidents either are the products
of the author;s imagination or are used fictitiously, and any resemblance to actual persons, living or dead, events, or locales is entirely coincidental.

This book is printed on acid-free paper. ∞

For Sue Ann,
my wife of over 28 years.
You've always provided an outlet
to live my dreams.

PROLOGUE

The slight movement of the evening breeze accented the sudden tone change ringing out from the dark green metal casing. Silence. He hadn't mistaken the sound of the Stinger missile locking on the unsuspecting heat source almost a mile above the earth. Shaking his dark shoulder length hair, heightening his level of concentration, the dark complected man let his hand begin the backward movement. Slowly, his mind almost in a trance, his fingers tightened on the cold metal, allowing the trigger mechanism to release the surface-to-air missile. The deadly heat-seeking projectile blasted free from the three sided hunting shack, blowing out the back of the dilapidated old building. It continued to rush upwards into the night air at more than one thousand feet per second. Lighting a match to check the time, he failed to smile as he noted the hour, 9:53 p.m.

1

FRIDAY NIGHT

Carson Jeffers pushed the smoke-gray sunglasses farther up the bridge of his sun-tanned nose as he glanced at the green and white sign advising him, "Rental Cars Keep Left." Ignoring the blaring horn of the muddy cream colored ford pick-up he abruptly cut off as he moved to the far left lane, he absentmindedly ran his strong right hand through his sandy hair. Regardless of how refreshing the April evening breeze felt, Carson frowned and continued to replay the events of the past few hours.

Neither father or son acknowledged the other's presence in the green four wheel drive Toyota Land Cruiser as they passed by the turn-in to both National and Hertz. Pushing the black collar of his blue goretex ski parka back over his blond hair, Carson started to say something to his sixteen-year old son as they moved farther into the parking structure across from the terminal. Kelly promptly turned away, glaring out the shaded window cutting off Carson's attempt to communicate with his son. Carson's facial features hardened as he bit his lower lip in disappointment at Kelly's overt rejection.

Carson observed the double row of cars lined up in front of the empty check-in booth admitting there was no winning mind games played with a teenaged son. Kelly's fingers drummed up and down the arm rest of the vehicle as his young mind raced back and forth over the sudden change of plans forced upon them during the past few hours. A hurried look toward the young boy revealed his inability to change the strained relationship with Kelly. Frustrated and disappointed over his inadequacy as both a sounding-board and a father, Carson turned his thoughts to his Portland based business.

He was the forty-four year old Chairman of the Board, Chief Executive Officer, and single shareholder of the privately owned multi-national company, ManTech, Inc. It was openly regarded in business circles as the "solution source" for import-export questions. Once the problem could be identified, ManTech went to work quantifying a rational approach to turning a business problem into an economic opportunity. Trying to recall his earlier conversation with Michael Randall at the headquarters of the business consulting firm, he failed to notice Kelly's fixation on the rows of Omega aircraft silently guarding the gates of the Salt Lake Terminal.

Three long years had passed since Lynda Jeffers had left Carson a widower and last looked into Kelly's deep blue eyes. If she were alive today she would certainly marvel at the added foot in height her son added to his slight, but wiry frame. Kelly's eyes remained glued to the waiting aircraft, a silent admission that neither male understood how to broach the topic of the death of a caring mother or a loving wife. Turning off the ignition, Carson grabbed a pen from the inside pocket of his parka while scanning the mileage shown on the odometer as well as the fuel level. He marked the information down on the orange and black envelope that held the Budget rental contract. Hastily he added both the return time and date to the appropriate boxes and slid the completed document into his front coat pocket. "Grab your bags and I'll meet you at the entrance to Omega's terminal," Carson murmured to his silent and brooding son. He knew full-well the young man was upset about going home.

"OK," Kelly answered flatly without looking directly at his father.

"Don't forget to get your ski boots out of the back." Carson didn't wait for an answer, but used the remote to pop open the rear entry of the sport utility vehicle.

"I won't. What do you think I am, an idiot?" blurted the 5 foot 9 inch high school sophomore, his voice clearly indicating his state of mind.

Carson's blood pressure took a momentary jump as he stopped to answer with "No comment!" but instead changed his mind, said nothing, and headed for the Budget rental counter and its express check-in box underneath short term parking. Quickly jamming the express folder in the empty mail slot, he threw his black leather garment bag over his shoulder and hurried to catch up with the frustrated and unhappy dark haired youth.

Carson reflected on Kelly's short temper, recognizing that his futile attempt to bridge the chasm between them during the past week had failed. It was as if Kelly had consciously slammed a heavy metal door between them in an effort to keep his father out of his painful world. "Let's try again. What do you say?" Carson asked as they passed by the hanging monitors that were continually flashing gate numbers and updated departure times.

Kelly slowed his determined gate, while taking a deep silent breath. No longer was he marching cadence like a decisive military cadet. "What do you mean?"

"Deer Valley didn't turn out like either of us had planned." Carson hoped that Kelly noticed the use of the words *either of us*. He reached out to touch his son on the shoulder, a natural hand gesture from a concerned parent. Kelly effectively blocked the move by transferring his red nylon knapsack from his left shoulder to his right. "This week was supposed to have been a vacation for you from school and for me from work, and I thought you would enjoy just getting away for the last week of spring skiing at Park City," he continued while unconsciously ignoring the disappointing body language.

"You mean, getting away from my friends, don't you?" interrupted his son.

Raising his voice an octave, Carson resolutely retorted, "You may think those boys are your friends, Kelly, but I can assure you such is not the case! They are using you and as long as they know you'll chip in and support their habits, they'll keep coming around. But, I promise you, the moment you finally come to your senses, they will split so fast, it'll make the hair on the back of your neck stand up!"

Kelly stopped and glared defiantly at his father. "You don't have to yell," he muttered under his breath.

Carson lowered his voice as he slowed his walk. No doubt everyone in the baggage claim area to his left could hear his lecture. Two young girls, each holding one of their mother's hands, started walking again. When Carson had started his tirade, the young mother had been forced to stop and listen or to rush around him. She had chosen to wait and listen.

As the father-son duo reached the moving metal steps of the escalator rising to the second level of the terminal, Kelly stepped closer to his dad. He wanted to tap his father on the back and admit that he knew his warning was correct, but he just couldn't. Instead, he lowered his head and kept quiet. Deep down in his gut, he had known for some time that neither Brad nor Terry were the friends they vocally claimed to be. Kelly knew that Carson thought he was using drugs, and, yes, he had tried them, but he was satisfied with the temporary oblivion he got from a six pack or two of beer.

When Carson and Kelly first arrived at the condo in Deer Valley on Monday, Kelly had been sure that Carson had planned on having some business clients meet up with them. After all, the ski chalet had six massive bedroom suites, each with its own rock fireplace and sitting area, and it was entirely owned by ManTech, Inc. Carson had quickly assured his son that such fears were misplaced and the week was to be just for the two of them. Kelly had acted like it was not a big deal either way, but he was pleased there was no one else sharing his dad's time. Despite their frequent disagreements, Kelly had enjoyed the long sunny days he spent with his dad on the expertly groomed slopes. Weather was perfect, spring snow conditions couldn't have been better, and even this afternoon the higher runs had been extremely fast and smooth. All week long Kelly had thought they weren't going home until Sunday.

During a late lunch Carson received a phone call in the midmountain Stein Erikson lodge. Michael Randall, Carson's closest friend, right hand man, and President of ManTech, Inc. paged Carson alerting him of the Portland problem. Suddenly the ski trip was cut short by two days, and there was absolutely nothing Kelly could do about it. "Nothing's changed after all," the boy thought to himself. "If only Dad would put me before his work," he silently mouthed to the world as both he and

Carson stepped off the escalator and headed for the security check point directly in front of the C concourse.

Carson retrieved his keys and the metal coins from the plastic tray the uniformed security guard held out to him. Grabbing his leather carry-on, he turned right and headed for the gift shop. "I'll just be a minute. I'm going to get a newspaper." After passing the book rack with the latest suspense thrillers he knelt down and found the stack of *USA Today* newspapers stuffed under the shelf on the opposite side of the back register. It just didn't seem like the two of them could reach a common understanding. Carson desperately wanted to bring Kelly into his world, but it never seemed to happen the way he planned. He sensed Kelly's disappointment when they left Park City two days early, but then Michael wouldn't have called unless the contract negotiations between First Pacific Net and Western Regional Manufacturing were hopelessly deadlocked. A Saturday conference session focused on a comprehensive Internet joint venture agreement in Australia appeared to be the only answer. Michael believed that Carson could calm the friction between the two global trading partners. He had to go back. Kelly should understand!

Still silent, Kelly fell in beside his father as they got on the moving sidewalk leading from the C to the D concourse. Despite his failure to tell Carson in so many words, Kelly really did love him. The sixteen-year old outwardly still blamed his father for the deadly illness that had abruptly ended his mother's life. Kelly knew that Carson couldn't have prevented Lynda's cancer from spreading, but he needed to blame someone, and Carson was all he had.

After exiting the flexible jetway leading from gate D-8 to the wide bodied jet, Carson and Kelly waited while the other first class passengers made their way on to the plane. As they boarded the massive jet, a flight attendant smiled at both the young boy and his silent father. Nichole Lewis asked, "Can I help you two find your seats?"

"Thanks, but we're all right," Carson responded while simultaneously showing the attractive dark-haired attendant the two boarding passes.

"Seats 4E and F." Nichole pointed to the same seats on the far side of the plane that Carson had suggested with his earlier head gesture. She had no doubt that this rugged man had flown many times. Not waiting for someone to hang his coat in a closet, Nichole watched him take off his parka and place it in the overhead bin. There wasn't even a trace of a smile to lighten his facial expression. Something heavy was on his mind.

Julie Richards continued ushering the incoming passengers onto the L-1011 aircraft, while at the same time noticing Nichole as she visually followed the sandy haired man to his seat on the isle. Julie lightly touched Nichole, the senior flight attendant, on the shoulder and smiled. Julie had been trying to get Nichole to get out and meet someone, even going so far as to set her up with three separate pilots, but it was a losing battle. It wasn't that Nichole wasn't attractive, because she was. The truth was that Nichole Lewis was just not interested in starting another relationship.

Still wondering what was bothering the man in 4E seated next to the dark haired teenager, Nichole smoothly pivoted towards the other passengers entering the plane from the accordion-style gateway. Turning to the first class section of the plane to indicate where an older couple could find their seats, she noticed that the teenaged boy had finally taken his seat by the window, 4F. Pushing her short auburn hair back across her forehead with her right arm, Nichole just knew that the good-looking sandy haired man in 4E had to be married.

It had been over a year since her divorce from Raymond Lewis. Ray was an electrical engineer working for Boeing in Seattle. From the beginning they had both thought they could make the marriage work, even with her constant traveling. Unfortunately, they were both wrong, the traveling had driven them apart. Julie had once told Nichole that absence makes the heart grow fonder. She had been right, fonder of someone else! Nichole really didn't blame Ray. They had both tried, but she was never home long enough to keep the sparks lit, let alone the flames burning in the fireplace.

Ray had fallen in love with Nichole for her strong and independent personality, and the fact that she was five foot seven, one hundred twenty pounds, and prided herself on keeping fit, had only made him that much more interested. The problem had always boiled down to her work. She was just gone too much. Twelve months ago they had formally dissolved the marriage, for once, thankful there had been no children. Quitting her job at Omega might have been an option earlier on, but the marriage had disintegrated too far for that now. Nichole still loved her job, and after twelve years she didn't want to start all over again, especially at age thirty-four.

The bell on the intercom system sounded and Nichole knew they were about ready to push back. Omega Flight 421 to Portland, Oregon with continued service to Seattle and Anchorage was ready for departure.

• • •

Moving his dark hair away from his eyes, the Latin effortlessly adjusted the binoculars, easily identifying the Omega flight as it pulled back from D-8. The hunting shack was dark and damp, but the location some three and one-half miles from the busy terminal gearing up for the future Olympic traffic was perfect. Placing the strong German-made field glasses on the narrow ledge normally used by hunters with shotguns, the athletically built Peruvian casually shook his shoulder length hair from side to side. Using the hand held radio he listened intently to the air traffic controller on ground frequency twenty-one point nine. One by one the planes were handed off from Ground to Departure Control. Suddenly, Omega Flight 421 was told to switch to thirty-five point five.

Holding the small black radio receiver in his left hand, Esteban Moreno contemplated that certain fireball and massive destruction that was about to fall from the skies northwest of the Omega Airlines terminal hub. When the decision to launch the missile had first been made, Esteban was adamant in his choice of Salt Lake with the small hunting shacks hidden in the marshlands near the airport. Dirt roads ran in all directions connecting the tiny huts, and if not familiar with the partially soggy terrain, Esteban knew that it would be impossible to maneuver through the near frozen swamp land.

From the operation's beginning, Esteban had planned three separate escape routes leading away from the small dark weathered shanty where it would all begin. He was confident that he would only need the one exit route, but he had found over the past forty-three years of his life that there is always safety in numbers. Peering out into the darkness, Esteban knew that tonight would be no different!

Esteban kneeled down and removed the thirty-five pound Stinger missile from the make-shift carrying case that appeared to be nothing more than a container used to transport shovels, rakes and other landscaping tools in the back of a standard pickup truck. In reality that is exactly how the missile had been hidden in the shack earlier that day. Methodically he lifted the weapon of destruction and balanced it on the ledge with the European binoculars, remembering how he had become associated with *La Libertad Occidental.*

He had grown up in a wealthy suburb in Lima called Mira Las Flores. His family was one of the so-called *forty families*, who together had once controlled more than 90 percent of both the prime real estate and the corresponding wealth of Peru. Esteban's features were light, almost more European than Latin. He received a classical education at the finest schools in Europe and the United States. He spoke both Spanish and English like a native, was fluent in German, French, and Italian, and as a boy had developed an appreciation of classical literature. Being an international businessman and renowned big game hunter, Esteban's father was almost never home. Accompanying his father into the field provided Esteban with his first exposure to weapons that kill. A bright boy, it didn't take him long to realize that few people in his South American country shared the luxury he and his family enjoyed. It was so unfair that so many people starved when his family had such an abundance. His father shrugged off his son's concerns, thinking he would outgrow his youthful foolishness. But Esteban Moreno became resentful, which later turned into a calloused indifference for life.

When the *LLO,* as *La Libertad Occidental* was known in the American media, began to grow and spout forth an emotionally charged leftist political dogma, it was only natural that the twenty-five year old student would find a home, a secret retreat he had steadfastly maintained for the past eighteen years.

The miniature radio crackled sharply as the unseen controller continued to bark instructions into the silent darkness. Effortlessly, the well muscled Latin changed frequencies on the portable black and silver receiver, quickly following the Omega Flight's switch from Ground to Departure Control. Not permitting a hidden smile to appear on his chiseled features, he put the missile he had stolen from the Marine Corps Air Station at El Toro, California on the shoulder of his faded blue Utah Jazz sweatshirt. "It won't be long now," he told himself.

• • •

Captain Tom Nickle adjusted the left seat restraint with his right hand, while fishing for a laminated departure chart from the black leather flight bag positioned between the two pilots of the L-1011. Phil Bradford, First Officer on the Omega Airlines jet, nodded acknowledgement of Tom's last instruction, and used the in-flight public address system to ask the flight attendants to make final preparations for take-off and cross-check. The L-1011 didn't have the safety record of the newer 747, but Omega elected to pick up a number of the cumbersome wide bodied aircraft when Eastern Airlines had gone out of business. Financially, the move had been a wise business decision for the international airlines as the L-1011 was really nothing more than an updated DC-10, but Tom Nickle and Phil Bradford would both have much rather been flying the 747.

9:44 P.M.

"You've got it, Phil," Tom announced over the intercom while continuing to move his fingers methodically down the printed taxi checklist.

"Check," responded Phil. He glanced out the windshield of the aging aircraft and noted that the sky was clear, almost assured of a smooth take-off.

The two uniformed Omega pilots continued their individual duties completely confident of each other's actions. Jason Newell, a three year veteran with Omega, served as the flight engineer and sat behind Tom and Phil as they orchestrated the departure from Salt Lake International Airport. He thought to himself that Tom and Phil's continued efforts to bid the same routes and fly together for several years paid safety dividends for all concerned. Working together like smooth bearings on a well-oiled machine, the two experienced pilots left nothing to chance, knowing full-well that it takes a complete flight crew to put several hundred thousand pounds of metal in the air and keep it there. Checking his flight information, Jason relaxed as the powerful ground tug pushed Omega Flight 421 back from the gate to start the first leg of their flight to Portland, with continued service to Seattle and Anchorage, Alaska.

Tom acknowledged Ground Control on the headset, switched the radio to frequency 35.5 and reported in to Departure Control. The clearance was standard. Flight 421 was to climb and maintain 8,000, turn to heading 280 at the marker and then turn northbound along the shore of the Great Salt Lake.

• • •

Carson pressed the button on the left side of his arm rest, raising the seat to an upright position, and handed Kelly the sports section of *USA Today*. The young man took the red and white section of the paper and lit the overhead light above his seat as he opened the section to page 3. Kelly had watched *Sportsnight* on ESPN during the week as the announcers tried to guess which players would get taken in the upcoming NFL draft. Kelly checked to see if there was any new information as to who would draft the number one quarterback in the nation from Washington State. As a sophomore at Portland High, Kelly had tried out for the junior varsity team, but failed to make the final cut. Carson wanted the boy to try out for the team again next year, there was no doubt as to his athletic ability. With his latest growth spurt, all he lacked was the determination to stick to a task, and lately that determination hadn't been demonstrated to the frustrated father.

As the plane taxied south toward Runway 34, Kelly folded the paper in half and started to read the update on the San Francisco Forty Niners' coaching change . This late at night there was only one other plane waiting for clearance to take off.

• • •

9:48 P.M.

Both pilots and the flight engineer heard the simple instruction on the radio. "421 Heavy switch to tower on nineteen point five."

Tom keyed the mike. "421 Heavy going to nineteen point five."

As the L-1011 continued taxiing to Runway 34, Captain Tom Nickle and crew heard the air traffic controller announce, "Position and hold."

9:50 P.M.

Salt Lake Tower cleared Flight 421 for immediate departure. Phil Bradford used his left hand to push the power forward as Captain Tom Nickle started to read off the V speeds. Even after 24 years in the cockpit, Tom still loved the thrill of instant acceleration. Take-off was an immense high, almost an instant injection of adrenaline, and a complete focusing of physical movement with the management of an enormous amount of raw power.

• • •

Carson put the green and white *Money* section of his *USA Today* in the vinyl pouch on the back of seat 3E and starred thoughtfully out the window of the aircraft, totally aware of the physics of flight. The evening was clear and the Salt Lake City lights seemed to flicker like fireflies as the plane darted down the runway. He felt a supercharged sensation as the aluminum tube seemingly defied the laws of earth's gravity and rose majestically into the sky, and almost immediately he experienced the same *rush* he felt from his first flight in the Air Force. His stomach seemed to separate from his body as the huge wide bodied L-1011 lifted off from Salt Lake International Airport. Carson glanced down at his son, and saw that Kelly was still engrossed in reading about the approaching NFL draft. Every few seconds the boy would look up from the paper and peer out the window.

• • •

9:51 P.M.

Esteban smoothed the fabric of his sweatshirt under the missile and went through a mental check list, insuring he had left nothing to chance. Turning up the volume on the portable radio receiver, he heard the command from Salt Lake Tower. Omega Flight 421 was rolling on Runway 34.

• • •

9:52 P.M.

As *Pilot in Command,* Phil continued the pressure on the yoke until the L-1011 passed through 7,800. First Officer Phil Bradford watched the altimeter settle evenly at 8,000 feet as he trimmed up the plane and turned left to the heading of 280 degrees. Across the cockpit Captain Tom Nickle alerted Salt Lake Control as to the aircraft's new heading, while simultaneously scanning the instruments from left to right. The secret of being an excellent pilot is to do the same thing the same way, time after time, and both Tom Nickle and Phil Bradford were excellent pilots.

Each of the 274 passengers felt the plane bank and then turn north along the shore of the Great Salt Lake. The group of Japanese tourists looked out the window, trying to capture the lights of the disappearing city with their 35 millimeter cameras.

• • •

The slight movement of the evening breeze accented the sudden tone change ringing out from the dark green metal casing. Silence. He hadn't mistaken the sound of the Stinger missile locking on the unsuspecting heat source almost a mile above the earth. Shaking his dark shoulder length hair, heightening his level of concentration, the dark complected man let his hand begin the backward movement. Slowly, his mind almost in a trance, his fingers tightened on the cold metal, allowing the trigger mechanism to release the surface-to-air missile. The deadly heat-seeking projectile blasted free from the three sided hunting shack, blowing out the back of the dilapidated old building. It continued to rush upwards into the night air at more than one thousand feet per second. Lighting a match to check the time, he failed to smile as he noted the hour, 9:53 p.m.

Esteban dropped the expended missile housing callously to the ground and patted his cotton gloves together, to keep the circulation moving in his fingers, not as any indication of remorse. Not hesitating to see what he had initiated, he rested his weight on his left foot, while at the same time pushing down with his right. The Kawasaki dirt bike roared to life and Esteban spun the bike out of the shed, brushing the expended missile as he escaped the partially demolished wooden structure. He wasn't concerned about the authorities finding what was left of the Stinger missile, after all, they had been warned. Fifteen seconds later Esteban Moreno made his second turn to the southeast and was headed towards the highway, away from the flash in the sky!

• • •

Tom and Phil both felt the plane buck as they saw warning lights blink and emergency buzzers sounding in the cockpit. Not recognizing the explosion in the rear of the aircraft for what it was, they both believed they had lost the number three engine over the tail. Phil fought the controls of the plane as Tom started to shut down what was left of engine number three and turned the transponder to 7700. Flight 421 was squawking an in-flight emergency.

Tom reacted immediately and knew that whatever was happening was worse than anything he had been exposed to in the simulator on his recent semiannual check ride. Phil seemed to be fighting a losing battle and was having no luck in getting the yoke back. Omega Flight 421 started to fall out of the sky. "I've got it!" yelled Tom across the noisy cockpit. Authoritatively he gave instructions to Phil and Jason. Already the airspeed and altitude were decaying, and the stick shaker and bank angle warnings were frequent. Tom continued to fight the controls as Phil finished securing what was left of the tail engine and locked down the leading edge flaps. Jason got Salt Lake Control on the radio and declared the emergency. Miraculously Tom managed to get some kind of control over the plane, but it still continued its deadly sink. The vibration emanating from the huge jet was deafening. "Full power!" screamed Tom, even though he had the controls. Something was wrong, seriously wrong!

The back of the plane was in total bedlam as the plane continued to buck and lurch as it thundered towards the ground. As soon as the plane had started loosing altitude, Jason sounded four bells over the PA system, using the signal for an in-flight emergency. There wasn't time for personal communication with the remaining flight crew as Jason immediately began his hurried conversation with Salt Lake Control. Nichole Lewis and the other members of her flight crew were on their own as Flight 421 struggled to make an emergency landing.

Screams and crying shrieked above the storm erupting from the back of the plane. Nichole used the intercom and tried to talk to the crew in the back, but had no luck. Even as the massive mass of metal lurched downwards, Nichole tried to insure that everyone was still fastened in. Fortunately, the seat belt warning light had still been lit when she heard, what later would be found to be the engine exploding from the rear of the plane. Cabin pressure was dropping, and the gale of wind rushing through the plane gave further evidence to Nichole of the crisis that Tom, Phil, and Jason were combating. Just before she fastened herself into the jump seat she made one last check to make sure all the passengers in the first class cabin were in the ready position. She noted that the sandy-haired man in seat 4E had his arm around his son, holding him tightly. The boy was sobbing and shaking uncontrollably as the plane continued to plummet downward. There was nothing else Nichole could do. She pulled the straps tightly over her shoulders and leaned forward to clutch her knees.. Never one to pray vocally, Nichole ignored the sounds of insanity and pleaded silently that Tom could gain control over the disaster.

●   ●   ●

"Oh God!" Tom screamed to no one in general and to the Almighty in particular. "I can't get the nose up. Phil, we've lost the elevators and most of the rudder control."

"Number two is gone too," answered Phil as he shut down all remaining electrical systems and the fuel lines running to both number two and number three engines. "Tom, get the nose up! The runway is almost dead ahead."

"Hell, I'm trying!" Tom cut in as he manhandled the yoke back even further. "Are they ready on the ground?"

"Emergency vehicles rolling," Jason responded as confidently as he could.

"Get the gear down! Now!" Tom ordered. Still in emergency power, Tom had delayed gear extension until 300 feet AGL (above ground level). He was hoping with ground effect they could get some control over the violent vertical movement. "Unless we can get some attitude control, we're never going to make the blacktop. This baby is not centering on the line." Continuing to issue instructions, Tom finished, "We better hope the crew has the passengers prepared for a hard landing. We might be setting down on the frozen marshlands just north of the runway!"

Jason was already announcing to Salt Lake Tower that Flight 421 might not make the runway. None of the three crew members questioned what they could have done better. Hopefully, that would come later. Right now, each of the three men prioritized their tasks with the remaining time, fully aware that some procedures were being disregarded.

"It's over, set your......" Captain Tom Nickle never finished giving the instructions to set the landing flaps. A few more seconds and they might have made it. The nose had started to come up, and even though they were way right of center, they were at least partially lined up on the runway.

Omega Flight 421 slammed into the ground a quarter mile short of the end of Runway 34. The nose gear shattered immediately, making steering virtually non-existent. The rudder was barely working before 421 hit the ground, and when the nose gear collapsed, the left wing crashed into mother earth. Seconds later, the massive L-1011 began to cartwheel towards the fast approaching strip of concrete. Most observers stated that it seemed like the whole thing took place in slow motion. On the first cartwheel the flight deck was crushed to half its original size, killing all three flight officers. The plane continued to turn end over end as it broke into sections. What was once a beautiful winged creature now appeared to be individual metal boxes, each one attempting to fly independently. The passengers directly above the wings never had a chance. Massive fuel tanks exploded in the wings, engulfing the screaming passengers in bright yellow fireballs as the wreckage careened off the left side of the runway.

2

The screeching sound of the bending and twisting air frame was deafening! The rapidly slowing jumbo jet, what remained of its first class cabin, gauged a three foot deep valley across the 150 foot wide strip of burning concrete. It then twisted upside down one final time as it slid off the molten runway into a high stand of near dead weeds. A Salt Lake County emergency vehicle was parked directly in its path. Two officers in their late twenties, both female, leaped out from beneath the flashing red and blue lights just as the moving mass of metal from the L-1011 folded over their white pick-up. Fire was burning everywhere, and the small reserve gas tank that the maintenance shed maintained in the back of the county truck exploded violently on impact. Three hours later two charred bodies were found 250 feet from where the aluminum and steel coffin had come to rest.

Carson fought to clear his head and maintain consciousness. Coughing from the build-up of deadly smoke, peering into the darkness he quickly realized that he was still strapped upside down in his seat. Blood rushed towards his head. He was oblivious to the deep gash on his right leg and the burned hair on both arms. He came close to blacking out from the unnatural position of his body. Foul and wretched smoke continued to fill the metal cavern. The severe darkness inside the crushed metal container proved a stark contrast to the noon-day light created outside the plane by the numerous fires burning on the runway. Carson struggled to find the release handle on his seat belt, but was jolted upwards as the forward section of Flight 421 rocked violently.

Another severe air blast from an explosion farther down the runway propelled the first class wreckage another 30 yards, off the now bloody strip of concrete.

Carson jerked his head to the right where Kelly should have been buckled in the adjoining seat. Broken glass and metal were scattered everywhere. Billowing black noxious smoke poured through the jagged hole in the metal fuselage, and for the second time in seconds the plane lurched forward. It continued to dig a grave into the partially frozen ground. Fearing another explosion and the accompanying fire, Carson was approaching a near panic!

"Kelly, Kelly!" Carson's screaming was the only human sound resonating through the darkened carnage. He suddenly found the safety release of the belt that continued to dig harshly into his stomach and ribs. He took the long drop to the ceiling, now the floor of the cabin. His fall was partially blocked by the limp, but lifeless body of Julie Richards. Her head was twisted almost 180 degrees backward and her flight attendant's uniform was almost completely gone, as if torn loose by a giant rushing tornado. Ignoring the obvious death around him, Carson rolled onto his left side and shoulder, yelling his son's name, and searching for his now non-existent presence. "Kelly, answer me!"

Muffled screams emerged upwards from a row of four seats that had come loose from the floor and landed upside down. Carson stumbled over the dead and scrambled forward, all the time exploring the source of the whimpers that were coming from under the seats. Rapidly he heaved the pillows, blankets, and carry-on garment bags over his shoulder into the blackness. "Kelly, are you there?" He stopped momentarily to listen for the faint voice.

Bending forward under the darkened floor, recently turned ceiling, he coughed and gagged on the ever thickening smoke as he grabbed hold of a broken arm rest. Using strength he had no idea he possessed, he lifted the complete row of seats, turning them upright. All three passengers who had been sitting in the bulkhead row of the main cabin were dead. Blood was everywhere and he almost vomited as he stared at what he had uncovered. The top section of the seats had been sheared off by some piece of flying metal. All that was left of the young family were headless torsos still strapped to their seats.

Once again, Carson heard the muted voice coming from underneath the duffel type satchels that must have belonged to an athletic team. He could barely make out the white "U" on the red bags that were still pinned to the bottom of the wreckage by a corner of the bloody seats.

"Help me!"

He heard it again. The voice was getting stronger. "Maybe it was just louder," he thought as he continued to throw the red and white carry-on's into the darkness. Biting the bile in his throat in disappointment, he finished removing the baggage from the struggling body. The flight attendant who had taken his boarding pass, and then showed he and Kelly to their seats, looked up at him from the floor. Carson reached under her shoulder to pick her up, but she determinedly grabbed his arm and struggled to her feet.

"Are you all right?" Carson asked as she gained her balance in the smoke congested cabin.

"Alive," Quickly resuming control of her senses she coughed and stated, "You've got to get out of here right now. A fire can start any minute!"

Carson was no novice to the danger of a fire in a plane crash. When he had first arrived in Vietnam in the mid seventies, he had seen first-hand what happens when an aircraft explodes and burns. North Vietnamese rockets hit the Da Nang airfield just after he landed his F-4 Phantom jet. He was still taxiing beside the active runway when the large cumbersome cargo plane ahead of him buckled and started to burn. Three of the flight crew escaped from the inferno through the small windows on the flight deck. Explosions had rocked the rear of the C-130, sealing shut the rear ramp of the plane. The hot air was impaled from the rear of the plane to the front and caught the men as they were still exiting the wreckage. Overly heated air seared the delicate lung tissue of their bodies, and all three servicemen had walked away from the fire only to die shortly thereafter in the Da Nang Hospital.

Carson shook his head from side to side, acknowledging the concerned flight attendant's warning. However, there was no way he was going to leave the plane without his son. "I've got to find my boy! He was sitting right beside me," he stated in a determined voice.

Nichole Lewis looked into Carson's pleading eyes and knew that he wasn't going to exit the wreckage until he found his son, or was at least convinced that he wasn't inside. She pulled his arm forward and motioned to another section of seats. "Let's look over there!" They continued to move backwards into what was left of the plane. Baggage and bodies were strewn everywhere. Nichole stopped to check for the living among the passengers, both those who had come loose from their safety belts and were laying in the aisle, as well as those still buckled to the wreckage. Each time, she felt for a pulse and moved on. "No life anywhere," she thought. "What had gone wrong?"

Carson stopped to pick up a young child who couldn't have been more than five or six years old. She was still alive and secured to a seat. He hurriedly checked to see if the man and woman next to the little girl were still breathing. They weren't. Gently, he lifted the whimpering, but still conscious child in his arms. He bent down and futilely tried to get a breath of cleaner air. Eyes watering, he passionately started towards the opening in the plane where the cabin door should have been. A fireman breathing compressed air and dressed in yellow protective gear emerged through the smoke and took the child from his arms. He motioned for Carson to follow him.

"I've got to find my son!" Carson screamed at the retreating fireman. The man never heard a word he said. Carson lunged back into the smoke-filled metal cavern, moving past the flight attendant who was now showing another fireman where to search. Stumbling forward, he knew that he wasn't going to be able to continue breathing the wretched air much longer. Smoke and fire had virtually consumed the oxygen, foam was now being sprayed on the wreckage from fire trucks positioned all over the runway. Bending down, almost crawling along the floor, Carson tried unsuccessfully to catch his breath. Arriving at a mass of metal and plastic divider walls, he paused momentarily and then started crawling even faster. Carson recognized the bright burgundy and green parka Kelly was wearing as they boarded the plane less than twenty minutes earlier. Ignoring the smoke, he wiped the tears from his eyes

as images flashed through his now-numbed mind. Carson had purchased
the coat as a gift for Kelly from Cole Sports on Main Street in Park City.

He knelt beside the body squeezed into what had once been a lavatory. Carson already knew it wasn't going to do any good, but he had to
get Kelly off the plane. The folding twenty-four inch door had crumpled
like an accordion. Carson kept hoping that his son was alive, while
simultaneously praying that death had been instantaneous. The prayer
must have been answered. When the plane collapsed at impact, the steel
bolts holding Kelly's safety belt to the seat had been sheared off as
quickly as a hot knife slices through butter. Kelly lost consciousness
when his head slammed into the ceiling. By the time he had fallen into
the small bathroom he was already slipping into the afterlife. The blunt
trauma to the head had spared Kelly all pain. Less than two seconds after
Kelly shot out of the seat beside his father, the door to the cubicle collapsed, stopping the young football player from flying out of the plane as
it continued its deadly tumble down the airstrip.

Fortified by a sudden rush of adrenaline, Carson wedged his hands
behind the plastic door and ripped it from its hinges. Kneeling on the
floor of the L-1011 he pulled Kelly to his chest and began to sob. First it
had been Lynda, and now God took his only son. "It isn't fair!" Carson
screamed to the heavens blanketing the Salt Lake Airport.

Nichole took a breath of compressed air from the man dressed in
yellow rubber gear. "Help him, I 'm all right," she said quietly to the two
Salt Lake Firemen who were attempting to guide her out of the plane.
She looked down at the lonely man who was kneeling on the floor.
Releasing herself from her temporary protectors, she gently placed her
hand on Carson's shoulder. Tears flooded her eyes, not from the smoke,
but from a deep inner emotional reservoir. It was as if he was crying in
pain to the Almighty.

Nichole's heart moved in heavy anguish as she heard Carson sob
again and again, "Why, God? Why did you take my son?" She moved to
try and comfort him, but the firemen were already helping him carry the
broken body of his only son out of the smoldering rubble.

She continued to wind her way systematically through the debris,
searching for the living. Unwilling to admit defeat to the grim reaper,

Nichole worked her way methodically towards the rear of the wreckage. It was doubtful many others could have survived the horrendous impact, but at least the fire hadn't engulfed the first third of the plane like it did the sections over and behind the wings. She spotted more and more floodlights illuminating the darkness as additional rescue workers wound their way among the dead and dying.

Nichole stopped by one of the Japanese tourists who would never reach twenty-two years of age. Kneeling beside the body to feel for a pulse, she tripped over his camera, and not knowing where to put it, strung the black leather strap around her neck as she lifted his head. "Nothing! Not again!" she cried to herself as she lowered the young boy back to the *ceiling* of the plane.

Another fireman, dressed in the same yellow protective clothing, finally got her to move towards the light. "There isn't anything else that I can do," she sobbed to the wreckage of Flight 421. As soon as she reached the exit and was helped through the now enlarged jagged hole, she ran across the runway. Her stomach couldn't take anymore!

"How many made it?" she asked herself as she crumbled to the grass. There was no one to answer her question. Men and women just kept working under the bright flashing lights. Tomorrow Nichole Lewis would find out that only 42 of the 274 passengers, including herself and one other flight attendant, survived the impact. Unfortunately, eighteen of the initial survivors and the other member of her flight crew would die in the next twelve hours.

Nichole pushed herself to her feet and walked wearily across the field to the waiting ambulances. She noticed the sandy haired passenger zipping a plastic bag shut around his son. Her heart ached for him, but there was nothing she could do.

3

SATURDAY MORNING

The vibrant spring sun shining through the partially opened hanger doors provided a stark contrast to the dark and bloody mayhem dropped so unexpectedly on Salt Lake International Airport only 14 hours before. Nichole Lewis fell in silently beside the tall African-American executive from Omega Airlines, and the two of them followed quietly as one of the six morticians provided by the international carrier directed them midway across the makeshift tomb. Row after row of tables, each covered with gray rubber containers, forced her to think of the silent memorial politicians constructed in Washington D.C. This time the dead hadn't been serving any higher cause, they were just trying to get home to the west coast. Holding back a flood of tears, she nodded lamely as the professional undertaker unzipped the rubber-like plastic container. "That's Julie Richards," she added as she bowed her head and finally allowed the tears to flow down across her high cheekbones and pool on her lower lip.

Acknowledging her response with a downward motion of his head, the thin Omega executive motioned for the mortician to grasp the metal handle and close the air tight container on the fourth table. "I'm sorry to have to put you through this so soon after the crash, but it's important to make the identification as soon as possible," the Omega employee commented as he handed Nichole the form requiring her signature at the bottom.

The eerie silence was deafening. It was as if the more than two hundred bodies in the vast and almost empty chamber could hear the thoughts of Nichole and her companions as they strained to carry on a whispered conversation. Still, the soft tone of Nichole's identification blended with the hushed voices around the hundred foot high room, provided a mood of deep reverence and respect for the dead prior to their bodies being identified. Soon transportation would be arranged to waiting mortuaries around the nation and three foreign countries, including Japan and Australia. The huge cavern-like edifice would continue to be the last waiting room for Flight 421's passengers.

All the Omega aircraft had been moved from the hanger during the preceding ten hours, and would not be returned for many months in the foreseeable future. Once the initial identification process was completed, the hanger would be used to reconstruct the giant L-1011 from the wreckage strewn across the airport. Hopefully, a determination as to the cause of the crash could be found, and any such future catastrophe could be avoided. Only after the initial identification could the families arrange for transportation to the deceaseds' home cities. Omega would naturally pay all expenses. The remaining nameless victims would later be moved to a more secure location where the use of dental and health records would be used to establish exact identities.

"That will do it," Nichole heard the official from Omega tell her. "We'll arrange for Miss Richards' transportation back to Seattle. Her family can take possession later this evening."

"The word *possession* seemed terribly wrong," she thought, as she moved her head up and down to signify that the man didn't need to repeat his comment again.

"I understand that you're flying back to SEA-TAC late today or first thing tomorrow?" the Omega executive continued, asking the question more to comfort Nichole than to solicit an answer. Even though Nichole and Julie Richards were both based out of Seattle, Omega would not ask Nichole to accompany Julie's body to the Northwest.

Nichole silently answered the man's inquiry by nodding her head, "yes." Biting her lip and wiping the tears from her eyes she went on, "The doctor wants to make one final examination of my shoulder and insure that there is no infection in the stitches. As soon as that's done, I'm free to go home." She kept her voice low, not wanting to disturb the

other people now wandering among the tables, all doing the same thing
for their friends and loved ones that she had just done for Julie Richards.
Sadly, such identification was not always possible. Every few minutes
she heard soul-piercing cries of anguish and despair.

Recognizing their next appointment, the Omega executive touched
his shorter companion on the left shoulder and pointed to the Hispanic
couple standing in the doorway. "If you'll excuse us?" he said as they
shuffled off to complete a task neither of them were prepared for or
wanted.

"Sure," Nichole answered mutely to their backs. She paused one last
time to look at the table where Julie Richards' young body lie waiting
for transportation to Seattle, and then started to head for the door where
her recent companions were already greeting the middle aged couple
who had recently sent their 13 year old daughter to meet her grandpar-
ents. A trip that had ended in heartache and sadness. Midway to the
hanger entrance she recognized the sandy haired man that had been sitting in 4E the night before, and quietly moved to his side, once again
putting her arm around his drooping shoulder. In any other environment,
the move might have been called forward, but on this particular Saturday
morning it was understood for what it was — a touch of understanding.

Carson raised his head from the gray rubber-like bag holding the
already identified body of his sixteen-year old son. Turning to look
Nichole in her eyes, he was not surprised to see tears slowly running
down her face and slipping off her chin. "You OK?" he asked, reversing
roles with the emotionally drained lady.

Haltingly she answered, "I guess as well as could be expected. I'm
sorry about your son." They both felt the enormity of the loss manifest
by the countless tables in the shadowed room, and neither of them spoke
for several moments. Nichole tightened her arm around his shoulder in
an effort to relieve the grieve she saw in the father's eyes, eyes that were
red and sunken. She correctly guessed that he had already cried himself
out, his tears long since dried up, but still ever present.

"Kelly Jeffers," he stated quietly as he pointed at the gray bag on the
folding table. "He was not even seventeen years old. It's not fair. I
walked away with a few cuts and bruises."

Nichole nodded her head in sympathy and understanding, but wisely said nothing, still keeping her arm around the dejected and mourning father. She knew that this man needed to purge his thoughts, and at the moment there wasn't anyone else.

Looking right through Nichole, Carson seemed to be talking to the universe. "God? God? Right now I can't believe there is a god," he stated quietly. "Yet, last night I prayed fervently to someone up there that Kelly would live. I didn't care if I made it or not, but why did a young boy who had already lost his soul mate die so suddenly?"

"Soul mate?" questioned Nichole, not understanding the reference of his last statement.

"She died three years ago from cancer. For thirteen years Lynda had lived for the boy. It was as if a bond existed that couldn't be broken. No matter what she was doing, I guarantee that Kelly was always in her thoughts," he replied, motioning silently to the young man entombed in the flexible gray air tight coffin. Carson continued talking, not fully aware whether Nichole, or anyone else was listening. Every once in a while he would glance down at the three-foot high table where his boy lay motionless. Fighting to keep his voice steady, he would catch himself and look back into Nichole's eyes. She would smile gently, and the father would continue.

After several moments, Carson relaxed his shoulders, and Nichole removed her arm. "Nichole Lewis," she stated placing her slender fingers over her heart.

He nodded in understanding to the introduction and replied, "Carson Jeffers. I didn't get a chance to thank you last night, but I really did appreciate your helping me look for Kelly," he remarked in a voice that was still partially breaking. "I imagine you were close to losing your patience with me, what with all the other people you were helping."

"Not at all. I just wished the night had turned out differently. Up until we started careening off the runway, I really did think that we were going to make it," she responded, not sure why she had added her last statement. Possibly the ongoing wake being conducted in the hanger required some kind of response.

Carson was non-responsive to Nichole's recent observation. "I apol-

ogize for monopolizing your time, Nichole. I guess I just needed someone to talk to," he stated evenly as he once again wiped non-existent
tears from his eyes. The use of first names was a natural and unassuming
liberty that both the man and the woman felt comfortable with. Refusing
to separate himself from the boy on the table he continued, "I'm taking
Kelly home to Portland in a couple of hours."

"How will Kelly's mom take the death?" asked Nichole, aware of
the harshness of the question, but wanting to know the answer just the
same.

Carson swallowed softly, and then unconsciously moved his right
hand through his slightly disheveled blond hair.. "She was the soul mate
I was talking to you about. My wife died almost three years ago next
month."

"I'm sorry," she responded, not knowing how to comfort the strong
sandy-haired man.

"It's OK. At least when she went, I was able to prepare myself. We
knew for nearly six weeks that her death was inevitable. Kelly was thirteen years old, but he just didn't understand. Not that I understood either,
I just came to grips with the loss. Anyway, before she closed her eyes in
the hospital, she took Kelly in her arms to say goodbye. She kept saying,
'I'll always be there to watch over you." Carson again looked down at
the table and nodded his head back and forth in some ritual form of
denial.

"She was comforting your son," Nichole commented softly as
Carson struggled to continue the story.

"Possibly, but Kelly never forgave me just the same."

"Forgave you?" questioned Nichole, not understanding.

"Kelly always believed I could do just about anything, and somehow
I just let Lynda die. In his young mind he never forgave me for letting it
happen. This last week was my feeble attempt to get closer to the boy.
We weren't supposed to fly home until Sunday night, but I just had to
get back to work!" Carson stated as he raised his voice slightly while
touching the cold plastic covering on the table. Continuing he added,
"As if ManTech couldn't make it without me."

Feeling his tension rising, Nichole touched his elbow and said,

"Let's leave. Right now there's absolutely nothing that either of us can do for your son."

Carson nodded his head in agreement, wiped away the non-existent tears one final time, and held his hand on what appeared to be Kelly's chest for three or four seconds. The final goodbye said, he took Nichole by the arm and backed away from the table.

Nichole glanced across the room to where she had recently said her farewell to Julie Richards, and then allowed Carson to guide her from the darkened tomb. Suddenly two men approached her from the end of the table. "Are you Nichole Lewis?" the taller one with the buzz haircut asked in a voice altogether too loud. His authoritative demeanor indicated that he already knew the answer to his own question.

"Yes." she answered, as Carson stopped walking.

"You were the supervising flight attendant on 421, weren't you?" he quizzed almost mechanically in a voice that would have been suited better to making itself heard in a busy sports stadium.

She responded in a much lower voice than that issued by the interrogator. "What can I help you with?" Didn't they realize what everyone in the hanger was going through? Why were they asking her questions about the flight while they were still standing among the grieving and the dead?

"We need to ask you some questions about the accident last night," broke in the shorter of the two. His suit was unwrinkled, as if it had just come from the cleaners, or off the shelf at an expensive men's store.

"Now?" questioned Nichole, unable to fathom why the questioning was taking place in such an inappropriate setting.

Realizing the need to establish some rapport with the upset young woman, the taller man took a leather folder from his inside suit pocket, and introduced himself and his well dressed shorter partner. His badge said FBI. "Once again, we need to ask you about the accident?"

The way he continued to emphasize the word "accident" instead of calling it what it really was bothered Nichole. In reality she was put off by their very intrusion into an extremely somber moment. "We crashed, don't you understand? Why beat around the bush? Say it like it is." she said to herself as the taller man put his identification away in his suit.

Carson straightened his shoulders and tensed his back muscles, still remaining quiet. They weren't talking to him, but it angered him that they continued to be so abrupt with this flight attendant. Of the ten or twelve people he had talked to in the past fourteen hours, from doctors to airline executives, she had been the most understanding of the lot.

"Ma'am, once again. We need to ask you some questions about the accident on Flight 421," asked the shorter agent, his raised voice more than making up for his physical stature.

Realizing they weren't going to go away until they finished their inquiry, Nichole responded, "I was the supervising attendant last night. What is it you want to know?"

After a few questions dealing with the schedule of Flight 421, the shorter agent stopped writing in his pocket planner. Finally lowering his voice a degree, he asked, "Did you feel anything funny before the crash?"

Nichole paused, more because it was the first time that the word crash had been used, than because of the question put to her by the government agent. "What do you mean by funny?"

"Just answer his question." Mr. Buzz Haircut emphasized.

"Tell me what you mean by funny," retorted Nichole, finally starting to lose her patience.

"Don't get short with us!" the immaculate dresser stated in a voice that could be heard in all four corners of the hanger.

Carson had had it. There was absolutely no reason for them to be badgering Nichole like she was some kind of a witness to a federal crime. She was just a flight attendant who had been doing her job, and unfortunately, that job put her in harm's way, the wrong place at the wrong time. Separating himself from Nichole's grip on his arm, he moved a step closer to the two insensitive males. "If you will kindly tell the young lady what you mean, then I'm sure she can try and answer your questions, but don't persist in this badgering interrogatory." Sensing no acceptable change of attitude, Carson added, "Why don't you be so kind as to just leave us alone? I'm sure that your questions can be answered in some more appropriate location?"

"Who are you?" the taller agent demanded, shortening the distance between the two men. It was a move that was intended to establish control of the situation, but was a failure from the man's first step.

Carson remained stationary. "Carson Jeffers. And unless you can begin to conduct yourselves like the professionals you pretend to be, neither of us are going to talk to you. Come on Nichole, let's get out of here." He took her once again by the arm and walked straight towards the open door of the hanger-turned-morgue, knowing full well he would have a final chance to say his last goodbye to his son.

The two government agents stared at the couple as they walked into the light and left the building. Both men were amazed that they had been put down so effectively. Mr. Immaculate was the first to speak, "Don't sweat it. She doesn't know anything."

Carson and Nichole caught the special bus, and waited quietly as it made its way across the taxiway to the terminal. Three other couples and an older gray-haired man with a well-kept beard kept them company. No one spoke to each other, there wasn't anything to say. The older gentleman with the Kenny Rodgers-type beard continued to cry softly, even as they stopped beside the steps alongside gate C-1. The white van normally used to go back and forth between long-term parking for lot A would continue transporting the grieving back and forth to the hanger. As they walked up the silver and gray stairwell leading to the terminal, Carson asked Nichole if she would like a drink. Nodding yes, they exited the concourse, turned right past *Mrs. Fields's Cookies* and walked down the hall to the President's Club Room.

Carrying two drinks, one in each hand, Carson sat down on the couch beside the attractive dark haired flight attendant. His physical demeanor had changed once they entered the terminal. It wasn't as if he had forgotten his personal grief, but he had placed it in a corner of his heart where he could recall it at will. Somehow Carson and Nichole had melded together, and were relating more like close friends, rather than like a couple who had known each other for less than 24 hours.

Taking the glass from his hand, Nichole commented, "I'm sorry about that. They should have been more cognizant of what was going on in there." She was referring to the two men they had just met across the tarmac in the cold hanger. "I guess sometimes people doing their jobs just don't consider how they might be coming across to others."

"They may have been doing their job, but they were downright rude in the way they went about asking questions," he responded while taking a long drink from the clear glass. Rolling the ice cubes from one side of his glass to the other, he looked out the window and studied the airport landscape. "What do you think they might have been referring to when they talked about feeling something funny?" he asked, avoiding any immediate conversation about his son.

Placing her partially empty glass on the table by the couch, she wrapped her arms around her chest and added, "I imagine they were just trying to find out what caused the crash. Did you notice they kept referring to it as an accident? It seemed like a sterile word to me. It was as if they couldn't bear to say the word *crash*. What do you think they might have meant?"

Carson looked puzzled by her question. It was exactly the same question he had just asked her, all-be-it phrased in a different manner. Running his hand through his dusty colored hair, he responded. "Don't know for sure, but it might have something to do with the way that the pilot lost attitude control."

"Do you mean *altitude control*?" she quizzed, thinking of the way the plane plummeted to the ground.

"No," Carson answered. "Attitude control is entirely different than altitude control. Attitude in flying refers to the plane's relationship with the horizon. Did you feel the way the nose pitched down?" Acknowledging the nod of Nichole's head, he continued, "It was as if the plane's elevators just abruptly stopped working."

Puzzled by his last response, Nichole asked, "Are you a pilot? You sound like you know a lot about the L-1011?"

"Not a professional pilot like you might think, and I know very little about the kind of jets that Omega flies." Removing the sun glasses he had put on when they exited the Omega hanger several minutes earlier, Carson explained, "I started flying over 20 years ago in the Air Force, and since that time I've managed to keep involved in aviation. In 1990 I flew in the Gulf, and my company leases both a King Air and a Citation jet. We share the actual flight expenses on a per hour basis with three other companies in the Portland area, a business arrangement which allows me to fly both of the planes as often as my schedule permits. Most of the time, however, I leave the flying to pilots who don't have their mind on some kind of business dilemma, as I often do. It's safer that way." He paused abruptly, the impact of his last sentence hitting him squarely between the shoulders. "Safer," he said under his breath, as he renewed his thoughts of the crash of Flight 421.

Nichole released her self-imposed grip on her chest, and laid her hand across Carson's lower arm. "Still, you said that you felt the plane drop immediately. What would cause that to happen?"

"Somehow, there was an elevator failure. Absurd, but it happened."

"Is there anything else you remember about the crash?" Nichole asked, as she sat thinking about what he had just said.

Carson pondered her question while reviewing the events of the previous evening. "Only that the pilot was having an extremely hard time managing the rudder. Try as he might, he couldn't keep the plane centered on the runway as we came in." Shuddering slightly, he said, "I was holding my son and noticed that the runway appeared to be coming up on the side of the plane."

"Is that odd?" Nichole asked, unable to see the significance of seeing the runway.

"I should never have been able to see the runway from where I was sitting. When I saw the runway, I knew it was over and we were going in."

Reviewing Carson's explanation in her mind, Nichole looked him in the eyes and asked, "Do you have any idea what could cause the loss of both the rudder and the elevators at the exact same time?"

Carson nodded his head from left to right, indicating he didn't, but in the back of his mind he briefly considered one possible alternative explanation. Subconsciously, he convinced himself that it was too improbable a scenario to even consider, let alone voice aloud.

Changing the topic of conversation back to the present, Nichole asked when the funeral for Carson's son would be.

Carson said the funeral would be held at the end of the coming week.

Nichole asked, "Can I attend? I live up near Seattle and would really like to, that is if you don't mind?"

Without questioning her motive, Carson answered, "I would like that. I still don't know the exact day of the service, but I'll put an announcement in the Portland paper.

4

The bluish-gray haze caused by the afternoon sun reflecting back off the pavement buried the black asphalt of Las Vegas Boulevard. Esteban had driven through the night in the old blue Ford pick-up and was currently dressed as a migrant farm worker looking for work in one of the new upper-class subdivisions that were surrounding Las Vegas. A chain of events had been started in Salt Lake that would have shattering consequences all over the globe, and right now, manual labor was the last thing on the South American's mind. In a matter of weeks fear would put a stranglehold on the United States - fear every bit as compelling as the emotion a swimmer feels while paddling in the moon-lit surf as the theme music from the movie *"Jaws"* resonates over the sound of the crashing waves. "This time," Esteban thought to himself, "the cause of the fear will not be some Hollywood prop found on the lot of Universal Studios."

The tall Latin had his shoulder length hair pulled back into a tight pony-tail, held in place by a faded red and blue checkered handkerchief. Stepping off the curb onto the sweltering pavement, he noted the hour was straight up, and turned to watch the man-made volcano and fire erupting behind him. "How appropriate," he mused as he viewed the spectacle sponsored by the *Mirage.*

As the eruption blended into the hazy fog blanketing the pavement, Esteban continued south down the Strip and strolled up the curved drive-way leading to *Caesar's Palace.* The cascading water fountains partially obscured the afternoon Vegas traffic. Hesitating to allow a long white

Lincoln limousine access to valet parking, he smiled to himself, and remembered how easy it had been to load the splattered bike into the back of the pick-up.

La Quinta Motor Inn catered to truckers and was located alongside McDonald's next to the entrance to the I-15 freeway. After leaving the muddy road in the Salt Lake marsh he followed 40th West to 21st South, turned right on Redwood Road, and then headed directly south to 72nd. By the time he got to the motel, sketchy details of the Omega crash were being broadcast on every radio and TV station in the Salt Lake area, as well as on national feeds across the nation. He drove the grimy Japanese motorcycle up the oil-stained 2 x 8 plank and cinched tight the tie down straps to the bed of the small truck. Using a kryptonite lock, he deliberately secured everything against theft, and then entered the motel room he had previously paid for with cash and slung himself across the queen sized bed. It wasn't important to tune in the news broadcasts, they were, after-all, irrelevant. Two hours later he got up and drove south on the I-15 freeway, obeying the recently increased speed limit at all times. Emergency vehicles with red and blue flashing lights were still traveling back and forth in all directions.

Six tedious hours later, night was starting to turn to day as he drove out to the shore of Lake Mead. Ten minutes and three-and-one half miles above the damn he found the seldom used dirt trail leading to the secluded rock outcropping. Following a final reconnaissance of the area he silently pushed the dirt bike off the cliff and watched it sink to the bottom of the dark waters below. Only the week before, Esteban had been diving and found that the bottom was more than 75 feet from the surface of the ever expanding Colorado River. Now, double checking to insure there were no witnesses who had seen him dispose of the bike, he drove into Las Vegas and registered at the Mirage. It had been an extremely long and tiring day!

Absorbing the ever present air conditioning, he returned to the present and entered the luxury casino designed to extract millions from wealthy gamblers across the world. The casino operator told him that she would ring Mr. Cleaner's room. As the call was put through, Esteban allowed a smirk to appear on his chiseled face. "Mr. Cleaner!" Esteban had been introduced to the man, known simply as *"The Cleaner,"* some fifteen years earlier. He had covertly learned The Cleaner's given name, or at least the one he went by. But Esteban never used it, understanding from the beginning the need to remain nameless in this fight for moral equality.

Waiting for an answer, he starred at the communications device and wondered why all house phones were constantly the same color. It didn't matter what country or hotel he was in, the phones were always the same. "Cleaner here," he heard through the beige handset.

"Shortfall," he stated, speaking directly into the mouth piece.

"Coffee shop in five." There was a click as the phone high above the kidney shaped pool was hung up, and then the line went dead.

Esteban casually replaced the receiver and gave a courteous nod to the elder gentleman waiting to use the in-house service. Exiting from the bank of mostly pay phones, he walked through rows of clinging slot machines and headed towards the coffee shop located near the entrance to the pool area. Observing everything that went on around him, he marveled that there were no casinos with windows or clocks. The effect was to slow down time, keeping customers ignorant of the world going by them on the other side of the solid walls.

He got to the restaurant before the Cleaner. The various smells circling the eating area made the lean Latin suddenly realize he was hungry. After briefly glancing over the plastic-covered menu, he opted to forego the evening buffet on the opposite side of the room, and instead ordered a breakfast omelet and coffee. The waitress in the shortened Roman Toga hadn't thought the order out of the ordinary. After all, in Las Vegas a great many of the workers start their day at five or six in the afternoon.

Both Esteban Moreno and the Cleaner were careful men. They had no fear of anyone recognizing them, but if the unforeseen did happen, it was always good to give people something to remember. Thus, the red bandanna and migrant worker outfit. Esteban could afford to dress however he chose, and today he chose to be a farmer.

Not bothering to ask permission to seat himself, the Cleaner slid

back the chair and thanked the girl in the short, tight Roman outfit for
the menu.

Esteban lowered his fork and studied his companion as he ordered
coffee. The Cleaner had on the brightest pair of red and white pants possible. The small white checks were almost invisible against the fire
engine color of his slacks. His shoes were white wingtips, and he had on
a purple pullover. If anyone were ever asked what color hair he had, they
wouldn't be able to remember. It was turning gray. "Nice effect,"
Esteban remarked after the Cleaner returned the menu to the toga
dressed waitress.

"Each to his own," the cleaned commented, noting the torn Levis,
faded denim shirt, and red and blue bandanna in Esteban's hair.
Placing the USA Today front page he had been carrying in his left hand
when he sat down on the table between them, the Cleaner asked, "Any
problems?"

Esteban read the headlines, 242 DIE IN SALT LAKE AIR CRASH,
and then answered the fifty year old man dressed in red pants, "None."

"Don't be so quick. You have a possible problem in Los Angeles."

Esteban didn't miss the inference left by the word, you, in the elder
man's statement. "What type of problem?" frowned Esteban, as he once
again lowered his fork and deposited it beside his omelet.

Waiting for the waitress to leave his coffee on the table, the Cleaner
slid his wooden chair closer to the formica table and leaned forward to
whisper something in the ear of the migrant farm worker from south of
the border.

Esteban deepened the frown now occupying his total facial counte-
nance. He didn't want to believe what the Cleaner had stated, but he
knew that the man never passed on information that wasn't verified and
highly accurate. The Latin had long ago been convinced that his life
often depended on the veracity of what he learned from this audaciously
dressed individual. As he contemplated the serious potential problem
remaining in Los Angeles, he recounted to himself what had taken place
three days earlier.

Esteban and Ricardo Gutierrez had been able to simply drive on to
the Marine Corps Air Station at El Toro exactly as Gunnery Sergeant

Adrian Baker promised. Baker had arranged for them to pick up the dry cleaning at the off-base laundry without any problems, and the uniforms belonging to the two marine officers were close to perfect fits. Esteban remembered Baker explaining how both junior grade officers were going on TDY duty, and would have to take clean uniforms. Once the uniforms were in the cleaners, all you had to do to pick them up was to give the last name. Despite the occasional *snafu,* the retail clerk never asked for the claim tickets, after-all the laundry always made good on the loss.

Once Esteban and Ricardo had the new uniforms, they simply purchased rank insignias and waited for the night when Sergeant Adrian Baker was to have guard duty at the Marine Corps Air Station Armory. Shortly after 2200 hours, 10:00 p.m. for civilians, the two Latins stole a captain's Grand Am that was parked in off-base housing, and dressed in their new uniforms, they simply drove up to the main gate. Esteban's hair was stuffed up under his utility cover and when they approached the waiting MP, he snapped to attention and saluted the sticker attached to the front bumper, waving the two middle-aged officers through the chain link fence. Smooth as silk!

Esteban and his younger companion had driven directly to the motor pool. When they got there, they parked the Grand Am, used the Request For Vehicle Form Baker had provided and claimed a small green cargo van. Still remembering the events of the evening, he recalled that they were to arrive at the Armory at exactly 12:40 a.m. Esteban backed the truck up to the ten foot metal doors and rang the buzzer. A twenty year old marine corps corporal looked through the small plate glass window, puzzled at the appearance of the green van in the middle of the night. The young corporal went down in a heap as Gunnery Sergeant Baker clubbed him from behind.

Sergeant Baker stepped over the unconscious marine and inserted his blue and white security card into the computer terminal by the door. After punching in a series of numbers, the heavy steel aperture slowly rose from the ground, allowing the senior non-commissioned officer to drag the fallen marine to the side of the loading dock. Esteban gunned the engine, increasing the rpm of the green truck, and backed into the loading bay.

As soon as Esteban stopped the van, Ricardo swung open the door, leaped from the passenger side of the vehicle and in a fury bent down and seized the semi-conscious marine by the collar. He pressed the fat tube of the silencer firmly against the side of the man's head and fired. The young enlisted marine from the Midwest should have gone to Sick Bay rather than taking duty as Fire Watch. Sergeant Baker turned away from the bloody execution. He hadn't been surprised when the Latin terminated the corporal, as it had been arranged earlier out of necessity. The marine had to die, it was part of the plan, and he was just grateful the roles of the two servicemen hadn't been reversed. Ricardo raised the back of his camouflage utility jacket and smoothly fitted the weapon back in his belt. Sergeant Baker slid the blue and white magnetic coded card into the opening in the wall a second time. As soon as the numbers were entered, the door to the Armory closed silently against the night air.

Almost in a stutter, Baker demanded the balance of his money. Esteban had earlier paid him $25,000 cash and promised him another $225,000 when the Armory was opened and the remaining witness silenced. Esteban didn't acknowledge his emphatic request with an answer, instead he tossed him a gym bag containing the promised amount. Baker unzipped the cloth container and started to count the money, but quickly surmised that it was all there, just as the Latin had agreed. Less than ten minutes later the military cargo van was loaded with fifteen shoulder launched Stinger surface-to-air missiles.

Baker picked up the yellow gym bag he had safely stowed on the floor beside the van, and led the way back to his office at the rear of the building. Opening a green file cabinet, he removed a false bottom he had prepared ahead of time, and deposited his new found wealth under the military file folders. Assured that the hiding place was secure, he tossed the gym bag back to Esteban and told him to tie him up as they had agreed.

Using duct tape, which Esteban always said was quicker and more secure, Ricardo lashed the gunnery sergeant to the green metal chair behind the desk. Ricardo asked him if he was ready, and Baker nodded in the affirmative. Knowing that he was going to have to take a substantial beating for a quarter of a million dollars, Gunnery Sergeant Adrian

Baker was glad that he passed out after the first few blows from Ricardo's pistol. Ricardo continued pounding Baker's head and shoulders as Esteban pulled open the file cabinet and quickly stuffed the used currency back in the yellow bag. Esteban raised his head as the sound of sirens blared in the distance. It sounded like the commotion was coming from the base motor pool, and all Esteban could think of was that the car they had stolen from the marine captain must have been reported missing and found by the MP's at the motor pool. Ricardo sensed Esteban's new found urgency and clubbed Baker one more time before stepping on the running board of the van and vaulting into the moving truck. As soon as they approached the outer door, Esteban leaped from the driver's side, rushed back into the office of the Armory, and shot Baker twice in the chest. After leaning down and retrieving the blue and white card from Baker's bloody shirt, he ran back to the front of the Armory. Ricardo had understood what was happening and had moved into the driver's seat while Esteban was in the back office. Esteban used the card and then quickly punched in the computer numbers he had seen Baker use to lower the door. As soon as Ricardo moved the van to the outer driveway, Esteban repeated the process, dropping his shoulders to walk under the descending door to the passenger side of the truck. They could still hear the sirens growing louder in the distance.

There was no problem in leaving the base; they were not even stopped. Ricardo drove to a truck stop off the I-5 freeway where there were no lights in the parking area. Esteban noted that Ricardo had extinguished all the overhead lights some two hours earlier with the same silenced pistol that he had summarily used to pistol whip Gunnery Sergeant Adrian Baker, USMC. Ricardo waited for Esteban to lower the metal ramps leading into the moving van, and then drove into the darkened interior. Everything had worked perfectly. Nothing had gone wrong!

Snapping his fingers as if to bring himself back to the present, Esteban watched the Cleaner pick up a pen and write on the Keno pad, "Sergeant Baker - Los Angeles Memorial Hospital. Below Baker's name the Cleaner added a short list of instructions. Esteban waited for him to finish writing, and then picked up the paper and studied the abbreviated directions. Reading silently, he memorized the details. Marine Gunnery Sergeant Baker would never recover.

The Cleaner lit a match and burned the Keno paper Esteban had placed in the ashtray. He finished his coffee as Esteban once again dug into his cheese and mushroom omelet.

5

MONDAY MORNING

Michael Randall used the left shoulder of his trim African-American frame to nudge the pine door open, and quietly stuck his closely cropped head into Carson Jeffers' private office. Michael had twenty-four hour access to Carson and seldom stopped at a closed door, but this morning he had imposed a self-made restriction on this privilege. There had been an unwritten understanding between the two men ever since Carson had invited Michael to join ManTech, Inc. If the door was closed and the small red bulb, partially obscured by the professionally arranged silk plants, was on, Michael knew that Carson needed privacy for either personal or business affairs. When the light was off, it didn't matter if the door was closed or not, Michael didn't need to worry about knocking. As President of the small, but extremely successful, business and consulting firm, Michael Randall was the only person granted this privilege, one that he didn't take lightly in view of the tragedy that had recently befallen his employer and best friend.

He stepped onto the hand-dyed red and black Navajo rug, not sure of exactly what to say. He knew Carson was going through a personal pain unfathomable to anyone who had never experienced the sudden death of a loved one. Having been with Carson three years earlier at Lynda's death didn't make this morning any easier. His close personal friend sat stoically on the burgundy leather sofa gazing out the window. Even the view of the Portland skyline centered against the Columbia River didn't seem to be registering an impression. "Not any easier today than it was two days ago, is it?" Michael asked as he sat down on the wooden coffee table across from his chief executive officer.

Carson's frame was silhouetted against the city as he stood and turned away from the massive floor to ceiling window. "Everyone always says that time heals the wounds, but it's a lie, Michael, a complete fabrication!" The tone of Carson's voice carried the depth of his despair far better than any poem written by some time honored author. "All time does is thicken the skin, and possibly harden the heart. Before Lynda died, I swore to her, by all that was sacred, that I would raise Kelly so that she would be proud." Raising his voice without yelling, he stared into his friend's dark eyes. "Michael, I failed both of them!"

Michael wanted to interrupt his friend and tell him that he was wrong, but he sensed that Carson was just venting a personal frustration. Placing the Internet projections, spread sheets and financial papers beside him on the clear stained pine table, Michael responded, "I understand, but..."

"There's no *but* about it. I failed Kelly and I outright lied to Lynda." Carson started to slowly pace back and forth across the 12 x 16 foot Indian rug, turning first to face the window and then Michael. "Sure, I knew there was nothing I could do about the cancer," he said as he did a final 180 degree turn away from the window. "We both accepted the fact she undoubtedly got sick because of heredity and her family health history." Pausing momentarily, he continued, "I don't know if I ever told you, but her grandfather and her mother both died from pancreatic cancer. We knew when we were married that she was an extremely high risk candidate for the same type of malignancy." He stopped speaking as he turned towards the Columbia River. "Michael, it didn't make it any easier, just understandable."

Michael rose from the low wooden table and took two steps across the rug, where he was able to clutch his companion tightly on the arm.

Carson stopped him before he could say anything. "Hear me out," he said as he picked up the coffee cup that had been resting beside the picture of his wife and son on the square table at the opposite end of the leather couch. "I failed Lynda when I didn't take the time to spend with Kelly. Somehow, I got trapped into thinking that if I could build

ManTech into my legacy, Kelly would always have something. It was bull shit! Kelly didn't need toys and all those things I associated with success, he needed my time! God damn it, Michael, I didn't give it to him. I failed both of them!"

Ignoring the unusually harsh vocabulary, Michael nodded and let the man continue. Carson's eyes took on a determined glare that made his angular shaped face stand out against his colored hair, but the image was immediately forgotten as he dropped his bombshell. "I know that Kelly didn't have to die. Something went terribly wrong on that plane last Friday night. During the past 72 hours I have had an awful lot of time to relive those brief minutes before Kelly's life was taken from him." Pausing, but not waiting for any kind of acknowledgement from the 6'2" ManTech president, he continued, "Michael, I am going to find out why we crashed!"

Michael nodded as if to signify an understanding that was non-existent. He noticed that Carson said *he was going to find out*, not that he wanted to find out.

Carson used a common hand gesture and pointed upwards through the window at the Portland sky. "There are numerous and redundant safety devices on an L-1011. Every member of that flight crew was trained to handle even the most complex emergency situation, but none of it did any good three days ago! Why not, Michael, why not?"

Carson's friend stared back at his boss. "I'm sure the FAA and every other government agency in the country wants to find out exactly the same thing, Carson. What more can you do?" he answered, knowing as he spoke that Carson had something else in mind.

"I don't know for sure, but, if there's any way that I can find out how to stop something like this from happening again, I've got to try. Will you help me?"

Michael walked over to where Carson was once again looking at the steel and concrete Portland Skyline. Raising his arm, he touched his friend's shoulder. "You know I will," he answered, still not sure what either of them could possible do. Michael had known Carson Jeffers for more than 13 years, and was by now convinced that Carson never started any kind of project without a detailed road map on how to finish it.

Recalling his first encounter with Carson, he thought back to when he was in the MBA program at Thunderbird, one of the most highly respected business schools in the country. Despite being raised on the streets of Philadelphia, Michael had never allowed his minority standing in society to cloud his vision of business success. At the conclusion of a two-day symposium on developing international trading partners, Carson Jeffers, one of the visiting experts, had asked Michael if he was interested in joining ManTech, Inc. Impressed by Michael's grasp of international economics, Carson explained that ManTech was a new company, but one that would provide long term benefits for both Michael and society in general. After careful consideration, Michael accepted the offer, and joined the firm immediately following his graduation. It was a move he had never regretted. Their relationship had started out as purely business, but over the years Michael and Carson had become the closest of friends. Carson had helped Michael work through a painful divorce, and now it was Michael's turn to lend the moral support he knew his friend desperately needed.

"Close the door, Michael," Carson said as he walked across the corner office and placed his half empty coffee cup on a corner of his desk. Slowly, he picked up a yellow legal pad and turned to face Michael, who had returned to his seat on the coffee table.

Michael noted that the top sheet of 8 1/2 by 14 inch pad of paper had a list of items marked in red. Some of them had a star next to them.

It was evident that Carson had studied the list for some time as he had it completely memorized. Tearing the top sheet from the rest of the pad, he handed it to Michael. "Let's take it a step at a time." For the next two hours Michael lived every moment of the crash, again and again. It was almost as if he had been on the plane, seated in 4E with Carson. Michael listened carefully as Carson used a clinical voice to describe the details of life, death, and suffering in a manner that was almost void of feeling. Filling the borders of the yellow paper with hand scribbled notes, Michael heard Carson describe his feelings as he sensed the plane start to fall.

Carson handed Michael the remaining portion of the blue lined legal pad, and then unconsciously ran his right hand through his hair as he talked. "I know that the FAA and several other organizations are looking into the details of the crash, and this includes the FBI." He then retold, for a third time, how the two FBI agents had almost accosted Nichole Lewis in the Omega hanger.

Staring at the picture of his wife and son, Carson asked, "Now tell me, Michael, why would the FBI be investigating an accident of an L-1011? They were in Salt Lake within hours. Why?"

He waited a moment to allow Michael time to evaluate the information, and then answered his own question, "Because the accident just might not have been an accident. Michael, what are the two causes of virtually every plane crash?"

No novice to aviation, Michael quickly responded, "Pilot error and mechanical failure."

Carson's expression reflected an ever slight smile as he congratulated his friend on his answer. "Correct. Many people list weather as a third reason, but I personally believe that a good pilot will not fly in weather that exceeds either his abilities as a pilot or the structural limits of the aircraft." Referring to the crash of Flight 421, he added, "Neither of these causes would require any type of coordination with the FBI. Yet, there they were, less than twelve hours later in the Omega hanger, haranguing Nichole Lewis and demanding answers to questions about the crash."

"Why were they there, then?" Michael asked as he pondered the importance of Carson's astute observation.

Carson recalled how agitated the two agents had been when Nichole asked what they were insinuating by their questions. It had seemed a little strange then, and now it seemed even more odd. Instead of answering Michael's rhetorical question, Carson stated, "I want to use every resource available to us here at ManTech to get answers to the questions on your pad of paper."

He gently pounded his right fist in his left palm to emphasize each point, once, twice, and then three times. "First, what happened mechanically to that L-1011 that caused the plane to lose pitch and attitude control? Let's find out everything in the NTSB report as it happens."

NTSB stands for National Transportation Safety Board, and Michael

was already plotting how he could access the encrypted computer information, using the Internet security device that First Pacific Net wanted to
market to the major cable companies in the world. The secret debugging
encryption mechanism could yield countless secrets when combined
with high speed fiber optic technology.

"Second, I want to know everything about the history of the pilots
and flight crew of Omega Flight 421. If they had ever been stopped for
pissing beside the freeway, I want to know it."

Pounding his fist in his hand repeatedly, he said, "I want to know
why the FBI is investigating this crash, literally before the NTSB even
got set up! If they know something strange or *funny* about Flight 421, we
have to find out what it is!"

Michael tapped his pen repeatedly on the pad of paper now resting
on his long legs, while following the pacing movements of his boss.
"Who else do you want to bring in on this?"

"That's up to you, Michael, but I want you to take charge of our in-
house investigation. You can pull anyone from any department you think
necessary," he answered, and then almost interrupted his own response
by saying, "Keep the group small and make sure that everyone is fully
aware of what everyone else is doing."

Michael considered which particular skills might be necessary to
investigate an air crash. It wasn't going to require a lot of people
doing legwork, better to let the government agencies spend their time
doing that. He had already determined that he wanted immediate
access to every piece of information in the government's comprehensive investigation reports. After another minute, Michael responded to
Carson's admonition, "I think that we need two other people right
now. We have got to, excuse the term, break into the government's
computer files and search through every entry, byte by byte, concerning the crash of Flight 421."

"Who do you have in mind?" Carson asked, having complete confidence in Michael's computer skills. Once he got started, there was virtually nothing he couldn't find out from a computer. There was, however,
one person working for ManTech who could come close to matching his

skills, and Carson had correctly anticipated at least a portion of the response to his inquiry, Jim Tedrow.

Michael stopped writing on the yellow pad. "I want to use Jim to help me evaluate alternatives and access the secured data banks maintaining these files." Michael knew that Carson understood that he was referring to the 27 year old computer programmer they had hired away from MicroSoft. Michael paused, and then swallowed as he finished his answer, "I think we are going to also need Blake Terry."

Carson stopped Michael before he could continue his reasoning behind the inclusion of the two ManTech employees. "You do realize, don't you, Michael, that what we are going to do is illegal, and in all probability could end up putting us behind bars?"

Michael nodded, fully comprehending the recent penalties addressed in the latest Internet technology legislation passed by a Congress, fully aware of public fear about the intrusion into private and public lives. "That's why I'm suggesting we bring in Blake." Blake Terry had been an FBI agent for sixteen years, and when he couldn't stand the blind bureaucratic ambition of some of his supervisors, he had left the Bureau and started a small private investigative company in Portland. Carson had quickly recognized his talents in finding out why certain business executives made stupid conclusions. After a few successful investigations, Carson and Michael had hired Blake as head of ManTech Security and Investigations. As the company grew and information became of an ever increasing value, they had never regretted their decision.

"Does he still have any contacts in the government that owe him any favors?" Carson asked, referring to Blake's previous employment.

"I'm sure he does, and besides, if what you are hinting at is true, I think we may need some professional help, and I hope you understand what I mean by professional."

"Blake and Jim are fine, but make sure they understand what the repercussions will be if we make a mistake. If they're still in agreement after they have all the facts, then make them part of the team. Let's meet late this afternoon and see what we can dig up. Say 4:30. I'll start by calling Hank Grishhold."

Michael picked up the spread sheets and financial projections he had planned on discussing with Carson when he entered the room. It was ironical that the suggestions he was going to make for protecting the technology breakthrough of First Pacific Net would provide the same access to secrets the government seemed unwilling to share with the American public. Still, he knew that right now, Carson was only concerned with finding out why Kelly died. As he closed the door behind him, he wondered what luck Carson would have with Hank.

Hank Grishhold was the same age as Carson. Both of them were ex Air Force jockeys and had maintained a friendly relationship over the years. When Carson got called back to duty to fly in the Gulf War, Hank stayed at home, maintaining an elected presence in Washington, D.C. He had served two terms as a congressman from New Mexico, and one term as a U.S. senator. When Governor Rolland Attwilder was elected to the highest office in the land, he picked Hank Grishhold to be his Chief of Staff. Not only was Senator Henry Grishhold from his native state of New Mexico, he also had the congressional experience that President-elect Attwilder valued.

Carson hit the intercom button on his phone and asked his secretary and long time assistant, Janelle Robbins, to try and get hold of Hank Grishhold. Most executive assistants would have been flabbergasted to be asked to get the Chief of Staff for the President of the United States on the phone. Janelle was not. She had done it five or six times in the past two and a half years, and actually found it easier to get Hank Grishhold, Chief of Staff, on the phone, than Henry Grishold, U.S. Senator from New Mexico.

"Mr. Grishhold is on line four," Janelle announced to Carson over the intercom.

Lifting the receiver from its cradle on his desk, Carson heard Hank's first comment. "Carson, you old desk jockey. How are you?" the President's Chief of Staff yelled into the phone.

"Not good, Hank. Not good."

"What's bothering you, old buddy?"

It always amazed Carson how a person in such a high office could still act like the happy-go-lucky pilot he had first met in Da Nang, Vietnam. The line took on a deathly silence as Carson explained how he had been on Flight 421 from Salt Lake to Portland. For the next few minutes Hank listened to Carson's near clinical account, and remained quiet, except for an occasional, "I'm sorry."

Finally, Carson had gone through the entire accident and got to the reason for his call. He wasn't sure what he should tell Hank about his and Michael's efforts to conduct their own secret investigation, but wisely decided that he only wanted to tell enough to get some help from Hank. In no way did he want to put Hank in a position that would jeopardize his position as Chief of Staff to The President of The United States. "Hank, I have a suspicion that something funny happened to 421 in Salt Lake." He had used the term funny almost as a reflex statement as he was still thinking about what the two FBI agents had asked the Omega flight attendant in the hanger on Saturday morning.

"What are you referring to, Carson?" Hank responded.

Carson didn't answer the question directly. Instead he switched the phone to his opposite ear, and said, "I just want to find out what happened, and why my son had to die."

In a much subdued voice, Hank answered, "Carson, let me explain what is happening. The FAA is investigating the accident and will release the results as soon as they have something. I'm sure you realize the efforts they take to make an NTSB report that is accurate. But rest assured that when I get that report, I'll review it, and then send you a copy."

It only took a few minutes before Carson could sense that Hank Grishhold had to attend to his other duties as Chief of Staff. Before he hung up the phone, Carson knew he wouldn't be able to get anything immediate from Hank. Hopefully, Michael, Jim, or Blake were having more success.

• • •

Michael once again pushed open the door to Carson's office, only this time he didn't hesitate as the door swung from left to right. Michael was upset. As soon as he had left Carson's office that morning he had called Blake Terry and Jim Tedrow together. He explained what they were up against, including the possible legal entanglements involved in their search, and then asked if they were in or out. Both men joined their senior executive in his decision, and then promised to get some kind of preliminary report back to him in three or four hours. He hadn't expected a lot of information, but he had thought that he would get something more than he had in his hand.

Michael had just left the meeting with Blake and Jim. Jim had started by telling him that access to the FAA and NTSB files was extremely restricted. He had been able to completely bypass the highly classified security system of the FAA and gain access to a preliminary report from the NTSB. After reviewing the file, Jim was convinced that his entry into the government mainframe had corrupted the file, as it now contained the service record of a marine gunnery sergeant by the name of Adrian Baker. Flight 421 was an Omega Airlines flight.

Listening carefully to Jim's explanation of how he had used the encryption device belonging to First Pacific Net, Michael wondered if the corruption explanation was entirely accurate. "Why would the service record of a marine sergeant be included in the NTSB file?"

Jim had no logical explanation, and assured Michael that he would continue trying to access each of the data banks they had already identified, but he had to do it in such a way as not to leave a return trail. Even using the highly secret encryption tool, Jim had some trepidation as to the computer trail they were weaving across the global communications network, known simply as the Internet.

Michael understood Jim's security concerns completely. He had worked along the same lines from a separate terminal for more than three hours and ran into the same security protection measures. His computer search had been centered on any and all FBI investigations concerning Flight 421. He couldn't get anything to make sense on his terminal, and had finally decided to try and broaden the scope of his search to all FBI investigations of any airplane accident or crash in the past 12 months. His screen kept coming up with the error message, "CLASSIFIED S12." Michael didn't know what that meant, but he was determined to find out.

Blake Terry had struck out, too. He called his friends who were still working for the Bureau, and after he started asking questions about

Flight 421, they treated him like he had some kind of plague. He only received one solid piece of information, something that had to be *disinformation*. When pressed hard enough, an old FBI partner had told him there was absolutely no investigation taking place concerning the crash of Omega Flight 421. Blake remembered Michael telling him about the two men who had identified themselves as FBI agents in the Salt Lake hanger. He wondered, "Why would the Bureau start asking questions, and then deny it?"

Carson watched Michael force the door open. "Sit down. What have you got?"

Michael fell into a wingback chair matching the leather couch by the glazed window. He noticed that Carson needed some rest. His sandy hair had gone flat and seemed to fall across his eyebrows, an effect that combined with his drooping shoulders, left the image of total despair. Ignoring Carson's haggard look, Michael quickly brought him up to date as to the problems the investigation was facing.

Carson listened closely, then told Michael how he had also struck out with Hank. "Either he doesn't know anything, or he is not willing to find out," the tired sandy haired executive stated. "Have you got anything else?"

Michael told Carson about the cross file on the marine that had ended up in the NTSB preliminary report.

"Why would the crash of an Omega L-1011 contain the file of a marine gunnery sergeant, Michael?"

"I don't know. Quite possibly, it is a mistake and it shouldn't even be there. We'll keep looking at it." Tossing the *Time* magazine he had brought with him to the table in front of the couch, he asked, "Have you read this?"

Carson, still seated at his desk, pointed to a duplicate copy, partially hidden under some papers on his oversized pine desk, and nodded that he had. He pulled the papers off the cover of the magazine and looked at the color picture of the burning wreckage of Flight 421. Picking up the magazine, he asked Michael to come around behind the desk.

"That's Nichole Lewis. The flight attendant who appears to be running across the runway."

"She's the one who helped you find Kelly?" Michael asked, as he leaned forward to get a clearer picture of the cover of the weekly periodical.

"Right. She is also the one that was rudely interrogated by the non-existent FBI agents in the hanger," Carson stated angrily. He continued to stare at the picture of Nichole on the edge of the runway.

"What does she have around her neck?" asked Michael as he took the magazine out of Carson's hands.

Together they examined the photo. "It looks like a camera." replied Carson.

6

olland J. Attwilder was no stranger to stress. Even when he first ran for the elected office of Mayor of Santa Fe, his intestines had started to tie themselves into knots when he felt his anxiety level increasing. The President of the United States of America was supposed to remain cool under pressure, and fortunately, only the First Lady had any inkling of his idiosyncrasy. This Monday morning President Attwilder continued to hold his anxiety in check. He looked up from the morning briefing papers Henry Grishhold had dropped on his desk at 6:30 a.m. Both the Chief of Staff and his boss were early risers, but this habit hardly accounted for their lack of sleep over the weekend. The disaster in Salt Lake City had claimed far more than two hundred lives, a fact that wasn't overlooked in the Oval Office.

"OK, Hank. What do we have on this group calling itself *La Libertad Occidental?*" President Attwilder asked, as he quickly reshuffled the pages of Hank's recent update.

Using a duplicate copy of the same information, the Chief of Staff flipped to the second page of the briefing that summarized what the President had just read. Looking across the desk at the taller man, Hank reviewed the facts, "They are commonly known as the LLO and first made themselves known to the public when they bombed President Acosta's personal residence in Lima, Peru, almost sixteen years ago. Since that time they have claimed responsibility for bombings, kidnappings, and assassinations all across the western hemisphere."

President Attwilder stopped Hank from continuing. "Have they spread their ideology across the Atlantic?"

"It appears so. Last year they were linked to the Red Brigade's bombing of the Vatican. I guess political insanity doesn't respect geographic boundaries," answered his highest appointed aid.

"I see they are claiming responsibility for the events that lead to the crash of the Omega flight out of Salt Lake on Friday night. Do you think they are serious?" President Attwilder asked, once again turning the pages of Hank's morning report.

"Once again I'll say that it appears so. According to Tom Folger, they sent a letter that can definitely be construed as a *warning,* to the Regional Office of the FBI in Los Angeles last Thursday."

The nation's chief executive tugged several times on the collar of his shirt in an abortive attempt to loosen his tie, and then closed the report and dropped it on his desk in the Oval Office. President Attwilder was lean and rugged and stood six-foot three-inches tall, even without the boots he commonly wore in the upstairs living quarters. Even in a suit, he still looked like he belonged on the 1,400 acre ranch he maintained just outside Santa Fe, New Mexico.

Moving his chair back far enough from the desk to stand, the President asked, "Have you gotten hold of everyone?"

Anticipating the President's next instruction, Hank stood and walked towards the door. "They're all waiting outside, Mr. President. Are you sure you don't want anyone else?"

"Let's keep the group tight for the time being," responded the western politician, knowing full-well the importance of the meeting Hank had orchestrated on his behalf. "Bring them in."

Hank Grishhold opened the side door separating the President's inner office from the desk of Sandra Kennard, his long time secretary and closest female friend, aside from the First Lady. Sandra had worked with Rolland Attwilder on his congressional campaigns and gubernatorial races, and when he was elected to the office of President of The United States, she naturally came with him. If you wanted something from President Rolland J. Attwilder, you first had to go through Sandra Kennard.

"Sandra, ask the Vice President and the others to come in." Hank attempted a smile, an exercise that didn't fool the female aid. She had been closely involved in the crisis situation ever since Friday night, when the President first received the news of the devastating accident. Only now it appeared it was no accident.

Seconds later Vice President Jason Wright, along with Thomas Folger and Seymour Dillan, followed Sandra Kennard into the President's office. She offered them coffee as they each took a seat. All of them accepted, understanding that the President's personal secretary had arranged the seating. Vice President Jason Wright had taken the floral print high-backed chair to the left of the President. It was assumed that Hank Grishhold would return to the chair he regularly occupied on the right side of the President's desk. Seymour Dillan, director of the CIA, and Thomas Folger, head of the FBI, each took one side of the eight foot sofa. Dillan could have gotten by with a quarter of the couch. Seymour was only five foot seven and weighed just over 130 pounds, but no one let the director of the CIA's size fool them. His experience as a field operative in the intelligence service earned him total respect from those who served under him. Thomas Folger, most often referred to as Tom by the other people in the room, and Mr. Director by the rest of the world, was a large man who took up most of his half of the couch. Not only was he taller than the President, he was also in better shape. If he wasn't almost fifty years old, he could have still been playing semi-pro football. When Tom talked to you, you listened carefully to what he had to say.

Jason Wright, the Vice President, lifted his coffee cup from the silver tray that Sandra was passing around the room. Jason and President Attwilder had served on several committees together when they were both still in Congress. After the Party nominated Rolland Attwilder as their candidate for President, Jason Wright was the natural choice for his running mate. Not only could Jason bring in all the electoral votes from New York and most of the northeastern part of the country, his slightly more liberal views balanced the conservative rhetoric espoused by President Attwilder.

President Attwilder moved around the room, greeting each of the men graciously, but in a tone of voice that indicated they had a lot of work to do. "Hank, why don't you bring everyone up to speed?" the President requested, once again taking his seat at the powerful desk in front of the window.

Chief of Staff Hank Grishhold nodded his head, and handed out the briefing paper he had previously cleared with President Attwilder. This was not totally new information to either Seymour Dillan or Thomas Folger. For the past several days, their agencies had been running independent investigations that had provided much of the intelligence contained in the briefing. Once Hank finished distributing the report, everyone in the room had a condensed summary of what everyone else knew. The briefing paper was titled, *"TERRORISM AND THE THREAT TO AIR TRAVEL IN THE UNITED STATES."*

Hank unconsciously cleared his throat to insure he had the group's attention, and then jumped right in. "Last Friday evening an L-1011 flown by Omega Airlines crashed just after take off from Salt Lake International Airport. What preceded that crash, along with the actual destruction of the aircraft itself, will undoubtedly alter life as we know it in the United States. This briefing paper establishes the scenario that was independently arrived at by both the CIA and the FBI."

President Rolland Attwilder raised his lanky frame from behind the oak desk and started pacing the room. Hank and the others remained fixed to their chairs as they waited for him to speak.

Fifteen seconds later, a period that seemed far longer to each man in the room, President Attwilder quit pacing and stood directly beside the Vice President. "Jason, we have to stop anything like this from happening again. As of this moment, you are to delegate all outstanding projects to your staff. Your major responsibility will be to coordinate the efforts of the group in this room." Frowning out of frustration, he continued, "You are to stop the LLO, and any other similar organization, from duplicating the cowardly and contemptuous act demonstrated Friday night in Salt Lake City."

The President's instructions were already being implemented. Early Sunday morning, President Attwilder and Vice President Wright had met with Hank Grishhold and formulated a potential plan of action, and during the last twenty four hours, Jason had taken the ball and started it rolling. His position as Person In Charge of the task force on terrorism was now formalized.

Vice President Jason Wright assumed the role of task force supervisor instantaneously. Nodding acceptance to the other members of the group, he rose from the straight backed chair and stood beside the President. Turning to address the Chief of Staff, he began, "Hank, I hope you will excuse me, but Seymour and Tom have both provided me with some additional information that I can add to this briefing. Here are the facts as close as we have determined.

"One. At approximately 1:00 a.m. last Wednesday morning, an unidentified group of potential terrorists broke into the armory at El Toro Marine Corps Air Station and stole fifteen shoulder fired surface-to-air missiles, commonly referred to as Stingers. The perpetrators of this theft are still at large.

"Two. A Marine Gunnery Sergeant Adrian Baker is a possible witness to the robbery. He and a Corporal Isaac Jefferson were standing watch in the armory. Corporal Jefferson was pronounced dead at the scene. Gunnery Sergeant Baker was beaten, pistol whipped, and then shot twice in the chest and left on the armory floor for dead. Baker is still alive and is under a security watch at Los Angeles Memorial Hospital. Memorial specializes in coma victims, and as your briefing paper already states, Sergeant Baker lapsed into a coma before regaining complete consciousness.

"Three. Thursday afternoon a messenger service delivered a letter to Tom's regional office in Los Angeles. I will have Tom read the letter that was forwarded to FBI headquarters in just a moment. After a spectrograph analysis and a complete battery of tests, all we know about the letter and its author is that the letter was pieced together from words extracted from individual copies of *The Los Angeles Times*. The courier service has been unable to provide any information that has proved useful in locating the sender.

"Four. Friday evening just before ten o'clock, Mountain Standard Time, Omega Flight 421 from Salt Lake to Portland departed on Salt Lake Runway 34. After leaving the heading of 280 and heading north along the shore of the lake, they lost control of the plane. Attempting to return to the airport, Captain Tom Nickle executed a 180 degree turn, but crashed upon landing. Two-hundred-forty-two people died that night. There were 42 survivors, of which another 18 have since died from injuries related to the crash.

"Five. A thorough investigation, encompassing a radius of eight miles from the Salt Lake crash site, turned up a spent Stinger missile in a hunting shack approximately 2.7 miles northwest of the runway. It has now been confirmed that this missile was used to down Flight 421. As you all are aware, the Stingers stolen from El Toro are heat seeking, proximity fused missiles, and this Stinger has been traced to the missiles stolen from El Toro." Pausing to make sure the group was still with him, he continued, "This particular missile appears to have exploded just aft and above the rear engine of Omega Flight 421. The way the missile casing was left in the hunting shack leaves little doubt that the shooter wanted us to find it and identify it as one of the El Toro missiles.

"Six. We believe *La Libertad Occidental,* or the LLO, to be responsible for the missile launch. We have been unable to identify any individual suspects.

"And seven. We have been able to contain all references to the crash being anything other than an accident. I don't have to tell you what the state of panic would be, if and when the true cause of the crash of 421 were ever leaked out."

Vice President Wright looked up at Tom Folger, who was now also standing. "Tom, would you brief us on the investigation of the actual theft of the missiles from El Toro?"

Tom waited while Jason took his seat, and then began, "First, let me read you the letter from the LLO, which was received at the Bureau office in Los Angeles." Thomas Folger then reached in his black leather attache case resting on the couch he had vacated, and passed out a copy of the letter Vice President Wright had just referred to. In block letters cut from a newspaper they all read:

"BE WARNED:

"FOR THE PAST 20 YEARS THE UNITED STATES HAS SUP-PORTED PUPPET DICTATORS AND WORKED TO REPLACE

DULY ELECTED OFFICIALS IN THE COUNTRIES OF OUR
SOUTH AMERICAN NEIGHBORS.

"LA LIBERTAD OCCIDENTAL HAS RECEIVED 15 STINGER
MISSILES. DO NOT FLY IN THE SKIES OVER YOUR COUNTRY.
ONE OF THESE MISSILES MAY BE LAUNCHED WITHOUT
WARNING. THE DEATHS OF MANY INNOCENT PEOPLE WILL
BE ON YOUR HANDS.

"EXACT DEMANDS WILL BE SENT IN THE NEXT FEW
DAYS. IT IS IMPERATIVE THAT YOU UNDERSTAND THE SERI-
OUSNESS OF YOUR SITUATION. WE REGRET THE LOSS OF
LIFE, BUT UNFORTUNATELY, WE MUST DEMONSTRATE THE
WEAKNESS OF YOUR POSITION.

"LA LIBERTAD OCCIDENTAL
"VIVA LA LIBERTAD!"

"Was this letter taken seriously when it was received?" President Attwilder demanded of the director of the FBI.

Jason Wright broke in before Tom had a chance to answer the outbreak from the President. "Completely! The only problem is that there was nothing in the letter that indicated where or when a possible launching would take place. Only an idiot would tell John Q. Public that 15 Stinger missiles are unaccounted for and might very will be used to shoot down an airliner in his own neighborhood!"

There was silence in the room as each person questioned the logic of the Vice President's retort. Everyone understood the dilemma the Bureau had faced when they first received the letter. The Federal Bureau of Investigation receives literally thousands of letters every year warning of future acts of terrorism, or taking credit for acts already completed. Most of these letters are pranks, but each one is investigated as if it were a serious threat.

Vice President Wright calmed down, thanked Tom for his input, and immediately asked Seymour Dillan to update the group as to the status of his efforts in finding the base of operations of the LLO.

Standing to address his peers, Seymour began speaking in a low resonate voice that left no doubt as to his disdain for the act they were all investigating. "First of all, the LLO has maintained a base of operations in the jungles of Peru. To date, the government of Peru has not allowed us access to specific areas of their country we believe to be probable strongholds of the organization. To the best of our knowledge the LLO has over 300 active soldiers operating in Peru and other South American countries."

"And in the United States?" questioned President Attwilder, while simultaneously squeezing a hard rubber ball he kept in his desk. It was supposed to relieve tension, but it didn't seem to be working.

"Still, questionable, Mr. President," Seymour stated matter-of-factly. Looking down at his own prepared notes, he continued, "Second. Until this last week, there have been no known terrorist acts committed on the soil of the United States that could be positively identified as belonging to the LLO. Tom Folger has explained in his briefing that there are a number of suspicious bombings, but absolute responsibility has not yet been determined. "Last night a team of CIA operatives left a Navy submarine and secretly landed in Peru. NASA had reported an increased amount of possible foot activity in this sector. It coincided with the landing of a small transport plane on Sunday morning." Seymour Dillan unfolded a map of Peru and laid it on the antique coffee table in the center of the room. Pointing to a portion of the map outlined with a red marker, he stated, "Here!"

Looking up from the color map, he went on, "Ninety minutes ago, we were notified that this suspected stronghold was in reality just a drug processing operation." He once again used a hand gesture to indicate the area marked in red. "We still don't have any confirmation that the LLO was behind the theft of the Stingers, nor do we know where those missiles are located." Seymour Dillan sat back down on the cushioned sofa. "Yes, but we believe that confirmation is forthcoming," he added from his seat on the couch.

"We do know that they have 15 Stinger missiles," interjected Thomas Folger, attempting to clear up any possible doubt left by the director of the CIA's last remark..

President Attwilder put a large hand to his reddened forehead and said sternly, "Fourteen, Tom. Fourteen."

Everyone understood the significance of the President's comment.

President Rolland Attwilder and Vice President Jason Wright stood looking at each other, each hoping the other had an answer to the threat facing the nation..

Sandra Kennard opened the door and entered the office unannounced. Walking quickly to the left of the desk, she whispered something to the President and left.

"Tom, there is a call from your office. I think you had better take it." President Attwilder sat back down and pointed to the phone on his desk, indicating that Director Folger should pick it up.

For the next few minutes there was near silence as the other four men listened intently to the one sided conversation.

Finally, Tom Folger hung up the phone and reviewed what had just transpired. "The Chicago office just received another letter. It is apparently from the LLO. A copy is being faxed to Sandra right now."

Sandra Kennard again entered the office from the side door and handed the fax she had just received to the President. Frowning, President Rolland Attwilder read it, and solemnly handed it to Tom Folger. It was just like the last one. A warning cut from the pages of a newspaper.

Tom read:

"YOU WILL DEPOSIT $2 BILLION U.S. DOLLARS IN A NUMBERED SWISS ACCOUNT. THIS MONEY WILL BE USED TO CORRECT YOUR IMPERIALISTIC MISTAKES IN SOUTH AMERICA. WHEN YOU ARE READY TO MAKE PAYMENT, PLACE A PERSONAL AD IN USA TODAY. IT SHOULD START "DEAR NEIGHBOR, I HAVE WHAT YOU WANT." DON'T DELAY. OUR INSTRUCTIONS WILL FOLLOW.

"ONCE AGAIN, WE FEEL IT NECESSARY TO DEMONSTRATE THE SERIOUSNESS OF YOUR SITUATION. FLIGHT 421 CRASHED OVER 72 HOURS AGO. YOU HAVE FAILED TO WARN THE INNOCENT PEOPLE OF THE UNITED STATES TO QUIT FLYING. WE ARE LEFT WITH NO ALTERNATIVE.
"LA LIBERTAD OCCIDENTAL
"VIVA LA LIBERTAD"

"Let's get on this. I doubt if we have much time!" Vice President

Wright said as Tom finished reading the letter. The Vice President knew that they would all do everything humanly possible, but their efforts to stop the next air disaster would prove useless. There was really nothing they could do. They couldn't possibly warn the public!

"President Attwilder sat down at his desk as the men filed from the room, each one determined to use the full power of his office to confront this hideous threat. Jason Wright, being the last one out, closed the door behind him, leaving the President sitting in the chair behind his desk, his body leaned forward with his arms supporting his sagging head.

President Rolland Attwilder was thinking, "Where will it take place? How many innocent people are going to die?"

He muttered aloud to a now empty room, "Damn it to hell! What can we do?"

7

TUESDAY AFTERNOON

A surging wave of bodies rippled through the twenty foot wide passageway leading to the narrow escalator. Any anxiety or fear of flying, that may or may not have been harbored by the Omega passengers, was certainly not detected as the men, women, and children jostled for position around the moving turntable in the baggage claim area of La Guardia International Airport. In reality, the crowd was just behaving in a normal fashion, they were,after all in New York City. Esteban pushed his way through the noisy throng waiting for their baggage as it came off Flight 1067 from Las Vegas. He switched his black carry-on garment bag from his left shoulder to his right, straightening the slightly wrinkled collar of his gray-pin striped gabardine suit as he headed for *ground transportation*. Even with his hair neatly pulled into a pony tail, Esteban Moreno appeared to be nothing more than a busy executive.

Esteban edged his way to the curb and waited for a middle-aged black man to motion for the next cab to move forward. Reaching into the pocket of his expensive slacks, he pulled out two dollars and palmed them to the would-be porter as the man turned and yelled for the young couple next in line to move it along. Esteban Moreno pulled the rear door of the dented yellow cab shut as he slid across the rear seat. "Sixty-first and Madison," he told the East Indian cab driver, just as the horn blared from the yellow and black vehicle. Forcing his way into the line of traffic, the cabby nodded, and speaking surprisingly good English, said, "No problem. Might take a few extra minutes, with the bridge construction."

Esteban settled himself into a semi-comfortable position in the black vinyl seat. "Things haven't changed," he thought. For more than 20 years he had flown in and out of La Guardia and Kennedy airports, and in all that time he couldn't remember when there wasn't some kind of bridge construction going on.

"This the place?" questioned the driver as the cab slowed to a halt.

Esteban nodded his head in agreement, checked the fare on the meter, and tossed two twenties across the seat. "Keep it," he said as he grabbed his leather garment bag and stepped out on the pavement. The brownstone building was only four stories tall, and from the outside, it didn't appear to have any distinctive features. In New York City appearances are oftentimes deceiving, as was evidenced by the opulent lobby. A polished marble staircase circled up through the center of the building, however most people used the natural wood grained elevators that opened on the right side of the dark green pile carpet.

The security guard studied the identification card, and checked the name against a master list he had been given earlier. Satisfied, he pointed towards the bank of elevators and sat back down at his desk. Esteban fingered a hidden scar under his right shoulder and moved in the opposite direction from the Otis built machines. He had learned from a sad experience in Santiago, Chile, to never take an elevator in a strange building. This afternoon, despite his familiarity with the converted office building, he walked up the two flights to the conference room in the rear of the 100 year old historical landmark.

The secretary quit typing on her computer as he came through the door. Standing effortlessly, she walked around the L shaped desk, recognition already established. "I'll take your bag, go on in, the meeting is just getting started. He told me to tell you to go on in as soon as you got here." She sounded much younger than her fifty-five years.

Esteban slipped into an empty seat at the far end of the 12 foot long glass topped table, and listened intently as the distinguished silver haired executive solicited reports from each of the seven people who were already seated around the raised platform. Most people would have been startled, if not extremely frightened by the tone and contents of the reports being delivered. Esteban experienced none of these emotions as it was, after all, part of the plan.

Fifteen minutes after Esteban took a seat at the table, it was evident that the individual reporting process was ended. After waiting for the papers to be returned to the table, the silver haired gentlemen stood and moved to an empty space between the two women in the group. "You all understand the importance of your assignments. Our business is based on trust, and trust is based on loyalty." His tone of voice left no doubt that he was referring to loyalty to the organization that controlled the corporation, that acted as trustor, for the same brownstone building on Madison Avenue. Esteban observed their reactions, quietly filing them away for future reference. Some nodded agreement and others merely remained quiet, but no one seemed puzzled by the Latin's appearance at the end of the table. Previous meetings in this same room had established his right to attend.

The speaker continued, "The seeds are in place." Using a laser pointer, he moved the red triangle from one section of the map that had silently dropped from the ceiling at the head of the table. "Flight 421 set the ball in play. It is now in our court," he stated, using a basketball analogy that was familiar to them all. "A belief in madness rules our world. It is important that the United States government understand the difference between acts of madness and demented minds. When we arranged for the delivery of 15 Stinger surface-to-air missiles, we were not mad. When we approved the crash of the L-1011 in Salt Lake, we were not mad. And when we approved Shortfall, I most assuredly guarantee you that we were not mad!" The urgency of his delivery convinced each person seated at the table to pay close attention.

Moving slightly to his left, he came to rest behind the slender olive complected lady with short dark hair. "Now," he continued, placing both his arms on the shoulders of the lady still sitting in front of him. No effort was made on her part to regain her freedom. Instead, she turned her head upwards to catch his next comment. "We all understand the importance of security." He still didn't remove his hands from her shoulders. "Martha Willburg was responsible for recruiting Gunnery Sergeant

Adrian Baker, United States Marine Corps." He patted the dark skinned lady twice on the shoulder, signifying a form of congratulations. The information she provided was crucial to our success."

The silver haired speaker stopped and looked for the first time directly at Esteban, silently acknowledging his presence. Turning once again to his captive audience, he raised his voice slightly, while tightening his grip on Martha Willburg's shoulder. "Sergeant Baker should be dead! He is not, but I can assure you that he soon will be." He paused and again looked at Esteban as if to solicit a look of agreement.

Focusing his dark eyes on each person seated at the polished conference table, he continued his speech, still maintaining his grip on the woman's shoulder. "We shouldn't be having this conversation." The grip was now more frightening to the people around the table than to Martha herself.

Martha Willburg tried to slump out of the grip of the orator. It was a futile effort.

Never releasing the pressure, the silver haired man continued, "Sergeant Baker gave instructions on the specific car, a Grand Am, that was to be used to gain entrance to Marine Corps Air Station, El Toro. The marine captain who owned the car was supposed to have been in North Carolina on leave." Digging his strong fingers into the soft tissue of Martha Willburg's shoulder, the speaker continued, "He was not! Captain Edward Parker cancelled his leave two days before El Toro. Apparently, his young son got sick with the measles. One week ago tonight, last Tuesday, at approximately midnight, Captain Parker's son got worse. The Captain dressed the boy to take him to the base hospital. When he went outside, his Grand Am was gone. Stolen!

"Now, if you were Captain Edward Parker, Martha, what would you do?" he asked, finally lightening the pressure of his hands.

The man continued speaking, without waiting for her answer, "Right, Martha!" he stated in a voice that could barely be heard. Leaning down as if to whisper, he suddenly returned to a normal speaking voice, and while smiling, he continued, "He called the MP's and local law enforcement officials and reported the loss of his car. That in and of itself wouldn't have been too bad. The MP's, however, were kind enough to send a car to take Captain Parker and son to the emergency room at the base hospital.

Grabbing her head in his vice grip hands to face his accusations, the man roared, "Now, Martha, guess where the hospital is located on the base? No idea? Let me tell you. It is directly across from the base motor pool where the Grand Am was still parked, as per the instructions from Sergeant Baker. Five more minutes and we wouldn't have gotten the missiles off the base. And now Sergeant Baker is still alive. Probably a vegetable, but alive, nevertheless.

Fright was hardly the word to describe the dark haired lady's state of mind, but still she remained seated at the table. "Martha, you should have known that Captain Edward Parker never left town," he whispered as he finally removed his right hand from her shoulder, and stuck it in his pants pocket.

Esteban was the first one to see the six inch stiletto knife flash through air. No one said a word, watching in amazement as the knife was jammed into Martha's neck and then violently slashed upwards. Blood gushed everywhere. Martha Willburg's head fell forward banging the table top and splashing blood that had already gushed onto the now wet surface. Still, no one moved.

The well dressed gray haired executive wiped the razor sharp instrument on the back of Martha's business suit. Addressing the group in a level tone of voice, he stated, while shaking his head at the corpse leaning across the bloody table, "She was in charge of Baker, and she should have known!" He dropped the knife loudly on the glass table top beside Martha's head, her face still frozen in fright. "Shortfall will succeed. Let this be a lesson to all of you. I will not accept stupidity!"

Esteban nodded his head to The Cleaner, who was still standing behind the bloody, but lifeless body of Martha Willburg. He understood why The Cleaner had almost severed the guilty member's head. Both men knew what was at stake!

8

WEDNESDAY MORNING

Carson used his right index finger to wipe the moisture clear from the corners of his eyes. Now, with his son laying in the casket, his light blue eyes closed as if to protect them from the misty fog, Carson knew it was over. Kelly was gone. Soft choral music emanating from the speakers fell down over the quiet graveside. Nodding his head slightly, his eyes partially closed, Carson signaled the minister that he could lower the lid. This simple act of closing the mahogany and chrome memorial ended a chapter in Carson Jeffers' life. The ever present Oregon fog continued to dampen his blond hair, and as the result of a lifelong habit, he used his fingers to brush it back across his head. Wiping the water from his hands on the side of his dark blue wool pants, he failed to notice the attractive dark haired lady standing in the back of the crowd. She was dressed in a light blue suit and carrying an unopened umbrella. Nichole Lewis was not bothered by the Oregon mist.

Nichole had read the *Oregonian* and found the obituary notice Tuesday morning. Her first impulse had been to send a card and forget making the three and a half hour drive. As she read the announcement for the second time, she had the distinct impression that it was important for her to be at the service. She knew that Carson Jeffers would undoubtedly have many friends and business associates at the service, but she said to herself, "They don't understand, they weren't there. You'd have to have lived through the horror of the crash." So she made the drive to Portland.

A large group of teenagers stood to the right of the burial plot, crying openly for their lost friend. It was undoubtedly the quietest the high school students had been in months, and by the number in attendance, you could tell that Kelly had been well liked. Two boys dressed in jeans, white shirts, and ties stepped from the group and walked in front of the casket. Heads bowed, the boys almost appeared to be twins in their Portland High letter jackets. Navigating a path between the floral arrangements, they approached Carson and handed him a large card. He took the hand-made remembrance and opened it to read the words of sympathy. Once again the grieving father wiped the tears from his dark blue eyes as he re-read the thoughtful words signed in the scroll of several hundred adolescents. Nichole watched Carson thank the boys and shake their hands. Reverently the young athletes rejoined the group of Portland teenagers who were by now completely stationary on the grassy knoll.

Nichole was touched by the gesture and wiped her eyes in sympathy. The dark haired flight attendant silently moved through the group of friends and loved ones until she was standing ten feet behind Kelly Jeffers' mourning father. Sobbing softly to herself, she listened to the minister finish reading from the Bible. When he finished reading the passage, he bowed his head and said, "Let us pray."

She didn't hear the exact words offered in remembrance of this man's son. She, like the rest of the mourners, was trying to make sense of this terrible loss of life. The more she thought about it, the harder she wept. Gaining some composure over her emotions, she noticed that Carson leaned over and whispered something to a six-foot-two-inch short haired African-American companion. Nichole considered the display of true compassion manifest in his body language, and knew that he must be an extremely close and dear friend.

Soft music continued to fill the cemetery as the graveside service ended. Father and friend stepped forward, and placed white roses they had been wearing in their suit lapels on the now closed casket. Slowly the audience retreated from the freshly dug burial plot, many of them stopping to pay their respects to Carson. The younger dark haired man stepped back and stood behind Carson, staying close enough to offer support, but not interfering with the compassionate greetings of both Kelly's and Carson's friends.

As the group became smaller, Carson recognized Nichole standing quietly beside the draped mound of cool earth that would soon cover his young son's body. Raising his hand in the late morning moisture, he motioned her forward to his side. Nichole didn't say anything, she just put her hand around Carson's shoulder, and he responded with an embrace of appreciation. Nothing else needed to be said. Her presence was a statement in and of itself.

On the other side of Portland Memorial Cemetery, a twenty-eight-year old observer focused the zoom lens of his Nikon camera a second time. He had taken the first group of pictures when Nichole opened the door of the jeep pick-up and joined the people surrounding the six foot deep grave. Following instructions carefully, he continued snapping pictures, one after another. A permanent record of the physical contact between the attractive flight attendant and the grieving father was instantly captured on film.

Carson rotating his head from left to right and beckoned to his friend who was still standing behind him. Leaving his right arm resting on her shoulder, Carson spoke softly, "Michael, this is Nichole Lewis. She is the flight attendant who was with me in the crash last Saturday. I told you how she helped me take care of Kelly."

Michael gently wrapped both of his large palms around Nichole Lewis' right gloved hand and gave it a squeeze, almost as if it were in appreciation. "Nice to meet you, Nichole. Michael Randall. I wish we could have met under a different set of circumstances."

"Likewise," Nichole responded as the well dressed man released her arm.

"Michael is the president of my consulting firm," Carson explained to Nichole as the three of them stood by the open grave. "Saturday morning is still a haze in my mind. Did I tell you about ManTech?"

She nodded that he had.

"Michael is the closest friend I've got. Now with Kelly gone, I guess he is the closest person I could call family."

The two ManTech executives and the Omega flight attendant started moving towards the long gray limousines parked under the row of pine trees. Before reaching the cars, Michael excused himself and went to talk to the drivers.

Stopping at a green metal bench next to the cars, Nichole asked, "Would you like to talk for a minute?"

"That would be nice," Carson said as the two of them sat down on the slightly moist bench.

"I'm glad you could come," Carson told Nichole. "It wasn't necessary."

Wiping her eyes with the wet tissue she pulled from her pocket, she responded. "I would have come to the memorial service, but the notice in the paper just gave the time and address of the graveside service and internment."

Carson held her arm briefly and apologized, "That was my fault. I didn't do a very thorough job of the obituary notice. But I really do appreciate your taking time to drive down here to Portland."

After several moments of condolences, Nichole asked, "Are you able to sleep? I can't."

"It's hard. I spend half the time feeling guilty about even being on the plane, and the rest of the time making promises to somehow get even," Carson answered.

"What do you mean by getting even?"

"Getting even probably isn't the right way to say it. But I want someone to pay for the death of my son."

Nichole Lewis noted the look of determination that had suddenly replaced the tears on his rugged face. It was the first time that she had been aware of the faint but jagged scar running from just above his left eye into the right edge of his hairline. She would later learn that the scar was a souvenir from southeast Asia.

"Do you mean financially?" she asked, hoping the answer was no.

"No. I'm not talking about money. I don't give a damn about that." Carson paused and reflected on what he really meant, unaware of his abrupt vocabulary. "Nichole, I know in my gut that something very odd happened on Flight 421 that caused us to crash, something that never should have happened. It was something that neither the pilots nor the plane were able to handle. I want to find out what caused the crash of Flight 421. It must never happen again."

Nichole once again wiped the mist from her face, mixing tears with the clear water from the sky. She was relieved to hear that Carson wasn't just intent on extracting a pound of flesh from Omega. "Omega and the FAA will find out what caused the crash," she said.

"And if they don't?" interrupted Carson, looking up the slight hill to the partially obscured flower covered casket.

Nichole didn't know what to answer. Carson's hurried tone disturbed her, but it was understandable after everything he had lost. She thought to herself, "There is really nothing you can do. When the NTSB review findings are finally released, everyone will get the answers they are searching for." Finally responding to his question, she vocalized, "They will."

Feeling the momentary tension surface between them, Carson attempted to change the subject of conversation. "I saw your picture on the cover of *Time*." He paused and asked, "Did you read the article?"

"Yes. Why?"

"Nichole, the *Time* article keeps calling the crash an accident. I have spent quite a bit of time rethinking our conversation with those two FBI agents." Pausing as if to regroup his thoughts, he continued, "I thought it strange that your comments in *Time* so strongly supported Omega's position that the crash of Flight 421 was an unavoidable accident."

Nichole placed the still unused umbrella on her lap and smoothed her blue jacket, brushing the water droplets to the ground. She distinctly remembered telling the reporter that she didn't know what caused the crash. When he had asked her if she had some kind of opinion as to the reason for the accident, she had said that she found it odd that the plane reacted so strangely right after take off. It was as if the crash had taken place without any warning. She continued to explain that she had been involved in more than a dozen serious in-flight emergencies. They never happened without some kind of warning. When the interview was published, she, too, found it curious that her comments were edited in such a way as to make her almost the spokesperson for Omega. A spokesperson who firmly believed that Flight 421 was an accident, and nothing more!

Taking Carson's hand in her own, she said, "Don't believe every-thing you read in the press." She then explained, "When I was inter-viewed, I voiced the same concerns we discussed after we talked to those two men in the Salt Lake hanger. Not one of my suspicions was even alluded to in the *Time* article. I found the piece to be particularly biased reporting, especially after I had told the reporter how we seemed to lose such sudden attitude control."

"Following the crash, were you debriefed by Omega?" Carson asked as he considered the implications of her recent revelation..

"Yes, at least three separate times. My direct supervisor along with several Omega executives asked me repeatedly what I had observed just prior to the crash. When I told them my supposition that there might have been something strange about the accident, I was told to concen-trate on getting ready to go on my next cross country."

"When is that?" asked Carson, as he turned to acknowledge Michael's gesture that they were ready to leave.

"I am scheduled to fly from Seattle to Atlanta the day after tomor-row."

"Yet Omega never published a word about the possibility of the crash being anything other than an accident?" quizzed Carson, returning to her earlier explanation about the debriefing.

"Nothing at all, In fact I received a very strange phone call Monday afternoon."

"What's that?" Carson inquired, momentarily calculating what he was personally doing at that same time.

"Pierce Ekholt called me."

"Pierce Ekholt, the Chairman of the Board of Omega Airlines?" questioned Carson while leaning forward waiting for her to go on.

"The same. Anyway, he called me at my cabin on the sound and thanked me for my help with the rescue operations on the runway. He said that I had saved several lives that might have been lost if I hadn't used my head."

"What's so strange about that? I'm sure that Pierce Ekholt was indeed thankful?"

"It's what he said just before he hung up. He said that I was not to keep spreading unfounded rumors about the crash of 421."

Carson saw Michael walking towards them, indicating they needed to leave. There were still some details to take care of at the mortuary.

As Carson started to get up, Nichole put her gloved hand on his now rain soaked leg and stopped him from leaving. "Carson, he told me specifically not to talk to you about the crash." Waiting for her comment to sink in, she added, "Now, why did he do that? And why mention your name?"

Unable to fathom an answer, he replied, "I don't know, Nichole. I just don't get it." Recalling the cover of the news magazine, Carson posed another question, "Was that a camera around your neck on the cover of *Time*?"

Nichole nodded, "Yes, I didn't realize it was even there until I saw the magazine."

"Why did you have it?" Carson asked, intrigued by her reply.

Nichole thought back to Friday night. "It belonged to a young Japanese tourist who had been taking pictures out the window of plane just before we crashed. I guess he wanted to remember the Salt Lake City skyline."

A thought entered Carson's mind as he thought about the propensity the Japanese have for taking countless photographs. Troubled by his memories, he posed another question, "Did you give the camera back?"

"No. I couldn't. The young man died in the crash. To tell you the truth, I didn't know what to do with the camera. In fact, I still have it."

Carson thought back to how 421 seemed to nose down all of a sudden. "Nichole, would you do me a favor?"

"If I can," she answered.

"This may sound strange, but I want you to take the film in that camera and get it developed."

"Why?" Nichole responded with a puzzled look on her face.

"Probably for nothing at all. Kelly was sitting by the window, and I would like to see what he was looking at before he died." Carson knew that this was not entirely accurate, but it was all he could say. "Not a great way to build a friendship," he thought to himself..

"I'm returning home this afternoon, and I'll take the film in when I get there. If you could spare the time, why don't you come up tomorrow?" Nichole asked, not entirely sure of the reason behind her invitation.

"I would like that," he said, thinking that he really would enjoy the drive up to Seattle. He didn't really expect to find anything on the film, but it might give him a chance to sort out his feelings.

Carson offered his arm as Nichole stood on the flower lined walkway. Taking a piece of paper out of her purse, she drew a map showing how to find her cabin on the Puget Sound. Before she walked back to her jeep, she paused and looked back up the hillside to the flower covered coffin. "I am truly sorry about Kelly,"

It was the most natural thing in the world. Carson took her in his arms and held her tight, all the time thinking about the son he would never see again.

The reddish haired photographer snapped another picture and then picked up his cellular phone. He punched in the area code and phone number. When the ringing stopped, he heard, "Security - Omega Airlines."

9

The slight screech that rose from the massive tires under the Boeing 767 was enough to bring Esteban to full consciousness. He felt the sleek American Airlines jet attach itself to the Dallas/Fort Worth runway. With the hour time change and a 6:00 a.m. New York departure time, it was still early morning in east Texas.

Esteban knew that Ricardo would have everything arranged. He exited the accordion style gateway, tossing his black garment bag loosely over his shoulder. Today he was wearing cowboy boots, Wrangler jeans, and a dark blue denim shirt with the sleeves rolled halfway up his strong dark arms.

"Como estas, companero?" Ricardo greeted as he fell in beside him.

"Not bad. Not bad." It sometimes annoyed Esteban when Ricardo would lapse into his native tongue. But here in Texas, it was doubtful if anyone would find it strange to see two Latins greeting each other in Spanish. Just the same, better to stay with English.

Ricardo was three or four inches shorter than his six-foot companion. Dressed in dusty ranch style boots and a weathered black cowboy hat, he left the impression that he was almost the same size as his Peruvian partner.

"Everything cleaned up in New York?" he asked casually, knowing Esteban wouldn't have been on the early morning flight if there had been any loose ends in the Big Apple.

Esteban noted that Ricardo had immediately switched to perfect English. Ricardo and Esteban had been companions in this business since that day some twelve years ago on the train ride from Machu Pichu to Cuzco, Peru. Esteban had been meeting a group of financial support- ers of the LLO as they returned from seeing the Inca Ruins set high on the slopes of the Andes. It had been the perfect cover for the purpose of their rendezvous. Ramon Gutierrez, Ricardo's father, was from Santiago, Chile, and had promised to fund the bombing of the Brazilian Embassy in Montevideo, Uruguay. Ramon's only requirement for releasing the money was for Esteban to take the twenty-two year old younger Gutierrez into the LLO. Unaware of the young Chilean's capabilities, Esteban had refused. Ramon, the father, would not release the funds. Finally, Esteban compromised and told the father that he would take his son with him to Montevideo. The boy would have to prove himself. Ricardo hadn't disappointed Esteban and the two men had remained constant companions.

"It was a worthwhile trip," Esteban finally replied.

"I've got everything set for one o'clock this afternoon. Drove straight through and arrived last night about 7:30. Do you want to look it over?" Ricardo asked, opening the door to the dusty, gray Jeep Grand Cherokee.

"Let's see how it lays out," Esteban answered above the roar of a departing jet. Exiting the terminal area, the two men in the silver colored all wheel drive vehicle smiled at each other, each thinking of the surprise awaiting the DFW airport shortly after lunch.

•   •   •

Sandra Kennard picked up the phone and listened to the frenzied voice on the other end of the line. Quickly she hung up and rushed through the door to President Rolland Attwilder's inner sanctum.

"Slow down, Sandra."

"Rolland, you better turn the television on!"

President Attwilder knew there was something out of the ordinary happening. Sandra had stopped calling him by his first name when he was inaugurated as President of the United States two years ago. It didn't bother him that she used his first name, but she had wanted to show her respect for what he had become.

"Tom Folger just called. It's happening again," she continued as she switched the set to CNN.

President Attwilder stared in resignation as he saw a video description of total mayhem. The CNN reporter was literally screaming into the microphone, sirens blaring from all sides as fire engines and ambulances sped past the reporter.

A young well dressed lady gripped the microphone. "We are here outside the NationWide Terminal at the Dallas/Fort Worth Airport. Air travel has suddenly been hit with a second major accident in less than a week. A NationWide Boeing 757 jet arriving from Atlanta has just crashed. The plane is believed to have been carrying 175 passengers. First reports suggest there are no survivors. This is Patricia Sanderson live with CNN News."

The picture on President Attwilder's television switched to the local NBC reporter in Dallas. He continued the story explaining how CNN's Entertainment News team was at the airport to film the arrival of country pop singer Garth Brooks, who was finishing his world tour in Dallas. The Dallas-based television announcer continued, "CNN had literally been able to film the disaster as it was happening. American's jet carrying Garth Brooks and his band landed at 12:50 p.m. Exactly ten minutes later, NationWide flight 488 from Atlanta was on a long final approach. Flight 488 crashed, strewing wreckage across both runways and the adjoining taxiway. Dallas/Fort Worth Airport is closed. The exact number of dead is still unknown. There is little hope that any of the passengers on 488 survived, and first reports indicate that more than 100 people on the ground may be missing and, in fact, are assumed to be dead. The carnage is unbelievable..."

Both President Attwilder and Sandra Kennard remained glued to the live video coming from Texas. Finally, President Attwilder said, "Get Jason Wright, Hank Grishhold, Tom Folger and Seymour Dillan. I want to see them all in this office, now!"

•   •   •

Esteban marveled at how lax the security around the Dallas airport had been. He had called the secret voice mail number late last night and provided the final details of the mission. Ricardo picked up the call as soon as he arrived in Dallas. The Cleaner had once again provided not only a perfect mission but also arranged an escape that was flawless. Only sixty minutes earlier he and Ricardo had been hiding beside the old water tank just off the airport. And now here he was in a motel some ten miles east of the airport.

"Not so rough," the naked girl whispered in his ear.

Esteban shoved her red head back against the mattress, violently restraining her struggles with his rough hands. Mentally, he thanked Ricardo. His Chilean companion had known what he would need when they finished at the Dallas/Fort Worth Airport.

Esteban slid his long tight legs up under him and mounted the young whore. His thigh muscles bulged as they folded around the slender torso of the Dallas teenager. Leaning forward, he took her left nipple in his mouth. Sucking, then biting, and finally pulling until blood droplets ran down her smooth skin. Grabbing the pillow with his left hand, he covered the young redhead's face, while simultaneously thrusting ever deeper into her frightened loins. It was as if his movements could purge the memory of Lima. Again and again he moved, ever faster, ever harder. He thought he could hear the screams that must have been coming from NationWide Flight 488. They were, however, only the muffled sounds of terror shrieking out from the king sized pillow. Pushing and rocking, he kept going, finally erupting like an exploding volcano. The girl was quiet. She had stopped moving. Esteban rose from the bed and walked into the bathroom, pausing to stand naked in front of the full length mirror. Shaking his head slightly, he turned on the shower and returned to the bedroom where he flipped on the TV. Changing channels until he found CNN, he smiled to himself, "It's nice that the networks schedule their reporters in advance."

Continuing to sit on the edge of the bed, he rolled the muscles in his shoulders and then relaxed to listen as his recent handiwork was explained to the world. The young prostitute Ricardo picked up in Dallas still hadn't moved. Ricardo had paid her $300 to wait in the hotel room, promising her another $1,000 at the end of the afternoon. Esteban removed the pillow from her head, once again remembering the screams he heard coming from his mother's room in Lima. His father was always gone, but he never failed to leave a key for his wealthy friends. The screams never stopped. Esteban covered the young girl with the rumpled sheet and rolled her body off the bed. Ricardo would clean up the mess. He always did.

● ● ●

The Oval Office was never intended to be a parlor for a wake. To the group of five men watching the latest reports from Dallas, it seemed as though that was just what they were attending. A somber mood, every bit as heavy as an unwieldy wet woolen blanket, permeated the room.

President Attwilder continued to pace from his desk to the fireplace on the east wall, as if his lanky movements would somehow lessen the tension. Vice President Jason Wright sat on the edge of the long couch staring at the carnage still being shown on the television. Hank Grishhold sat forward, occupying only the first third of his customary chair near the President's desk. Tom Folger and Seymour Dillan stood next to the window, both hoping that the light from the Washington, D.C., sun would somehow soften their spirits. All five men knew they had just lost a battle and were losing the war.

President Attwilder stopped walking and turned the sound partially down on the set. "You all just heard the reporter say that wind shear is suspected in the crash of 488. I assume that was your doing, Tom?"

"It was the best I could do. I leaked something that was plausible, even though we all know it isn't true. We need time!" The director of the FBI emphasized his point as he moved in from the glare off the outside window.

Vice President Wright sat up and broke in. "Mr. President, we all know what caused the crash of 488 in Dallas. I think we had better consider meeting the demands of these lunatics."

"We can't do that, and you know it," interrupted the President's Chief of Staff.

"We may be left with little choice if we don't get some leads on these people damn soon," joined President Attwilder. "These nut cases know that we aren't going to be able to keep this whole thing out of the press much longer. I think the only reason they haven't forced our hand before this is to allow us the time to raise the money. Hank, I agree with the Vice President. We don't have much time left."

Turning once again to the director of the FBI, President Attwilder asked, "Tom, what have you learned from the sergeant who was on guard duty at El Toro? Has he been able to give us anything?"

"Nothing. He is still in a coma. When he first arrived at the hospital, he muttered a few words about Stinger missiles, South America, and some numbers. We think he was trying to warn us about the theft of the missiles."

"And the numbers?" asked the President. "Any idea on what they are?"

"Still unknown. There is some supposition that they may be part of a telephone number. We are trying to complete a number through a computer scan, but haven't got anything yet. Until he regains consciousness, all we can do is speculate. The doctors are doing everything they can."

"Well, keep on it. This Sergeant Baker may be the only possible lead we have as to the identity of the actual people shooting off these missiles." Everyone knew that they had to find the individual assassins, not just identify an organization.

"Mr. President, let's get back to keeping a lid on the true cause of both crashes." Tom Folger walked away from the window and slumped onto the couch. "So far no one has questioned the delay of the FAA in releasing new information on Flight 421. I'm afraid that little hiatus is about to end. We will continue to report that wind shear is the suspected cause of this crash in Dallas." He paused as if to consider the gravity of his remarks. "We have to call in every favor and contain all speculation about the likelihood of two crashes in a week being anything other than a coincidence."

The Vice President turned and stood by the television, now almost completely void of sound. "Tom, in your briefing you said that Nichole Lewis had told a *Time* reporter that the crash of 421 seemed strange or even suspicious?"

"Yes," Tom answered, thinking back to the FBI Intelligence briefing he had recently shared with the Vice President.

"Is *Time* still holding on the story?"

"For the time being. I'm sure that they may try to reach the Omega flight attendant, now that a similar crash has happened in Dallas." Tom knew what the Vice President was getting at. He remembered briefing the chairman of Omega Airlines on what they were really up against. "I personally talked to Pierce Ekholt and explained how Nichole Lewis had been interviewed by our agents. He understands the gravity of the situation. I brought him up to date on our efforts to stop any and all rumors from spreading. The threat of terrorism is something the airlines have been living with for years."

"You briefed him on the true cause of the crash?" questioned the Vice President.

"I did. We couldn't expect him to play ball if he were kept in the dark," Tom answered.

"And this Nichole Lewis, what do you think she really suspects, Tom?" interjected President Attwilder.

"Not much right now. Pierce assured me that she would be all right. As of now, the only contact she has had, other than with the *Time* reporter, is Carson Jeffers."

Hank sat up in his chair and listened carefully to what Tom Folger was saying. When Tom paused, the Chief of Staff immediately jumped in. "Carson called me Monday morning asking for my help in finding out what caused the crash."

The President joined back in the conversation, addressing his comments directly to Hank. "We both know how much help Carson was in expanding our trade agreements in South America. Why was he calling about the Omega disaster?"

Hank reminded the President that Carson had been a personal friend for over twenty years. "As you will recall from the names listed in the last briefing report, Carson was one of the survivors last Friday on Flight

421. He had been skiing with his son in Park City. Kelly, his sixteen-year-old, died in the crash. Carson has it in his mind that he needs to find out what happened. He told me that it is important he know what caused the plane to react the way it did."

"I'm sure we all understand the tragedy of his personal loss, but what did you tell him?" asked Tom Folger, previously unaware of the phone conversation between the Chief of Staff and Carson Jeffers.

"I told him that I couldn't help him. He seemed to understand, especially when I assured him that the FAA and NTSB reports would be made available to him. I think he'll back off and leave it alone," Hank replied.

"I sure as hell hope so!" emphasized the President, remembering how thorough Carson had been in investigating the real reason Argentina had threatened to walk out of the trade discussions in Punta Del Este some thirteen months previously.

Seymour Dillan, who had remained remarkably quiet, now joined the discussion. "Carson Jeffers is investigating the cause of the crash of 421, and he is one of the leading experts on Latin American trade? Sounds too coincidental to me."

"My God, Seymour!" Hank exclaimed, straining his voice in frustration. "His only son was killed in that crash. What are you insinuating?"

Seymour Dillan raised his hands chest high with the palms extended, as if to say, "I don't know, but let's not ignore any possibility."

President Attwilder waved Dillan off with a shrug. "Let's not jump to conclusions."

Jason Wright knew the meeting was ended. Everyone in the room had work to do. "We all know what needs to be done," he said as he moved to the door of the President's office.

Everyone took his comment to mean the meeting was over. The two directors of the country's intelligence services followed the Vice President out the door. They were already deep in conversation as to how to deal with the media about NationWide Flight 488. Hank Grishhold was the last of the group to leave the room. He paused to talk to President Attwilder.

Rolland Attwilder never noticed him. The President had turned up the volume on CNN. The announcer seated in front of the rows of video monitors was speaking. "Wind shear is believed to be the cause of this second air disaster in less than a week...."

10

Carson and Michael turned away from 6th Avenue as the limousine headed north towards the river, and after stepping across the pooling water on the sidewalk, Carson followed Michael through the smoke colored double glass doors and headed for the bank of elevators. The executive offices were still virtually deserted, and except for a skeleton staff who had remained to handle the phones, the balance of the ManTech employees were yet to return from the service at Portland Memorial Cemetery.

Speech was unnecessary as the two men exited the elevator on the eleventh floor and walked directly into the outer brain trust of the consulting firm. Passing the empty desks, Carson pushed open the door of his office, and motioned for Michael to join him in front of the large window overlooking the Columbia. "Michael, do you believe in a life after death, you know, an afterlife?" he asked, while gazing at the moving blue water.

Moving the soft turquoise drapes aside from the right side of the large window so he could see exactly what Carson was looking at, Michael answered, "I came to the conclusion some years ago that nothing else makes sense." Watching the rippling water weave its way toward the ocean, he continued, "Kelly is not gone. Somewhere his spirit lives on. Where and how I don't know, but I firmly believe that in some form, he still exists." It wasn't a lot of comfort, but under the circumstances it was all Michael had.

Facing his friend, while simultaneously running his right hand through his wet hair, he commented, "I hope so, Michael. I want to believe, but sometimes it's just so hard to accept. The alternative, however, is no easier to comprehend. Is this it? Does it all end here? I guess I'll just have to go on faith."

Michael considered Carson's troubling question, undoubtedly prompted by the recent experience at the Cemetery. His close friend had lost a son, his only child. First it was Lynda, and then Kelly. Carson had to wonder what had happened to them. "It's all you can do," Michael finally responded in a somewhat reassuring tone.

Carson turned away from the overcast sky, while taking off his suit coat and tossing it over the back of the couch, suggesting that he was ready to get to back to work.

Picking up his friend's jacket from the leather sofa, Michael asked, "Why don't you go home? There is nothing for you to do here."

"And at home, Michael? What's there?" Carson responded, while holding up his arms to refuse the return of his jacket.

Michael didn't have an answer, knowing the grieving father was right. Instead, he turned his attention to the noise he heard erupting through the open door of Carson's office. The front office staff were returning to their desks and the commotion seemed totally inappropriate considering where they had just come from. Moving through the door to ask them to hold it down, Michael was immediately drawn to the cause of the group's disturbance. A radio was blaring from one of the desks near the file cabinets, and Michael could clearly hear the frenzied voice of the newscaster. One of the secretaries held up a hand to quiet the group. Voices hushed to utter silence as the announcer continued, "We interrupt this program to bring you more live coverage from our CNN reporter in Dallas, Texas..."

Carson had followed Michael into the outer office, and when he heard the announcer state that they were interrupting the program in process, he had quickly found a place near the front of the group. Seconds later Carson ran back to his office and flipped open the pine door that concealed the television monitor in the wooden bookshelf opposite his desk. Quickly realizing where Carson had vanished to, Michael hastened to stand in front of the large color screen. Both men were oblivious to the noise in the outer office as visual images flashed on the screen. The hysteria of the same national newscast was now being broad cast, live, to the entire world. Carson and Michael stood glued to the set, watching in horror as death was once again forced brutally into their lives. Neither man moved until the reporter stopped speaking.

"No way, Michael. No way!" Carson blurted while waiting for the newscast to continue.

Michael understood what Carson was saying. Two air crashes in less than a week. Impossible it was not. Improbable it was, and the likelihood of two similar air disasters in a week was too remote for either Carson or Michael to consider, let alone believe.

Finally Carson sat down on the front corner of his desk, still absorbing the images that were bring broadcast from the Dallas/Fort Worth Airport. "You better get Jim and Blake in here, Michael," he instructed. "We have to get on this. It's now time to drop everything. Something or someone has gone stark raving crazy, and unless we move fast, I have a premonition that our country is going to experience even more of this madness."

Michael wasted no time as he moved quickly to the outer office and gave instructions to Janelle. In less than two minutes he was back in Carson's office watching the same terrible drama that was unfolding in front of millions of other viewers. Silently he thought, "Such a terrible loss of life." It was now 12:15 p.m. Pacific Standard Time and according to Patricia Sanderson of CNN, the crash took place almost an hour and a quarter earlier. As Michael watched the report, he was immediately concerned that the horror of a tragedy similar to the disaster of flight 421 five days earlier might throw Carson into a total state of depression. Nothing of the kind happened. In fact, it seemed as if Carson had once again detached himself from the emotion of the moment in order to analyze the meaning of the separate events.

Michael appeared to interrupt the announcer as the audio portion of the program was temporarily returned to the local Portland NBC station. "Jim and Ted should be here any minute. Janelle said they had just checked in."

"Did you hear what the she just said?" Carson asked, referring to the comments of Patricia Sanderson, the CNN reporter, not Janelle, his secretary.

"About the suspected cause of the accident?"

"Exactly. She said the cause of the crash may have been wind shear, inferring that the Dallas/Fort Worth Airport has a reputation for being notorious for extremely severe wind conditions." Pausing to let Michael compare his analysis to that description just given by the reporter, Carson continued, "Michael, she is blowing smoke, and I don't know where the fire is coming from."

"What do you mean?" asked Michael, surprised by Carson's verbal attack on the reporter.

"I've flown into DFW a number of times and I admit there have been incidents of sudden wind shear, but the airport is not infamous for those conditions. Denver, yes. DFW, absolutely not. Besides, the crash happened less than ninety minutes ago. Why would anyone release a statement about the probable cause of the accident, or crash, in such a short time frame?" The sandy haired executive continued, while at the same time rolling up his white shirt sleeves. "There must be something else." He lowered his voice, as if talking to himself. "What is going on?"

Jim Tedrow and Blake Terry hurried through the group still congregated in the administrative area, and entered Carson's office together. Blake was the first to speak, "We just heard on the radio. What's going on?"

Carson pointed to the television and let Patricia Sanderson bring the men current on the situation, "The death toll is mounting. Unconfirmed reports now total over 377 people dead with more than 400 injured. All 182 passengers and crew on NationWide Flight 488 are assumed dead. When the plane touched down, it broke apart, spewing fire in all directions. Two commuter planes operated by TEXAIR were engulfed in the flames." Gasping for a breath, she continued with her live update, "There were no survivors on either of those flights. The list of casualties has not been released as of this time, but they continue to mount."

Blake was already loosening the tie he had purchased just for the early morning memorial service. He had given up wearing a suit and its accessories when he quit working for the FBI more than ten years before. Casually he threw the navy blue tie over the back of the oversized leather chair, while simultaneously extracting two sheets of paper from a file folder he had placed on the 18 inch high rectangular table. "I think you had better see this," he said to the other three men.

"What have you got?" Michael asked, fully aware that Blake was ready to give them a briefing on his findings about the investigation into the crash of Flight 421 in Salt Lake.

Speaking first to Carson, the ex-government official launched into his report, only briefly referring to his hand-prepared notes, "First of all, I am absolutely convinced that the two agents who tried to interview both you and Nichole Lewis were, in fact, on assignment with the Bureau. I didn't get anywhere with any of the people I knew in either the Salt Lake or Los Angeles offices. Denials were everywhere. Finally, I asked Jim to access the travel records of all FBI investigators starting the day of the crash." Referencing his notes, he turned to include Michael and Jim in the briefing, "Fourteen separate agents were detached from other FBI offices, and they all ended up in Salt Lake City within ten hours of the accident. We opened their case files and found that none of them shared more than one or two similar investigations. Absolutely nothing was recorded for their reasons to be in Salt Lake. Absolutely nothing!"

Jim Tedrow, the twenty-seven-year old ex-MicroSoft programmer, now turned computer investigator, removed the wire framed spectacles from his freckled face and pointed to the names of the agents listed on Blake's summary sheets. "Thank you First Pacific Net," he said in such a way that both Carson and Michael knew that the information could never have been retrieved over the Internet without the supposedly non-existent encryption tool. "Each one of these agents has at least nine years active service as a field investigator for the Bureau, and not one of them has less than three meritorious commendations."

"How did you find that out?" Carson asked, already knowing that the answer was illegal.

"I was able to break into source files for cases without alerting someone to what I might be searching for. By the way, if you were looking for a testimonial as to the power of First Pacific's technology, I guess I could give a pretty good one," he interjected in such a way as to try and lighten the mood that had settled in the room. "Anyway, I finally used a password that has been confirmed to be that of the director of the FBI, Mr. Thomas Folger. I figured that if something was going on he would certainly be involved. No one would be suspicious of entries in the computer log under his name."

"Where did you get his password?" asked Carson. "No, don't tell me. Let's just hope they don't change it."

"If they do, I can get that one too," Jim stated very matter-of-factly. No one in the room doubted that this mild mannered M.I.T. dropout could do what he promised.

Digesting the information Blake and Jim had uncovered, Carson turned to face Michael, who by now was sitting on the pine coffee table next to Blake Terry's discarded tie. "Michael, what have you found out about the NTSB report? It has been almost a week since the crash, and based on the secrecy surrounding the whole incident, they must have found something?" Carson waited for an answer.

Michael saw no need to stand as he addressed the group. "As you might guess, the final report has not been finished, but the preliminary report lists the cause of the accident as hydraulic failure in engine two."

"The loss of hydraulics would cause the plane to lose some steering control and could possibly affect the elevator control. It would not happen instantaneously as took place on 421," interjected Carson, recalling his air force training on hydraulics.

Michael nodded his head in agreement and then continued with his portion of the impromptu briefing. "The report itself specifies that all inquiries concerning the findings are to be forwarded directly to the White House. Now what would prompt such an entry?" asked Michael.

"That's what we need to find out," responded Carson, as he once again stared at the latest casualty counts being given by Patricia Sanderson in Dallas.

For the next fifteen minutes the group huddled around the coffee table, now turned conference table, discussing their additional discoveries, which really didn't amount to very much. Finally Carson asked, "What about the file on the marine gunnery sergeant? Was it still cross referenced with the preliminary NTSB investigation?"

"All references to it are now removed from the report. At first I assumed that it must have been part of a corrupted file, and dismissed it outright," answered Michael, not waiting long enough for Carson to ask another question. "However, just out of curiosity, I accessed the Marine Corps Service Record Division and called up information on this Sergeant Baker. Now get this! He doesn't exist. Not only is all reference to his service record missing, it appears that there was never any such person. I ran a program last night to try to match hospital records, drivers' licenses, and credit cards to any such non-existent person."

"What did they show?" asked Blake, looking at Carson, knowing he was wondering the same thing.

Michael answered, "Every last one was negative. However, I thought I would add a search of ambulance records, 911 calls and utility records. I should have the results late today or early tomorrow. It is going to take some time. Our computers are fast, but we are talking about examining literally billions of records under multiple name combinations. Right now, I would guess that the entry was a mistake."

Patricia Sanderson was back on the television summarizing the last two hours' events. Michael picked up the remote from the bookshelf and turned up the volume. As they watched the pictures of the disaster in full color, Carson pulled Michael aside and told him that he was going to go to the Sound the following morning and talk to Nichole. He quickly related Nichole's explanation of how she acquired the camera she had around her neck in the *Time* photo. "She said she would have the pictures developed by the time I arrive." Carson added.

"What do you expect to find?" Michael asked, still not sure why Carson was going to make the drive to upper Washington state.

"Probably nothing. But I'm hoping that the owner of that camera took enough pictures of the skyline to show when the nose started to pitch down. Just possibly those pictures might give us something else to build on."

Carson looked back at the television monitor. Two commuter planes were burned beyond recognition. Nodding his head from side to side, Carson said, "We don't have much time."

11

The latch on the motel door closed quietly behind him, allowing Esteban to stand on the weather stained sidewalk and breath in the humid air of east Texas. The temperature was not as hot as Las Vegas, but the oppressive moisture was already caking the blue denim shirt to his back. Passing Ricardo's room, he paused at the red and white vending machine. Searching his pockets, he found several quarters and deposited three of them, one after another, until the frosted can slid to the bottom of the machine. He picked up the Coke, carefully scanned the parking lot and surrounding area, and when he was confident there was no surveillance, he walked back and knocked on Ricardo's door.

"It's time to move," Esteban commented, as Ricardo sat back down on the bed visually searching the motel room for his discarded clothes.

"And the girl?" questioned Ricardo as he stood and shook the legs of his pants down over his still dusty boots. Esteban's younger companion in the LLO waited for an answer. It certainly wasn't the first time he had purchased a woman for his partner. Sometimes he just paid them, and then other times it was something else. Ascertaining which action was now required, he added, "Do I need any money?"

Esteban shook his head, a stoic expression on his face. "No need. Just dump the trash."

Ricardo finished adjusting his dark brown Mexican boots under his clinging Levis. "Is there a timetable?"

"Drop me at the Anatole and then come back and finish here. I will be registered under the name of Ethan Mabry."

"You've got it," Ricardo answered as he reached behind him and extinguished the overhead light before following his much taller mentor out the door.

•   •   •

The Loews Anatole Hotel is world renowned for both the quality of its lodging rooms as well as its ultramodern convention facilities. At any given time three to four thousand guests will be wandering the halls and shops, each with a slightly different agenda in mind. Esteban walked through the lobby, primarily designed as a giant atrium, and stopped at the registration desk where he listened to the other people in line talking about the catastrophe out at the airport. He waited for the elder couple from Minnesota to check back into the hotel, now unable to get a flight back home. He then finally was able to get the room he had reserved while in New York City the day before. Leaving a cash deposit and specifically requesting a smoking room, he showed the uniformed receptionist a Florida drivers license issued to Ethan Mabry. Before he walked away and headed toward the hotel shops, she handed him a plastic coded card that would never be returned.

"You must like to read a lot?" questioned the young girl as she gave him change in the gift shop.

"When you are away from home, there's not a lot more to do," he smiled. The good looking Anglo-American girl returned his grin and Esteban knew that she would be more than happy to help him find something else to occupy his time. "Now was not the time," he thought. He picked up the copies of *USA Today, The Wall Street Journal, the Los Angeles Times,* and the Spanish newspaper, *La Prensa*, and put them under his arm. The bell over the glass plate door chimed softly as he walked out of the gift shop. "She didn't even notice the latex gloves," Esteban thought to himself, but then, he knew she wouldn't. They were perfectly clear and only paper thin, and unless the girl had actually felt them, she would have no way of knowing that Ethan Mabry had no fingerprints.

Room 816 faced the Expo Mart across the freeway, now almost completely filled with frantic emergency vehicles trying to get to or from the airport some 12 miles to the west. Esteban pulled open the white plastic rods hanging from the center of the drapes, and allowed what remained of the Texas sunlight to filter into the room. Getting immediately to work, he placed the newspapers on the desk and tore off the top sheet from the Loews note pad. Next he placed an exacto knife, a roll of scotch tape, and several sheets of bond paper on the desk next to the phone.

In small, but clearly legible script, he drafted the letter, remembering the instructions he had received in New York.

"To the National Editor of *The Wall Street Journal*:

"*LA LIBERTAD OCCIDENTAL REPRESENTS THE OPPRESSED PEOPLE OF LATIN AMERICA. THE IMPERIALISTIC AGGRESSION OF THE UNITED STATES CAN NOT BE TOLERATED ANY LONGER. WE HAVE TRIED TO WORK WITH WASHINGTON D.C., BUT THEY FAILED TO HEED OUR WARNINGS.*

"*LESS THAN TWO WEEKS AGO, WE WERE FURNISHED 15 STINGER SURFACE-TO-AIR MISSILES. THESE WEAPONS OF DESTRUCTION WERE RECEIVED AT MARINE CORPS AIR STATION, EL TORO, CALIFORNIA.*

"*LA LIBERTAD OCCIDENTAL INFORMED THE UNITED STATES FBI THAT WE HAD THESE MISSILES. REASONABLE DEMANDS WERE MADE. THOSE DEMANDS WERE NEITHER OBEYED NOR ACKNOWLEDGED. WE WERE FORCED TO SHOOT DOWN TWO AIRCRAFT, BOTH PASSENGER PLANES. THE FIRST WAS IN SALT LAKE CITY, AND THE SECOND AT DALLAS/FORT WORTH.*

"*THE GOVERNMENT HAS DENIED THAT WE ARE RESPONSIBLE. IT IS NECESSARY THAT AIR TRAVEL IN THIS COUNTRY STOP IMMEDIATELY. IN ORDER TO PROVE OUR DETERMINATION, LOOK AT THE DATE AND TIME THIS LETTER WAS PLACED WITH THE COURIER SERVICE. IT SHOULD REACH YOUR OFFICE BETWEEN 3:15 AND 3:30 P.M.*

"*BELIEVE US! THIS LETTER IS NOT A HOAX!*

"*BY 3:45 P.M. EASTERN TIME, ANOTHER PLANE WILL BE*

SHOT DOWN. THIS TIME CERTAIN DEATH WILL FALL FROM THE SKY IN ONE OF THE 11 WESTERN STATES.

"WE ARE SERIOUS. THE GOVERNMENT MUST MEET OUR DEMANDS. UNTIL THEY DO SO, WE WILL CONTINUE TO USE THE STINGER MISSILES.

"TURN YOUR TELEVISION TO CNN. BY 4:00 P.M. YOU WILL REALIZE WE ARE SERIOUS. THE PEOPLE OF THE WORLD SUPPORT OUR CAUSE."

LA LIBERTAD OCCIDENTAL
VIVA LA LIBERTAD

Esteban reviewed what he had written. Satisfied it was correct, he began the tedious and time consuming task of duplicating the important message. *The Wall Street Journal* would verify the information, but they couldn't sit on the story, at least not for very long. Using the exacto knife, he carefully cut the words from the individual newspapers and placed then in separate piles on the writing surface of the desk. Finally he assembled the words and taped them to the sheet of common twenty pound bond paper he had taken from the copy machine in the business center on the second floor. It was the same paper sold in literally thousands of such centers across America every day.

"They'll get the message," he thought to himself as he reread the letter for the second time. Esteban then gathered up the remaining portions of the papers and went into the bathroom. Methodically he tore the mutilated pages from each publication, separating the unblemished newsprint from those sections where he had cut the block words for the ultimatum. When he had two piles, he placed the smaller one in the tub, and then started ripping the pieces into even smaller sections. The last thing he did was to add the note paper, where he had drafted his original message, to the smaller pile.. Slowly, he burned the remains of the messages in the tub, making sure to take his time. He didn't want the smoke alarm to go off. When he was finished, Esteban wiped the ashes into a pile, and carefully gathering them up to be flushed them down the toilet. Satisfied with his handiwork, he turned on the shower and washed away the last traces of his ninety minute labor. Momentarily startled by the ringing on the desk, he answered the phone. "Yes. Ethan Mabry here."

"I'm in the lobby. Are you finished?" Ricardo asked.

"I'll be right down. Meet me across from the reception desk." Picking up the remaining uncut papers still on the bathroom counter, he turned off the lights and closed the door. Passing a cleaning cart in the hall, Esteban stuffed the additional pages of the newspapers in with the trash from more than thirty other hotel rooms.

"We are scheduled on the red-eye flight out of Houston," Esteban told Ricardo as they drove away from the hotel. The freeways were still congested with traffic and emergency vehicles, but they still had plenty of time to drive and make their flight from the other major airport to the south of DFW. The letter to the Editor of *The Wall Street Journal* would be mailed for overnight delivery from the west coast. It would be marked *Personal and Confidential*!

12

THURSDAY MORNING

Carson reached around the steering wheel of the green and tan Ford Explorer and turned off the radio. The news media acted like a school of piranha, jumping on each morsel of information from Dallas/Fort Worth, and then dissecting it and tearing it apart. After a while, he tired of hearing the same news told again and again, each broadcaster adding his or her own personal spin to the story. Slowing down, he pulled the four wheel drive utility wagon onto the entrance to Interstate 5. The Puget Sound was almost an hour north of Seattle, a full five hours away.

Rain droplets ran first one direction, and then the other, as Carson used the windshield wipers to clean off what remained of the early morning moisture. The fog had lifted, leaving Portland clear and overcast. In the distance he could see a sign on the Bank of America recording a temperature of 51 degrees fahrenheit. As he pulled on the bridge to Vancouver, he heard the repeated sound of a fog horn, and looked to see a large ship in the middle of the Columbia being pulled by several hard working tugs. Thinking to himself that the wide river never looked more dull and gray than this morning, he said aloud, "An almost perfect reflection of the mood settling on the country.

●　●　●

Slowing to 45 and following the green and white sign telling him to keep right, Carson prepared to exit the freeway. Nichole's directions were clear and concise. Her cabin on the sound was still 30 minutes away, but the drive took closer to 45. Carson made one wrong turn, ending up in a stand of pine trees overlooking the crashing surf of the ocean on giant boulders propped against the shoreline. After 15 minutes Carson turned the green Explorer around to retrace his journey, and quickly corrected his mistake. Checking the handwritten sheet Nichole had given him, he turned off the small two lane road that wandered through the northwest woods. "I guess I'm not the only one that gets lost," Carson thought to himself as he passed the white Ford Taurus. The driver was sitting with the door ajar, studying a map. He looked up and nodded as Carson's four wheel drive vehicle made the turn in front of him.

Nichole's cabin was set back from the road. Carson pulled to a stop on the moist bark driveway, mentally recording the setting in his mind as if he had taken a photo. He pushed the door shut on the wagon and walked up on the covered porch. Lifting the heavy iron knocker hanging from the middle of the redwood door, he let it fall back onto the dark wood. Nothing. All he heard were the sounds of the leaves settling in the musty forest. It was not an unpleasant feeling.

"Anybody home?" he yelled as he walked around the cabin. He had called Nichole just before he left Portland, promising he would arrive around one o'clock. He was late, but not by much.

"Up here," the faint voice from the jagged cliffs behind the house answered.

Carson waved and followed the path that worked its way through the heavy woods to the rocks hanging over the sea. Heavy clouds were forming in the west, the sea looking rougher than normal. He tasted the salt on his lips, glad that he had put on the Nautica windbreaker before getting out of the car.

Nichole stood facing the mounting wind coming in from the west. "Any trouble finding the place?" she asked, trying to make herself heard above the sound of the wind and water.

"Made a wrong turn once, but your directions were not to blame," he replied as he scanned the horizon and watched a gull dive into one of the breakers. The waves crashing on the rocks made it difficult to hear.

"Let's go back," Nichole said, turning away from the powerful surf. Speaking less forcefully, she continued, "Sometimes I come here hoping to understand what life is all about."

"Have you figured it out?" Carson asked as they retreated back down the path he had just climbed, obviously making reference to the latest air crash to hit Dallas/Fort Worth.

"Not yet, but the power and majesty of the ocean makes it easier to keep asking." Pausing slightly, she asked, "Now it's happening in Dallas. My God, Carson, what is going on?"

Carson stopped and stared back at the cresting waves of the giant surf and said, "I'm not sure, Nichole, but I'm still determined to find out."

When they got to the log and timber cabin nestled in the woods, Nichole pointed at the Explorer and changed the subject. "Up here you sometimes need a four wheel drive. The roads can get pretty ugly when it starts to pour."

Carson remembered that he hadn't seen a car near the house as he drove up. "What do you drive?" he asked, searching for another car.

She swung the four foot wide front door open and led the way into the house. Answering his question, she said, "I've got a Dakota pick-up and it's got four wheel traction." She noticed him still looking through the window searching for her truck in the yard. "It's parked in a lean-to shed behind the cabin. Not much of a garage, but it keeps the weather and wet leaves off. Would you like some coffee?" she asked, leaning around the corner from the kitchen.

"That would taste good," he said as he removed his damp windbreaker.

"Have a seat. I'll be right there."

Carson hung his coat on the hall tree by the door and found a comfortable over-stuffed denim couch. It was well used, and he thought it fit with the rustic decor. The room had a 15 foot ceiling, extending from the front door to the massive rock fireplace that protected the opposite end of the 20 foot long chamber. He noticed the envelope laying on the coffee table in front of the couch. It said *One Hour Photo*.

"Here you are." Nichole offered the coffee, putting a tray of cream and sugar on the table next to the pictures.

"Thanks. Are these the pictures you were telling me about?"

"I picked them up early this morning, right after you called. To tell you the truth there's not much there."

"Do you mind?" Carson asked as he put down his coffee and picked up the envelope.

"Go ahead. Help yourself," she replied, lowering her cup to the table. Nichole wrapped her arms around her beige, heavy woolen sweater, remembering the reason for Carson's visit.

One at a time, Carson looked at the pictures. His face registered the disappointment as he thumbed through the photos. There were only six pictures in the envelope. The Japanese boy must have just changed rolls of film before boarding the plane. Two pictures were photos of three boys standing outside the gate of the D concourse in the Omega terminal. One picture was a blurry representation of the plane parked at the gate. It must have been taken through the terminal window. There were two pictures of Japanese passengers sitting in the plane. The last picture was a black picture with spots of light in the background. Carson guessed it must have been the picture of the Salt Lake skyline, but it didn't show much. He shuffled through the six photos one more time, and then dropped them on the green and white envelope that still contained the negatives.

"Not much there?" commented Nichole as she sat huddled on the opposite chair. She had pulled her knees up under the oversized sweater. Her short dark hair gave the impression of a woman much younger than 34 years.

"I guess I hoped for something more. I don't know what it was that I wanted to see. Maybe if he had taken more pictures?" he said, phrasing his comment more like a question.

"I can remember him pointing the camera out the window. For some reason I thought he must have been taking a number of pictures," she responded, leaning over to pick up the pictures Carson had dropped. "Just the one picture, and all you see are the lights on the mountain.

They're not bright enough to even see the hillside," Nichole said as she dropped the picture and took a drink of coffee.

Carson held up his hand as if to stop Nichole from speaking. Leaning down, he grabbed the pictures from the wooden table one more time. This time he threw all of the pictures with the Japanese friends to the side. He held up the dark photo with the pin points of light. Excitedly, he asked Nichole, "Can you pick out the lake at the bottom of the picture?"

She took the picture and looked closely. "I believe so. You act as if that is important?"

"You shouldn't be able to see it, Nichole. You shouldn't be able to! Can I borrow your phone? It's important!"

Nichole motioned to the phone hanging on the pine wall. She could see that he had seen something, but she didn't understand what it was. "What's the matter?"

"I'll explain in a minute, just as soon as I finish this call." The private line to his secretary rang three times before she picked it up. "Janelle, let me speak to Michael."

"He's in with Blake and Jim. Can you wait just a minute and I'll get him?"

"Sure. But hurry," Carson responded, tapping his knuckles against the light wood behind the phone. Thirty seconds later Carson heard the receiver being picked up. "Are you alone, Michael?"

"I am now. Blake and Jim just left. They were finishing explaining a possible problem."

"You can fill me in later," Carson blurted as Michael stopped speaking. "First, let me tell you that the crash of Flight 421 was no accident. We were shot out of the sky and based on what we've learned, the government has already figured it out!"

Nichole sat up and listened to what Carson was saying to his close friend. There was no doubt that he had seen something in the photo, but for the life of her she couldn't see it.

"Carson, slow down. What do you mean you were shot down? Are you saying that some plane, possibly military, fired on you?" Michael was thinking that there must have been some kind of accident. Hill Air

Force Base was only 30 miles from Salt Lake International Airport, and they oftentimes carried live ammunition.

"No, Michael. There was no other plane. Someone fired a surface-to-air missile from the ground northwest of the airport and shot down Flight 421 with a missile."

"What are you talking about, Carson?" The phone went silent for a moment. "Is it the pictures?"

"Yes. One of the photos from the camera Nichole picked up was taken just at the right instant and captured the proof." Carson considered how to summarize what he had subconsciously suspected ever since the confrontation in the Salt Lake Omega hanger. "The photo shows the lights of Salt Lake. None of them are bright enough to illuminate the background, with one exception. There is one light near the water of the Great Salt Lake that is many times brighter than all the rest. Michael, I've flown over that section of the lake tens of times, and there's nothing there. No lights. Nothing!"

Nichole picked up the photo that Carson had dropped on the table and tried to examine it as he explained how he spotted what he was sure was a missile of some kind. She now clearly saw what Carson had been referring to. The light next to the water was definitely brighter than any of the others.

Carson hung up the phone, clearly troubled, not hearing the distant machine stop recording the conversation. The man in the white Taurus took off the headphones and made a phone call using a cellular phone. The wires running down from the overhead phone lines were still attached to the recorder on the front seat. Someone was going to be upset.

"What's wrong, Carson?" Nichole asked.

"First of all, the crash of 421 was not an accident. Someone intentionally killed Kelly."

Nichole knew that he was referring to all the passengers on the Friday evening flight, even though he only used the name of his son. It was personal. She interrupted him. "I heard you explaining to Michael. How did you know?"

"When I was in the Gulf in 1990, I was almost shot down by surface-to-air missiles. Once you see them fire, you never forget it." He thought to himself, "And then there was Vietnam."

Carson sat next to Nichole on the blue denim couch. She had changed places when Carson started explaining about the picture to Michael. Carson went on, "Michael just briefed me on what they had been able to find out. He has been able to finally tap into a secret White House computer file. We think they already know that the crash of 421 was no accident."

"Tap in?" she said, not understanding either the content or the context of his last statement.

Realizing that he hadn't told Nichole of his private investigation, he quickly brought her up to date with the basic steps he had taken to find out what was happening. Nichole listened intently without asking for anything to be repeated, and without bringing up the legality of his actions. When Carson finished briefing her on his intentions, he wasn't surprised she had some questions.

"Why do you think the government already knew it was no accident?" she asked in a hushed voice.

Carson went on, omitting the exact details of the encryption device they had effectively stolen from First Pacific Net. "When we first tapped into the preliminary NTSB file, we found it was cross referenced with the military service record of a marine Gunnery Sergeant Adrian Baker. Later, all references to this Sergeant Baker were removed from the file. In the beginning we thought the first entry had been a mistake. Somehow the computer must have cross linked two separate and distinct files."

"Then what?" she asked, waiting for Carson to continue.

"Michael and another man who works for me, by the name of Jim Tedrow, were both bothered by the fact that this Baker no longer existed. I don't mean that he was now not referenced in the report, I mean there was no evidence that such a person ever existed. Anyway, early this morning Michael and Jim were able to identify a marine gunnery sergeant admitted to Los Angeles Memorial Hospital."

"Was his name Baker?" she asked, thoroughly intrigued.

"Not on the admittance records. This sergeant was admitted under the name of Ronald T. Chapman. But it's Baker."

"How do you know it's him?" she asked, now bewildered by the two separate and distinct names.

"Michael and Jim are extremely thorough. They tried to verify the records of a Marine Gunnery Sergeant Ronald T. Chapman. Now, get this. Up until ten days ago, there was no such marine. The first record of Gunnery Sergeant Ronald T. Chapman was the admittance record at Los Angeles Memorial. It appears that he is under some kind of protective custody orchestrated by the White House. By the way, Gunnery Sergeant Baker's original service record entry was recorded as being received on the first NTSB computer log on Wednesday, April 11th, the same day that Ronald T. Chapman was admitted to Los Angeles Memorial."

"It could still be a coincidence, Carson. What's to prove it's the same person?"

Carson stood and looked out the window at the now falling rain. Turning back to Nichole, he said, "Marine Gunnery Sergeant Ronald T. Chapman was listed as the ordinance NCO at El Toro. He was in charge of Stinger surface-to-air missiles. The marines aren't supposed to even have these weapons, but they do. They started in Vietnam and have kept them ever since," he stated in a voice that was sounding more remote and distant all the time.

"You seem very familiar with these Stingers?" Nichole said pensively, impressed by the resources that Carson had mustered together during the last week.

Deciding there was nothing to be gained by holding back, he decided to tell her the rest of the story. "In 1975 I was shot down by friendly fire 20 clicks north of Da Nang. It was from a shoulder-fired surface-to-air missile, a first generation Stinger." Carson brushed his hand slowly through his sandy colored hair, and pushing it back, showed Nichole the scar that ran into his hairline. "Anyway, that's where this came from. The launching was an accident and I was able to eject, but I made it a point to find out what had nearly ended my fragile existence on this planet."

Nichole stared in amazement. "You think that this Gunnery Sergeant Baker or Chapman may know where the missile came from, is that it?"

"I'd bet my life on it. Tomorrow morning I am going to fly down to Los Angeles and see if I can't visit this Sergeant Baker/Chapman. All we have is his admittance record, but it appears he was barely conscious when he arrived."

Nichole came and stood by Carson, taking his arm gently in her own. "I want to go with you."

"I don't think that's a very good idea, and besides you have to go back to work," he responded, looking into her pleading eyes, while at the same time remembering her upcoming cross country trip to Atlanta.

"It's important to me, Carson. I lost my dearest friends on that plane, and I want to know why. And I can't go back to work. My supervisor called this morning and told me to stay at home until the NTSB investigation on the crash of 421 is complete. I was promised full pay, and I understood very clearly that I wasn't to talk to the press again." Nichole took Carson by the arm. "She, also mentioned that I was not to talk to you again, stating very emphatically that it would be better if we didn't speak at all or the FAA investigators wouldn't be able to get a completely unbiased report from either of us." She pressed Carson's arm more firmly against her own.. "Omega knows, Carson. They know!" she stated, for the first time fully aware of Omega's motives.

"You're sure about this?" Carson asked, fully conscious that the *unknown* was staring them in the face, offering a truth that might be too frightening to even consider.

"I need to be there," she answered determinedly.

After a long silence, Carson responded, "OK, but as soon as we find out what this Sergeant Baker/Chapman knows, then you come back here. Agreed?"

She squeezed his arm gently. "Agreed."

"Nichole, how much of the news reports on the Dallas crash did you watch yesterday and this morning?" Carson asked, as they looked out at the dripping rain falling through the trees.

"Too much," she stated without moving from the window. "It was the same thing, wasn't it?" she shuddered.

Skirting around her question, he replied, "I wasn't really sure until now, but I can't believe the government didn't know. I'm not saying they're behind it, but there can't be any doubt as to their investigation into the entire affair," Carson answered. Listening to the noise of the building weather, he explained, "CNN said the crash was supposedly caused by wind shear, but I don't believe it." Carson continued to hold Nichole by the arm. "I don't think so," he repeated emphatically.

The sound of the rain drops sounding military taps on the roof increased as the gale from the ocean heightened it's fury. "Why don't you stay here tonight? We can fly down tomorrow from SEA-TAC." Nichole suggested against the backdrop of the storm.

"You're sure you don't mind? I really am not looking forward to driving back to Portland tonight," he asked as they stood framed against the window.

"I've got an extra room. Besides, I think I'd prefer not to be alone," Nichole answered, holding tight to the strength she felt coming through his body.

13

FRIDAY MORNING

The Cleaner used his right index finger to push the reading glasses farther up on his nose, the wire rim frames accenting his silver gray hair. Once again he scanned the morning editions of *The Wall Street Journal* and *USA Today*. Both papers used 90 percent of their editorial space to comment on the recent air disasters, but he found the difference in their editorial approach remarkably different. *USA Today* centered its coverage on the details of the separate crashes, concentrating on the stories of the victims. Families grieved and friends anguished in despair as Omega Flight 421 and NationWide Flight 488 gripped the nation in lamented sorrow. *The Wall Street Journal,* however, focused its efforts in detailing how the crashes could have been avoided if the airlines had only spent the funds necessary to invest in newer and safer aircraft. Editorials castigated the government bureaucracy for not having required the airports to purchase the new wind shear detection systems the FAA had recently completed testing. According to the New York journalist, had these actions been taken as he emphatically suggested, neither of the accidents would have happened.

Folding the *USA Today* inside *The Wall Street Journal,* The Cleaner dropped both papers on his desk and realized everything had worked perfectly. "Well, almost perfectly," he said to himself, thinking of the loose end Esteban still had to tie up in Los Angeles. Looking up from his desk to gaze out the fourth floor window of the Madison Avenue brownstone, he was momentarily distracted by the stock market index on the front page of the *Journal.* It was plummeting at a rate that demonstrated how totally inadequate the American people felt in understanding what was happening. "The Dow Jones average always reflects the public's feelings, and right now, that feeling isn't very good," he said to himself. Smiling, he thought privately, "It is about to get worse, a lot worse!"

The phone he kept locked in his right-hand drawer was ringing, however no one could hear even the slightest sound of the phone. He had removed the ringing device and replaced it with a small light, mounted under the middle desk drawer that could only be seen when a person was sitting in the chair directly behind the six-foot walnut desk. And only one person ever sat in that chair.

The gray haired man unlocked the drawer and removed the handset. He punched in a three digit set of numbers on the small electronic machine positioned next to the phone. Ten seconds later, a message appeared on the read-out. It said, "Clear."

"Identify," he said, as he spoke into the phone.

Quickly a voice repeated a second series of numbers. The display on the machine in the desk drawer now read, "Voice Pattern Recognition Complete - Esteban."

Knowing that the line was clear of bugs and listening devices, and that he was now speaking to Esteban Moreno, The Cleaner asked, "Did you receive the final instructions?"

A slightly distorted voice answered, "They came through last night. There doesn't appear to be any problem. We walked through everything just to make sure."

"Timing is crucial. I assume the letter to the *Journal* has been sent?" the cleaner commented as he once again reviewed the panic spread across the front pages of the national newspapers.

"It went yesterday. Delivery is guaranteed. There will be no trace." Both men knew they were discussing the next step in a plan they couldn't allow to fail.

"And our marine, how is his health?" asked the gray haired Cleaner.

"Guarded. It's unfortunate for them that he won't survive through tomorrow." Esteban knew the Cleaner would understand exactly what he meant.

"Don't delay. His condition must not improve, and I emphasize must not!" the Cleaner responded, allowing his voice to carry the seriousness of his last instruction. It wasn't necessary to ask the next question, but he did so anyway. "How are the pencils?"

Esteban smirked at the question, knowing that his compatriot was referring to the remaining missiles. "Still in storage," he answered confidently.

The Cleaner was pleased to know that the military missiles were locked safely away in the warehouse in National City, California, just 30 minutes away from Mexico. "Con Dios," the Cleaner said as he hung up the phone. It literally meant *with God*, but was shortened Spanish slang for *good luck*.

14

Vice President Jason Wright had suggested the meeting location be changed. Security measures were much more rigid in the basement, some 600 feet below the White House floor, and everyone in the room realized they were about to alter the course of history. Right or wrong, history was about to change.

President Attwilder was the nation's Commander in Chief, yet this afternoon, deep in the bowels of the earth, he was relinquishing a small portion of this responsibility to Jason Wright, the supervisor of the Special Terrorist Task Force. Vice President Wright stood next to the audio visual screen that had been lowered from the ceiling, dwarfing the five individuals surrounding the highly polished table. The below ground sanctuary was one of the most securely guarded locations on the east coast of the United States, and was normally used when the full security council was called into an emergency session. After careful consideration, both the President and Vice President had agreed that the inner group be kept to its initial size, and consequently the large oblong table appeared to be empty. Seymour Dillan and Tom Folger had already demonstrated the fact that absolutely no security breach would be tolerated in either of their respective services. Each of the two men had already sequestered more than one person who asked too many questions. Only the most trusted and senior CIA and FBI investigators were assigned to the case, and then, they only received partial briefings of the true extent of the terrorist threat on a *Need to Know Basis*.

Jason looked around the table to insure that everyone was ready.

Using the control panel at his left, he darkened the room so that the images on the screen could be seen easily. "We are all familiar with our findings in Salt Lake." The Vice President clicked the laser remote, and a bright, full color picture of the crash flashed on the screen. Despite their familiarity with the situation, the graphic carnage depicted in the photographs still made each of the men around the table extremely uncomfortable.

"You will notice that there is very little of the tail assembly in this photo. There is no doubt that the Stinger missile destroyed a large share of the rear section of the L-1011, virtually destroying the elevators, and rendering the rudder practically useless. It was amazing that the pilots were even able to turn the plane around."

Flashing the remote a second time, he continued. "The casing of the Stinger missile was found in this hunting shack northwest of the field. It has been positively identified as one of the missiles stolen from El Toro." The picture zoomed in to reveal a series of numbers imprinted on the side of the casing.

"There is absolutely zero doubt that the organization calling itself *La Libertad Occidental* has in its possession the remaining 13 missiles." The photo on the screen changed again. For the next several minutes Vice President Wright showed a series of photos taken at Dallas/Fort Worth Airport. Pausing the slide presentation, more to allow the group to digest what they had just witnessed than to regroup his thoughts, Jason went on. "The LLO has us by the throat, and they are tightening their grip. Seymour, would you bring us up to date on the CIA's efforts in locating the stronghold of the LLO and the thirteen Stinger missiles?"

Seymour rolled back the black leather and chrome chair from the walnut table and walked decisively to the front of the room. Jason sat down in the chair to the side of the podium. The Director of the CIA began by pointing the laser remote at the screen. "What you are looking at is the remains of the drug processing plant in Peru. Our operatives were able to ascertain that the LLO is backed financially by the drug cartels operating between Columbia and Peru."

President Attwilder became impatient and interrupted Seymour's slide presentation. "Do you know where the stronghold is located?"

Seymour clicked the remote a second time. "Up until three weeks ago, they were operating out of this jungle village on the Columbian border." Using the red triangle of the remote to highlight a section of the South American map, he continued. "Since that time there has been absolutely no trace of the group. We do know that the organization is divided into a form of cadres or cells, each one completely isolated from the next. No one person appears to know what is going on."

"No one?" questioned the President's Chief of Staff.

Turning to face his interrogator, Seymour went on. "Hank, certainly someone knows, but we have never been able to identify the top leadership of the organization. Every time we get close, our informants end up dead, or just disappear." The director paused to emphasize a point. "Whoever is running this operation has necessarily kept this cadre extremely small. I'll let Tom brief you on his investigation."

Jason Wright stood and took the remote from the smaller man. "Tom, would you please continue?" he asked, handing the director of the FBI the remote.

Tom Folger stood to his full height and walked around the table. "We are in a shit locker without a key! I would like to tell you that the FBI has been able to identify the assassins, but that is just not the case. I guarantee, we are using every possible resource in the investigation." He clicked the remote back several slides to illustrate his point. The five men stared at the wreckage burning on the runway in Dallas/Fort Worth. "What I can tell you is this, and it's not much. The marine sergeant who witnessed the theft of the missiles has lapsed into a deep coma. The chances of his regaining consciousness are a thousand to one, and if he does come out of the coma, the doctors think he will be no more than a vegetable." Tom used the remote to show a picture of Gunnery Sergeant Adrian Baker as they found him at the armory at El Toro. "We can't expect to get anything from him. We have had no luck in identifying the numbers he was supposed to have uttered when he got to the hospital. There was only a single attending physician on duty, and he was the one who wrote down what he said. The doctor doesn't even know for sure that it was a number. He said it might have just been a name or some unrecognizable phrase. We are striking out with Sergeant Baker."

Vice President Wright frowned. "Isn't there anything you can do?"

"Nothing. Everything that can be done, is," he answered. Tom clicked the remote to show two slides, side by side. "What you are looking at are the impressions of boot prints lifted from both the Salt Lake and Dallas firing sites. In Salt Lake there was only one shooter. That is the slide to the left. In Dallas we have identified two separate sets of boot prints."

President Attwilder asked, "What can you tell us about the shooters from the boot prints?"

"The same shooter from Salt Lake was in Dallas. He appears to be about six feet tall and weighs approximately 185 to 195 pounds. His companion in Dallas is somewhat shorter. Maybe three to four inches, and weighs less than 150 pounds." Tom placed the remote on the podium that remained stationary at the head of the table.

"And?" asked Hank, expecting the director of the FBI to continue.

"Hank, that's it! The prints match literally millions of possible boots. All we have is a description that could fit a huge share of all the men in the United States." Tom sat down and lifted the remote from the rostrum before handing it to the Vice President. He could have gone on, but it wasn't going to do any good.

President Attwilder stood up and walked up to the front of the table. "Is that it folks? Have you given up?"

No one answered the tall slender man who rightfully assumed control.

The President sat down in a chair and began speaking. "Tom was right on the money when he said we were in a shit locker. As soon as the public finds out what is happening, we are going to be crucified for withholding information that might have saved the lives of hundreds of innocent people in Texas and Utah. The fact that we could do nothing about it will not matter." He rubbed his reddish forehead and continued. "That is only the beginning. We are left with absolutely no doubt that these madmen will strike again, and it will only get worse. As soon as that happens, the economy of this country will start sliding into the cellar, probably never to recover." Tom and Seymour looked at each other and shook their heads trying to figure out why the President had switched to the topic of the national economy.

The President turned to the Vice President. "Jason, what is the financial condition of the airlines at the present time?"

Jason knew what President Attwilder was referring to. Remaining seated, he answered in a somber voice, "The last five years have produced record losses for the airlines. Each of the major carriers has been hit with increased fuel costs, coupled with forced downsizing and a flat economy. Their financial situation is precarious at best."

President Attwilder turned to the rest of the group. "Jason said it like it is, but let me tell you what else is about to happen. As soon as the American voters understand the threat they are facing, they will quit flying. Absolutely no sane person is going to get on a plane if they think it might be blown out of the sky! Many of the airlines won't be able to take the financial pressure. Massive layoffs will be a certainty. Stockholders' equity will evaporate overnight. The domino effect will be unbelievable. The depression of 1929 may seem like a picnic before this is over."

Silence hung over the conference table. Finally, Tom Folger spoke for the rest of the group, "Mr. President, I think we had better consider meeting their demands."

"Do you mean pay the $2 billion?" asked the President, scratching his chin with his right hand. President Attwilder acted taken back, but in reality Tom's suggestion was something that had been gnawing at him for several days.

"I'm afraid so. It may be the only option out of this mess."

Seymour spoke up, now completely cognizant of the economic crisis facing the country, "Mr. President, Tom has a point. We may be able to find the people behind this, but they may very well have destroyed our country before we do."

Hank knew the two directors were right, but they had a problem. Money. "There is absolutely no way we can come up with $2 billion dollars, Mr. President. Even if we wanted to pay the money, we couldn't do it. We just can't march up the hill and ask Congress to approve a special funding package earmarked to pay economic blackmail."

Jason Wright hesitated, and then made a suggestion he had been considering voicing for the last several minutes. "There may be a way. The President already explained how the economy is about to go south, permanently. What if we went to the top CEO's in the country? We start with the heads of all the airlines. They have the most to lose, and the fastest. Then we hit the other top corporations. Possibly we could get them to come up with the money. They could certainly raise it, and it would certainly be in their best interests."

President Attwilder considered what his second in command had just proposed. "It might work, but how do we approach the companies? We just can't go in and ask for billions of dollars to pay off a group of terrorists."

Vice President Wright continued brainstorming his idea. "There may be a way. The American Alliance is an organization attended by the top CEO's in American business."

President Wright caught on immediately. "You've hit on something Jason. Let's use them to solicit the funds. Is Drew Matthews still the chairman of the Alliance?"

"He is," the Vice President answered, now following President Attwilder's lead..

"See if you can bring him up to speed. Use your discretion in what you say. Do you think he can keep a lid on the problem, while still contacting the top CEO's?"

"I'm sure he can. He has too much to lose, just like the rest of the companies do," the Vice President replied.

Seymour Dillan cleared his throat, drawing attention to the pencil he was tapping on top of the solid walnut conference table. "We may still have a problem."

"Which is?" the President asked.

"Carson Jeffers," answered the director of the CIA.

Hank bristled in anticipation of what was coming. He thought this conversation had been put to rest at the last meeting in the President's office.

"Go on," President Attwilder instructed.

"I still think that Carson Jeffers may be connected to the LLO. We ran a background search on his negotiation efforts in Punta Del Este last year. It seems that the major benefactors of the trade agreements have been Peru and Columbia. Furthermore, the Argentine delegate who drowned off the coast of the Plat River was the only representative who originally opposed the agreement. Carson Jeffers flew out of Montevideo the day following his drowning." Seymour paused and said, "We have a letter on file claiming responsibility for the drowning. Up until now, it was never seriously considered to be credible. We might have been wrong. The letter was signed *La Libertad Occidental, Viva La Libertad*."

Hank started to stand, when he was motioned back to his chair abruptly by the President. "Is that it?" President Attwilder asked. "Carson's boy was killed on Flight 421. He wouldn't kill his own son, and don't forget, he was on the same plane himself!"

Waiting for the President to finish speaking, Seymour nodded to Tom Folger, and said, "Tom, why don't you explain what you found on the Salt Lake Air Traffic Control tapes?"

"Go ahead, Tom," President Attwilder said, keeping Hank in his chair with the motion of his eyes.

"It's possible that the downing of Flight 421 was an accident. Let me explain." Tom Folger clicked the remote until he found the aerial photo of the Salt Lake airport. Using the laser pointer to again illustrate his point, he continued. "You see where the missile was fired in Salt Lake. Realistically, there should have been no survivors. Stay with me," he said, using the pointer to illustrate his theory. "Flight 421 was departing on Runway 34. There was a second flight departing on the parallel Runway 35, Flight 377. Its final destination was Dulles Airport, here in Washington, D.C. Salt Lake Air Traffic Control tapes clearly indicate that Flight 421 had received a Position and Hold instruction. They were to wait for final clearance on Runway 34. When the controller released the flight, he cleared *Flight 421 to depart on Runway 35*."

Tom waited a second for everyone to follow his pointer. "Flight 421 was holding at the end of Runway 34, not 35. The controller cleared the wrong plane to take off on the right runway. Flight 421 should have been the second plane off the field, not the other way around."

"Did Flight 377 get off before the crash?" asked the President.

"It did. And guess who was on that plane?" Tom asked the President.

"Tell us," the Commander in Chief said, now intrigued by this latest revelation

"Senator George Daren Baird, Chairman of the Foreign Relations Committee. Just possibly, the Stinger missile was meant for Flight 377 not 421," the director of the FBI stated.

Vice President Wright jumped in. "Then what was Carson doing in Salt Lake, and on that plane?"

"My only guess is that he was there to insure that the mission went off without a hitch," Tom answered. "If his name ever came up, who would suspect someone who was on a plane that could have been the one shot down. The Dallas/Fort Worth crash of NationWide Flight 488 was not a random shooting. There is now absolutely no doubt that Flight 488 in Dallas/Fort Worth was selected because the CNN entertainment news team could film it. What makes you think that the Salt Lake target was not chosen just as carefully?" Tom Folger sat back down.

No one said anything. Hank had listened to enough. He stood and exclaimed, "Someone here has been smoking dope! Are you all crazy? Mr. President, you know Carson. You can't possibly believe this garbage?"

The President sighed in frustration. "Hank, I don't know what to believe."

Jason called on the President one last time. "Sir, we have to handle another problem."

President Attwilder couldn't believe there was more. "What else?" he said.

"Nichole Lewis. The Omega flight attendant has been voicing her suspicions again. She believes that the crash of Flight 421 was no accident."

The President was losing his temper. "Take care of it! For God's sake, Jason. You know what's at stake."

Suddenly, the red phone on the corner of the table started ringing. The President stared at it. Sandra Kennard was the only one who would interrupt this meeting, and it would have to be an extreme emergency for her to call. Slowly, the President raised the phone to his ear.

"Mr. President, I have Gerald Better, Senior Editor of *The Wall Street Journal* on the phone. You had better to talk to him. With your permission I'll patch him through."

"What does he want?" asked the President, instantly recognizing his secretary's voice.

"It's about El Toro. He said you would understand, and that he had to talk to you."

"Put him through, Sandra," the President said as he punched the speaker button on the phone. "I think you had all better hear this. If it's what I think it is, our timetable just might be running out."

The voice on the other end of the phone began. "Mr. President, this is Gerald Better. Five minutes ago, I received a letter from a group calling itself *La Libertad Occidental*. It was delivered to my desk personally by courier service. I think I'd better read it to you."

Everyone listened in horror. When Gerald finished reading the letter, the President said, "I will have an Air Force helicopter pick you up in 15 minutes. Don't let anyone else touch the letter, and above all else don't talk to anyone. Can you meet the chopper on the roof? You'll be flying to Washington, D.C."

"I'll be waiting, Mr. President."

Rolland J. Attwilder looked at his watch. It was 3:20 p.m.

15

steban honked the horn of the white cargo van twice as he pulled up to the service entrance of the Herbalife Building in Century City. A security guard was already opening the metal door at the back of the building. Esteban parked the truck belonging to *West Coast Air and Electrical* next to the 20 foot long metal trash bin. Ricardo slowly opened the passenger door and stepped down to the darkened asphalt, stained with ten years of paint and cleaning supplies. Esteban stayed in the van, thumbing through the papers on the dusty clipboard.

"What do you fellows need?" asked the overweight security guard dressed in a green polyester uniform.

Ricardo raised his arms and yawned while pointing at Esteban. "Better ask the boss man," he said as he stuck his hands in the pockets of the faded light blue coveralls. The name *Johnny* was embroidered on the left front pocket of the dirty uniform.

"Be with you in a second, just need to note down our arrival time," Esteban said, while flipping the clipboard pages back and forth. "If we don't mark it, they can't bill it. At least that's what the dispatcher says." He continued writing for a minute. When Esteban felt that the balding guard had just about lost his patience, he stuck the pen he had been writing with in the breast pocket of his blue coveralls.

"You guys here about the air conditioning?" the security guard asked.

Ricardo leaned against the truck and rested his arm under the words *West Coast Air and Electrical*. Esteban vaulted the two shallow steps and walked up to the door, pulling out the work order for the repair work as he moved. "Kind of miserable, isn't it?" he asked, referring to the heat.

"You said it. By the way, what took you guys so long to get here? The system was out when we opened the doors at 8:00 this morning." The guard looked at his watch and saw that it was 12:15 p.m..

"Hey, you gotta wait your turn. Do you have any idea how many calls we get here in the Los Angeles airport area?" Esteban retorted.

"Don't get upset, man. I'm just making small talk. It's no skin off my nose."

"If you'll just leave the door propped open, we'll get our things and see if we can't get this building cooled down," Esteban said, while moving around to the back of the truck. The guard was already sliding a wooden block under the metal door.

Esteban and Ricardo pulled a collapsible cart out of the rear of the van, neither of them surprised at the guard's concern about the air conditioning. Esteban and Ricardo had entered the building at 11:00 p.m. the previous night with the maintenance crew. Once they had a cleaning cart along with a bucket and a mop, they simply entered the elevator and pressed the button for the top floor. Access to the roof was restricted from the Otis elevator. Ricardo mopped while Esteban climbed the stairs to the roof. Once on top of the building he removed a pair of bolt cutters and snapped the lock to the air conditioning unit. He quickly pulled the breaker to the massive condenser and cut each of the electrical wires leading from the condenser. When he was sure the unit wouldn't start at the beginning of the next work day, he flipped the breaker back to its original position. Using a can of black spray paint, he turned the front of the central air conditioning unit into a mediocre piece of graffiti art. He and Ricardo had simply taken the elevator to the ground floor with their supplies. When the cleaning crew took a break to smoke, the two Latins never returned.

Ricardo poked his head in the service entrance, insuring that the bald security guard was back at his desk watching television. "Let's do it. He's out of the way," Ricardo told Esteban as he headed back toward the air conditioning service van.

"Put the two cases on the bottom of the cart and then cover them with the canvas tarp," Esteban instructed his companion.

Ricardo nodded and lifted each of the cases that weighed just over 50 pounds each onto the aluminum cart. When he was finished, he started piling the electrical wire, tool boxes, and cardboard boxes containing new air conditioning parts on top of the canvas.

Esteban slammed the rear door of the cargo van shut, tossing the two duffel bags on top of the cart. In less than an hour they would walk out the front of the building dressed in slacks, shirts, and ties. They would look just like the rest of the Herbalife distributors, who were already in the building waiting for the afternoon training session to begin.

"So far, so good," Ricardo commented as the two of them pushed the six foot aluminum push cart through the service door.

The security guard lumbered out of his chair and yelled down the hall, "Follow me, and I'll show you the service elevator. Sure hope you guys can undo the work of those kids that wrecked the system last night. These Herbalife people are really getting impatient, what with their training going on and everything."

Esteban replied back, "We'll do what we can. Chances are we can get it fixed in an hour or so, but you never know until you get in to it."

"Here you go," the guard said as he opened the elevator. He inserted a security key above the panel and punched the button marked R. "This will take you straight to the roof. I would go up and help, but I've got my job here."

Esteban and Ricardo grabbed hold of the cart and pushed it into the metal elevator. The guard was already heading back to his television set. Esteban hit the CLOSE button on the elevator control panel. As the elevator started for the roof, he marveled at how people believe what they want to see, not necessarily what they are really looking at. The Herbalife security guard had been told by maintenance that *West Coast Air and Electrical* would be coming to repair the system on the roof. *West Coast Air and Electrical* installed the central air conditioning system less than 18 months before. When the guard saw the cargo van and two uniformed personnel, he didn't even consider asking for ID. He was far too hot.

It had been an easy task to follow the air conditioning van as it left the main office. *West Coast Air and Electrical* had two vans taking service calls this Friday morning. The Cleaner had told Esteban the first van took all calls from Compton south. The second van took the calls north of Compton to the Los Angeles City limit, and that included the area surrounding the Los Angeles International Airport. Four miles and 12 minutes after the second van left the fenced-in enclosure at *West Coast Air and Electrical* it was hit from behind by a white Lincoln Town Car. There was no major damage, but the two *West Coast* employees would have to report it to dispatch.

Esteban and Ricardo had been apologetic. Ricardo, who was driving the long white rental car, said he had just dropped his coffee cup and looked away from the road. Neither of the two men dressed in the *West Coast Air and Electrical* coveralls thought it strange that they had been hit from behind just as they were parking to make their first service call. Everyone got out of their cars to exchange drivers' license numbers and insurance information. The street was completely deserted. Ricardo took down their information but couldn't find his license in his pocket. He told the driver of the van, a Johnny Rivera, that he must have left it in his bag in the trunk. When they walked around to get it, Ricardo and Esteban shot each of the two men in the heads. There had been little blood, but the uniforms fit reasonably well. After removing the two cases from the large trunk, Ricardo placed the bodies in the back of the Lincoln. The rear seat had been removed earlier to accommodate the plastic cases. He had then parked the Town Car in long term parking at the airport, where he waited for Esteban to meet him in the cargo van.

"Secure the elevator so it can't be called from any other floor," Esteban said as he rolled the cart to a spot beside the air conditioning unit. He checked the time. It was 12:30 p.m. Pacific Time. Quickly calculating the three hour time difference between Los Angeles and Wall Street, he knew that they were right on schedule. Both members of the LLO had rehearsed their movements several times during the last 12 hours. They knew what to do.

Ricardo removed all the miscellaneous tools, wire, and electrical parts and heaved them against the chain link fence. Esteban took the hand held radio receiver and changed the frequency to Los Angeles Tower. One plane checked in on final approach just as an American Air Lines 727 flew by the building to the west. All the planes were coming in from the east, landing into the wind. The breeze was coming off the ocean. It always did. Finally both men took out the green cases and removed the two Stinger missiles. Each did their final pre-firing check. Everything was on schedule. Esteban noted the time: 12:40 p.m.

They laid the missiles against the south wall of the building, and then removed the *West Coast Air and Electrical* coveralls and quickly put on the shirts, ties, and linen jackets. In the front pocket of each jacket was an Herbalife distributor badge with its accompanying gold pin. It was 12:43 p.m.

"Everything according to the plan," Esteban reminded Ricardo. They both understood that timing was essential to the success of their mission, which was why they were using two missiles for one aircraft.

Silently they waited, the Stinger missiles on their shoulders. High above the 405 freeway, neither man noticed the thousands of cars rushing to leave the Southern California cities for the desert, the mountains, and Las Vegas. Exhaust from all the cars drifted up to join the afternoon pollution. The San Diego Freeway was rapidly becoming a 100 mile long traffic jam. It soon would get worse!

The radio receiver sounded. World Air Flight 1058 had just passed the middle marker. Esteban looked at Ricardo and said, "This is it. Get ready."

Ricardo smiled and listened as the Stinger missiles locked to the heat generated by the huge jet engines of the plane on its final approach.

Esteban fired first. Ricardo waited the allotted two seconds and launched the second heat seeking missile. Neither man checked the time. They were already in the elevator heading for the training meeting on the 2nd floor. The time, however, was 12:46 p.m.

16

"**...Y**our tray tables, and raise your seats to their full upright position."
Nichole listened to the male flight attendant on Alaska Airlines
continue preparing the passengers for the landing at Los Angeles
International Airport.

"Sounds familiar, doesn't it?" Carson commented, as the flight attendants continued picking up glasses and napkins in the center aisle.

"We all train together. It cuts the expenses for the airlines and cre-
ates a comfort level with the passengers," she said. The blond German-
looking male stopped to say something to Nichole, and then moved on.

"He told us that we should be landing in less than five minutes,"
Nichole told Carson, nodding at the attendant moving back down the
aisle. They were flying first class. Carson had paid for the tickets, elect-
ing to choose an airline other than Omega. In the event they happened to
be recognized, he thought it better not to alert her current employer that
she was still maintaining contact with him.

Carson was sitting next to the window. He turned away from
Nichole to look at the houses passing by below them. They were getting
closer and closer. Suddenly he grabbed Nichole by the arm, and
screamed, "Oh, God, no!"

Nichole looked out the window, shrieking in fright, just as the plane
ahead of them exploded in a tower of flames. It was on a parallel final
approach.

Carson and Nichole clenched each others' hands as a second missile
flew toward the crippled airliner. All they could do was watch in horror.

Carson had witnessed the first missile rise from the city below and explode just above the right wing of the descending 737 Boeing jet. It had literally blown the wing away from the aircraft. An instant later, both he and the Omega flight attendant at his side reeled back in their seats as the second missile exploded close to the fuselage of the plane. It must have been locked on to the same heat source as the first missile, and when it exploded, the heat from the explosion kept the projectile coming. Carson watched in horror as the body of the other plane rocked and started to come apart. It was already in the first stages of a spin, falling to the earth. The pilot had no chance to recover. Aerodynamics had altered the angle of attack, the plane was no longer flying.

Nichole gripped Carson's arm and stared down at the destruction. She kept saying, "No! No! No!" Her supplication did no good. The first plane kept falling, once again in slow motion. Burning baggage, and what must have been bodies, were dropping from the hole in the side of the plane.

Carson said nothing. His jaw muscles were as defined as the back of a world class weight lifter exerting that final heave of the bar into the air. The Alaska jet from Seattle to Los Angeles banked to the north, trying to escape the smoke and flying debris from the remains of World Air Flight 1058. Carson's eyes remained fixed on the disaster, watching as the burning jet settled onto the moving thread of cars heading both north and south. Suddenly the 405 freeway was aflame, both the northbound and southbound lanes. Explosion followed explosion as the ruptured wing spilled burning fuel up and down the rows of standing cars. He could see people jumping from burning vehicles, only to be hit by flying pieces of metal and careening trucks. The destruction wouldn't stop. Parts of the plane landed on the houses surrounding Century Boulevard. Flames were everywhere. There was nothing he could do. He didn't turn away. He couldn't!

Nichole continued to scream. Her voice went unnoticed as the passengers gasped, yelled, and cried at the death and destruction that was rolling north up the San Diego Freeway.

Finally, the pilot of the Alaska Airliner tried to restore some kind of order to the panic that had seized the plane. "Please stay calm and remain in your seats," he announced over the public address system. "The aircraft that was landing just ahead and to the right of us experienced a major problem. We have not received any word as to what exactly happened. Due to the situation, we are being diverted to Ontario and should be on the ground in ten or fifteen minutes. Once again, please stay in your seats. We will provide further information as we receive it."

Carson stared at Nichole, still clutching her arm. "Whatever started in Salt Lake just took a turn for the worse!" he said. He brushed his hand through his sandy blond hair and continued. "God, what have they done? What have they done?"

The Alaska flight was only one of many flights to be diverted to Ontario. One after another, the jets landed. Those with more fuel were sent to San Diego. A few flights landed at Burbank and Long Beach. Los Angeles International was closed.

Carson guided Nichole down the metal steps attached to the truck parked next to the 737. He wondered to himself how he could be in one crash caused by a missile and then witness another? "Let's get out of here," he said as they went past the baggage claim area. They each carried a small carry-on. Both bags belonged to Nichole. When they left her cabin that morning, she had given Carson a small bag for his shaving gear, and on the way to the airport he had stopped at a mall and purchased two shirts and some underwear. He had not expected to be in Los Angeles more than a day. Now he didn't know.

"Taxi!" he called from the curb. Most of the passengers were waiting in the terminal, unsure of what to do next. He wanted to get away fast."The Red Lion," he told the driver as he opened the door for Nichole to get in.

Carson told the receptionist that he needed two rooms, adjoining if possible. She smiled and took his credit card, running it through the small gray machine. Seconds later the authorization was received. "I'll meet you in your room in a few minutes. I've got something to do," he told Nichole.

"Where are you going?" she asked as she took the key to her room.

"Alamo Rental Car is just across the street. I think we better get some kind of transportation while we still can," he replied. "In a few minutes you probably won't be able to get a rental car, no matter what you're willing to pay."

●   ●   ●

Gerald Better was escorted off the large helicopter onto the White House lawn. No one said a word. The crash of World Air Flight 1058 had just come over the radio. The Air Force flight crew didn't know what was happening. He couldn't tell them. Not yet!

"Sit down, Gerald. You don't mind if I call you Gerald do you?" President Attwilder asked, as he pointed to a chair next to Tom Folger in the conference room of the White House basement.

"Thank you, Mr. President." He took a seat where the lanky Commander in Chief had indicated. Sitting down, he noticed that the five men were all staring at him, as if he were on trial. He didn't know what to say.

Vice President Wright helped out. "Do you have the letter?"

Gerald Better nodded that he did.

"Please give it to Tom Folger, the director of the FBI. Let's see what we have to work with," the Vice President said.

Gerald heard the television playing on the monitor above his head. CNN was broadcasting from Los Angeles International Airport. He sank into his chair as he saw the pictures of the burning aircraft laying among the hundreds of destroyed cars on the concrete freeway. Gerald Better shuddered as the terrible images appeared one after another. He wasn't alone.

●   ●   ●

Nichole opened the door, the television playing behind her. Carson entered and sat on the bottom of the bed and watched in fear. He didn't say anything as Nichole sat beside him. She held his arm, trying to find some kind of safety from the horror coming into their room from Los Angeles.

"What are we going to do?" she asked, still watching the television.

Carson used the black infra-red remote to lower the volume on the set before answering. "As soon as I find this Sergeant Baker, I'm going to get you out of Los Angeles and home to your cabin in Washington. Then I'm going to try and stop this terror. I have no expectation, or even hope that I can, but I have to try."

"I want to help. Whatever is happening, I'm part of it," she said.

"You may be part of it, but right now there's nothing you can do."

Nichole started to argue, but could see that the look in his eyes was not one of debate. Instead she said, "All right. Let's see Baker, and then I'll go back to Washington."

Carson could tell he had got the best compromise possible, and nodded, "I need to get hold of Michael. He has undoubtedly heard about Los Angeles, but we need to find if he has learned any more background on this Marine Sergeant Baker. Before I came back to the room, I called Los Angeles Memorial Hospital and asked for the room of Gunnery Sergeant Baker. They have no record of any such person." Carson stopped for a minute to watch the carnage being shown on television and then continued. "Anyway, I remembered that Sergeant Baker was no longer Baker, instead he was Ronald T. Chapman. The nurse verified that Gunnery Sergeant Chapman was still in the hospital, but I couldn't get through to his nurse."

"Why not?" asked Nichole.

"The receptionist finally said he was in a special unit of the hospital and hung up. I think we've verified that the government has this Baker under some kind of watch or security."

Nichole stood and looked at Carson as if she had just got a brainstorm of an idea. "Why don't we just go to the authorities and tell them what we know?" she asked. "Maybe they don't know what is happening?"

Carson shook his head. "They know, Nichole. It's the government that is protecting this Baker/Chapman. They don't want anyone to know what is happening. Why? I don't know. But I don't trust anyone right now. Remember I told you about calling Hank Grishhold, my friend who is the Chief of Staff for the President?"

"Yes."

"If Hank can't level with me, we aren't going to get anywhere with anyone else. For better or worse, we are on our own here." Carson paused and then said, "Nichole, that's why you have to get out of this."

The strength of her response shocked him. Nichole looked at the television, and then turned to Carson. "Make the call to Michael!" Glaring at the television she stated, "I will see them burn in hell, Carson. Burn in hell!"

Carson picked up the phone and dialed ManTech in Portland. "Janelle, is Michael there? Yes, we know, we are in Los Angeles"

Carson waited a few seconds and heard Michael on the other end of the line. "Are you OK?"

"We are fine. Nichole and I were on a parallel approach. Michael, we saw it happen. The pictures on television can't begin to describe it. We have to find out who is doing this."

"Tell me what happened." Michael demanded.

Carson took several minutes and gave an entirely different story of the crash than what was being broadcast on the networks. He explained how they had actually seen the missiles explode, knocking the wing and a portion of the fuselage from the rest of the plane. He then recounted what he had found out about Gunnery Sergeant Baker/Chapman.

"Carson, let me give you an update of what Jim and I were able to access from the files, using the director of the FBI's password. We think that Sergeant Baker is still in a coma, but we're not sure. He is under a heavy security watch. It appears that he might have witnessed the theft of the Stinger missiles as we earlier suspected."

"Michael, can you get us in to see him? I think it's important."

"I'll do what I can. It is going to take several hours. Let me get back to you late this evening. What's the number there?" Michael asked.

Carson looked down at the base unit of the phone and read the number for the Red Lion, including the extension of Nichole's room.

• • •

9:35 P.M.

The phone rang in Nichole's room. She was watching the television replay the rescue efforts taking place at the Los Angeles Airport. The

405 freeway would be closed for days. All traffic was being diverted to the 110 freeway.

"Yes," she answered as she lay on the cover of the bed.

"Nichole, can I speak to Carson?" asked the voice she now recognized as belonging to the dark haired Michael Randall.

"He's in the other room. I'll get him."

Carson had heard the phone and was already coming through the adjoining door. He still carried the note pad he had been working on for the past two hours.

"Michael, what have you found out?" Carson asked, as he sat down on the bed and took the phone from Nichole.

"OK. This is what Jim and I have been able to do. It is impossible to gain entrance to the security wing of the hospital and the actual room of this Sergeant Baker without a special clearance. The clearance must be approved by the office of the director of the FBI. It appears that this marine is indeed an important witness. Anyway, you need to have the clearance, or I can guarantee you that you'll never get close the man. We have to take the chance and use your real names, as you will have to provide verification of who you are. Tomorrow at 7:00 a.m., you are to go to the main entrance at Los Angeles Memorial. Tell them that you need to see a Gunnery Sergeant Ronald T. Chapman. You will probably be told that they have no record of him, or that he is in a restricted section of the hospital."

"What then?" asked Carson.

"Tell them you need to see the security officer for Gunnery Sergeant Chapman. If they ask for your name, just tell them it is an S-12 visit."

Carson recognized the reference to S-12 that Michael had briefed him about earlier when he tried to get into the FBI files. "What is S-12?" he asked.

"You can thank Jim for that. He found that Tom Folger's password ended with S-12. Whenever we run into the classification of S-12, we enter the appropriate code and walk right through. We have put both your name and Nichole's in for a special visit from the office of the director. It is now part of the S-12 file. You are scheduled to arrive early tomorrow. We thought about putting it in for a visit tonight, but we thought that looked too much out of the ordinary."

"We'll try it in the morning," Carson said. "I don't want you or anyone else flying commercially. Charter an aircraft if you need to. The odds of being on a plane that is shot down is remote, but somehow I have been involved, or nearly involved, in two of the three crashes on commercial passenger planes. That's too much of a coincidence."

Nichole had been listening to the entire conversation, and sat up when Carson mentioned the two out of three crash situations. She watched him hang up the phone.

"Did you understand?" Carson asked.

"Most of it. We are going in the morning," she replied. "I'm frightened, Carson. Really, really frightened. Can we stop this?" she asked as she lay back down.

Carson looked at her lying on the bed, her short dark hair still accenting the angular features of her slender jawbone. She was still wearing a white cotton blouse and a navy blue skirt. The blouse was pulled out of her skirt, the top button having come undone earlier when she curled up against the pillow. She looked extremely vulnerable.

He moved closer to her and stroked the soft white skin of her forehead. "Nichole, I can't promise you I can do anything about this nightmare, but I'll try." He paused while starting to rub her neck, hoping she would relax. "We'll try. Nichole, we will all try."

Nichole rolled from her side onto her back and looked up at Carson. She took the hand that had been rubbing her neck and held it to her breast. "Please hold me."

Carson gently took his other arm and put it around her back, pulling her close to him. He pulled her tighter while laying down beside her.

She gently sobbed on his shoulder. "Please stay with me."

Carson turned off the light and whispered, "I will." He thought to himself, "Deep inside this self assured woman is a frightened lady. A very frightened lady!"

17

SATURDAY MORNING

Drying his freshly shaved face, Esteban smiled, looked at his watch, and tossed the towel in the basin. The time was 6:45 a.m. Glancing in the mirror of the dingy bathroom, he was pleased at what he saw staring back at him, a resident intern dressed in a green scrub hospital smock and matching pants. Inhaling the arousal of the morning air, he took a deep breath and rubbed cold water through his shoulder length hair. Combing it straight back into a neat ponytail, he used a thick rubber band to keep it in place, and made one last cursory perusal in the mirror.

"Vamos. Deja el espejo. Ya es tiempo," Ricardo said as he stuck his head around the corner and saw his companion inspecting his *new doctor's* appearance. He could see that Esteban didn't appreciate hearing him say they had to leave, but when he thought about it, he realized it must just be the use of Spanish.

His observation was right on the mark. "Deja el Castellano en Sudamerica! While we are in the States we speak English, OK?" Esteban stated emphatically, as he moved effortlessly through the sliding wood door separating the bathroom from the cramped hallway. "And yes, I realize it's time to go to the hospital."

Unconcerned about leaving any fingerprints or other clues to their early morning presence, the two Latins exited the small bathroom, and closed the door on the reflection of their hospital dress. Entering the kitchen, neither man seemed alarmed at the two bodies lying on the twenty year old linoleum floor. The Cleaner had confirmed that the two resident interns were assigned to the Security Wing of Los Angeles Memorial Hospital. Their hospital security passes were encrypted with a special computer code that would give them entrance to the wing on the second floor where **Gunnery Sergeant Baker**, now **Chapman**, lay sequestered in a coma. The marine still hadn't regained consciousness, and after this morning, he never would.

Ricardo pulled back the kitchen chair in the small apartment the recently deceased doctors had rented near the hospital. Pushing one of the bodies to the side with his left foot, Ricardo sat down and turned on the hair dryer. Assured that the dryer was heating properly, he waited for Esteban to furnish the necessary paperwork.

Esteban reached in his smock, "Here are the pictures we had taken at the mall," he said as he took out the two color passport photos from his breast pocket.

"Set them on the table," Ricardo responded as he continued to heat up the laminated ID badge of the first dead intern. It only took 90 seconds and Ricardo had separated the lamination and placed Esteban's picture on top of the picture of the blond resident. Using the hair dryer to keep the plastic moist, he pressed it all back together and set it on the table. While it was drying, he duplicated the process a second time. "Finished," he said, handing Esteban the ID bearing his picture, now encased in warm plastic. Adding his approval of handiwork he had just completed, Ricardo commented, "These IDs should get us into Baker's area without a hitch." Esteban's card was still fully encoded with Jay Prestwich's entrance authorization.

"Everything set?" asked Esteban, as he pulled the two bodies over to the table.

"It's ready. This place should go up in smoke at precisely 8:30 a.m." Ricardo answered, knowing that he had completed the preparations exactly as Esteban had outlined. There was no blood on either body. If the coroner looked carefully, he might find some small bruises on their necks. Esteban and Ricardo had surprised the two interns as they entered the apartment some six hours earlier. Both of them quit struggling immediately when they inhaled the chloroform. Ricardo had suffocated each of them with a pillow after the bodies were dragged across the covered porch into the kitchen.

Esteban opened the door to the gas oven while Ricardo took the gas barbecue grill and pulled it into the kitchen. He opened the valve on the stove one quarter turn until he could smell the nauseating gas oozing into the small room. Ricardo duplicated the procedure on the propane tank of the barbecue.

Esteban moved through the apartment, checking to make sure there were no windows open. When he returned to the kitchen, Ricardo was placing the small bomb he had previously fabricated on the oven door. In just under an hour and a half, the timer would ignite the incendiary flare, which would subsequently create a gas explosion of the highest magnitude. By the time the bodies were recovered, Esteban and Ricardo would have left the hospital. It was extremely doubtful that anyone would ever check to see when the two interns arrived at the hospital. If they did, they would find nothing suspicious about the time of the interns' death.

Ricardo left the apartment first. Esteban followed behind. The Cleaner's instructions had been very specific. Los Angeles Memorial was less than a five minute walk away.

18

"**W**e have no patient here at Memorial by the name of Ronald Chapman, marine or not!" stated the short gray haired receptionist, as she closed the card file found on the desk behind the cutout in the wall. She shut her mouth and glared sternly at Carson and Nichole, believing her belligerence would force them into leaving her station. Her hostile attitude might have had something to do with the fact that neither Carson nor Nichole were dressed in suits, but in reality she was just not a friendly person. Carson had on the same beige cotton pants he was wearing when he went to see Nichole in Washington. He had now put on one of his new shirts, a light blue Polo. Nichole was dressed almost like the day before, the same blue skirt together with an off-white blouse, and she was still wearing her light windbreaker.

Carson had tried taking the friendly route, and it had not worked. He was tired of this woman's attitude, and was ready to do an about face. "Now, you listen lady, and you listen good. You are an obnoxious cretin who somehow lost sight of the fact that you are here to help people, not the other way around!" He leaned closer to the lady dressed in the white uniform.

"Now you listen.." the lady responded angrily, already retreating through the hole in the wall.

Carson leaned forward and pressed his right index finger against her open mouth. "We are here at the express orders of the White House and we will, and I emphasize the word WILL see Marine Gunnery

Sergeant Ronald Chapman. Now please direct me to the secured wing of this hospital!"

The moment Carson used the word *White House*, the receptionist's attitude took an abrupt change for the better. No longer was she rude. Instead, she stood and apologized, immediately directing Nichole and Carson to the corridor on her left, "Climb the first set of stairs, and take the last right. You will come to a metal door with a guard after 30 or 40 yards. Your Sergeant Chapman is in that section of the hospital. Once again, I do apologize for the misunderstanding. We were told to deny the existence of Sergeant Chapman. But if you're from the White House, I'm sure it will be all right."

Carson decided to let her continue thinking that she had made a terrible mistake. He frowned and marched down the hall. Nichole caught up with him just as the grouchy receptionist picked up the phone. "Will we be all right?" she asked Carson as they approached the guard at the door.

"Unless I miss my guess, the gray haired receptionist has already called the person at that security desk and told him what happened," Carson answered, motioning to the guard who was standing to greet them.

"You must be the couple that gave Alice such a hard time downstairs?" the man remarked as Carson and Nichole came to a halt beside his desk.

"That's correct. My name is Carson Jeffers and this young lady is Nichole Lewis. We are here from the White House to see Marine Gunnery Sergeant Ronald Chapman," he stated as authoritatively as possible. Nichole took the lead and folded her arms in a gesture of *let's get moving*.

"That may all be true, but I've not received any information as to a visitor for Sergeant Chapman. I'm sorry, but without specific authorization, you can't see him," the well dressed young man in the suit said. "Can I see your authorization?"

Carson noticed the copy of *The Los Angeles Times* lying on the desk next to an empty coffee cup. The headlines read 839 PEOPLE DIE IN LOS ANGELE⌣ ᴵR CRASH. He correctly guessed that the man was on loan from the FBI and had been on duty at the hospital for several hours. Answering his request, Carson replied, "What you can do is the following. First, you will enter the code S-12 and then punch in both my name and that of my associate. That's CARSON JEFFERS and NIC- HOLE LEWIS."

The young FBI agent worked the keyboard on the computer. Almost instantaneously he looked up and said, "I'm sorry. The authorization must have come through in the night. If you will show me some identifi- cation and sign the log, you can go right in."

Carson showed his drivers license. Nichole did the same. "Which room is the marine in?" Nichole asked, realizing that they didn't know where Gunnery Sergeant Baker/Chapman was.

"Second door on the left," the man in the suit replied.

"Thank you," Nichole answered.

Carson noticed a second guard, dressed in camouflage utilities posi- tioned at the door to Baker's room. He had some kind of radio receiver in his ear.

"You can go right in," the marine guard said as the couple approached, indicating he had already been informed of their clearance.

Nichole pushed the door open and saw the figure lying on the bed next to the window. There was an IV tube running from his left arm to a clear bottle of salient solution hanging from a chrome hook Various tubes and electrical wires ran from his body to a display console on the right side of the bed. Glancing at the monitor that was shooting a green vertical line up and down, she could see that he seemed to be breathing, even though he was unconscious.

Carson crossed the room and lifted the medical charts attached to the bottom of the hospital bed. Running his right hand through his sandy hair, he said, "Nichole, come look at this. Michael was right when he said that Sergeant Baker or Chapman might be in a coma. Apparently, he never did regain full consciousness. It doesn't look like he is going to be of much help to us."

Nichole took the chart from Carson's hand and moved to the win- dow behind the display console and started to read. "He may not have regained full consciousness, but he did speak when he got to the hospi-tal," she said as she turned the pages of the chart.

Carson left the side of the comatose marine and went to see what Nichole was talking about.

"See the words, Stinger, followed by a group of letters or numbers?" she asked Carson, as she handed him the clip board.

"At least we know where the missiles must have come from," Carson said, reading the individual yellow pages. "According to the chart, Gunnery Sergeant Chapman was stationed at El Toro Marine Corps Air Station.

•   •   •

Esteban and Ricardo entered the hospital and headed directly for the secure wing. The Cleaner had given them complete instructions as to the geography of the hospital. As they approached the man in the suit, Esteban took the stethoscope from the front pocket of his green smock and put it around his neck.

The two fraudulent interns barely acknowledged the man at the desk. Instead, they simply placed their ID cards in the coded slot beside the computer, continuing to carry on a conversation about the need to fight all forms of socialized medicine.

"Doctors are all the same," thought the FBI agent as he listened to the two doctors talk. When the authorization cleared, he punched a code into the computer terminal, and the door clicked.

Esteban pushed it open, nodding thanks to the officer as they walked by. The agent in the suit couldn't see the .44 caliber weapons, both with silencers, that were concealed under the green surgical smocks. It was good he didn't.

The marine corporal stopped them at the door. "Can I help you?"

Esteban walked right up to him and said, "We need to see the sergeant. There are some tests to be completed."

"Let me just check with the main desk," The marine responded as he lifted the transmitter to his mouth.

Ricardo had already removed the .44 from his belt under the back of his green smock, and quickly placing it behind the young corporal's left ear, he pulled the trigger. The bullet passed through the brain and out the far side of his head, the slight noise went unheard in the empty corridor.

Ricardo caught the already dead sentry with one arm as he fell. "Grab his legs and help me pull him into the room."

Esteban dropped the marine's legs as they entered the darkened hospital room. He saw Gunnery Sergeant Baker attached to the beeping electronic display. The bed containing the weakened body of Sergeant Baker was the main focal point of the room and neither Esteban or Ricardo had expected to see anyone else. Unfortunately, both men were taken by surprise. Ricardo was the first to react. Seeing the man and woman standing next to the window behind the large electronic machine, he turned, surprised, and fired the .44 magnum at the shapes silhouetted in the window.

A split second before he fired, Carson recognized their desperate dilemma. He squatted and sprung several feet to his left, twisting in mid air, dropping the medical chart as he moved. Plaster and sheetrock splattered behind him as the lead slug from Ricardo's pistol imbedded itself in the thick wall directly behind where his face had been. In the enclosed hospital room, the shot was nothing more than a whispered bark. Carson reacted from instinct and training. Nichole stood in front of the six foot wide window as Carson jumped. He uncoiled with the tension of a compressed spring, pushing her backwards. A desperate burst of power in his movement, Nichole was lifted off her feet and knocked through the closed window onto the fire escape. A corner of curtain caught around her body and ripped from the top of the window frame. Because of the force of the shove, most of the falling glass missed her body and showered near her feet.

Esteban knew he had to finish the job started in El Toro. In rapid succession he fired three rounds into Baker's head. Quickly, he refocused on the man pushing the woman out the window. Before the monitor attached to Baker's head turned to a flat line, Esteban was moving to the window, firing as he went.

Carson dove through the window, a piece of jagged glass ripping a three inch gash in his right forearm.

Nichole was still stunned from the fall. Carson grabbed her and pulled her up the steps of the rusted fire escape as she tried to clear her head. "What's happening?" she screamed.

All he knew was that if they didn't move fast, they would be dead. "Come on," was all he could think to say as he dragged her around the corner of the building. Pulling her frantically behind him, he finally asked, "Are you OK?" He could see that she had hit her head on the iron rail guarding the window, but he didn't see any blood.

"I think so," she answered as clearly as possible, quickly following Carson up the ladder to the roof. Despite the determined movement of her body as she followed Carson up the building, her mind fought to understand the reason for the attack. Together with the crash witnessed over Los Angeles International Airport, Nichole was lost, unable to comprehend any of it.

Carson leaned back and pulled her forward, urging her to move faster. "We have to go up. Down takes us past the window again. Let's hope there is an exit on the roof," he exclaimed.

•   •   •

Esteban checked one final time to make sure that the comatose marine had stopped breathing. "Ricardo, see if anyone might have heard the breaking glass of the window." He knew that the sounds of the silenced .44 went unnoticed in the large hospital.

Ricardo opened the door of the room and found the hall empty. Grabbing the chair the marine corporal had been sitting on, he pulled it into the room and propped it against the door, wedging the chair back under the door handle. No one would be able to get in for several minutes.

Both men knew that they had to go after the witnesses to the death of Sergeant Baker. There was no choice. "Who were those people?" asked Ricardo.

Esteban didn't answer immediately. He was still rehearsing in his mind what had just happened. The lady was the flight attendant on the Salt Lake crash. He had read all the news accounts of the crash and remembered seeing her picture on the front cover of *Time*. Her name momentarily escaped him, but he remembered her face. Backdropped against the wreckage of his missile, he couldn't forget it. The man, however, was almost a blank. Esteban thought he remembered him from the Punta Del Este Trade Conference last year. "But what would he be doing in Baker's room?" he thought.

"I'll fill you in later. Cover me," Esteban said as he crawled through the broken glass of the window, knocking the larger pieces of glass from the frame with his pistol.

Less than 30 seconds had passed since the man pushed the woman through the window. Esteban ran up the fire escape, still wondering what in the hell the two were doing in the room. Ricardo surveyed the fire escape leading down the building to insure that they hadn't gone that way. Confident that they went up, he followed closely behind Esteban.

• • •

"Your arm, it's bleeding. Were you hit?" Nichole asked as she felt the drops of blood falling onto her white blouse.

Looking down as he climbed the last steps of the ladder leading to the roof, he answered, "I'm all right. The blood is from my arm. The broken window got it as I climbed out of the room." He could feel the vibration of running feet coming through the metal ladder. "Hurry, Nichole!"

Carson scrambled up the last section of the 15-foot ladder, sliding over the two foot lip onto the tar and rock surface. Landing on his side, he grabbed Nichole's outstretched hand and yanked her over the small wall. Chips of brick and mortar exploded to the right of his head. Whoever was firing at them was not asking questions.

Clutching Nichole's arm in his now bloody hand, he ran for the small square structure in the middle of the roof and grabbed the door to pull to open it. It didn't budge. "It's locked!" he yelled. "Stay here."

Running back to the ledge above the ladder, he looked down to see the two dark haired men climbing the ladder below. The one with the pony-tail was almost to the top. Both men were dressed in the same green outfits normally worn by doctors. Carson heard a slight spitting sound. His head was already back over the ledge as the top of the wall started to crumble from the pistol shots. "Shit!" he yelled, unable to think of a better word to describe what was happening to them.

Crouching under the ledge, he asked himself why were two doctors shooting at them? And why did they kill Sergeant Baker? He couldn't answer the questions, but he seriously doubted that either of the men were really doctors. "This thing is getting more bizarre by the minute," he said aloud.

The sounds on the ladder were getting closer. He heard the panting sound of breathing as the fingers eased over the edge of the precipice. Fighting the urge to grab the hand, he waited. A second fist came over the edge of the wall, this one holding some kind of a pistol. Carson remembered his hand-to-hand combat training and knew that he would only have one chance. Seizing the barrel of the gun, he dropped to his back, his right foot already rushing through the air. The dark haired Latin had already grabbed his wrist. Carson focused on the spot directly behind the man's head as it rose above the wall, his foot kept coming, until he felt it hit bone. He accelerated the force of the kick even more, remembering the man was trying to kill them. The pony-tail snapped in the air as the man's head jerked back over the wall. Suddenly Carson felt a tremendous weight pull on his arm. The Latin must have fallen off the metal ladder. Carson rose up above the wall and clubbed the man over the side of the head with his right forearm. Blood from the gash in his forearm flew in all directions. He felt the weight on his arm decrease. The man must have dropped. Carson was still holding the gun. Running, he rushed to the door on the roof.

Nichole gasped when she saw the blood splattered all over Carson's shirt.

"Move!" he yelled, pointing the gun at the door handle. Pulling the trigger twice he fired into the lock. It loosened, but still the door didn't give way. He pulled the trigger a third time. Nothing happened. The gun was empty. Dropping the useless weapon on the tar covered gravel, he backed away from the door, Adrenaline surging through his body. With a giant snap, Carson kicked the handle of the metal door. It flew open.

• • •

Esteban stopped falling after six feet. Ricardo had grabbed his arm and was still holding on. Using all the strength he could muster, Esteban reached out and latched onto the metal ladder. The world was spinning. He felt his jaw and knew that it was dislocated or broken. Fighting to regain his equilibrium, he focused on the shorter Latin holding him onto the metal ladder. Together they struggled over the edge of the roof.

Ricardo moved quickly to the roof exit, pistol drawn and at the ready. "They must have gone down. Do we follow them?"

Esteban moved to the edge of the roof and stared at the street four stories below. A man and a woman ran from the alley running along the side of the hospital and climbed into a white four door sedan. Esteban guessed it was a rental car. He got a good look at the man as he looked up at the roof before closing the door. It was the man from Punta Del Este. A name suddenly matched the face. "Carson Jeffers!" he muttered. "What in the fuck was he doing here?" Moving his slightly dislocated jaw from side to side, Esteban made a silent vow to kill both of them.

"They're gone. Let's get out of here before they find Baker's body. I know who they are," exclaimed Esteban, already walking to the open door on the roof.

"Who are they?" asked Ricardo.

Esteban stopped to retrieve the .44 caliber pistol laying on the hot roof. "Carson Jeffers and Nichole Lewis. What the fuck they were doing in Baker's room, I don't know."

"Going to call The Cleaner?" asked Ricardo as they hurried down the stairs.

"Immediately," muttered Esteban. He continued to rub his jaw until he felt it snap back into place.

19

"**H**e's what?" yelled Tom Folger into the speaker box on his large oak desk.

"Mr. Director, I just got on the scene. Our agent cleared both Carson Jeffers and Nichole Lewis into the secure wing of Los Angeles Memorial. It appears they shot Marine Gunnery Sergeant Baker in the head three times." Special Agent John Feather had been on the phone for five minutes with the director of the FBI, and he knew the director was fuming.

"Damn it to hell! Didn't anyone try to stop them?" Tom screamed across the phone lines. Towering over the open files on his desk, he crushed the paper he had been writing on into a ball, and heaved it at the closed door of his office. The paper sphere bounced three quarters of the distance back across the room.

"Special Agent Hathorne checked the computer for entrance authorization, and it came up positive." Pausing slightly, Agent Feather said, "Sir, the authorization is still in the system. It is an S-12 authorization."

It was the first time that Tom Folger talked in a normal tone of voice. "An S-12 authorization?"

"Yes, sir," the agent in charge of the west coast FBI Office answered.

"What about the guard at the door? Surely, he must have tried to stop them?" Tom asked as he slipped down in the chair at his desk.

"Marine Corporal Williams is dead, sir. He was shot through the head at close range. This Jeffers fellow must have used a silenced weapon. No one heard a thing. Apparently, Carson and the woman pulled Corporal Williams' body into the room, and then secured the door with a chair." Describing the scene in detail, he continued, "The window leading to the stairs on the side of the building was apparently locked, which didn't stop the two of them from smashing it open and escaping on the fire escape to the roof. The door on the roof was locked leading down to the street, but they just summarily shot the lock apart and strolled out of the building. It appears it was a full five minutes before anyone had any suspicion that something was wrong. Finally, the supervising nurse noticed that the electronic monitor on Baker had flat lined. It took three or four more minutes to get maintenance to open the door, and by then Baker was dead and Jeffers and Lewis were probably miles from the scene."

"Fax me a complete report," Tom instructed the FBI agent on the west coast, fully aware that he already had been given a comprehensive report covering all the discouraging details. The FBI had blown it.

"Yes, sir," Agent Feather replied.

• • •

Carson continued to drive, heading north on the 101 freeway. Nichole had torn the extra blouse in her carry-on into strips and was wrapping it around his arm. For the moment, the blood was stopped. "We've got to get to a doctor," she stated emphatically as Carson continued moving from lane to lane, keeping ahead of the slow traffic on the right side of the thoroughfare. "Your arm is bad. It's liable to start bleeding again soon," Nichole stated as she straightened up the mess in the front seat. "Besides, there is the danger of infection."

"The arm is OK. We'll stop and get some antiseptic and some more bandages, but we've got to get out of Los Angeles first. Whoever killed Sergeant Baker can't let us get away. We witnessed the murder," he replied as he edged the rental car into the high traffic lane on the left side of the freeway.

"Where are we going to go?"

"Santa Barbara has a small airport. We'll stop there and see if we can't lease a jet to get us back to Seattle. It's only a couple of hours up the coast."

For the next two and a half hours Carson and Nichole reviewed in detail what had happened at the hospital. Analyzing the sequence of events, Carson was more convinced than ever that Sergeant Baker had known something that could have helped them. "Why would someone kill a person who was already comatose?" he asked as they made the exit into Santa Barbara.

Nichole looked across the car at Carson and answered, "Someone was afraid that he might come out of the coma. And if he did, he must have known something." Thinking back to Sergeant Baker/Chapman's medical chart, she asked, "What were the words that he had supposedly uttered when he got to the hospital?"

"Stinger and South America. Stinger refers to the missiles, but what does South America have to do with the three crashes?" he responded.

The charter office was located right across from the main terminal of the Santa Barbara Airport. Carson grabbed the remaining long sleeved, forest green polo shirt that was still in the small bag on the back seat, and pulled it on over his sandy hair. He had already thrown the bloody light blue shirt on the floor behind the front seat. "Come on in. Let's see what we can arrange," he told Nichole as he opened his door. She nodded and got out. Together they walked up to the office of the FBO.

"You don't have anything until tomorrow?" questioned Carson. "Surely there is someone that can take us to Washington."

"If you want to fly backseat in a Cessna 182, sure. But you realize that will take five or six hours?" the short sleeved attendant asked.

Carson had learned from personal experience that he didn't really like flying long distances in single engine planes. He decided to wait until the next morning. Using his American Express card to guarantee payment for the charter of the Citation II jet, he asked the attendant, "Can you recommend someplace close by where we could get a room?"

"Why don't you try the Cathedral Oaks Lodge? It's only a few miles away up on state road 192. Being located right in the foothills of the Santa Ynez Mountains, you'll find it quiet, and the rooms are set right among the gardens," the helpful young man answered.

Carson and Nichole liked the idea of someplace peaceful.

•   •   •

"A king, with a view of the water," he told the receptionist.

The young girl of Asian heritage returned his American Express card after running it through the machine. "Room 212 is down on your left. You can park in front." She handed Nichole the key. Carson was busy putting his credit card back in his wallet, and was quickly finding that his arm had stiffened up a lot in the last three hours.

•   •   •

"It's not bad. And the boy at the airport was right when he said it was quiet. All I can hear are the ducks out on the pond," Nichole murmured as she slid open the sliding glass door to the small second floor patio. Turning to Carson she added, "Why don't you take a bath and soak that arm? I saw a small strip mall down the road. I'm almost positive that it had a pharmacy and a clothing store. We need something else to wear, and you need some first aid supplies."

Carson didn't argue. His arm was really throbbing, and they would need some more clothes to get home. "See if you can find some pants and a shirt. 33 x 34 on the pants and an extra large shirt," he said.

He started to get some money out of his wallet, but Nichole waved the effort off. "I'm fine. Besides, my plastic is as good as yours," she said, grabbing the car keys off the desk by the television.

Carson was already moving to the bathroom. It had a large combination circular tub and shower on the far side of the white tiled room. Kicking off his shoes in the corner, he proceeded to pull the polo shirt over his head. In a few moments all of his clothes were discarded near the door. He took a moment to survey the damage he had received a few hours earlier at Los Angeles Memorial. It seemed strange that he would leave a hospital with cuts and scratches he didn't have when he got there. "Not your normal hospital experience," he said aloud to himself as he filled the wash basin with water.

He turned on the shower across the room. The razor and toothbrush Nichole had given him the day before were still in the small carry-on he had put on the counter. Steam was starting to fill the room. Taking a wash cloth from the metal rack, he rubbed the mirror and stared at himself from behind the glass.

• • •

"Why don't you give me both the shirts." Nichole said as she laid her purchases on the counter beside the sack containing the bandages and ointments she had found at *Long's Drug and Pharmacy*.

"That will be $204.57," the clerk said as she packaged up the two pair of pants, shirts, a blouse, and underwear.

Nichole handed the lady her VISA card. While the receipt was being printed, Nichole kept wondering what was happening to her life. All of a sudden, it was completely out of control and she had always prided herself on being the person who commanded the situation.

• • •

She could hear the shower running when she opened the door. Throwing the new clothes on the bed, she took the sack with the bandages and ointment and opened the bathroom door. Her first thought was that the early morning fog was coming from the ocean, just like it did off the Sound. Her mind returning to the present, she realized it was just the shower, and her clothes were starting to get soaked.

"Find what you were looking for?" she heard through the mist.

"Almost," she said as she unbuttoned the waist band of her skirt and let it slip to the floor. Pulling her blouse up over her dark hair, she released her bra and dropped both items on the sack of first aid supplies. "Can I join you?" She pulled open the curtain surrounding the large shower. Small droplets of water were forming on the light skin of her shoulders, preparing to cascade down the smooth curves of her breasts.

Carson smiled for the first time all day.

Nichole thought to herself, "Maybe everything is not as out of control as I thought."

20

SUNDAY MORNING

Silence hung in the air of the conference room. The quiet was amplified by the lack of traffic on Madison Avenue. The Cleaner continued to stare at the empty chair last occupied by Martha Willburg only a few days before. None of the five men, nor the single woman, wanted to be the first to speak. Each of them had just listened to an explanation of what took place at Los Angeles Memorial.

Finally, the gray haired executive standing at the front of the table on the second floor of the brownstone spoke. "Mistakes are like pebbles dropped in a quiet pond. At first the stone drops out of sight, hidden in the depths of the cool water. But, if you watch carefully, a growing circle of ripples skim across the surface of the water, impacting the entire shoreline of the pool."

Each of the members of the council clearly understood what The Cleaner was referring to. If Martha had insured that the owner of the Grand Am had left on leave, the car wouldn't have been reported stolen, which would have avoided the extreme urgency in leaving El Toro. Baker would have died cleanly and perfectly. Los Angeles Memorial would not have happened, and there would not be two witnesses who could unravel the entire Shortfall operation.

"This will be the last mistake," the man at the front of the room stated. There was no debate from those seated around the table. "For your information, a sanction on this Carson Jeffers and Nichole Lewis has already been ordered. It will be carried out immediately, and I hope that it will put an end to this matter."

The Cleaner took a second to clear his throat and continued, "What we are most concerned with is why Carson Jeffers was in Sergeant Baker's hospital room to begin with. It is our speculation that somehow he has launched a rogue investigation into the crash of Flight 421 in Salt Lake. His own son was killed on that plane. After the crash, this Nichole Lewis began to feed suspicions that the crash wasn't an accident. I would guess that Carson Jeffers was a captive audience." The Cleaner showed a picture of Carson and Nichole together.

"We have determined that Carson Jeffers' investigative efforts are being coordinated from the offices of his Portland based business, ManTech, Inc. It is imperative that any such investigation be terminated immediately. To do this we must destroy his company, before or after Carson Jeffers' departure from this earth."

The Cleaner turned to the middle aged man with the slight New England accent. Several years earlier The Cleaner had crowned this man with the code name of Butterfly. Everyone believed that it was because he could float through the realms of government without raising doubts and suspicions. "What have you found out about ManTech, Inc?"

The Butterfly put down his pen and recited from memory the vital statistics about the Portland business consulting firm. They paid their taxes, had very little debt and were extremely good at what they did.

"Can they be destroyed?" the woman sitting at the table asked.

"They can," answered The Butterfly, while looking at The Cleaner. "Tomorrow morning ManTech is about to run into major problems. Within 48 hours I can assure you that ManTech will, for all practical purposes, be out of business."

The Cleaner flashed a map of Europe on the screen. "We all realize how important Geneva is to Shortfall."

21

og rolled in from the coast and covered the patio with a light mist. Carson stood next to the Spanish stucco wall of the second floor deck, trying to see through the moist cloud. Unable to clear his thoughts any more than he could clear the air, he went back in the room and sat on the edge of the bed. He was dressed only in the pants Nichole had purchased the day before. The scars on his chest, along with the bandage covering his lower right arm, still bore witness to what had happened in Los Angeles.

Nichole pulled the extra pillow up behind her back. "It doesn't make any sense, does it?" she asked while wrapping the sheet around her nude body. Carson had left the patio door open, and cold air was now filling the room.

"I'm afraid not. The worst part is that we really don't know what is happening or why. Let's look at what we do know and see if we may have overlooked something."

"Go ahead," she said, holding his bandaged arm against her body.

"OK. This nightmare started just nine days ago when someone launched a missile at our flight from Salt Lake to Portland, and I say missile, as we can effectively discount any other explanation." Carson stopped talking for a moment. Nichole pressed his arm a little tighter against her breasts, stating that she understood what he was thinking about. When Carson was able to put the death of his son aside, he went on. "These same madmen shot down another plane in Dallas on the following Wednesday. Both crashes were attributed to causes other than from the missiles. Finally, two days ago, a third plane was dropped from the sky with two surface-to-air missiles, which could have just as easily taken us out instead." The reality of the disaster at Los Angeles was something they hadn't really discussed, but Carson thought it prudent to put the catastrophe in perspective. They had been, after all, on a parallel final approach just behind the plane that was destroyed by the same two stinger missiles. Carson finally went on, "We also know that the government has some knowledge about the reason for the disasters, but so far they haven't spoken out."

"How do we know that?" Nichole asked, shivering from his emotional recapture of the last week.

"If they didn't know, they wouldn't have had the FBI involved in Salt Lake. Plus we know that Gunnery Sergeant Baker had some knowledge about the Stinger missiles and was under government protection."

"Not that it did him much good," she added.

Carson got up from the bed and stood just inside the glass door, looking out into the fog. "Here's what we don't know," he said, turning to look at Nichole on the bed.

"We don't know who has the missiles that were probably stolen from El Toro Marine Corps Air Station. Nor do we know how many missiles we're talking about. Two of the people involved are the phony doctors at Los Angeles Memorial. Second, we have no idea what Sergeant Baker might have been able to tell us about this crisis. Third, we haven't the foggiest what the purpose is for these random acts of terrorism." Finally he stopped speaking and closed the sliding door, leaving the nebulous fog outside the room.

Nichole stood up from the bed, the rumpled sheet still clinging to her shaking body, and said, "What if they weren't random?"

Carson stopped to consider what she had just said. "You're right. But we need to know why. Let me add something else. Whoever tried to kill us in Los Angeles appeared to be of Latin descent." Stopping to consider how to say what he was really thinking, he went on. "Nichole, they are going to try again. Whatever we got ourselves in the middle of is going to kill us unless we can get some help."

She shuddered and wrapped her arms around him from behind, her slender form silhouetted through the light bed sheet. "What kind of help?"

"We need to get back to the northwest. I think we should go to Portland and see what Michael, Blake and Jim have come up with." Reaching for the phone on the desk, he continued. "I'm going to call Michael."

Nichole laid back down on the bed, covering herself with the light blanket while Carson dialed a number in Portland. She asked, "How are you going to get hold of him. Today's Sunday morning. Aren't your offices closed?"

He nodded in the affirmative while he finished pushing the last three digits of the phone number. "I'll try Michael at home. It's only 7:00 in the morning. He should be there."

"Carson is that you?" asked the voice on the other end of the phone line.

"Michael, let me explain where I am and what's happened to us," Carson said.

His Portland friend interrupted him before he could go on. "Is your favorite meal still breakfast?"

"What in the hell are you talking about?" blurted Carson.

Nichole couldn't make sense out of the one sided conversation.

"All night long I've been thinking about Western omelets and hash browns, and I guess it's on my mind."

"Really?" added Carson, realizing for the first time that Michael was trying to tell him something.

"Yea. I think I know where I can get one of those omelets in the next 30 minutes. Would you like one, Carson?"

"Michael, I'm in California. There's no way."

"Sorry. I forgot about that. Well, I'll talk to you later." The phone went dead.

Carson turned to Nichole and explained what was happening. "Michael couldn't talk. Unless I miss my guess, his phone was bugged. And if it was, my call might have been traced. Why, I don't know. But we better get out of here right away. How long before you can leave?"

Nichole was already walking towards the shower. "Give me five minutes. One thing I learned while flying was to shower and dress fast."

"I'll call the charter and see if we can leave right away. I'll explain everything on the way to the airport.

• • •

"Michael was telling me the name of the restaurant where we often go for breakfast. It's called the Oregon Grubstake, and is famous for its omelettes. The place is owned by a friend of ours named Joey Marshall. Joey, Michael, and I went to Alaska last year to go fishing. Actually there were supposed to be four of us, but Kelly refused to go at the last minute."

Nichole didn't say anything, understanding the problems that Carson and his son had been going through at the time.

"Anyway, I think Michael wants me to call him at Joey's restaurant 30 minutes after we talked. I got the pilot of the Citation at the Santa Barbara FBO, and he is pre-flighting the plane right now. I'll try reaching Michael as soon as we get to the airport." Carson turned off of Highway 192 and headed west to the small airstrip.

"What are we going to do with the car?" Nichole asked as they went in the terminal.

"We'll just leave it. Eventually, it will be reported missing and will show up here. I rented the car in my name in Ontario, and just right now, let's not broadcast to the rental company where we are. Whoever was on the roof at Los Angeles Memorial saw us get in this car."

"Do you have any idea who the man with the pony-tail is?" Nichole asked, as Carson pushed open the double glass door leading to the pilots' lounge.

"I don't know his name, but I know I've seen him before. Remember when I said I thought the two killers were Latin?"

"Yes."

"The man in the pony-tail looks like a person who was hanging around the Punta Del Este Trade Conference in Uruguay this past year. There was a man there that looked an awful lot like this guy, but I only saw him once or twice. It could be him, but that would really be a long shot."

Carson met the pilot of the Citation II as they entered the lounge area. The Citation II can be flown by one pilot, but on a commercial charter it's generally not done. When Carson had called the charter office and talked to Barry Stanford, the pilot, he was told that the co-pilot couldn't leave for another two hours. Barry had agreed to let Carson fly right seat in order to leave immediately. Carson told Barry they would be ready to leave in five minutes. All he had to do was make a phone call.

After dialing information to get the number of The Oregon Grubstake, Carson put the call through. Nichole pulled up a second metal chair to the wooden desk and listened to the conversation.

"Are you sure you weren't followed?" Carson asked as he listened to Michael telling him about the visit he had received from the FBI.

"As sure as I can be. I took my golf clubs and threw them in the jeep. Then I drove to the club. I was sure someone followed me from the house. After I got to the club, I quickly changed clothes and took a taxi right from the delivery entrance. I'm pretty sure that whoever was following me thinks I'm still dressing to go golfing. When I'm done here, I'm going back to the club."

"OK. Tell me again what happened," Carson said on the phone.

"Last night about 8:30 two men, who identified themselves as FBI agents came to the house, and asked if I knew where they could get hold of you. I asked them why, and they wouldn't answer. It was evident by their demeanor that they didn't want to give you any kind of award for being a good citizen. When I told them I couldn't help them, one of the two said that it would definitely be in my best interests to provide any information possible on your whereabouts."

Carson then explained what had happened at Los Angeles Memorial, leaving out any reference to his current relationship with Nichole. He detailed how he actually saw the pony-tailed man kill Baker as they flew out of the room. "The government knows what is happening," he finished telling Michael.

"Blake had a feeling something strange was going on as early as late yesterday afternoon," Michael told Carson.

"What do you mean?" Carson responded.

"Saturday afternoon he and Jim accessed the computer of Los Angeles Memorial Hospital, hoping to erase any evidence of your entry in the morning. They found that your authorization had been starred and sent by e-mail to Washington, D.C."

"So Washington, D.C. knows that Nichole and I were in the hospital when Baker was killed?"

"It appears so," Michael answered. "Anyway, Blake suggested that we set up an alternate method of communicating with each other. He also said that it might be good to have access to some ready cash, something non-traceable. I agreed, and Blake arranged for several cellular phones that have numbers that are not connected to ManTech or any of its employees, including you. I didn't ask where he got them, but I have three numbers for you to keep." Michael gave Carson the cellular phone numbers, indicating the first would reach himself and the other two would reach Blake and Jim. "Carson, I told Blake and Jim to get out of Portland. They are working out of some kind of *safe house* that Blake set up. I'm not really sure where it is, only that it is within an hour of Portland."

Carson was thinking about the money. He already realized that as soon as they ran through the credit card for the charter, his travel plans would be public knowledge. It was doubtful that anyone would cancel the card immediately, as the U.S. government might still be trying to track his movements. "How much money were you able to get put away?" he asked.

"Almost $250,000. I used all the cash we had in the safe."

Carson knew he was referring to the money they kept for emergency use. It seemed like a good amount of money, but in dealing with overseas clients, cash sometimes provided the last ingredient to put a deal together.

"One more thing," Michael said. "Don't come back to Portland just yet. Give me until tomorrow to discover from the local authorities what is going on. Let's find out what is happening before you walk into a hornet's nest."

Carson thought about his recent decision to do just what Michael suggested he not do. Thinking about it, he said, "Nichole and I will go back to her place on the Sound. I don't know if that will be safe or not, but I'll call you from there tomorrow." He added, "I'll use the secure number you just gave me."

Hanging up the phone, Carson briefed Nichole on what had happened. As soon as he was finished, he took her hand and led her out to the sleek Citation jet parked in front of the terminal. When they reached the plane, Carson asked Barry to change their flight plan to go to SEA-TAC in Seattle.

Fifteen minutes after Carson's American Express card was charged for the original deposit, they took off for SEA-TAC Airport in Seattle, Washington.

22

E steban listened carefully to the recorded message he was hearing on the phone at the Los Angeles Airport. There had been no doubt in his mind that Carson Jeffers was going to run. The only question had been to where? He and Ricardo were at the Los Angeles Airport ready to pursue Carson and this Omega flight attendant, but first they had to have some idea of where they were going. The Cleaner had verified that the white Buick was rented in Carson Jeffers' name at the Ontario Airport, but it had not yet been turned in. Esteban knew this Jeffers person was lucky, not professional. After all, the rental car had been paid for with an American Express card issued to Carson Jeffers. He either didn't believe he was being followed, or he was just plain dumb. Credit card receipts leave a trail every bit as clear as red paint across a white floor.

"What do we have?" Ricardo asked his taller Latin companion.

"The man and woman flew out of Santa Barbara Airport on a charter Citation."

"Destination?" asked Ricardo.

"Seattle. They should be arriving at SEA-TAC within the next hour." Esteban looked at the airline schedule in his hands and continued. "There is a direct Alaska Air flight leaving here in less than 20 minutes. I want you on that plane. Carson Jeffers and Nichole Lewis must be running to her cabin on the Puget Sound." Esteban handed Ricardo the detailed instructions he had written down while listening to the voice mail message. "Here's how you get to her cabin. You have a car reserved in Seattle at Budget under the name of Carlos Herrera."

Ricardo nodded and continued to listen to the detailed instructions. In his wallet he carried a valid VISA card and Arizona drivers' license issued to the same Carlos J. Herrera. When Esteban finished reviewing the directions to Nichole Lewis' cabin, Ricardo asked, "What will you be doing?"

"I have some business to attend to for the LLO. It won't take long. I should be no more than three hours behind you. I have a charter arranged to fly me direct to Seattle."

Ricardo knew that Esteban would have told him specifically what the LLO business was, providing Ricardo had a need to know. He didn't. There was, however, one thing he wasn't sure of. "What should I do about this Carson Jeffers and Nichole Lewis when I get there?" he asked as he started walking towards the Alaska Airlines ticket counter.

"When you get to Seattle, find a sporting goods store and purchase some kind of hunting rifle. If you have the opportunity to take either, or both of them out, do it! I will bring the other weapons on the charter and meet you near the cabin."

Ricardo answered, "OK." He had to go buy a ticket, and he knew there were plenty of empty seats.

•   •   •

Barry Stanford closed the cabin door of the business jet and walked with Carson to the general aviation terminal at the Seattle airport. "Nice landing. Your thousands of flight hours show," he said in an attempt to compliment Carson on his flying skills.

"Thanks. I appreciated the opportunity of taking the approach." Turning to Nichole, Carson continued speaking. "I hope you didn't mind being back there all alone."

"Not at all." She was going to tell Carson what she had been thinking, but thought it best to wait until they were alone.

"Santa Barbara will mail you a completed receipt for the charter. They will still charge you for the actual hours on the plane. You are aware that you have to pay for the flying time to and from Santa Barbara?" the pilot asked.

Carson nodded that he was. Barry Stanford turned left and entered the general aviation terminal while Carson and Nichole walked around the building to grab a cab. They needed a ride to the main lot in front of the SEA-TAC terminal where Carson's Ford Explorer was still parked in short term parking.

Carson opened the door of the all terrain wagon for Nichole. She thanked him, and then started explaining what she had been thinking about on the flight up from California. "If those two men could find this Sergeant Baker, it stands to reason that they are going to be able to find us just as easily."

Carson had been thinking the same thing. He had just elected not to scare Nichole with his fears for the present time. He nodded his head for her to go on.

"I doubt that it will take them very long to find out that we have returned to Seattle. When they do, they will quickly deduce that we have gone to my cabin."

Carson listened while she explained her logic. He was impressed.

"We probably don't have more than a few hours before this pony-tailed assassin shows up. You said you were going to call Michael tomorrow. We can't stay at the cabin," she finally said. "It isn't safe."

"I agree. What did you have in mind?" He knew she was thinking of something and wanted to know what it was.

"Do you remember seeing the small inlet behind my cabin?"

"Yes. There was a Boston whaler moored on the floating dock," he answered.

"Correct. The boat is mine. My dad gave it to me a couple of years ago. He always loved the ocean, and wanted me to have the same experiences."

"It sounds like your dad's done well for himself."

"He has," she countered without explaining more about her father's financial success. "Let's take the boat into the sound. I know a place where we can put the boat in and wait for a day or so."

Carson hadn't started the engine yet. He was considering what

Nichole had just suggested, and it made a lot of sense. Even if this Latin assassin discovered they had taken the boat, he wouldn't have any idea where they went to. There are literally hundreds of miles of coastline that would have to be searched. "It sounds good to me. We'll go back to your cabin and get the boat. What about food and supplies?"

"The boat's got sleeping bags and camping equipment. You can actually stay on the boat if you want. We will need to get a little food. We can stop on the way back to the cabin to do that."

"OK, let's do it," Carson said as he backed out of the parking space in the concrete structure.

•   •   •

Ricardo walked through the baggage claim area and headed straight for the rental car counters. None of them were busy. First of all, it was Sunday afternoon, and second of all, the airlines were already flying far fewer passengers than normal. Three major accidents in less than two weeks had weakened passenger confidence. Most people were either staying home or finding a safer method of transportation. The stocky Latin smiled to himself.

As he signed the rental contract with the name of Carlos Herrera, he asked the dark haired girl in the blue and orange blouse if she could tell him where he could find a sporting goods store that would be open on Sunday afternoon.

"Take the Pacific Highway three miles south and there is a Wal-Mart on the left. They have a pretty good sporting goods section. What did you need?"

"I thought I might try some hunting and fishing while I'm here," Ricardo answered.

"You'll find everything you want there," she said as she handed him the keys to the car.

•   •   •

"Just pull in behind my truck." Nichole pointed to the white Dakota parked under the lean-to.

Carson grabbed the two bags of groceries. "Where do you want these?"

"Follow me," she said as she led the way down the steps to the boat tied up on the dock. Nichole showed Carson where to store the supplies.

Carson zipped up the front of his Nautica windbreaker. There was little doubt in his mind that the weather was turning cold. "You'd better grab some warm clothes," he told Nichole.

"I'll change out of this skirt and blouse." She took his arm and they climbed the steps leading up to the wooden cabin.

Carson was as impressed by the cabin and its lush setting as he had been the first time. He got the impression that the sun didn't shine a lot. The overcast sky seemed to deepen the dark green of the forest. Opening the back door of the cabin, he noticed that the room seemed very dark. "Do you mind if I open the front drapes?" he asked.

"Go right ahead," Nichole yelled from the bedroom directly across from the large windows. "How much should I take?" she asked.

"Pack two or three changes of clothes. We will probably be back tomorrow, but let's be prepared in case Michael has some bad news," he answered. All Carson had was the clothes he had on and the extra shirt Nichole had purchased the day before in Santa Barbara.

•　　•　　•

Ricardo pulled the blue rental car into the trees above the cabin. He was positive that this was the cabin owned by Nichole Lewis. The directions he received from Esteban had been extremely detailed. He lifted the new Remington 30-30 rifle with the scope from the back seat and loaded it with hunting shells. The clerk at Wal-Mart had asked what he planned on hunting, and he said that he was hoping to get a deer. He wished he would have had time to zero the rifle in, but he was hoping to get to the cabin ahead of Carson Jeffers and the woman. Finding a fallen log on the small hill a hundred yards in front of the house, he settled down behind it to wait. The parking spot beside the house was empty. Ricardo felt confident he had beaten them to the cabin.

Suddenly, he sensed movement from inside the cabin. "How is that possible?" he thought. Using the scope on the Remington rifle as a telescope, he saw the curtains on the front window slide open. Someone had opened the drapes, but he couldn't see who it was.

Chambering a round in the hunting rifle, he said to himself, "There must be another parking place out back." He realized immediately that he should have checked around the house as soon as he got here. Still, he had time to finish the job.

"By the time Esteban arrives it will be over," he murmured softly, as he continued sighting the rifle through the open drapes.

•   •   •

Nichole pulled out a pair of Levis from the bottom drawer of the log dresser and placed them on the side of the quilt covered mattress. She had already put another pair of pants, two cotton pullovers, and a sweater in the small black bag she had used in California. "Going out on the ocean would be cold," she said to herself as she unzipped her skirt and slipped it to the floor. "The thin blouse wouldn't do either," she thought as she finished removing the light clothing she had been wearing. Quickly, she pulled on the Levis and laced up the Red Wing hiking boots. She decided to wear the *Washington State* sweat shirt hanging on the back of the closet door. Fastening her bra, she took the sweatshirt and pulled the closet door shut behind her.

•   •   •

Ricardo peered through the scope while steadying the weapon. Slowly he saw the lady from the hospital focus in his sights. She was wearing a black lace bra that did justice to her slender, but well, formed physique. His finger started to tighten on the trigger as the lady pulled a maroon sweater of some kind on over her head.

He never considered the morality of what he was about to do. She had to die, and that was all there was to it. Many years ago he had come to peace with himself that the end always justified the means, especially when it concerned *La Libertad Occidental*.

Still, he thought it a waste to kill someone as beautiful as this lady. "Asi es la vida," he said to himself. Placing the cross hairs of the scope behind her left ear, he knew he couldn't miss. Ricardo took a shallow breath and squeezed the trigger on the Remington 30-30.

23

Nichole's reflection exploded in all directions. There was a loud crashing as pieces of the mirror fastened to the closet door tumbled into the room. Glass splintered onto the floor chaotically and Nichole wondered if the glass was flying from yet another direction. She glanced through the bedroom door as she rolled back across the floor to the bottom of the pine bed. The front window had shattered, too.

Nichole's senses had not initially known that a bullet had been fired — only that something was deadly wrong. Normal windows and mirrors don't explode. After the breaking glass, there was the soft report of a rifle, the sharpness of the crack lost to the sounds of the surf hitting the rocks west of the cabin. She looked at the mess littering the floor and called out, "Carson, are you all right?"

He answered from a prone position under the broken window. "I'm fine. Our shooter is on the hill above the house. I'll pull the drapes shut and see if I can make it to the bedroom." Quickly, pulling the long cords from his hidden location, the curtains moved partially shut, snagging on the broken glass jutting out from the window frame. "We aren't going to have much time. In a minute they will move down and try and flank us," he exclaimed, trying not to yell. He didn't want to advertise their intentions to the men on the hill overlooking the cabin.

Carson rolled across the floor in the doorway separating the bedroom from the great room. Blood started to ooze through his shirt from the small wounds caused by the broken glass at the Los Angeles hospital. Fortunately, his arm was all right. It hurt when he rolled up against the log frame of the bed, but the wound hadn't opened inside his coat sleeve. "Do you have any guns in the house?" he whispered to Nichole.

She pointed to the gun rack now exposed on the inside of the closet wall. The door was once again fully open following the blast from the unseen rifle. "It's only a 12 gauge shotgun. I have used it for duck hunting and that's about it."

Carson nodded and asked, "Is it loaded?"

"I think so. There is another box of shells on the shelf above the clothes rack."

Carson could see what she was talking about. "We have to make the shooter think we are going to make a stand. If he believes that, then we have a chance to get to the boat."

"How many of them do you think there are?" Nichole asked in a surprisingly calm voice. Evidently, she was becoming numb to danger, at least it appeared that way.

"Only one of them fired. The second one is probably moving around the back of the house now." Carson crouched by the bed and pulled the mattress from the wooden frame. Shielding himself with the matting and springs he darted into the closet.

A shot ricocheted through the front room. Whoever was firing appeared to still be up on the hill. "He's firing to keep us pinned down. I don't think he knows what he wants to do yet," Carson said as he crawled back into the bedroom carrying both the shotgun and the shells.

"What do you want to do?" Nichole asked in partial shock, her calm demeanor now fading fast.

"Do you think he can see the rear of the house and the deck leading down to the dock from where he is shooting?" Carson asked.

Nichole thought for a minute and answered, "I'm afraid so. There are some trees between the hill and the deck, but whoever is up there is definitely going to spot anyone crossing the deck."

Carson finished pushing the shells into the shotgun. Nichole had been mistaken about it being loaded. He threw the box with the remaining shells in the small black bag that had fallen to the floor when he removed the mattress. "Take this and see if you can make it to the back door," he said as he slithered through the bedroom door towards the front window. He rested the shotgun between his elbows. "When I start firing, you head for the boat. The shotgun is not going to do any good from down here, but the noise should make him duck."

"What about the second one?" Nichole asked.

"Let's hope I'm wrong about that. We don't have any choice. Two or three more minutes and the shooter on the hill will be moving to the house."

Carson moved the edge of the curtain with the barrel of the gun. More glass fell into the room from the shattered window on the outside of the curtain. Hoping the shooter hadn't moved, Carson told Nichole to crawl to the back door. "OK, when you hear me start firing, open that door and run for your life."

"What about you?" she asked. "How will you make it to the boat?"

"Just get the damned thing started. I'll be there!"

When Nichole had the back door open, Carson half crouched below the window and stuck the shotgun through the hole in the glass. He fired three rounds, one second apart. Waiting a couple more seconds, he emptied the remaining four rounds of the weapon through the window. As he fired the last shot, he ran for the open door in the kitchen. He vaulted the three foot wall on the deck and fell six feet to the moist ground below. Clutching the shotgun, he ran for the edge of the hill leading down to the dock below.

•   •   •

Ricardo was already starting to stand when the shotgun blasts echoed through the forest. He didn't know what Carson was shooting, but he wasn't going to remain a target to find out. He dove for cover behind the rotting log. The girl should be dead, but he thought he saw her running for the hill behind the house. "I shot her right through the head," he said to himself. Whatever happened would be corrected as soon as he finished the job on Carson Jeffers. He started to look up over the log when he heard the man start firing again. By this time, he had figured out that Carson was using a shotgun. Ricardo decided to take his time. He knew that a shotgun couldn't compete with a 30-30-that is, unless he was stupid enough to get within fifty feet of the man. That wasn't going to happen.

The Latin started crawling down the hill above the cabin. Suddenly, he spotted Carson running across the back yard, heading for the same spot where the girl had gone. "They must have a car hidden down there!" he screamed aloud as he bolted down the hill, firing the hunting rifle as he ran.

• • •

Carson ran for the edge of the hill. He could hear his pursuer crashing through the underbrush. Any safety provided by the house was now gone. Several rifle shots reverberated through the woods. Two limbs fell onto the forest floor to his right. Carson ran as he had never run before, drawing strength from muscles that hadn't been taxed to this extent in more than twenty years. It wasn't going to be enough. His body was slowing. All of a sudden it seemed as if he were barely moving. The edge of the ravine leading down to the cove was only twenty yards ahead. He was already sliding down the dew covered ferns. He wasn't going to make it. Calling on the last of his energy reserve, he slid over the edge of the shallow cliff, dragging the shotgun with him. He couldn't tell how far back the shooter was, but he could see Nichole casting off the ropes on the boat beside the dock. The sounds of the throbbing engine rose from the water.

Another explosion of leaves and twigs came from the ground behind him. The shooter was getting closer. Carson bounded across the narrow dock, leaping into the bobbing vessel. He saw a man standing on the edge of the ravine. He was trying to load the rifle. There was no pony-tail.

Nichole pushed the throttle forward, and the boat shot out into the cove. The whaler cut through it easily and within seconds they were out of range of the shooter. The water was choppy. Nichole guided the small boat through the waves into the channel.

Carson stared back at the figure walking up the hill to the house.

• • •

Ricardo pushed the back door of the cabin open and walked into the room. Somehow, this couple had outsmarted them again, and as he recalled what had just happened, he was beginning to think that it was more than luck. Starting in the bedroom, he quickly discovered why the woman was still alive.

"Fuck! Of all the damned luck," he said to himself as he examined the remaining portion of the closet door mirror.

They were heading to someplace along the coast, and he had to discover where. Slowly and methodically he went through the cabin, a room at a time. He found the pictures that started the whole thing. They didn't mean anything to him, and he tossed them on the floor that was now littered with broken glass, papers, books, and pictures that had been hanging on the wall only a few minutes earlier.

Suddenly the front door opened. Esteban stood staring at the mess. Ricardo didn't know what to say.

Esteban solved the dilemma by asking, "What the fuck happened?"

Methodically, Ricardo led his superior through the events of the past hour. When he was done he added, "They are out on the water. They have to put in somewhere. We'll find them."

Esteban walked out on the deck above the dock. Staring down at the water below, he asked, "Is there a map of the Sound anywhere?"

Ricardo thought for a minute and went to the middle of the room, now littered with books and papers. He picked up a book titled *Washington State - Its Coast and Tributaries*, and handed it to Esteban. The book contained detailed maps of the Puget Sound.

• • •

Carson used the flashlight to check the reference points on the map as Nichole continued to coax the engine. It had sputtered several times in the last few minutes, a forewarning of an imminent problem. The fuel tanks had been closer to empty than full, and several hours working the waves in the growing wind had accelerated the problem.

He shut his eyes trying to regain his night vision. Even when he flew at night, he always kept one eye closed to compensate for the loss of vision that always occurred when the eyes are exposed to a sudden burst of light. "I think I see some lights up ahead," he told Nichole, trying to make his voice heard over the sound of the sea.

"I see them. It should be Ned's marina," she answered through the ocean wind. Nichole was straining at the wheel, avoiding rocks in the high tide.

Carson stood on the bow of the small craft, looking for the obvious signs of rocks - a rippling of the water, a foamy quality, a swirl where there shouldn't be, or a darker shade in the water. The moon helped, but it wasn't enough. He saw a swirl in the valley of an incoming wave— and the ominous tip of a rock. A rock several times larger than the whaler.

The bow of the boat nudged, then slammed into the rock with the incoming wave pattern. Carson tried to brace himself. The second wave rocked the boat so strongly, he twisted to the floor. His wounded arm was wedged between an ice chest and a large tackle box. Carson thought they were going to capsize. They were caught on the lip of the valley of waves, soon to fall into the depths of the darkness below. Suddenly there was a long haunting scrape, a shrill screeching sound. He felt a tremendous vibration as the boat jarred and banged with unimaginable forces against the immovable rock.

As the first waves started to grade the whaler over the hidden boulder, Nichole cut the engines and braced herself against the steering console. The boat was held against the rock as another wave pounded from the leeward side. The ocean relaxed for a moment and the boat dropped suddenly into the roaring sea. Nichole gunned the engine as the whaler sped away from the unseen danger.

She cut the engine a second time as they floated up against the creosote soaked pier of the fishing village. Nichole expertly secured the stern to the refueling dock while Carson tied up the bow.

"A man named Ned owns the marina here. I doubt if the pumps are locked, but I'll go up and get him. I'll only be a minute." She walked up the hill to the light at the edge of the village.

Carson looked at his watch. It was 9:45 p.m. Breathing in the heavy air from the sea, he could tell there was a cannery of some kind close by. He followed Nichole through the trees with his eyes. Suddenly she dropped out of sight as the moon went behind a cloud.

He could hear them walking down the sandy path before he saw them. Nichole's voice was clearly recognizable. The man's voice had the gravel quality that comes from a long exposure to the sea.

"We really appreciate this, Ned. I won't try to explain what we are doing out here, but for your sake, try to forget that we were ever here," Nichole told him as he started filling the fuel tanks.

"Do you want me to top off the Jerry cans as well?" the old man asked. It wasn't really phrased as a question. Ned was dressed in dirty, insulated coveralls. He was already opening the two cans fitted to the side of the whaler. The flood light above the pump left a shadow on the gas cans. You could clearly see where the red paint was peeling away on the side of the containers.

"Nichole, I think you should know that two men came through here looking for the two of you about an hour and a half ago." Ned looked at Carson and then said, "You don't need to worry. I hadn't seen you before, and I sure as hell, haven't seen you now."

The pump shut off as the last of the gas cans was filled. "You was really empty, honey," Ned said to Nichole.

She smiled and thanked him for his help. Carson took out two bills and handed them to the old man. They were both hundreds.

"You don't need to pay now. I'll send you a bill at the end of the month like always, Nichole."

Carson said, "It's better this way. And we do appreciate your help."

Nichole was already untying the mooring lines from the dock. "Carson, we had better go. If we can get past Killer Whale Point, I think we'll be all right." Earlier she had shown Carson the spot on the map they were trying to reach.

Ned stroked the edge of his gray beard and said, "The weather's getting rough. You had best find a place to hole up soon. And, you can stay here if you want." Everyone understood that wasn't an option. The two men might be back.

Carson jumped aboard as Nichole backed away from the pier. "What did you mean about this Killer Whale Point?" he asked, as they sped across the smoother water of the cove.

She spoke above the throbbing of the engine. "Killer Whale Point is a bottleneck of land giving way to the main channel. The left side of the neck is rocky and dangerous, so boats keep to the right within 150 yards of the rocky point. The problem we have is getting through the close outcroppings of land without being spotted by the shooter."

Carson broke in, "I would guess there are two of them now."

"Probably so. Anyway, there is a dead end road at the top of the point. If these madmen are smart, they will know that is the one place we will definitely be exposed."

"How long to make it to this place?" Carson asked as he came and sat on the rail beside Nichole. He had watched her handle the craft in the heavy sea and understood that she was in command until they reached the sanctuary she had earlier shown him on the map, before it became even darker.

She reached out with her free arm and pulled him closer. "Not more than twenty or thirty minutes."

•   •   •

Ricardo sat on the rock taking his turn looking through the field glasses Esteban had bought at the small general store. They weren't great lenses, but they helped illuminate the small opening in the water below. For the past hour, he and Esteban had traded off watching the hourglass rock formation. They switched every 15 minutes. No one would admit to seeing the boat. Once, about two hours ago, they had seen what might have been the ocean craft heading up the channel.

Esteban was excellent at interpreting maps, and knew that the one place they would have a shot at them would be the place on the map called Killer Whale Point. Esteban had concluded it got its name because the whales got caught up in the cove and couldn't get out.

"There, against the rocks on the right. There's something moving in the water," Ricardo said.

Esteban took the glasses and tried to focus in the dark. It was difficult, but he could see a small boat working its way along the cliffs. "It's them." He handing the glasses back to Ricardo, picking up the sniper rifle he had brought with him from Los Angeles.

Normally, the shot wouldn't have been a challenge, but the boat continued to bounce up and down as it was jostled by the waves. He knew he couldn't wait much longer. The whaler was almost through the opening in the rocks. Both the man and the woman were in the back of the boat. Esteban would try for a head shot on the man and then finish the woman.

You could now hear the faint sputtering of the engine. Esteban drew a bead on the man. He wouldn't miss. Carson Jeffers was a dead man. Steadily, he pulled back on the trigger, never hesitating. A sharp crack sounded from the cliff. The man in the boat lurched forward, knocking the woman to the deck. The whaler continued through the opening and headed out to sea.

Esteban swore to Ricardo. "Hijo de puta! At least, I got Carson. We'll find the woman in the morning. She won't get far. With Carson dead, her spirit should be about finished."

24

MONDAY MORNING

Michael slammed the phone down on the desk, fully aware that he had spent the last five minutes screaming at the chief of Portland Police. It was another dreary day in Oregon's largest city, and the continual drizzle against the large window of Michael's office seemed to emphasize the lack of cooperation he had been receiving from Chris Lindberg. Michael stood and paced back and forth across the hardwood floor of the office. The word, "frustrated" couldn't begin to describe the emotion he was feeling.

Janelle stuck her head in the door and announced, "Blake is on line 3."

Dropping back into the tan leather desk chair, Michael lifted the receiver and asked ManTech's Director of Security, "Did you find out anything?"

Fully aware that the ManTech offices might be bugged, Blake debated how much he could say. After he thought about what he had found out, he decided he wouldn't be revealing anything the government didn't already know. "Carson is being sought for questioning in the death of a marine in Los Angeles. As of yet, he hasn't been charged with anything, but the possibility exists that he will be," Blake stated over the phone.

"Chris Lindberg as much as said the same thing," Michael responded. "When pressed, he wouldn't give me much more than you just stated, but his attitude was definitely uncooperative. I wouldn't call us close friends, but ManTech has always supported the police charities. This morning he treated me like I was a resident of a penal institution."

"Someone has gotten to Chris," Blake stated over the phone. "For what reason, I couldn't hazard a guess."

"Me either," answered the president of ManTech, truly concerned about the recent turn of events.

Blake spent the next five minutes recounting how he had visited the offices of the FBI in Portland. Just as he was reviewing how the local FBI office wanted to talk to Carson, Janelle's voice broke in over the intercom. She sounded upset.

"Blake, I'll get back to you in the next couple of hours," Michael said as Janelle closed the door to his office and came and sat by the light pine desk. Both men understood that Michael would use the secure phone on the next call.

"What is it, Janelle?" asked Michael as he took the printout from First Interstate Bank.

"Look at the balance section. You will see the amount in our operating account on Friday night was $147,053.21." Janelle pointed to the far right hand column and a figure she had previously circled with a red marker.

Michael found the figure on the accounting report, and nodded his head. "I see the amount. It looks about right." He thought for a moment and continued. "We wrote all the payroll checks on Friday night. The amount is probably about $35,000 less this morning."

"Turn the page, Michael," Janelle said as she leaned across the desk and pointed to the figure circled at the bottom of the third page. "Christine Anderson, one of our employees in the research department, was at my desk when I came in this morning. She banks at First Interstate and had tried to make a deposit on the way to work this morning. She wouldn't have thought anything about it, but she needed some cash back from her paycheck."

Michael continued to stare at the last page of the report he held in his right hand. In a disturbed voice he said, "Go on."

"When she handed the girl her deposit slip, the teller went and got the manager. He told Christine that the check couldn't be honored. Christine asked for an explanation, but he wouldn't tell her what the problem was. When she got to work, she came to see me. I immediately requested a copy of our operating statement from First Interstate. What you have in your hand is the fax copy I received."

Michael's eyes were glued to the last figure. "Surely, there's a mistake," he said.

"That's what I thought, too. I just got off the phone with Adele Johnson, the manager of the main office at First Interstate. Michael, there's no mistake! Prior to the opening of business this morning, all the funds in our accounts were seized and turned over to the Drug Enforcement Agency. No explanation was provided to the bank other than the signed order."

"Are you saying that the entire $147,000 was seized by the government?" Michael asked, his face taking on a reddish hue.

"Yes, but it's not just the $147,000. I tried to transfer some of the money in the savings accounts at Bank One into a petty cash fund. I thought I could take care of the employee's paychecks that way until the problem is solved."

Keeping the devastating report in his hand, Michael began to pace around his desk. He said, "And?"

Handing Michael a second sheet of paper, she dropped her next bombshell. "There was over $600,000 in those accounts. It's all gone, too!"

"Janelle, we're talking almost three quarters of a million dollars. The government just can't walk in and take it," he blurted out over the top of the bank printouts. "Get Don Norway from Bank One on the phone."

"I knew you would want to reach him. Before I came in your office I tried to get Don on the line. He won't take our calls."

The intercom sounded on Michael's desk. It was Janelle's assistant. "I think you had both better come out here."

"What's wrong?" Janelle asked, speaking into the speaker box on Michael's neat and organized desk.

Michael was already striding to the door. He was mad. Someone had just taken almost a million dollars, and he was not in any mood for a disagreement.

He pulled the door open and started to yell, "What is it!"

Two police officers were standing just inside the double glass doors of the executive offices. They were accompanied by three men in dark business suits. Michael correctly guessed they must have been some kind of government agents. A slightly overweight lady dressed in a masculine blue blazer had positioned herself slightly in front of the entire group. She was holding an official looking set of legal papers. In an authoritative, but extremely bureaucratic tone of voice, the lady demanded, "Are you Michael Randall?"

"I am."

"If you will come here, I have some papers for you to sign."

"What kind of papers?" Michael asked as he crossed the office and towered over the shorter woman.

"Just sign here, indicating that you are accepting service," she said, without actually answering his question.

Michael grabbed the papers from her hand. One of the police officers took a step forward.

The lady who had just relinquished the papers went on speaking as if nothing had happened. "My name is Ms. Barbara Turner and I am from the Oregon Attorney General's office. The papers you have in your hand are a complaint filed this morning against ManTech, Inc., for fraudulent business practices. The last section of papers is a restraining order signed by Judge DeAnn Condor. As of this minute ManTech is restrained from conducting any and all business activity in the state of Oregon."

She paused to make her final point, while at the same time taking a deep breath in an effort to exercise the authority she fully comprehended. She then continued speaking. "ManTech, Inc., is an Oregon corporation, and the State of Oregon is asserting that all business operations of ManTech are Oregon operations. You will cease doing business as of this moment."

One of the men in suits handed Michael another set of papers. He took them without asking what they were. Michael had no doubt that the well dressed government agent would soon tell him.

"We have reason to believe that Carson Jeffers has used ManTech as a front to distribute drugs originating from South America all across the United States and Canada. These papers are seizure orders confiscating every piece of equipment in this building. That includes computers, software, diaries, all papers, books etc. Every ManTech employee must leave the building within the next 30 minutes. They may not take anything with them other than coats, purses, and family pictures. Notebooks and papers are specifically forbidden to be taken from the premises."

Michael couldn't believe what he was hearing. For all practical purposes, ManTech was out of business. What had taken thirteen years to build was destroyed with the signing of a few papers. He knew that Carson would not be able to start the company again, and there was no doubt that the entire operation of the last ten minutes would be front page news within hours. He finally sat down on the edge of Janelle's desk and thumbed through the papers he was still holding. When he got to the last page, he threw the entire stack on the desk and asked in an interrogative voice, "You can't be serious about this list of properties?"

The overweight, masculinely dressed woman picked up the discarded papers, and looked at what had drawn Michael's attention. Not backing down a bit, she answered on behalf of the government agents. "Every asset, personal and business, of Carson Jeffers has hereby been confiscated and will be turned over to the Drug Enforcement Agency and the United States Internal Revenue Service. This includes all bank accounts, money market funds, financial instruments, Carson Jeffers' home in Portland, the condo in Utah, all interests in boats, cars and planes, and every item presently attached to, or residing in, any of those properties."

Michael just stared at the pompous lawyer as she handed him the papers to sign again. "Just sign here. These men will testify that the papers were duly served, but this will make it easier for all of us."

Michael took the papers, realizing he couldn't help anyone by refusing to sign. He grabbed a red felt pen out of the pen holder on Janelle's desk and scribbled, *Michael Randall—Under Protest!*.

As he handed the papers back to the arrogant government attorney, he turned to Janelle and asked her to gather all the employees in the building. "Tell them to meet in the conference room here on the Executive Floor." He knew he would have to tell them they were all now out of work!

• • •

Police Chief Lindberg opened the door of the police car and walked through the rain to the entrance of the ManTech office building. He still wore a uniform. Along with many other police officers, he liked the authority it brought with it. The foyer was crowded with more than fifty well dressed men and women; all seemed to be wearing extremely long faces. Most of them appeared to be in shock. Chief Lindberg knew what had just happened and didn't slow down as he passed among the people exiting the building. It would take them a while to understand that they were now part of Portland's unemployed. He had to wait less than thirty seconds to catch an elevator that was going up to the top floor. Michael Randall would be one of the last people out of the building.

As the Portland police chief entered the double glass doors, he saw Michael Randall speaking to the well dressed secretary, he recognized as Janelle Robbins. Chief Lindberg crossed the room and reached out to shake Michael's hand. He quickly realized that it was a vain effort and lowered his hand to his side. The chief began, "Michael, I'm sorry if I was short with you this morning, but this whole situation caught us by surprise. I hope there is a logical explanation for what Carson has done, but I don't know what it could be."

"Explain to me just what Carson has done, Chief. Go on explain it to me!" Michael retorted.

Janelle had her coat and was standing by the door. Michael stopped talking to the Portland police chief. "Go on, Janelle, I will be all right. As soon as I finish with our PUBLIC SERVANTS, I'll go on home. Just as quick as I know anything, I'll let you know."

The secretary shared by both Michael and Carson tried to smile, and then turned and pushed open the glass doors to the foyer in front of the elevators. None of the original police officers, government agents, or the Assistant Attorney General had moved from where they had been standing for the past half hour. It appeared that they were afraid that someone would try to take something out of either Carson's or Michael's office.

Chief Lindberg was growing impatient in dealing with Michael. "It is now believed beyond any reasonable doubt that Carson Jeffers and your company have been involved in poisoning our youth with drugs for a number of years. At the moment, you personally have not been charged with anything. I can't say the same for your friend Carson Jeffers. Can you tell us where he is?"

Michael thought about denying that he knew anything about Carson's whereabouts, but he had no doubt that the police chief already knew that Carson had called him at home on Sunday morning. Michael started to pull on the light beige raincoat still hanging on the coat tree by the glass doors and said, "Carson called me yesterday morning. He hung up before I could really talk to him. He did say he was in California. Where he is right now, I couldn't tell you." Michael would let them sort out who called who, and who hung up on who, later.

The chief knew he was getting nowhere and commanded, "Don't leave town without letting us know where you can be reached. We may need to get in contact with you again."

Michael nodded, knowing he wouldn't tell them anything. He would need to reach Blake immediately. Fortunately no one was searching the employees as they left the building. The cellular phone Blake had given him was still in the pocket of his overcoat.

"By the way," the chief said, as Michael was halfway through the door. "An arrest warrant for Carson Jeffers has now been issued!"

Michael stopped and turned back to the chief, waiting for the rest of the story.

Chief Lindberg enjoyed the drama of the moment and slowly continued. "Carson Jeffers has been charged in the death of a Marine Gunnery Sergeant Ronald T. Chapman in Los Angeles, California. Any attempt on your part to help your boss will be construed as an accessory to a felony, and appropriate charges will be filed!"

Michael didn't say a word. Instead, he pushed through the door and waited for the elevator. He wondered how he was going to tell Carson what happened. It had all taken less than an hour from start to finish.

25

"I can't wait any longer, Mr. President. Several eyewitnesses to the crash on Friday afternoon have come forward. None of them can say for sure what happened to World Air Flight 1058, but several passengers on an Alaska Airlines Flight have stated that they saw an explosion prior to the plane falling from the sky."

President Rolland Attwilder sat forward on his chair and drew large stars on the yellow pad laying on his desk in the Oval Office. He waited for Gerald Better of *The Wall Street Journal* to finish telling him what would be in Tuesday's edition of the most credible paper in the country. When Gerald finished reading the gist of the editorial, President Attwilder spoke. "Gerald, I understand that you can't hold back on the article. I would appreciate it if you could indicate that you have personally talked to me, and emphasize that every resource at our disposal is being used to apprehend the perpetrators of this nightmare."

"I'll do what I can," the voice said through the phone. "You do realize, Mr. President, that we have no choice but to publish a copy of the letter from the LLO."

"You kept a copy?" the President of the United States asked incredulously.

Gerald Better made no effort to answer the President's question. Instead, he asked one of his own. "Can you give me any specific information about this Carson Jeffers?"

President Attwilder stopped his doodling and dropped his pen on the paper, trying to maintain a steady voice. "What do you mean?" he asked.

The senior editor of *The Wall Street Journal* answered, "Our Los Angeles news bureau received information early this morning that names Carson Jeffers, CEO of Portland based ManTech, Inc., is a suspect in the terrorist attacks on all three planes."

President Attwilder was already pushing the button on his phone, summoning Sandra Kennard into his office. "I don't know what you are referring to, but I will check it out and get back with you."

"If I don't hear from you by this afternoon, *The Journal* will name Jeffers in our story tomorrow morning," Gerald stated very matter-of-factly.

"We'll get back to you," the President said.

"Thank you, Mr. President."

Sandra Kennard entered the Oval Office carrying a note pad and pen. "Yes, Mr. President."

"Call Jason and ask him to have Tom Folger and Seymour Dillan meet here in my office in one hour. Also, let Hank know about the meeting."

●   ●   ●

Jason Wright knew that he was in charge of the intimate group that had assumed the responsibility of eliminating the terrorist threat, but he waited for his boss to quit pacing. When President Attwilder finally took a seat, Jason began. "We have run out of time. You just heard the President recount his conversation with Gerald Better. By this time tomorrow the country is going to start slipping into total panic. The only thing we can do is to find those missiles and apprehend the leaders of the LLO." Each of the men in the room comprehended the full impact of the Vice President's words. The only problem was that there didn't appear to be anything they could do about it. "Tom, bring us up to date on your investigation," the Vice President said, turning to the large ex-football player.

The director of the FBI remained sitting, while correcting his posture on the large eight foot couch. "I have prepared a briefing report for each of you," he said, referring to the numbered copies of the top secret paper each person had already received. For the next ten minutes Tom reviewed in detail the steps being taken by the FBI to solve the theft of the missiles. Finally, he got to the section dealing with the death of Gunnery Sergeant Baker in Los Angeles. "There appears to be no doubt that Carson Jeffers gained entrance to the secure wing of Los Angeles Memorial Hospital and killed both Sergeant Baker and the marine corporal standing guard at the door of the room. Somehow he was able to access the computer clearance program, and he simply walked into the hospital room."

"I see he was not alone," commented the director of the CIA, as he continued reading Tom's briefing.

"That's correct, Seymour. Nichole Lewis was with him. We don't really know why she was there, but we doubt that she knows what Carson is up to. It is our opinion that Carson somehow gained her confidence and is planning on using her later on."

Hank Grishhold had been biting his tongue for the last several minutes but finally had to speak up. "I still find it hard to believe that Carson Jeffers is involved in these terrorist attacks."

Vice President Wright answered on behalf of Tom Folger. "Hank, I think I can speak for both the President and myself when I say that it seems unbelievable to us also. The facts, however, can't be ignored. Friday afternoon Carson Jeffers was on the Alaska Airlines flight that was following World Air Flight 1058 in the landing approach. It is just too much of a coincidence for him to be at both the Salt Lake and Los Angeles airports at the exact same time as the attacks."

Hank sat down and listened to the Vice President continue. "Following the crash of 1058 on Friday afternoon, Carson checked into the Red Lion Inn in Ontario. He subsequently went to Los Angeles Memorial Hospital and entered Sergeant Baker's room. The marine gunnery sergeant died three minutes later. Yesterday morning, he flew to Seattle with Nichole Lewis. He hasn't been heard from since."

President Attwilder nodded for Jason to go on. "Early this morning, we issued an arrest warrant for both Carson Jeffers and Nichole Lewis in conjunction with the death of Gunnery Sergeant Baker. I'm sorry, Hank, but I believe that Carson Jeffers is our prime suspect. At the very least, he is connected to the LLO."

When Hank listened to everything presented in such a factual manner, he had to agree that it looked very incriminating for his friend.

Tom Folger had waited for the Vice President to finish explaining the evidence to the Chief of Staff. When Vice President Wright finished, Tom continued. "We named both Nichole Lewis and Carson Jeffers in the arrest warrant. To date, we have not mentioned anything about the LLO in the warrant. That will have to change as soon as *The Journal* releases the story tomorrow."

President Attwilder had remained quiet during most of the meeting. He stood from behind his desk and walked over to the fireplace, still not speaking. Finally, he said, "Tom, don't wait. I want you to name Carson Jeffers as the prime suspect in the terrorist attacks. Work with Jason and draft a statement that we can read at a press conference later this afternoon. We are going to have to play our hand before Gerald Better publishes tomorrow. Right now, we have to play by their rules."

Vice President Wright walked over to the President and whispered something in his ear. President Attwilder nodded in agreement as Jason went to the door leading to Sandra Kennard's office. "Come on in," the Vice President said to the visitor sitting in Sandra's office.

Jason took the visitor by the arm and escorted him to the fireplace. The well dressed executive shook hands with Roland Attwilder and said, "I wish we were having this meeting under more favorable circumstances, Mr. President."

"So do I, Drew," the President responded to one of the most powerful men in American business. "I believe you have met everyone before, with the exception of Seymour Dillan, the director of the CIA. Seymour, this is Drew Matthews."

Both men shook hands.

"We are just discussing the grave situation that we are facing in the country today," the President stated. Turning to the Vice President, he asked, "Did you brief Drew on the letter that *The Wall Street Journal* received on Friday?"

"I did, Mr. President. I felt he needed to know as much as possible."

Everyone in the office already knew why Drew Matthews was in the meeting. The time had come to consider paying the ransom demands of the LLO.

Vice President Wright handed Drew a copy of the briefing report that everyone else was reviewing. Drew took the paper and skimmed it quickly. Satisfied that he understood the basics of what was going on, the middle aged businessman asked, "Do you want me to bring you up to date on my efforts to raise the $2 billion?"

"Please," answered Vice President Wright.

Drew was still standing beside Seymour Dillan when he began. "I have been able to get firm commitments for almost one and one half billion dollars. All of the money can be made available within a time frame of 24 hours, once the approval from President Attwilder is received to pay the money."

"How were you able to get the companies to commit to the payoff?" asked Tom Folger, immediately regretting his use of the term *payoff*..

Drew put down the briefing paper on the glass coffee table and answered, "I started with Pierce Ekholt from Omega Airlines. He volunteered to put up $200 million. The other airlines soon kicked in another $900 million. I was able to get another $400 million from the oil companies. They all realized that they couldn't afford to have the airlines go broke."

"We're still short about $500 million," interjected Hank.

"I am confident that I will have the total amount subscribed to within the next couple of hours," Drew answered. "I am going to keep the number of companies involved in this transaction to twelve or less."

President Attwilder raised his hand in a motion of "wait a moment." Looking directly at Drew, but speaking to everyone in the office, he said, "We are not ready to make the payoff just yet. We want to be ready, but let's give the FBI and the CIA one more chance."

Jason added, "I agree with the President. However, I do think that we should be ready to make the payoff immediately. Drew, can you leave for Geneva this afternoon and set up the account necessary for the transfer of funds?"

"As soon as I have the remaining commitments in hand," answered the businessman. "Do you have a preference of which bank to use in Geneva?"

"I don't," answered the Vice President. "Does anyone else?"

Everyone shook their heads, no. "Do you have one you can suggest?" asked the Vice President.

Drew thought for a moment and answered, "I have used The Bank of Switzerland before. It is located right in Geneva and has offices in New York. If I set up the account in Switzerland, we can move the money directly in and out of Wall Street. It should work OK."

"Set it up. We may need that account very soon. Is that it?" asked the President of the United States.

Everyone took his question to mean that the meeting was finished, and each man stood to leave. Drew Matthews looked troubled, and then said, "Mr. President, you should be aware that this money is not coming without a quid pro quo."

Silence flooded the room. President Attwilder asked, "What do you mean by *quid pro quo*?"

The chairman of the American Alliance looked at the President, unsure of how to tell him what he meant. Finally, he just laid it out. "Mr. President, in order to raise these funds, the companies demanded certain concessions that must be met within the next six months. No one is expecting anything immediately, but when this situation is resolved, they need a way to pay this money back."

"What is it, specifically, that they want?" asked the President.

"Each of the companies is going to need to raise additional capital to replace the money they are committing to this project. This money must come from the debt and equity markets. I agreed that your administration will support a bill to completely eliminate long term capital gain taxes. They all believe that with this incentive they can raise the capital necessary to bury these expenditures."

"That's it?" interrupted the Vice President, clearly upset with what Drew had just said.

"Not quite. They also want a corporate income tax break that would in fact roll back taxes to the level of five years ago," answered Drew Matthews.

President Attwilder and Vice President Wright looked at each other, each wondering how the country got into a situation where it was being held ransom by both terrorists and American industry.

26

The roar of the engine, combined with the flutter of the large whirling rotors, made hearing almost impossible in the blue and white chopper Esteban had chartered at Oak Harbor. Search and rescue operations usually kept the small helicopter service busy, but flying time had been minimal in the late spring. John Skoely, the pilot, was more than willing to look for a fishing partner who had been separated from his Latin companions. John looked at his watch and then checked the fuel on the rescue craft. "We have been out for almost three hours now. I don't mind taking your money, but we are going to have to refuel within the next thirty minutes. What do you say we head back and start again after getting some lunch?"

Esteban would like to have just kept searching for the boat, but he too realized that they had to get some fuel. "Let's make another pass in the area north of Killer Whale Point. Roberto and his wife told me they planned on camping somewhere close to the Point."

"You're sure they didn't put out to sea? We can organize a full search and rescue operation," the pilot said.

Esteban looked at Ricardo and replied, "No, they are just camping somewhere close." He knew that if they didn't find the girl soon, he would have to call the Cleaner and do just what the helicopter pilot suggested. It had been more than twelve hours since he had shot Carson Jeffers. He had no doubt that the man was dead, but the job wouldn't be finished until he took care of the Omega flight attendant. Besides, it had become a personal matter now.

John banked the chopper and turned back down the channel towards Killer Whale Point.

•   •   •

Nichole pulled the large branches up beside the beached boat and fought to keep from screaming in frustration. She had heard a helicopter pass near-by several times during the morning. The last twelve hours of her life had been more difficult, strenuous, and physically exerting than any other single event, and that included the crash in Salt Lake. Flight 421 had gone down in a matter of moments, but this was going on forever! She took the small hand saw she kept in the foot locker of the boat and cut the branch off the long limb. Lifting the water-soaked wood above her shoulders, she threw it on the boat. Looking at what she was doing, she doubted that it would do any good at all. However, when she stepped back from the pile of brush, it looked like a pile of driftwood. There was a good chance that it could be missed from the air. If, however, a full scale search was started, her camouflage activity would do absolutely no good at all.

From the south, she heard the whipping of air as the helicopter turned north up the small inlet. Diving under the edge of the boat, she shielded her body with the dead driftwood she had piled on the Boston whaler. Minutes seemed like hours, and finally the sound of the helicopter biting through the air grew more faint. Whoever was searching for her hadn't spotted the boat. There was no doubt in Nichole's mind that the pony-tailed Latin and his partner were going to try and kill her, too!

Slowly she pulled herself to her feet and stood among the rocks and wood that had washed up on the shore of the ocean inlet. Any other time she would have taken a seat on one of the smooth stones and wondered at the beauty of the sea. The sun was shining, the water was fairly smooth, and you could hear the gulls as they fished in the water. Today, she didn't notice any of it. She was going to die, and she couldn't do anything about it.

• • •

"Let's head back," Esteban said to the search and rescue pilot. "Can we start again in an hour? I'm sure we'll find my friends this afternoon."

"You're paying the bill. If you want to keep looking, it's fine with me. I'll get the bird serviced, grab some lunch, and meet you here about 12:30. Sound alright?"

Esteban nodded OK and then turned to finish his discussion with Ricardo, who was sitting in the rear seat of the aircraft. "I want that woman dead," he stated in a voice that couldn't be heard over the rush of the rotors. Checking to be sure he wasn't broadcasting his intentions on the aircraft's intercom, he added, "Before we leave here, we will have the bodies of both Carson Jeffers and this woman, Nichole Lewis."

Ricardo accepted the fact that Esteban was getting emotionally involved with the sanction. Carson Jeffers had gotten the best of them at the hospital, and then again at the cabin. Now he was dead, and if Esteban wanted to vent his frustration on the woman, he couldn't blame him. For the woman's sake, he hoped that she died before Esteban could question her.

• • •

Nichole took the dry clothes from the branches where she had hung them the night before. She had been able to guide the boat almost fifteen miles up the coast to its present hiding place, all the time navigating in the dark. Several times during the night, she had felt like giving up, but then she looked down at Carson lying on the deck of the small boat and knew that she just couldn't.

Neither of them had heard the shot from the rifle above the sound of the waves and the surf breaking on the rock cliffs of the Point. Just before Carson fell forward and knocked her down, she had seen a flash high on the cliffs, right where the road dead-ends on the Point. She knew instantly that they were too late. The dark haired men who had killed the marine in the Los Angeles Hospital were on the cliffs.

She was sure that Carson was dead. Blood was everywhere, and

Carson was not moving. Knowing there was absolutely nothing she could do until she made it through the opening, she had kneeled on the floor and gunned the boat through the waves. A whaler is made to withstand an extreme pounding, and she had given it the true test. Her father would have been proud of her. She shot over one breaker after another. Finally she was free of the surf and shot out into the channel.

Once she was clear of the cliffs she cut the engine to see if Carson was still breathing. She knew he wasn't, but she was wrong. A head wound is usually serious and almost always produces a tremendous amount of blood. Examining Carson, she found that his breathing was regular, but he was not conscious. He had been hit in the head behind the right ear. She knew that the man must have been using a scope. The boat must have moved just enough for the bullet to only produce a grazing head wound. Carson's head was split open to the bone in back of the ear. She got the first aid kit from under the steering console and cleaned him up the best she could. Using a pressure bandage, she was able to stop the bleeding. The problem was that he hadn't regained consciousness.

It was still dark, but the storm had abated and the moon had come out. She was able to recognize the inlet and made for the beachwood littered cliffs. Gunning the engine at first, she headed for the shore. She cut the engine as she banged on the smaller rocks under the cliffs. Using the mooring lines, she tied up both the stern and bow of the boat at the high tide level. She realized she would have to leave during high tide if she wanted to get off the beach. Carson was breathing steadily, and the bleeding was stopped. His clothes were soaked with salt water and blood.

After she tied up the boat, she found the cave she had been hoping for. It was still above high tide and was dry inside. Using strength she hadn't really believed she possessed, she fastened a type of travois, using the emergency oars and a canvas tarp, and started dragging Carson to the cave. It took almost thirty minutes for her to get him into the shelter. Once she was sure that he was still breathing all right, she started unloading the boat. He must have received a concussion when the slug hit the bone under his ear.

For the next two hours Nichole had used what driftwood she could find near the boat to at least break the regular lines of the whaler from the air. She would finish the job in the morning. Finally, almost three hours after she pulled into the cove, she made a fire in the back of the cave using small pieces of wood soaked in some of the gas from the red Jerry cans. The smoke filtered through a small opening in the rocks of the cave. It was close to five in the morning, and she doubted that the smoke would be spotted from the air in the dark.

Carson still hadn't regained consciousness. Nichole removed his wet clothes and tried to wash them in the ocean. She knew that they would be grimy with salt, but it was the best she could do. She washed her soaked outfit too, knowing she could change into the spare clothes she had packed in the small black bag where Carson had thrown the extra shotgun shells. Piling more wood on the fire, she opened the large double size sleeping bag and pulled it around Carson. Before dawn she had finally curled up beside his scarred body and slept. She was exhausted, but comforted by the steady up and down motion of his chest as it moved against her body.

Nichole finished gathering up Carson's shirt, pants and windbreaker from their concealed location on the lower branches. They still had faded blood stains here and there, but at least they were dry. She took them into the cave and went to check on Carson. If he didn't wake up soon, she would have to try and get him to a hospital. She thought the cure might be worse than the sickness. After all, Sergeant Baker had been killed in a hospital.

A moaning sound came from the down sleeping bag. "Carson, are you awake?" she asked as she knelt beside the weakened corporate executive.

Something that sounded like the word, *almost*, came from his mouth. Nichole started crying. Slowly at first, and then the tears wouldn't stop. It was as if she had held everything in for the past twelve hours, and now it started rushing out.

"Where are we?" Carson tried to ask the weeping lady.

"In a cave about 15 miles north of Killer Whale Point," she answered, trying to hold him at the same time.

Carson felt the bandages around the side of his head and asked, "I was shot?"

"Yes. It just grazed your head. The bullet caused a great deal of blood, but it didn't enter the skull. You must have gotten a concussion."

Carson was now almost fully alert. "How did you get us here?" he asked, looking around at the inside of the cave.

Nichole spent the next few minutes telling Carson what had transpired during the last twelve hours, finishing with the description of the sound of the helicopter.

Carson tried to stand up but almost passed out from nausea. "I guess I'm not quite ready to go anywhere," he said as he regained his equilibrium. "If you only heard the one helicopter, I would guess that just the two shooters are looking for us right now. It's possible that they might call in some help real soon. And if they do, we will be found."

Nichole knew that he was right.

"I think we should stay here until tonight and then try to make it to somewhere where I can get hold of Michael. It's time we tried to fight back. First, we have got to find out who these people are, what they are after by shooting down these planes, and why in the hell they are trying to kill us!"

"Do you think Michael has found anything out?" she asked as she started to open the igloo cooler she had brought into the cave from the boat.

"I hope so, but until we can talk to him, we won't know."

Nichole passed Carson a slightly moist ham and cheese sandwich that had been made the day before in the deli outside Seattle. "You'd better eat this," she said.

Carson took the sandwich, suddenly realizing that he was famished. Pausing after a couple of bites, he asked Nichole, "Where do you suggest we try and go tonight?" Nichole was familiar with the area, and he wasn't.

"How about Port Townsend? We can make it in the dark. It has a few motels, and it's on Highway 20," she answered, handing him a Coke from the cooler.

"I've landed at the airport there. As I recall, they had a pretty decent charter business going. I don't know for sure where we are going to go next, but we better have some way to get there," Carson responded.

Several times during the afternoon they heard a chopper pass by. Nichole must have done a pretty good job at covering the boat, as the helicopter never hovered over the inlet. Fortunately, the tide was high. As soon as it became dark, Carson helped Nichole clear the branches off the boat and drag it the few remaining feet into the water. There was still a slight throbbing in his head, but he felt a hundred percent better than he had when he first woke up. During the last several hours, he had tried to separate what they knew from what they didn't. Until he could talk to Michael, he still felt they were in the dark.

· · ·

Esteban placed the call to the Cleaner at 9:00 p.m. Pacific Time. The secure voice mail system came on immediately. When the signal sounded, Esteban recited a series of numbers. Before any action was taken on the information he was about to leave on the recorder, appropriate authentication would be completed.

"Carson Jeffers is believed to be dead. He was shot off the coast of Washington late last night. His body has not yet been recovered. It is believed that the woman, Nichole Lewis, is still holed up somewhere along the coast near Killer Whale Point. I believe it would be wise to initiate a manhunt or search operation for the two fugitives," Esteban stated into the mouth piece of the phone. He then outlined what steps he and Ricardo had taken to capture Nichole Lewis. Long ago he found it better to provide as much information as possible when he needed to ask for help. And he was asking for help in finding the woman!

· · ·

Nichole guided the whaler into the dock at Port Townsend. It was almost 8:30 in the morning, and the harbor was already bustling with activity from the fishing village. They were going to leave in the middle of the night but decided to wait until just before dawn so that they would blend in with the boats leaving for the early morning fishing. Nichole had laid out the fishing net across the bow of the boat. Carson tried to stay out of sight, hidden along the edge of the boat. From the air, the boat would look just like another small one-person fishing operation. They had not been spotted.

Carson wrapped his windbreaker around the shotgun and stepped onto the dock. Looking up and down the pier, all he saw were locals going about the duties of the day. Nichole followed him onto the wooden structure floating on old barrels and tires. Together they finished tying up the boat.

"When we turned into the harbor, I saw a small motel just up the road. Let's see if we can get a room," Carson said as he took Nichole's arm.

She changed the small black carry on bag to her other shoulder and pulled closer to Carson. She suddenly felt they might have a chance. Maybe it was just hope, but still she felt better. Looking at Carson, she could hardly see the bandage under the faded black baseball cap she had found in the footlocker of the boat. The embroidery that originally said *Mariners* was gone. It now identified him as a *Marine* instead of as a member of the Seattle baseball team.

A weathered plastic sailor was planted in the yard of the motel. It was supposed to be a welcome sign for the motel, but it looked more like a warning to continue on. The statue's feet were caked in cracked cement, and the whole structure was wired to the ground. Carson knew that it was to protect it from the wind, not to stop anyone from stealing it. A vacancy sign was displayed on the side of the dirty white siding of the office. Pulling open the screen door, Carson saw a lady about forty years old puffing on a cigarette. She didn't seem at all interested in helping them.

"Do you have a room?" Carson asked as he went to the counter holding the complimentary match books.

"Yup," the lady said. "Do you want one?"

"We do. Do you have something away from the road? We have been fishing all night and would like to avoid the road noise," Carson answered.

"Just sign here. That'll be $51.00 plus tax," she said as she handed Carson the registration card.

Carson filled out the card using the first name that came to his mind, Kelly Lewis. He realized it was a symbol of how confused his life had become, but he knew that he didn't want to use his own name. He handed the lady four twenty dollar bills. "I need to make a couple of phone calls, so just put the balance down as a deposit," he said.

The lady continued puffing on the cigarette as she wrote out the receipt and handed him the key to the room. "Room number 12 is around the corner facing the trees," she said, placing the registration card and the money in the drawer under the gray counter top.

Carson took the key and led the way to the room. It was even less than they had expected. There was really no need to get a key for the room. The lock was broken. A vinyl chair and a black and white television faced the small double bed. There was a rusted metal lamp on the chipped wooden nightstand. Carson checked the phone under the lamp and was pleased to see that it really was working. He was sure that it wouldn't be if he hadn't left the deposit.

Nichole checked the bathroom and found there was a shower, but no tub. "It will have to do," she said through the door, lifting one of the thin white bath towels. She came back into the small motel room, noticing the worn carpet for the first time. "While you try and get hold of Michael, why don't I see if I can get us something to eat and maybe a new shirt and jacket for you?" she asked.

Carson took the shotgun out of his coat and laid it on the bed. "That sounds great." He really wanted to clean up, but he needed to find out what was happening. He dialed the number of ManTech's offices in Portland as Nichole swung open the screen door protecting the room from the flying insects.

Carson waited for someone to answer the phone. He let it ring ten or fifteen times before he gave up. "Someone should be in the office," he said to himself as he replaced the phone. He thought about calling Michael at home but knew that wasn't safe. Shaking his head, he realized he must not be fully awake. He took out the telephone numbers that

Michael had given him over the phone on Sunday morning. Memorizing the number, he placed the call.

"Yes," the voice answered.

Carson recognized Michael's voice immediately. "Michael, why doesn't anyone answer the phone at ManTech?" he asked. It wasn't the most important thing he wanted to find out, but it was still on his mind.

"I'll get to that in a minute," Michael answered. "First of all, have you seen a paper this morning?"

"No. What is it?"

"Where are you now?" Michael asked.

"Port Townsend in a small run down motel. Michael, tell me what is happening."

"Let me pull off the road, where I can talk," Michael said as he parked in front of the convenience store. He knew he was being followed, but until he knew where he was going, he thought it best to stay in the Portland area.

For the next twenty minutes Carson and Michael brought each other up to date. Carson told Michael about escaping into the sound and how he had been slightly wounded.

Michael then explained how ManTech had been shut down. Carson just sat on the bed in shock as he learned of the total destruction of his company.

"They took all of the money in all the accounts?" asked Carson, not believing what he was hearing.

"Every last dime. They wouldn't even allow the banks to honor the paychecks I signed on Friday. We're finished. But that's not all. They seized all your personal assets. They have taken your home, the cars, the condo at Deer Valley, everything. Carson, they have agents going through every scrap of paper, every transaction, and every business deal we have done in the last thirteen years."

"That's it? That's what's in the paper?" Carson asked.

Michael had waited to tell Carson about the arrest warrant until the end, but now he knew he could explain everything. "Chris Lindberg, the Portland chief of police, told me that they had issued an arrest warrant for you in connection with the death of Gunnery Sergeant Chapman."

Carson wasn't really surprised. He took a pencil and started doodling on the pad of paper by the phone. "We had as much as expected that to happen, especially after the computer log was sent to Washington, D.C.," he said.

"I'm afraid that is just the beginning. Get a copy of a this morning's paper. It is a real shocker. Nichole is also wanted for the murder of Chapman/Baker."

Carson knew there was more. "What else is in the paper?"

"A group known as La Libertad Occidental has claimed responsibility for the attacks on the three planes."

"They are from Columbia and Peru," Carson uttered aloud.

"Carson, you have been identified as a high ranking member of that terrorist group and are being sought as the prime suspect in the attacks on all three of the aircraft," Michael stated.

"My own son was killed! Who would believe such an absurdity?" Carson screamed into the phone.

"Apparently, Kelly's death was a mistake, but they present a very compelling case in the paper," Michael responded to Carson's outburst.

"Let me get a paper and then call you back," Carson said as Nichole entered the room. He hung up the phone and stared at the shock registered on her face. She couldn't have heard everything that Michael said. It had to be something else.

Dropping the bag of groceries and sundry items on the bed, she tossed Carson a copy of the *Seattle Times* and *The Wall Street Journal*. "It can't be!" she said.

Carson picked up *The Journal* and started reading the main article. Nichole sat on the bed, in every bit as much shock as when she had first picked up the paper at the small market.

"Carson Jeffers, CEO and Chairman of the Board, of the Portland, Oregon, based ManTech, Inc., has been charged in connection with the death of a government witness in the recent terrorist attacks. It is speculated that a Marine Gunnery Sergeant Chapman could have provided crucial information concerning the theft of several Stinger missiles stolen from El Toro Marine Air Corps Station. Sergeant Chapman was killed three minutes after Jeffers entered his

room with an accomplice by the name of Nichole Lewis, a 34 year-old flight attendant.

"In the last five years Carson Jeffers' company, ManTech, Inc., has experienced meteoric growth with numerous international connections. Reliable sources have stated that ManTech, Inc., has been largely financed by South American drug operations.

"The Wall Street Journal has learned that Carson Jeffers was present and witnessed the crash of World Air Flight 1058 in Los Angeles. This was less than 24 hours prior to the death of Marine Sergeant Chapman. Government sources have stated that Carson Jeffers is considered to be to be armed and dangerous. Anyone having information as to his whereabouts should contact the local office of the Federal Bureau of Investigation.

"The radical terrorist organization, La Libertad Occidental (the LLO), has assumed responsibility for all three air crashes. The reasons for their actions are outlined in the letter received by this newspaper last week. Unfortunately, neither we nor the government could stop the Los Angeles tragedy from occurring. President Rolland Attwilder, in his news conference last night, outlined the safety precautions being taken to protect travelers. He also delineated the efforts being made to apprehend Carson Jeffers and the other members of this extreme organization."

Nichole and Carson didn't know what to say. They had believed that Michael was going to be able to help them sort out this entire affair. Now they could see that wouldn't happen.

"What are we going to do now?" asked Nichole as she picked up the local Seattle paper. It had drawn her attention lying on the bed. Both her and Carson's pictures were on the front page. They weren't great photos, but they were certainly recognizable. She pointed to the pictures as Carson started to speak.

"The first thing we have to do is get out of the Northwest. The search for us is only bound to get worse in this part of the country. By now the government knows that we escaped into the sound, and with any luck on their part, they will know we are in Port Townsend within the next few hours."

Nichole nodded that she understood, while at the same time reading the copy of the letter that was sent to *The Journal* by the LLO. It was an exact copy of the blocked out newspaper words received by Gerald Better last Friday afternoon. "Where do we run to?" she asked.

Carson had started pacing the room. The look on his face gave visual evidence that he didn't know. Nichole noticed that he appeared to have aged ten years since she met him two weeks earlier. The scar he had received in Vietnam seemed even more visible.

Finally Carson said, "We'll try to figure out something in the next few hours, but first we have to get out of this motel. If they start looking for us, they will find the boat on the dock, and it won't take them five minutes to locate our room here."

Nichole said, "I was thinking the same thing when I saw our pictures in the paper." Dumping the sack out on the bed, she picked up some hair coloring, new hats, sun glasses, make-up, and scissors. The few groceries and the backpack she had purchased before she had seen the newspaper were ignored.

Carson grabbed the two bottles of hair coloring. One was for a blond and the other for dark brown hair. He correctly guessed that he was to change from a dusty blond to a dark brown. Nichole was about to become a blond. "This will slow them down for awhile, but they will eventually figure out what we're going to do."

Nichole picked up the scissors and told Carson to follow her into the bathroom. He grabbed the small metal chair and sat it in the shower. Five minutes later he was no longer able to run his hand through the blond hair and push it back over his head. There wasn't any hair longer than two inches on his head. Nichole stood in the shower and cut off two inches of her already short hair. It wasn't a butch haircut, but it was short. Carson thought that it hadn't hurt her appearance at all.

Removing the chair from the shower, Carson washed all the hair down the drain. Nichole read the directions on the hair coloring boxes.

"Strip to your shorts," she said. "I don't want to get any of this on your clothes." She hadn't been able to get any new ones before she returned to the motel. "On second thought, take everything off and get back in the shower." She sat the chair back in the shower against the wall. Carson could still lean forward enough for her to do the coloring, still keeping his head in the shower. Ten minutes later, he showered off and washed the remaining hair coloring down the drain.

Nichole quickly completed the same process without the use of the chair. She had always wondered what she would like as a blond, and the result was amazingly striking. While she got dressed, Carson gathered up their things, including the packaging from the hair coloring.

They put on the sun glasses and Puget Sound baseball-style hats. Carson loaded the shotgun and stuffed the remaining shells in the backpack that Nichole had purchased at the market. What they couldn't take with them they put in the sack from the store. Finally, Carson wrapped both of their windbreakers around the gun.

"We'll take these things and dump them in the dumpster down by the dock," he said. "The packaging from the sun glasses, hair coloring, and baseball caps will go in separate containers behind the convenience store on the corner."

"What then?" Nichole asked.

"We'll walk downtown and try and catch a cab out close to the airport. We won't go straight there, but we should get close."

Leaving the lights on, they left the room separately and walked through the woods to the secondary road that ran down to the pier. No one had seen them leave. So far so good!

27

TUESDAY MORNING

Michael pressed the *end* button on the cellular phone and put it in the front pocket of his raincoat. He wished he could have helped Carson understand what was happening, but none of it made any sense. Watching the windshield wipers move the water off the glass in front of him, he could see that he, Carson, and Nichole were just raindrops being pushed first in one direction and then in another by some giant powerful hand. For several minutes he was mesmerized by the motion of the blades cleaning the window. Finally, he pulled down the visor and removed a pen from the white plastic holder attached to the top side, and using a napkin left in the car from his sandwich of the night before, he started writing. Somehow, he hoped it would clear his mind. He put a big question mark in the center of the napkin, while in the top right corner he wrote the word *Port Town*. In the other three corners he scribbled *Salt Lake*, *Texas*, and *LAX*. After staring at the paper for several minutes, he eventually gave up and wadded the napkin into a ball. Deciding he wanted a cup of coffee more than he minded getting wet, he opened the door and headed for the warmth of the convenience store. Dropping the soiled napkin in the waste can by the door, he went in and got the black coffee to go.

● ● ●

"Yes, sir. That's all that was written on the paper," the dark haired man in the slightly rain drenched suit stated. "Immediately after he finished talking on the cellular phone he appeared to be taking notes, and what I just recited was it. I couldn't locate the frequency soon enough to know who he was talking to, but I can tell you that Michael Randall was extremely upset when the conversation ended."

The voice on the other end of the phone answered, "Keep up the surveillance, and don't get in anyone's way."

Maintaining five or six car lengths between them, the man in the suit got ready to follow the Jeep Cherokee onto Interstate 5. Turning up the heat in the car, he pulled off his moist jacket and laid it over the front seat, settling into a routine he had done many times before.

•   •   •

Most of Port Townsend's seven thousand citizens had either left on the fishing boats, or were at work in one of the related outdoor trades. However, there were still several hundred people walking the main street of the community. Only a very few were dressed in suits; the rest looked much like Carson and Nichole. The fugitive couple's appearance did not seem the least bit out of the ordinary.

Carson stopped near the front of the same market where Nichole had found the papers. Satisfied no one was paying them any attention, he handed her two twenty dollar bills, and told her to go in and buy a couple of umbrellas. She looked much different now than her picture in the paper. While she was in the store, Carson found a seat on a cement wall that was simultaneously guarding the parking lot and watching the ocean.

"You know it's not raining right now, don't you?" Nichole said, as she handed him the two umbrellas, more than a little puzzled with her purchase.

"I thought it looked funny to be carrying windbreakers that seemed to be hiding something. If we put the umbrellas beside the windbreakers, the outline of the shotgun should not be visible to the good people of Port Townsend. Now, let's see if we can get a taxi."

"It might be best if we take the cab from somewhere other than near the docks," Nichole said as Carson finished disguising the shotgun.

Picking up the knapsack she had purchased with the groceries at the market, she walked with Carson away from the water. They looked like a couple of tourists, not trying to hurry, stopping to window shop and carrying on a conversation that must have been centered on the attractions of the small ocean village. None of that was true. They had no idea what was in any of the shop windows, and their conversation had nothing to do with the scenic attractions of Port Townsend.

For the past three hours Carson had silently been formulating some kind of a plan of action. His combat experience had taught him that before you could launch a counter attack, it was usually necessary to regroup and review your assets. That was exactly what he wanted to do now. "Nichole, we have to find someplace where we can go and organize some kind of a defense. Once we do that, hopefully, we can do something to turn this situation around."

Keeping her arm locked around Carson's elbow, she asked, "Where do you want to go?"

"I'm not sure. At first, I thought about trying to go to the Portland area, because that is where Michael, Blake, and Jim are. That's out now. I doubt if there's any place less safe than Oregon right now, with the possible exception of where we are standing this morning," he said as he took her arm and guided her into the deserted city park.

Nichole sat down beside him on the wooden bench facing the picnic tables and questioned, "Is there anyplace else?"

"I was thinking about the ski condo in Utah, but Michael said that everything we owned has now been seized by the government. So, that's out. I suppose we could try and get out of the country, but that would probably aggravate our problems."

"I agree," commented Nichole. "Somehow, we have to fight back, and we can't do it from some other country."

Carson looked around to check and make sure that no one had approached them from another section of the small city park. "I once wrote an economic paper titled *Success Through Manipulation*. It was presented at a senior management seminar held in San Francisco."

Nichole wasn't quite sure where he was going, but she could tell by the tone of his voice that he had something concrete in mind.

"Every successful company uses the art of manipulation to achieve the end result - increased sales. Manipulation does not have to be negative. When a parent teaches a young child how to talk, some form of manipulation is used to reward the child for his success. The most successful companies use the art of manipulating events to sell their product or service to the public, and hopefully, the end result is positive. Advertising, public relations, employee benefit programs, and even rumor mills are used to achieve specific results."

"I think I understand," Nichole commented as she followed the logical line of reasoning. "You're saying that results don't just happen. Events are staged, advertising is used, and rumors started that are not the end result, only the catalyst to produce the result."

Carson was amazed at her ability to grasp a concept that most businessmen never truly understand.

Nichole continued speaking, now able to apply the management principle to the events of the past week. "I think I get it. Whatever is happening to us is taking place because someone wants to achieve a certain result."

"Absolutely. Right now, we don't know what that objective is, but we will. Nichole, we will! Everything that is happening to us is part of some master plan. We are a contingency, or possibly some form of liability. I have negotiated enough business deals and been involved in the marketplace too long, not to know manipulation when I see it. And this is manipulation of the highest magnitude. Somehow we stumbled onto something we shouldn't have."

Nichole looked puzzled. "Once you recognize the fact that manipulation is taking place, what options do you have?"

Carson unconsciously ran his hand through the shortened dark brown hair. "You basically have three options. First, you can do nothing and just wait for the results to happen. We don't have this option, because, the result, in our case, would be fatal."

Nichole moved closer to Carson on the bench, and asked, "What is the second option?"

"In a business situation, you can remove yourself from the game. This means that you take yourself out of play. For manipulation to work, you become much like a chess piece. If you aren't on the board, then the player has to select completely different options. In our case, the choice of this option would mean that we would run and hide, preferably outside the country, until the game is finished. The final results might, however, have lasting consequences we don't want to consider. This option is certainly better than the first, but I don't like it."

"Neither do I," Nichole stated, watching the boats leave the small harbor.

"Let me explain the third option," Carson said as he turned to face Nichole. "In my paper I called it the *D&R Selection*. If you are being manipulated, and you want to stop the objective from being accomplished, you must first discover who is doing the manipulating and why. Once you have finished the *discovery* phase, you must use that information to *reverse the roles* of the manipulator and the person being manipulated. That is why it is called the *D&R Selection*. Discover and reversal is by far the best option, but it is almost always fatal if you lose. In a game of chess, you simply lose the game, but in our case, we lose our lives, and possibly thousands of others will lose theirs. And that is only what we can expect right now. We still don't know why the game is even being played."

"I don't see that we have any choice," she said quietly, knowing the first two options were out of the question. "How do we start?"

"The key to successfully applying this option is to gather all the information possible. Michael, along with both Blake and Jim, have been doing just that. We need to get together to evaluate just what we have." He thought aloud, "We are almost back to where we started. We have to find somewhere to go and regroup." He noticed the excitement in Nichole's eyes. "What is it?" he asked.

"I know where we can go. It is less than 500 miles from here. That's close enough that we could even drive."

Carson couldn't figure out where Nichole might be referring to, but he knew that they couldn't very easily drive. They would have to stop a number of times, and every time they did, they could be identified. "We can't drive, Nichole. It's too dangerous."

"How about Michael, Blake, and Jim? Couldn't they?"

"If they could slip away without being followed, yes, they could. But where are you talking about?" he asked, intrigued by her change in attitude.

"I told you a little about my father. He gave me the Boston whaler so that I could enjoy the ocean."

"So?" asked Carson.

"Dad's name is Neil Sorenson."

"The author of the historical novels centered in the Northwest?" Carson asked, having heard of the famous writer.

"The same. Anyway, I kept my married name after I got divorced. It just seemed easier at the time."

Carson nodded, remembering their discussion in Santa Barbara about her earlier relationship. He surveyed the park for any newly arrived visitors, and finding none, waited for Nichole to continue.

"At any rate, Dad owns, or better said, he shares ownership in a hunting and fishing lodge near Flathead Lake in Montana. It's about seven or eight miles outside the village of Swan Lake. The place is isolated from the main town of Kalispell and can easily accommodate all of us," she said excitedly.

"I don't want to burst your bubble, but the government will already have done an investigation of who you are and will certainly know all about the lodge."

"I don't think so. I haven't been there in five or six years. Actually, my last visit was before my marriage to Ray. Dad's name doesn't show up on any deed or land document. For all practical purposes no one knows about the place. Dad goes there to write periodically, but most of the time it's empty."

"How about his partners?" Carson asked, starting to get interested.

"They are two writers who live outside the United States. They only come back during the middle of the summer and at Christmas time." Anticipating Carson's next question, she continued. "The lodge is owned by an off shore trust on the Isle of Man."

Carson knew that this was a preferred tax haven off the British Isles.

Nichole went on. "Dad and his partners are all writers and they became extremely concerned about the United States tax structure. Since a great deal of their income comes from international sources, they set up the trust. Later they purchased the lodge in the name of the same off shore trust." She paused for a second and then added, "The Canadian border is less than a hundred miles away if we have to switch to the second option."

Nichole's last thought had not escaped Carson. The more he thought about it, the better it sounded. He didn't doubt that Blake could get Michael and Jim to Montana. There were no pictures of them in the papers, but he and Nichole were an entirely different matter. "How far is it to the airport from here?" he asked the new blond who was sitting with him on the green park bench.

"Probably four or five miles, I would guess," she answered, not understanding why he asked the question.

"That's probably farther than we want to walk along the highway. Someone is sure to remember us," he said, noticing the phone booth across from the picnic table. "Let's see if we can't get a taxi to drop us off somewhere close to the airport."

"Are you going to charter a plane?" she asked as he rose from the bench.

"Afraid not," he replied, helping her to her feet and picking up the umbrella package at the same time. "I would have to leave a credit card, and that's not possible just now."

"Then what?"

"I am going to steal a plane, or better said, borrow one!"

Nichole didn't understand, but she could tell that Carson was definitely serious. "How?" was all she could think to say.

"I'll explain later. First, I'm going to call Michael and get him moving to Montana. After that, we'll see if we can't catch a cab here in Port Townsend." Carson reached in his pocket and was relieved to find almost four dollars in coins. Usually he hated carrying it, but today was different. Fortunately, Nichole had combined her change from the market with his. After dialing the phone number of Michael's new cellular phone, he deposited the quarters and dimes asked for by the operator. Even with nearly four dollars in change, he realized that he would have to keep the call short. As the call was being routed, he lifted the receiver away from his head and spoke to Nichole. "Think of someplace fairly inconspicuous where I can tell Michael to meet us near the lodge. I don't want them asking anyone how to find the place."

Nichole took a minute to mentally review the geography of the area around Swan Lake.

Michael must have known that it was Carson calling by the way he answered the phone. "Wait just a minute while I find a place I can talk."

Carson answered, "Make it quick. If I get cut off, I'm out of change to call you back."

"What's the number you are calling from?" Michael asked as he pulled the car into the automatic car wash.

"I can't tell you, the number's gone on the phone."

"OK, it really doesn't matter, I can talk now. I have a tail on me, but he can't tell if I am talking now or not." The sun had just come out, and Michael's Jeep Cherokee was truly filthy. Talking on the phone, he watched from inside the vehicle as the soap from the automatic car wash foamed over his jeep.

"Listen, Michael. We need to get everyone out of Portland and meet someplace where we can put together a plan."

"I agree, but where do you want to meet?"

Carson took a minute and explained about the lodge in Montana. Michael thought it sounded like the best idea he had heard of.

"Can you reach Blake and Jim?" Carson asked quickly, fully aware of the evaporating time.

"No problem. I know where they are, and to the best of my knowledge, no one else does. I'm sure that Blake can get us to Flathead Lake. Where and when do you want us to meet you?"

Carson thought for a moment and answered, "At 9:00 tomorrow morning." Nichole whispered something in Carson's other ear, and then he continued. "There is trading post just north of the little community of Big Fork. It is on Highway 83 at the four corner stop. Meet us there tomorrow."

"How will you get there?" Michael asked, already figuring that it would be dangerous for Carson and Nichole to drive.

"We'll be there."

Michael knew they couldn't speak much longer. "Carson, I don't know if you realize it yet or not, but the country is acting like we are in a total state of siege. President Attwilder has declared a National State of Emergency. National Guard troops are attempting to protect all the major airports. I'm sure it is just for show, because if these maniacs want to take out another plane, they will find a way."

"Sounds pretty bad," Carson said.

"It is just the tip of the iceberg. People are refusing to fly on any of the airlines. The mood of the country is one of total despair. They closed the stock market early today. It was the single worst day since 1929. Even Black Monday in 1987 couldn't compare. Unless something happens soon, the country will be totally paralyzed."

"We'll bounce back," Carson said, trying to encourage his best friend.

"Maybe. But everyone in the country is after your head. There isn't a news broadcast on the air that doesn't start with something about Carson Jeffers and the LLO," Michael said.

Realizing they hadn't turned on the television in the motel, Carson said, "Nothing we can do about it now. Just be in Big Fork tomorrow. And, Michael, bring the cash. I think we are going to need it!" He hung up the phone.

Rolling the two remaining quarters between the thumb and index finger of his right hand, he turned the yellow pages open to the section marked "Taxi." There was only one listing. Carson dialed the number of the Port Townsend Taxi Service.

28

"The weatherman said you aren't going to need those," the cab driver commented, pointing to the umbrellas that Carson carried across his lap in the back seat of the yellow and black cab.

Nichole smiled at Carson as he answered, "We have got plenty wet in the last few days and decided it was better to be prepared."

The young blond-headed boy driving the cab said, "I can certainly understand that. Luckily, I keep dry most of the time, but still, I have to help carry bags. I've got soaked more than once in the last week. By the way, where do you want me to let you off?"

Carson had used the map in the front section of the yellow pages to familiarize himself with the area. There was a small industrial park about a mile north of the airport. "We need to go to the Puget Industrial Park. Can you find it?"

"Sure. It's just this side of the airport. Not much there except for the real estate office and that small software firm."

Not wanting to get caught in a mistake, Carson just smiled and turned to speak softly to Nichole. He had been worried that the driver might recognize them. Apparently, the change in hair coloring must have helped. Also, Carson knew that most people would not recognize someone from a newspaper photo unless they were looking for that person. That's the reason that more people aren't arrested from the pictures on display at the local post office.

Fifteen minutes later the cab stopped under the pine trees surrounding the three concrete structures. None of the buildings were larger than

3,000 square feet. To call the complex an industrial park was stretching the use of the English language. Carson tipped the driver and walked towards the second building. As soon as the cab turned around on the asphalt strip leading into the parking lot and headed back towards Port Townsend, Carson and Nichole started walking south. There was something else bothering Carson. Nichole could tell it by the distant look in his eyes. It hadn't been there when they were driving in the taxi. "What are you thinking?"

"How well do you know the area around Swan Lake?"

"What do you mean?" she answered, slowing her walk slightly.

"Is there a small airport close by? And I mean small. Something that is used by just local people. We need a place to land, and the moment we touch down, we stand a good chance of being picked up. I know that I can steal a plane, but eventually it will be reported, and when it is, the people who didn't recognize us the first time will the second."

Nichole almost grinned. "Dad has a landing strip right at the lodge. It is a grass strip that is only used by himself and his partners. All of them fly. In fact, Dad told me that they were thinking about keeping a small plane right there at the place. It is set back in the woods, and only the locals even know its there."

"Do you know how long it is?"

"Not exactly, but Dad chartered a Merlin and brought in a group of his friends from San Francisco a couple of years ago. It was long enough for them to fly in and out of."

The look of concern that had darkened Carson's face seemed to evaporate in the sun filtering through the large pines shading the path from overhead.

"I'm more than curious as to how you are going to steal a plane. Are you just going to walk up and take one?" Nichole asked as they walked beside the tall pines.

"Almost. Do you remember the scandal recently where a mechanic and a reservation agent at United took a 747 and went on a joy ride around the Denver airport?"

"Yes. They were fined, fired, and received a suspended jail sentence." She moved off the shoulder of the road as a truck passed them from the rear.

"Exactly. But none of that happened until after they taxied around the airport for almost thirty minutes. If they had done the same thing at an uncontrolled airport, they could have even received clearance in the Air Traffic Control System."

"What does that have to do with stealing a plane in Port Townsend?"

"Airplanes are not like cars," he explained as he pointed to the path in the trees that paralleled the road. Nichole followed him off the hard surface to the shaded area on their left. Carson went on. "An automobile uses an ignition key to start the car, and a door key to keep out intruders. An airplane only has the key to the door. There is no ignition key. If you can open the door to the plane, you can fire up the engines and leave."

"If you can open the door?" she said.

"I'll get to that in a moment. Let's assume that we can find a plane that is open. We do not have to file a flight plan to take off, and if we keep below 18,000 feet, the pilot is never required to file one. Providing of course he flies VFR, or visual flight rules, which we will do." The trees were thinning as they got closer to the 6,500 foot runway. Looking through the trees, Carson could see three rows of single and small twin engine planes. Just to the left of the first group of planes he spotted a Cessna Conquest and a King Air. Either of the turbo props would do, but it wasn't what he was really looking for.

Nichole took his hand as they walked straight up to the FBO. He hadn't had time to tell her exactly what he was going to do, but she didn't doubt that it made sense. At least to him.

"Do you have any hangers for rent?" Carson asked the young girl at the desk filling out a fuel order.

"How large do you need?"

"We're considering moving up to the sound from Southern California. I've got a Citation II and would want to find someplace that could accommodate the plane, plus an office for my maintenance man."

The girl thought for a second and then pointed to the large hanger at the end of the row of metal buildings with large bi-fold doors that opened onto the taxiway. "The only possible place would be Eldon

Stubbs' hanger. He keeps his Citation V there. From time to time he has leased out space to other aircraft. I'm pretty sure he has the space now. Mr. Caldwell had a Lear in there until two weeks ago. But he sold it and the new owner was from out of the area."

Carson listened to the young girl talk for several moments, fully aware that she hadn't found his face familiar. Finally, he asked, "Is Eldon Stubbs around today?"

"No, he's gone on a cruise and won't be back until this weekend. If you want to see the hanger, I have a key," she offered.

"If you don't mind?"

"Not at all." The girl reached behind the desk and opened a wooden key locker. Searching through the rack of keys, she found the one that read STUBBS. "Just bring it back when you're done looking. If I'm not here, just put the key on the desk."

•   •   •

Ricardo slowed the rental car that had been rented to one Carlos Herrera in Seattle, Washington. The junction of Highway 101 and 20 was less than a quarter mile away. Esteban pointed to the sign that said Port Townsend was 13 miles to the north. Ricardo made the turn without stopping. Seven minutes later they passed the Port Townsend General Aviation Airport.

•   •   •

Carson slid open the small side door of the large hanger. The girl at the desk had been correct. There was plenty of room to park a Citation II alongside the Citation V already stationed in the large hanger. Nichole followed him into the metal building, pulling the door shut behind her. There was no need to even look for the key to the plane. Carson knew from his own experience that most pilots never locked a plane when it was already secured in a hanger. Eldon Stubbs was no different. The cabin door of the silver and blue Citation V jet was open.

"Are we going to steal this plane?" Nichole asked as Carson opened the cabin door.

"Not steal, Nichole. Borrow. Mr. Stubbs can have the plane back when were finished. There is one other problem that we have to deal with."

"Which is?"

"Fuel. We can't very well ask the girl at the FBO to fuel up Eldon Stubbs' jet so that we can use it. Let's hope the last time the plane was used it didn't come back empty." Carson climbed into the cabin. Two minutes later, he stepped down from the plane and started his pre-flight and walk around.

"How's the fuel?" Nichole asked as she watched him go over the plane in a familiar pattern.

"The tanks are about half full. That should be enough to get us to Swan Lake, providing we don't run into weather or some other problem." Carson continued with his inspection of the aircraft.

Nichole wondered what he might have been referring to by his comment, *some other problem.* She had been carrying the shotgun and umbrellas ever since Carson opened the hanger door. She went in the small room that was labeled *Rest Room* and set them against the wall.

• • •

Esteban had Ricardo drive directly to the docks in Port Townsend. Esteban had come to the conclusion that Jeffers might not be dead after all. He doubted that Michael Randall would have been talking to the Lewis woman, but stranger things had happened. In all likelihood, Carson had been hit in the head. And if he was able to speak on the phone, it must have just been a grazing shot. The man must have as many lives as the proverbial cat. Today, the last of them would be ended.

"Over there!" Ricardo said, pointing to the Boston whaler moored against the docks.

"Let's check it out," Esteban answered.

The two Latins got out of the car and walked down the water soaked dock. Esteban was the first to jump across the water to the boat. Seconds later, he smiled to himself. "They're here. And the man was hit. Look here, back of the steering console."

Ricardo bent down to see what Esteban was referring to. The boat had dark stains on the lower wooden railing and around the console on the deck. The marks were almost black, but both men knew they were blood stains. "He's alive then?" asked Ricardo.

"For the moment, companero. For the moment."

Standing up in the boat, Esteban looked around at the small fishing town. "All right," he thought. "If I were this man, where would I go?" It didn't take him more than a minute to make a decision.

The woman at the desk of the motel behind the statue of the sailor wasn't planning on being of any more help to the dark haired man with the pony-tail than to her previous customers. She quickly changed her mind when Esteban laid his pistol on the counter. The tone of his voice was even more sinister than the dark blue revolver. Answering his demand, she said, "A couple registered early this morning. They are in number 12 back by the trees. They said they had been fishing all night."

Esteban took out the picture from the *Seattle Times* and showed it to the lady. "Are these the people?"

"Could be. I'm not sure. They haven't checked out. Why don't you look yourself?"

Esteban was planning on doing just that. Ricardo stayed in the lobby, insuring that the woman didn't call the police just yet. It only took Esteban a minute to realize that they must have left. Either they saw them as they drove up, or they left earlier in the day. Since they were facing the woods, he correctly guessed that they had been gone for some time.

Returning to the motel office, he changed his attitude to the woman. "My name is Ethan Mabry, and my partner and myself are with the Terrorist Division of the Federal Bureau of Investigation. We believe that this man and woman are Carson Jeffers and Nichole Lewis, the terrorists responsible for the recent airplane crashes."

The motel clerk had been listening to the news and never asked the two Latins for any identification. When Esteban repeated Carson and Nichole's names, her attitude changed immediately. "Is there anything I can do?"

"Just contact our office if they come back. Try to act like nothing is out of the ordinary." Esteban didn't try and explain that they wouldn't be back. The room had been empty.

• • •

"No, sir. I operate the only cab here in the town. Actually, it belongs to my folks, but I do the driving. And I didn't pick up a blond man and a dark haired woman."

"You're positive?" Esteban repeated as he stood next to the black and yellow cab he had stopped as it drove down the street.

"Yea, I'm sure. There was one other couple I picked up on the south side of town, but the lady was a blond and had real short hair, and the man had dark hair. At least it looked dark under the baseball hat."

Esteban showed the boy the picture of Carson and Nichole. "Is this the couple?"

The boy took the picture and moved his head from side to side indicating that he couldn't really tell. "I suppose it could be, if the hair were different, but I don't think so."

"Where did you drop them?"

"At the industrial park south of town. It's just this side of the airport."

Esteban and Ricardo were already heading for their car. Esteban stopped to ask one final question. "How long ago was that?"

"Maybe an hour," the boy answered.

• • •

Esteban exceeded the speed limit by thirty miles an hour on the way to the airport. Ricardo hadn't argued when Esteban took the driver's seat. He knew they were close. Both men hoped they weren't too late.

"You start with those hangers on the end," Esteban ordered. "I'll check with the flight office and see if anyone has seen them wondering around."

The office of the FBO was empty. "Everyone must be out with the planes," he thought. Esteban decided he would have to do it a plane at a time. He headed for the rows of planes tied down across from the parking lot to begin his search.

•   •   •

Carson had already pulled the hanger door open. He fastened the tug to the nose wheel and pulled the plane out in front of the hanger. He had kept thinking that someone would be walking around the corner from the front office, but so far so good. As he pulled the tug back against the side wall, he knocked on the door of the rest room and told Nichole they had to leave. "I'll meet you in the plane," he said through the door.

Ricardo watched the man walk towards the plane. He knew it was Carson Jeffers, even with the brown hair. The woman must be on the plane. Stepping out from behind the hanger door, he placed the .44 caliber pistol in the middle of Carson's back. "Stop right there. Put your hands on top of your head and turn around."

Nichole heard the voices as she started to open the door to the bathroom. Slowly she edged the door open, only to see one of the two men putting a gun in Carson's back. Closing the door, she tried to quickly decide what to do. She separated the umbrellas from the light jackets and removed the shotgun. It was her gun and she knew how to use it. Checking to make sure it was loaded, she breathed a sigh of relief. Then she realized she couldn't shoot the man without hitting Carson, who was right behind him.

Knowing she had to do something, she silently opened the door. It wasn't the man with the pony-tail. This man was shorter and was only ten or twelve feet away from the doorway. Raising the gun like a club, she started to inch her way towards the dark Latin.

Ricardo had sensed a change in the facial expression of Jeffers. It was slight, but it was noticeable. Just as he began to turn his head to see what the man might have been looking at, he went blank. The sound of the butt of the shotgun cracking against his head sounded like an ax splitting a pine log. Only it wasn't as effective. Ricardo was down, but he was still alive.

"What are we going to do with him?" she asked as Carson rushed to her side.

"We can't take him with us. Help me drag him into the bathroom. There is a roll of packing tape on the work bench against the wall." He pointed to the adhesive. Less than two minutes later, Carson had closed the cabin door of the Citation II and was turning on the injectors.

"Fasten yourself in. We've got to get out of here. The man wasn't by himself. I've got a feeling we will be using every bit of the 2,900 pounds of thrust that each of the Dash 5 engines produce."

"Are you going to turn on the transponder?" she asked, noting that the readout was still black.

"No. We want to avoid identification if possible. I had thought we might be able to make a straight approach to Flathead Lake, but that will be impossible. Someone is going to be looking for us in the next few minutes." Carson turned onto the taxiway heading for Runway 06. No one tried to stop them as they made the turn.

A dark haired man with a pony-tail started running from the flight line towards the runway.

29

E steban ran past the white enamel metal hangers and turned towards the runway. The metal buildings were all closed except for the end one with the large bi-fold doors. There was no doubt in his mind that Carson Jeffers and Nichole Lewis were in the jet that was taking off to the north. He raised his .44 magnum pistol and immediately dropped it back to his side. The distance was too great. Slowing down, he tried to read the call numbers on the tail of the sleek silver jet. The plane would be recognized as Three Charlie Alpha Two Seven Zero. He wished he had taken the sniper rifle out of the car. It was a mistake he wouldn't make again.

He watched the jet accelerate to almost 110 knots before the nose started to lift from the black surface of the runway. He hoped that Ricardo was all right, but it was doubtful, with the jet having left the same hanger that Ricardo was searching. Under his breath he swore in Spanish, "Hijo de puta!"

• • •

Carson pulled back on the yoke and started to climb through the dense, humid Washington air. For the next few minutes he was going to use the full thrust capacity of the dash engines. He could climb at 3,700 feet per minute, and he wanted to get to twelve or fourteen thousand feet as fast as possible. "Our best hope is to let them see us," he said to

Nichole as she watched the ground disappear below the right side of the plane. "Let's give them something to follow on their radar scopes."

"You want them to spot you?" she asked, puzzled by his intentions.

"I doubt if we have more than three or four minutes before they spot us. In all likelihood, they will scramble a flight of F-15's to check us out, unless they are already following us on radar. In that case, we may have twenty or thirty more minutes of breathing space," Carson answered as he raised the landing gear and trimmed up the plane for the maximum angle of attack.

• • •

It took Esteban less than forty-five seconds to find Ricardo in the small rest room of the open hanger. His Latin companion had regained consciousness, even though he had a terrific headache. As soon as he removed the tape from the shorter man's hands, he picked up a telephone on the maintenance desk. Checking to insure there was a dial tone, he placed a long distance telephone call to Washington, D.C. The Cleaner had given him The Butterfly's number in the event that he needed to get something done through government channels in a hurry. It was getting late in the afternoon, and Esteban didn't think there would be time to get the Cleaner to intervene. If he didn't act immediately, Carson Jeffers would be gone.

It took several seconds before the man known as the Butterfly picked up the phone. He listened intently for almost a minute as Esteban recounted what had happened at the Port Townsend airport. Finally, he asked, "What is the identification number of the plane?"

Esteban repeated the number *3CA270,* using the military abbreviations for the call sign. "Are you sure you can get the military to intervene in the hunt for Jeffers?" He asked, after repeating the number a second time.

The man in Washington, D.C., smiled to himself and answered, "I guarantee I can get to the right people immediately. When I let them know that they are tracking Carson Jeffers of the LLO, we'll get all the cooperation you ever dreamed of. I think you should go to Whidbey

Naval air station to coordinate the search. I'll set it up in the computer. Do you know how to get to the air station?"

"Get the search started now. We'll be there in a matter of ten or fifteen minutes." Esteban hung up the phone without waiting for his Washington contact to respond.

•   •   •

Seaman First Class Nick Shuck took the paper from Lieutenant Sanders and moved immediately to his scope. He was sure that he could find the Citation V among the clutter of images on his screen. Almost all of the civilian planes were identified by a call sign that was uniquely noted next to a transponder code. Military aircraft used the same system, only the codes were not assigned through Air Traffic Control.

"Do you think you can pick him out?" asked the company grade naval flight officer.

"If he's out there, I'll get him. Once we have him identified, what are we supposed to do?" asked the seaman seated at the radar scope.

"We notify the Pentagon we have the Code Red located, and they will then decide how to handle the situation. It is my opinion that if Carson Jeffers is in the Citation, Washington will want us to follow him on the screen, hoping that he will lead them to the rest of the missiles. Anyway, that's what I would do," answered the young officer wearing the double silver bars on his uniform. Both men had listened to the latest news reports about Carson Jeffers. According to *The Wall Street Journal*, there were still eleven missiles missing. Missiles that were threatening the very fiber of America's existence.

•   •   •

Esteban gave their names to the MP at the gate of Whidbey Naval Air Station. As soon as they provided identification, the two Latins were escorted to the office of Captain Seth Hatcher. Captain Hatcher was not annoyed by the appearance of the two men, and didn't find the long hair out of place, considering the top secret orders he had just received from the Pentagon. Captain Hatcher waved the two men into his office as he rose from his desk. "I understand you are tracking this Carson Jeffers in a Citation aircraft?" he asked, omitting any reference to the fact that the two men in front of his desk had recently returned from a covert assignment with the CIA in South America.

"That's correct, sir." Esteban understood military protocol and was following it to a letter. "Jeffers stole a Citation V aircraft from the Port Townsend Airport. He took off to the north in an extreme rate of climb less than ten minutes ago."

"We'll find him," the older navy officer stated. "Follow me and we'll go to the control center."

•   •   •

Carson leveled off at 14,000 feet. He had banked the plane to the right, and flown up the middle of the channel between Vancouver Island and the city of Bellingham, Washington. Five minutes after he took off from the small airport in the Washington woods, he turned east towards the Cascade Mountain range.

Nichole felt the plane bank to the south. It was the second major turn Carson had made in the past ten minutes. "Will they spot us on their scopes without us turning on the transponder?" she asked.

"The transponder would certainly help them. But we want them to think we are trying to evade them. There is no way we would have the transponder turned on in that situation. Using the process of elimination, they'll find us. We'll give them just a few more minutes. Make sure your seat belt's fastened as secure as possible. I can guarantee you that the next hour or so will be some of the worst flying your stomach's ever experienced."

•   •   •

Seaman Nick Shuck never looked up when Captain Hatcher entered the darkened control room with the two civilian dressed men. He had started his search along the Pacific coast and then moved into Canada. In a matter of minutes he had eliminated those areas. Moving along the coast from Bellingham to Seattle, he encountered much more civilian traffic. He eliminated every plane using a transponder, and then knocked out those aircraft that were flying at under 200 knots. In all likelihood, the Citation would be traveling at 250 knots or more.

Captain Hatcher, the lieutenant who had watch duty, Esteban, and Ricardo all stood behind the twenty-two year old radar operator. None of them said anything. They knew Nick Shuck would tell them the moment he had something. Seaman Shuck had tried broadcasting a warning to Carson in the Citation, but it wasn't known if he was listening or not. Even if he was, they knew that he wouldn't answer.

Nick used his right hand to wipe away the sweat that was appearing on his brow. He never took his eyes from the radar screen. "I've got him," he yelled as he pointed to the green mark on the radar screen. "He's heading south, straight towards the lower Cascade Mountain range."

The four men standing behind Seaman Shuck's shoulders watched as the radar operator showed them the blip traveling at over three hundred knots.

"Every other plane has been accounted for that could be making that signature," explained the seaman as they watched the screen. "What's he doing? It looks like he is trying to land or something. He is dropping fast. If there isn't a landing strip real close, our terrorist is about to crash in the mountains."

All the eyes were glued to the screen, Esteban's more closely than the others. He was the first to notice the green blip on the screen disappear. "Damn!" Esteban muttered.

"Lieutenant, is there an airport or landing strip anywhere near where we lost the plane?" asked Captain Hatcher.

The young officer ran towards the second computer and punched in the coordinates last seen on the screen. "No, sir. Nothing within 100 miles. And that country is really rough. If he was going to put the plane down on a road, he would never be able to take off."

Esteban kept watching the screen, along with Seaman Shuck. "He's not landing. I think he just realized that he can be spotted without the transponder. He'll show up again in a few minutes. No way can he keep the plane down on the hardtop for long." Turning to the radar operator, he said, "When you get him, try to determine the exact direction he is heading. Let's see if we can't figure out where he is going."

"No sweat, sir." Nick didn't mind giving the pony-tailed man the military respect reserved for officers. He could tell by the way that Captain Hatcher treated him that he was at least the equivalent of a senior grade officer in some branch of government service, probably intelligence.

Three minutes later Nick stated confidently, "There he is. I estimate that he is flying less than one thousand feet above ground level, and in that area of the Cascades, that's a good piece of flying."

"Can you plot his heading?" asked Esteban as he watched the color display.

A few seconds later, Nick answered, "He is maintaining a heading of 163 degrees true."

Captain Hatcher watched the monitor and then stated, "I would bet he is heading for Mexico. He can fly along the spine of the Nevada mountains and then slip through the Arizona desert straight into Sonora. Being dusk, I doubt that many people would even spot him, and if they did, who are they going to report it to?"

"Damn it to hell!" exclaimed the young Seaman. Turning to the senior officers, he said, "Sorry, sirs, but I lost him again. He slipped below our coverage."

Esteban told the young radar operator to keep watching. "Do you have a secure phone that I can use?" he asked the Navy captain. "And I mean a secure phone!"

Captain Hatcher pointed to the phone on the watch officer's desk in the glass enclosed office. "Give me 15 seconds, and you can use that one. I guarantee you will have total security."

Esteban entered the office and waited for Captain Hatcher to clear the lines. As soon as Hatcher left the room, Esteban placed the call. He started the conversation with the words, "They're trying to escape to Mexico...."

30

Neither Seaman Nick Shuck nor Captain Seth Hatcher noticed Esteban closing the door behind him as he reentered the control room. Ricardo had taken a seat just to the rear of the electronic monitor and was listening to the two men compute the course of the Citation V. Esteban closed the distance between himself and the military personnel, stopping just behind the senior Navy captain. "Anything new on Carson's direction?" Esteban asked.

"He's definitely heading south towards Nevada. A minute ago he popped up on the screen between Spanish Peak and Strawberry Mountain," Seaman Shuck answered, without looking up from the display.

Captain Hatcher realized that Esteban and Ricardo probably didn't know exactly where the two southern Oregon Peaks were and continued the explanation that the young seaman had started. "Both of these mountains are approximately parallel to Grant's Pass and Medford, Oregon. Strawberry Mountain is the taller of the two peaks at just over 9,000 feet. Jeffers flew through the saddle two minutes ago. He was still heading south."

Esteban listened intently as Captain Hatcher explained how they had spotted the Citation. Esteban then asked, "How about his speed, has it changed?"

Seaman Shuck answered without looking up from the color monitor in front of him. "As a matter of fact, it has, sir. He is now doing over 400 knots. And at that low altitude, he is burning fuel as fast as it can be pumped through the turbines."

Esteban waited for the radar operator to finish, and then posed his next question. "How much fuel does the Citation V carry, and would it be enough to get him across the Mexican border?"

"If his tanks were full, he started with around 5,900 pounds," Captain Hatcher answered. "But at this rate of consumption, there's no way he'll ever make the Mexican border. We have calculated that he'll go down somewhere west of Las Vegas. In all likelihood, he'll have to chance landing and get fuel at a small private airfield."

Ricardo whispered something to his taller pony-tailed companion and then asked the Captain if anyone had checked to see how much fuel was on the Citation when it left Port Townsend.

"The plane wasn't fueled before it took off. No one can say for sure what the fuel status was. The owner of the plane is out of the country on a cruise and doesn't even know the Citation is missing. Right now, we are operating on a worst case scenario. And that is that the plane had full fuel tanks."

Esteban and Ricardo understood the importance of stopping Carson from refueling the Cessna Citation. Esteban asked, "What can we do to stop him?

Captain Hatcher answered for the two men still standing at the scope. "We'll contact both Hill Air Force Base in Ogden, Utah, and Nellis Air Force Base in Nevada. They'll send up surveillance aircraft, and when Jeffers pops up again, they'll arrange for ground forces to be at all possible landing sites. They will have no trouble in apprehending both Jeffers and Lewis."

Esteban listened as the military leader explained how easily it would be to take Jeffers and Lewis into custody. "If only it were so simple," he thought to himself, recalling his own failed attempts.

• • •

Nichole gripped the arm rest on the right side of the co-pilot's seat and gritted her teeth. Carson had warned her that the flight was going to be rough, but she never expected anything like this. Almost without warning, Carson put the business jet into a descent, much faster than the plane had ever experienced before. She looked at the vertical speed indicator and saw it pegged at 4,000 feet per minute. There was no doubt that they were dropping faster than that. She almost felt like the plane was in free fall. In her mind she knew she was totally helpless. A sense of panic started to rise from the bottom of her stomach, and then she felt Carson pull back on the yoke while adding power to the huge turbine engines. Carson seemed to have forgotten that she was even there. She could see that his total being was consumed with controlling the 52 foot wingspan of the Citation V.

"Are we all right?" she asked as she felt the plane start to level out on the desert floor.

"We're fine for now. The Citation was designed to handle emergency situations beyond most pilot's wildest fears. So far it is performing beyond its specifications." There were no buildings of any kind on the horizon, and at two hundred fifty feet AGL, he would see them. Carson took a minute to explain what had just happened. "I'm sure they spotted us as we passed to the west of Strawberry Mountain. With any luck, they have us pegged on a south easterly heading. Now we need to turn north and head for Montana." He took a moment to consult the chart he had tucked in the clipboard fastened to his knee. "We'll pass north of both Boise and Salmon, Idaho. Just south of Trapper Peak in the Bitterroot Range there is a place called Lost Trail Pass. Our only hope is to make it through the opening before they pick us up on radar."

"Will they be able to see us as we go over the mountains into Montana?" Nichole asked as she looked at the map Carson had removed from the black flight bag he had found behind the left seat.

"Undoubtedly. But if they are looking for us in another state, it will probably take them a little while to decide that it was us, and by then we might be able to make it to Swan Lake."

"I hope so."

Looking at the Jeppeson manual on his lap, Carson added, "The landing strip at Swan Lake is not shown on the charts."

"It's there. I promise," Nichole said.

"I don't doubt you. It's better that it doesn't show up. This way, no one will suspect that is where we are planning on setting down." Carson continued to fly the plane across the desolate terrain. He looked at the fuel gauge and then tapped his fingers on the glass, hoping that the indicator would move. It wouldn't, and he knew it. But it was a habit he had learned many years before, and he had never given it up.

"You look worried," Nichole said, watching him eye the readout.

"I thought we would have enough fuel to make it to Swan Lake, with a little reserve. But now it appears that we are liable to end up a little short. Flying at this speed and this low altitude is really burning the fuel. The worst part is yet to come. We are going to have to dart over the Bitterroot and Sapphire Mountains, and that will burn fuel faster than we are using now."

"Can we make it?"

"We'll try, that's the best I can say." Carson continued to concentrate on his flying. The fact that the Citation V had a longer horizontal tail and elevator helped reduce the rotational force, making the plane more stable than the Citation II.

•   •   •

Michael continued to explain everything Carson had told him on the phone. Blake and Jim both listened, right up until they pulled alongside the farmhouse outside Kelso, Washington.

Michael had called Blake and told him to be prepared to leave as soon as they all got together at the old home where Blake and Jim had been staying for the past few days. Blake had told him to park at the downtown Portland Mall. He then waited for the government agent who was following him to find a parking place and follow him into the mall. Once he was inside, he went to the food court and ordered a club sandwich. He saw the man in the suit watch him order the food. While it was being prepared, he went into the rest room area. There was an exit to a service hallway that led to the underground parking structure. After running down the hall, he dashed to his jeep and sped out of the parking lot. Five minutes later he parked the jeep with the valet at the Marriott on the

Columbia River. The man in the suit was just discovering that Michael was not going to pick up his sandwich.

The driver stationed in front of the hotel waited for the bellman to open the door and let the tall, African-American executive into the cab. He was expecting a fare to the airport but was glad to make a trip up the freeway to downtown Vancouver. The eight mile trip took less than twelve minutes. After being dropped at the convenience store just off the I-5 freeway, Michael walked six blocks to the Residence Inn on North East Parkway Drive. No one paid any attention when he opened the back door of the white four door sedan and drove away with two men dressed in Levis and cotton pullover shirts.

●   ●   ●

Nichole was becoming more nauseated by the second. For the past ten minutes, Carson had followed a course that kept climbing through the western slopes of the Bitterroot range. Suddenly the plane would pull up and then abruptly fall, almost dropping onto the tree-covered terrain that was zipping by them at many hundreds of miles an hour. She wasn't going to say anything, but she knew that she was about to lose what little food they had eaten in the cave 24 hours earlier. Suddenly, she felt her head start to spin. It was almost like she was going to lose consciousness. Grabbing a hand towel that Carson had used to defog the side windows, she started to vomit into the cotton cloth. The next descent was worse than the climb. She kept the cloth pressed to her mouth as the plane dove down. She felt like she was being lifted and then ripped apart from her seat. A great weight seemed to press and squeeze against her lungs and heart, exerting a wrenching pressure on her inner organs. Blood continued to rush to her head. Instead of all the blood being sucked from her brain, it was being forced there.

She dry heaved a final time, and then started to black out. Carson couldn't do anything about it. He was too busy trying to get the plane down the western slope of Cleveland Mountain.

Carson felt himself start to get light headed. He knew they were pulling 2 or 3 g's. The Cessna wasn't designed as a fighter, and he knew full well that the plane couldn't take much more pounding. When he pulled the yoke back and edged the nose up, it took longer than he planned to flatten out, bringing them closer to the deck than he had ever imagined. If he had the landing gear extended he could have skimmed the taller of the trees in the Montana foothills. Slowly, he took the plane back up to three hundred feet AGL.

"Are you all right?" he asked, simultaneously watching the fuel indicator. It was almost at zero pounds fuel. He knew they weren't going to make it much farther, not and climb at the rate he had as they cleared the Bitterroots.

Nichole put the cloth rag she had been clutching in the small air sick bag she found fastened to the back of her seat cushion. "I'm better now, but that last bit was terrible. I didn't think that we were going to be able to pull out of the dive."

Carson didn't voice any opinion, but the same thought had entered his mind as the plane started to vibrate just before clearing the stand of pines. He watched the green trees and purple sage fly by below them. Interspersed among the foliage there were patches of snow, shielded from the sun by the larger trees and bushes. Glancing at Nichole, he could see that she was starting to relax, at least until the next climb.

"That's the Mission range just in front of us. We just went through the northern end of the Sapphires. If we can find a way through those smaller peaks, we should be able to set down within ten or 20 miles of Swan Lake. I don't think there is any way we'll make it to your dad's landing strip."

"Where will you land the plane?" she asked, considering his last statement.

"We only need a little less than three thousand feet, and that's according to Cessna. If we can find a straight road a couple thousand feet long, we should be all right."

Nichole only nodded, and then quietly dug her fingernails into the palms of her hands, literally drawing blood. Carson continued to fly towards the upcoming hills.

• • •

Seaman Shuck had been glued to the color display for over an hour. Once or twice he thought he might have picked them up, but the aircraft were almost immediately identified as civilian craft heading for Las Vegas. Both times, their transponders were not working - not because of any willingness to evade authorities, but rather due to mechanical and electrical problems.

Esteban, Ricardo, and Captain Seth Hatcher were seated around a six foot table looking at a topographical map of the western United States. The lieutenant on duty watch had found the map and brought it into the control room. Using his finger to follow the line that Captain Hatcher had plotted on the chart, Esteban didn't think it possible that someone hadn't spotted the Citation. "You're sure this is the heading they were following?" the taller Latin asked.

"That's the heading. Nobody has seen them or spotted a thing. Both Hill and Nellis report negative sightings," the Captain said, scratching his head in amazement.

"Sir, you better see this," Nick yelled from the scope across the room.

"What is it?" Captain Hatcher asked as he ran to see what the young man was referring to.

"Out of nowhere, I happened to spot a blip over the Bitterroot range. It would appear on my screen and then drop off just as suddenly. I thought it must be some kind of float plane, or light aircraft trying to clear the mountains. Here it is again, and it is doing more than 400 knots. I would bet a month's pay it's our man."

Everyone watched as the blip vanished from the screen a third time. Esteban was the first to speak. "It looks as if Jeffers has had a change of heart. He must have figured we would be looking in the Santa Rosa range in Nevada. The guy's smart, I'll give him that much."

Seaman Shuck spoke up. "I guarantee you that he is about out of fuel. Even if he had full tanks, he is going to have to set down pretty soon." Suddenly, the blip appeared and then vanished at the bottom of the screen. Nick raised his voice slightly, "Captain, unless I miss my bet, the Citation just went in the ground."

"Do you mean he crashed?" asked the senior officer.

"I think so, sir."

Esteban watched the screen, hoping that the mark of the Citation would suddenly appear again. There was no way he believed that Carson had crashed the plane. He may be on the ground, but he didn't crash. "Sir, who would handle the search for a downed military aircraft in this region?" he asked, walking over to the table and pointing at the northwest section of Montana.

"Hill Air Force Base. It would fall under their operational orders," Seth Hatcher answered.

"Can you arrange for a flight to get us to Hill Air Force Base immediately?" Esteban asked, using his hand to indicate that he was also referring to Ricardo.

"Consider it done. I'll call the Commanding General at Hill and let him know what's happening. He may also want to cancel the flights he has going over northern Nevada."

31

WEDNESDAY MORNING - SWITZERLAND

D rew Matthews looked out the window of Swiss Air Flight 101 that had originated in New York City. Geneva was for all practical purposes more French than it was Swiss. Most of Switzerland speaks a dialect of German, but not Geneva. They speak French. With the recent developments in the United States, the Swiss Air flight was more than three quarters empty. Panic never respects geographic boundaries, and the mostly empty flight from Kennedy proved it. The wheels of the wide-bodied air bus touched down lightly on the runway at Geneva International Airport, the minor impact forcing the businessman to concentrate on the purpose of the flight. Drew had been flying for almost eight hours and was anxious to get off the plane, and it wasn't just because he was tired. His responsibilities in Geneva couldn't wait for him to recover from jet lag. Besides, he doubted he would be in the city for more than twenty-four hours.

The flight attendant handed him his light overcoat and asked him in slightly accented English if he had had a good flight. He told her it was a smooth flight, but he hadn't gotten much sleep. And he hadn't. He spent most of the night going over the figures he carried in a small leather notebook. Drew had planned on leaving for Geneva on Monday evening, but the commitments on the remaining $500 million had taken longer than he had anticipated. Vice President Wright had pressured him to leave immediately, but Drew had felt that it was more important to make sure all the money was in place. Once President Attwilder made the final decision, the transfer was going to have to take place immediately.

Geneva's airport is directly connected to the modern underground train station. He thought about taking a taxi but decided on the EE train instead. They left every twenty minutes, and he could walk right to the Noga Hilton at 19 Quai du Mont-Blanc. From there it was only a short walk along Lake Geneva to the Bank of Switzerland. In the last two years he had made this same journey at least half a dozen times. None of those trips seemed at all relevant to his mission today.

"Do you want your regular suite, Mr. Matthews?" the attractive French receptionist asked as she returned Drew's Visa card to him.

"That will be fine." He liked the Geneva Hilton, even if it was one of the strangest hotels in the world. The inside of the rooms left the traveler with the impression that he was in the middle of a cruise ship. The walls and doors were covered with a hardened plastic, completely resistant to scratches. Chrome strips and door handles accented the blue interior of the halls, as well as the rooms.

"I would like to speak to Guido Meyer," he told the man on the phone. As he waited for Guido to answer, he turned down the heat in the hotel room. Guido Meyer's family had escaped from Germany prior to the beginning of World War II, and started investing in Switzerland. Guido had been born just before the war ended and had followed his father into the financial world. Now he was the managing director of the Geneva Branch of the Bank of Switzerland, and Drew wanted to let him know that he would be at the bank within the hour.

"Mr. Matthews. It's nice to hear your voice." Guido always called Drew by his last name, and Drew had adopted just the opposite habit. It seemed to work well for both of them. "I was expecting your call. Did you have a good flight?" the banker asked in perfect English.

"No problems," responded the American business executive. "Can we meet at 11:30?" Drew asked checking his watch. He had previously set the time piece to local Geneva time immediately after landing, a habit he found useful in fighting the effects of jet lag.

Guido answered, "11:30 is fine. Your preliminary instructions have been followed to the letter, but I must admit that I don't understand everything contained in your fax."

"I'll explain everything when I get there." Drew said good bye to the Swiss banker, hung up the phone, and decided to take a quick shower. It was imperative that he be completely alert during the meeting with Guido, nothing could be left to chance. "Not now," he thought. "Not with $2 billion dollars at stake."

•   •   •

The Geneva office of the Bank of Switzerland occupied the entire gray granite building across from the fountain springing up straight up through the waters of Lake Geneva. International transactions that required extreme secrecy and security arrangements were commonly arranged in the third floor conference room of the seventy-five year old building. Looking down on the spouting geyser, Guido thought it ironic that Drew Matthews was one of the top five most important businessmen in the world, yet he always came to the bank alone. He never brought any kind of entourage. He watched the distinguished-looking man cross the street from the boardwalk facing the lake.

Drew entered the dark wood paneled conference room, and handed his overcoat to the younger man standing next to Guido. Hanging the coat in the open cabinet behind the door, the man asked, "Would you like a cup of coffee, Mr. Matthews?"

"Yes. Black with sugar."

Guido's assistant left the room to complete his assignment. Quietly closing the door behind him, Guido handed Drew a set of legal papers containing several sheets of instructions written in English, two sets of legal forms, and a single piece of paper that was mostly numbers. Taking the papers from Guido's right hand, Drew sat down at the polished walnut table. Slowly, he read the papers, making notes in the small leather notebook that he had removed from the inner pocket of his suit coat. Before he finished, Guido's assistant opened the door and placed a silver tray with the coffee in front of the American businessmen. The younger banker knew that he wasn't to remain in the room and made a graceful exit, closing the door silently behind him. Drew never noticed. He continued reviewing the papers.

"Is everything satisfactory?" Guido asked.

"Perfectly." Drew took a pen from his coat pocket and began signing the first set of documents. When he got to the second set of papers, he turned to the Swiss banker and explained what instructions were to be followed.

"The total amount to be deposited in this account will be $2 billion in U.S. funds. It will be sent via wire transfer from eleven separate accounts in the United States. Once the total transfer to the account is completed, the funds can be withdrawn and transferred to a different bank by using this account number followed by the proper authorization." Drew used his index finger to point out the account number on the forms. He wrote a nine digit number that contained 6 numbers and 3 letters in the space on the form that was labeled *Authorization Code*. The procedure had been used a number of times between the two men seated at the dark wood conference table.

"Is that it?" Guido asked as he gathered up the original set of papers resting on the table. Drew had separated the duplicate copies of the papers, folding them neatly, and then placing them in the small leather notebook.

"That'll do it. Have a good day, Guido," Drew said as he stood and reached for his coat hanging behind the walnut stained door.

"I hope everything goes according to the schedule you have set out, Mr. Matthews."

"So do I, Guido. So do I." Drew closed the door to the conference room and walked down three flights to the ground level of the old historic building. After eight long hours in an airplane, he was tired of being confined in a metal container. The elevator just didn't seem like a good choice.

Rain had started to fall while Drew was in the bank, but it was now stopped. The sky was dark, and a new outburst was threatening to erupt any moment. The business executive pulled up the collar of his raincoat until it touched the lightened ends of his dark hair and crossed the street to the boardwalk of Lake Geneva. Walking briskly to beat the next rainstorm, Drew reviewed his actions of the past week. He hadn't been surprised at the ready willingness of the chief executives of the airlines and other major companies to contribute to the $2 billion fund. Each of the top CEO's of the companies had their total compensation package tied to the value of the stock of their employers. And when the confidence of the American people began to erode, their personal wealth literally was evaporating before their eyes. Using whatever means possible, they had to restore confidence in the American stock market, and then specifically to their own companies. The LLO had cost each of these men millions of dollars, a loss none of them wanted to take by themselves.

It was starting to drizzle a little harder, and Drew picked up his pace, stepping to one side for a girl on a black bicycle racing to beat the deluge that seemed imminent. He crossed the bridge and turned north to the Hilton.

•   •   •

Dialing the direct number that Vice President Jason Wright had furnished him, he called the United States. Not surprisingly, he had to wait for clearance on the other end. Dropping his raincoat on the chair beside the window, he used a hand towel to dry his face and hair.

"Jason, everything is arranged," he said as the Vice President picked up the phone. Drew only called Jason by his official title when there were other people present.

"Any problems at all?" asked the Vice President as he contemplated the assignment that Drew had completed.

"None. I guess we must remember that money still controls the world, especially when it concerns *La Libertad Occidental.*"

Jason Wright stood by the window of his office and looked out at the night lights of Washington, D.C. He was thinking that it didn't seem possible that the United States was about to pay a ransom demand of $2 billion to a group of South American terrorists. Finishing the conversation, Jason said, "President Attwilder has still not committed to the payment, but it seems inevitable at this point."

"Let me know when I should authorize the initial deposits into the Swiss account," Drew said as he finished drying his hair with the towel in his free hand.

"You'll be the first to know." Vice President Wright hung up the phone.

32

TUESDAY NIGHT

The left engine of the powerful Citation started to cut out and then it abruptly quit. Carson immediately applied extra rudder and continued climbing, trying with all his might to clear the ridge approaching from in front. He knew he didn't have much time left. Pulling back on the yoke, the Citation almost touched the trees jutting into the sky. Quickly, he lowered the nose and cut back on the power. He had been worried about stalling the large jet. Now, he was going to find out if the stall speed really was just 82 knots.

Nichole drew a little more blood in her palms as they dropped down into the deserted valley. She couldn't appreciate the beauty of the long narrow canyon. Pine trees towered over the green and purple sage brush on both sides of the isolated strip of Montana real estate.

Carson spotted a dirt road about a half a mile away. The plane was now less than three hundred feet from the earth and dropping fast. Quickly, he lowered the landing gear. Until he knew where he was going to end up, he didn't want to create any more drag then necessary. Using his left hand, he pushed the throttle forward and got a few extra knots before the speed continued to bleed off. 95, 94, 92, 90, 88, 86, 88, and then the right engine stopped altogether. "Hold on. This is it," Carson cried across the cockpit.

At 79 knots, the plane stalled and dropped onto the rough road that had been used for logging before the region became a national forest. Carson didn't say anything, but he could tell that they must have had a tail wind of more than 18 or 20 knots. They were going too fast. He wasn't going to be able to hold the plane on the road. "Brace yourself!" he yelled.

Nichole held onto the arm rests and prayed. She felt every vibration and bump coming through the plane. Closing her eyes, she waited for the inevitable.

Carson continued to use the rudder. There was no power to reverse the thrusters, which were also no longer functioning. If he could just keep the long wings from dipping into the earth, they would be all right. Without warning, the plane's left wheels hit a pot hole in the rough dirt lane. The plane bounced to the left and continued rolling down the mountain road. The speed was now less than 50 knots, but it was too much. Not more than fifty yards in front of them the old logging road turned due west. Standing on the left brake, he tried to make the turn. Quickly realizing the effort was useless, he decided the safest bet was to head straight into the sage brush.

Nichole could smell the sage as they jumped the embankment. She screamed, "Carson, help us!"

Carson grabbed one arm rest and threw an arm in front of Nichole's head to stop it from banging into the displays. With a stroke of luck, the nose wheel collapsed. If it hadn't, the huge plane would have dropped off the forty foot embankment, dropping down to the boulder lined creek below. With one final buck, the plane came to a halt, only thirty feet short of the four story cliff overlooking the cold water from the Montana runoff.

Smelling for smoke, Carson undid his safety belt and reached for Nichole. She was slumped against the side of the plane. "Are you all right?" he asked.

She nodded her head and opened her eyes. "Thank God. I thought we had had it. I opened my eyes for a minute and could only see the water rushing up to us from below."

Carson grabbed her hand and told her to follow him off the plane. He wanted to find out just how lucky they had really been. Taking a map in his hand, he stood and entered the main cabin area. He pulled the handle on the side door and stepped down from the aircraft. The first thing he did was to find out what kind of shape the plane was in. It only took a minute to discover that they were not going anywhere in the Citation. The nose gear was completely demolished, along with the landing gear on the left side. The tail had dragged across three VW sized boulders, and the outside metal of the plane had ripped open. He could only imagine the damage inside the structure. Forgetting about the seriousness of their own problems, he wondered if Eldon Stubbs had kept his insurance current, he was going to need it.

Walking back towards the old road, he estimated they had traveled almost a hundred yards before coming to a final stop. Looking in all directions, he could only see trees, sage brush, some snow, and rock. For all intents and purposes they were alone. He only hoped they could stay that way. Checking his watch, he noted it was almost 5:30 in the afternoon. The sun would be completely down in thirty minutes. Retreating back to the plane, he found that Nichole had found a canvas duffel bag in the back. Using some rope, she had fastened it into a form of knapsack and was filling it with matches, some blankets, soda pop from the fridge, and what remained of the packaged cookies and crackers. Her own knapsack was still in the rest room in the hanger in Port Townsend. "We're going to have to get out of here," he said as he spread the map out on the wing of the plane. Normally, he wouldn't have been able to use it as a table, but with the collapsed landing gear, it worked just fine.

"Where do you think we are?" Nichole asked as she looked down at the map, zipping the duffel bag shut.

Carson used his finger to point to a small canyon located to the west of Hungry Horse dam. "It looks like we are in this small valley. The road we just left leads to an old logging site, probably used when they were building the scaffolding for the dam." He pointed to an area west of the dam. "Swan Lake and Big Fork are about fifteen miles across those small peaks," he said, pointing to the ridge to the west.

"I take it we walk," she said, looking up at the high tree line.

"I'm afraid so. It's the only way out. We have to get to Big Fork by tomorrow morning to meet Michael, Blake, and Jim. Our main problem right now is to evade any people searching for us. Fortunately, it is almost dark. If we're lucky, we probably have until tomorrow morning before they find the plane."

Nichole looked at the Citation partially buried in the sage brush. "Should we try and hide the plane?" she asked.

"If we can give ourselves a few more hours in the morning, we better," Carson answered. "Did you find any tools in the plane?"

"There is a tool box in the rear baggage compartment," she said, pointing to the rear section of the cabin.

Carson moved off the wing and went to search the metal box. A few minutes later he returned with a small ax. "Let's try and drag some sage brush over the wings. I'll cut it if you will start pulling it to the plane."

Nichole dropped the duffel-shaped knapsack and followed Carson into the brush. They worked steadily for almost forty-five minutes and were both sweating profusely. Still, the effort had been worth it. Even from the road, you would probably not spot the plane without knowing what you were looking for, and from the air, it would be almost impossible to see.

"We have a long hike ahead of us, and I would like to clean up a little," Carson said as they finished placing the last of the sage brush on the plane. Their clothes smelled of sage, but it wasn't an unpleasant odor. Sage brush has small seeds that had shed down both Nichole's and Carson's shirts. They hadn't heard any aircraft flying nearby, and believed it highly unlikely they would be spotted before morning.

"Me, too," Nichole said as she started to hoist the duffel bag on to her shoulders. Carson reached inside the plane and picked up the loaded shotgun. "I'll carry the bag," he said as he stepped from the plane. Sliding down the steep embankment, they worked their way towards the cold pool of water in the rocks below. "It'll be cold, but I guarantee it will be refreshing," he told Nichole as he dropped the duffel bag and took off his clothes.

Nichole wasn't too enthused about stepping into ice cold water, but she knew she didn't want to walk fifteen miles in the dark feeling like she did now. She watched Carson walk into the ice cold stream. He ducked under the water three separate times, shaking his head as he came up the last time. Silently he walked from the stream and stood beside Nichole, naked but clean.

"I guess it's my turn." Resolutely she removed her dusty blouse and skirt, the remains of the sage brush falling to the rocks at her feet. She turned and hesitantly walked into the water. Suddenly she turned and stepped back onto the rocky shore. "I don't think I can do it."

Carson smiled for the first time all afternoon and pointed at the water. "In you go!"

Nichole took it as a dare, and she wasn't going to let him get the best of her. Besides, she knew she would feel a lot better. Thirty seconds later she stood on the shore shivering in the moonlight. Carson had taken one of the three blankets in the duffel bag and placed it over his shoulders. As Nichole stepped from the water, he pulled her close to him and sat down on a large smooth boulder. Wrapping the blanket around both of them, he soon raised her body temperature.

"Are we going to get out of this?" Nichole asked as Carson held her naked body from behind. She could feel the strength of his arms against her bare breasts. It just didn't seem possible that she was sitting nude under a blanket on a stream in the Montana mountains.

Carson turned her around and held her slender body against him. The pulse of his beating heart moved her breasts as if they were one. Nichole locked her hands behind his back and looked into his blue eyes.

"Nichole, we're not beaten yet. I promise you that we will get to Big Fork. After that, we'll see." Carson held her silently as they both watched the bright moon move behind the clouds. After a few minutes, he said, "We'd better go. It's a long way across those hills. Before we lose the moonlight, I would like to put as much distance between us and that plane as possible.

Nichole squeezed him tightly against her and whispered softly in his ear, "Then let's get going."

• • •

Esteban and Ricardo had stayed in the control room waiting for the Lear jet, that was recently transformed into a military aircraft. It was supposed to arrive any minute, and Captain Hatcher had promised to alert them when it was on final approach. Once the aircraft sent from Hill was in the air, Esteban had placed another call to his Washington,

D.C. contact. He thought they might need additional identification when they arrived at the Utah Air Force Base.

"Captain, there is a secure fax coming in marked for your attention only," the lieutenant said to Seth Hatcher.

"If you'll excuse me, gentlemen. I'll be right back," Captain Hatcher said as he followed the lieutenant into the duty office.

"Do you think we can find them?" Ricardo asked when they were alone at the table.

"I'm betting our lives on it. If they escape, there is a better than fifty-fifty chance that this whole operation will come apart. And if it does, I don't need to tell you what could happen to us."

Before the two Latin American terrorists-turned-government- agents could finish their conversation, Captain Hatcher reentered the dark control room carrying four sheets of paper. "I guess the Pentagon figured you might need special clearance at Hill. You just received special authorizations and identification papers."

Esteban took the papers, looking carefully at each one. There were two sets of almost identical documents. The smaller documents were twin identification cards in the names of Carlos Herrera and Ethan Mabry. They were personally signed by Seymour Dillan, director of the CIA. The larger documents were bar-coded with a specially encrypted code. They were entitled Presidential Seal. Each of the documents had a special notation, indicating that either Ethan Mabry or Carlos Herrera could speak on behalf of the President. All government and military personnel were to obey their orders as if they came from the President.

Captain Hatcher had read the documents when they came in and was visibly impressed by the power that the two men must have. "Someone in Washington wants you to have all the help possible in catching these two terrorists," he said, referring to the yet uncompleted capture of Carson and Nichole.

Esteban nodded and said, "It appears so, Captain. I just hope this will help in organizing the search for the plane. Have you heard from our transport yet?"

Captain Hatcher noticed Seaman Shuck waving to him from his console. "Unless I miss my bet, your plane is on final now. You can be out of here in the next ten minutes."

"We thank you for your help in this matter, Captain." Esteban put his new identification papers in the wallet he had in his pocket and turned to leave the room.

"Mabry," Captain Hatcher said in a loud voice.

Both Esteban and Ricardo stopped and turned around, unaware of why the Navy captain had detained them.

"Good luck, Gentlemen. It has been a pleasure working with you. I wish we could have provided more assistance," the captain said. "The lieutenant will escort you to the flight line."

• • •

Carson checked his watch and found that it was now almost 3:00 in the morning. According to the map they had been following, the small community of Big Fork shouldn't be more than a mile and a half through the dark woods to their left. Except for three fifteen minute breaks they had taken to rest, Carson and Nichole had been walking all night. The soda pop wasn't as nourishing as water, but it was certainly better than nothing. "Let's make sure that we are not too far from the General Store, then find some place we can get a few hours of rest," Carson said to the tired blond at his side.

"Whatever you say," she said, not fully aware of where they were. Carson had carried the duffel bag and the shotgun all night long. For the first three hours, Nichole had been able to keep up without any problem. They had followed a fire line that had been cut by the forest service for almost seven miles. But then they had to climb a thousand foot rock ridge. It had almost been more than she could take, but luckily they had been able to start down after a short break. Nichole's head was pounding. She knew she needed to rest soon.

• • •

Major General David Brown had been in communication with Ethan

Mabry even before the sleek twin engine jet touched down at Hill Air Force Base. As soon as the plane taxied to the open hanger, General Brown personally helped open the door to the small aircraft. "I trust you had a good flight," he said as he shook Esteban's hand.

"No problems. Have you been briefed on what we are up against?" Esteban asked while he showed the general the documents he had received before leaving Whidbey Naval Air Station.

General Brown moved to a computer terminal mounted on the wall of the hanger and quickly punched in the numbers that corresponded to the encrypted code on the Presidential Seal. Seconds later he got the authorization he now fully expected and turned back to speak to Esteban. "Mr. Mabry, for the past thirty minutes I have been organizing a search mission that will depart at first light in the morning. We will also be using enhanced satellite photography to try and spot the downed aircraft."

Esteban listened as the general continued to explain all the steps he had taken in organizing the search effort. The taller Latin quickly realized that General Brown had not gotten to be a general because he was someone special's son. General Brown was an extremely detailed and competent soldier. "There's no need to call me "Mister," General. I would appreciate it if you would call me Ethan, and my companion, Carlos."

"As you wish, Ethan. I have prepared a couple of rooms in the Senior Bachelor Officer's Quarters. I trust you will be quite comfortable until zero five hundred hours."

"I'm sure that will be just fine," Esteban answered, suddenly aware of the fatigue that was now invading his body. "We want to be on the first helicopter out of here, once recognition is confirmed."

"I guarantee you will be," General Brown answered, for the first time noticing the .44 magnum revolvers both men carried on their belts. The weapons were concealed under the shirts on their backs, but when Esteban shook his body to relieve the tension, the handle of the pistol caught on the fabric of his shirt.

• • •

Carson helped Nichole into the loft of the old barn. Through the weathered slats of the gray, two story building, he could see the dark strip he had identified as Highway 35. Big Fork was only two miles straight down the road. From the looks of the barn, it was only used in late summer or early fall. Still, there was enough hay left in the high loft to provide a soft bed. Carson knew they could sleep for a few hours and then hike through the woods to the general store. It would only take them thirty or forty minutes to make the 9:00 appointment. Checking his watch, he figured they had almost four hours to rest.

"Take my hand, and I'll pull you up," he said as he held out his arm to the extremely fatigued woman. The ladder had been broken, and he had had to scale the last five feet leading to the hay storage.

Nichole did as he instructed, and used her feet to try and help walk up the wall to the loft. "I can't believe we made it," she said as she collapsed on the soft cushion of year-old alfalfa.

Carson sat down and leaned against the wooden wall. "Neither can I." Waiting a moment to catch his breath, he opened the duffel bag he had taken from his shoulders and removed the blankets and remaining three cans of Seven-Up. "Let's make a bed," he said as he started laying out the first blanket.

Nichole crawled over to help him. For the first time she saw that the roof of the barn was gone over more than a third of the loft area. "Look at the stars," she said as she took the corner of the blanket and pulled it over the softest part of the hay covered floor.

Carson stopped what he was doing and laid back on the blanket, resting his body on his right side. He was immediately aware of the heavenly splendor that had caught her eyes. He drew Nichole close to him and gazed into the eternities, still not comprehending what they meant, but amazed at the grandeur, nevertheless.

Resting on her side, she gently pushed Carson onto his back so that he could gaze at the stars while still looking into her eyes. Raising her left thigh, she climbed onto Carson's chest, sitting upright in the same movement. Silently, she unbuttoned her blouse and removed her bra. She felt Carson's hands about her waist softly unbuttoning the buckle of her Levis. He continued his stellar discovery of her body, moving first up to her soft and supple breasts and then following the lines of her body down past her waist.

Without knowing exactly how it happened, Nichole realized that Carson had removed both her denim Levis and silk underpants. In an unhurried effort, she helped him remove the rest of his clothes. Nichole enjoyed the sensation of his strong, but gentle, hands moving up and down her body, exploring regions she had forgotten. She found her nipples getting hard. Carson continued caressing her body. The pain and fatigue she had felt for the past eight hours were now replaced by the most luxurious, relaxing thing she had ever experienced. The light breeze floating through the cracks in the slats and the opening in the roof combined with the fragrance of the hay to heighten her awareness of the moment.

Their coupling was as gentle as the moonlight falling through the broken rafters. For a while, both seemed to escape the pain, transported into a oneness. Sleep was as natural as their union, their body warmth making up for their lack of clothing.

33

WEDNESDAY MORNING

Esteban was awake instantly when he heard the shrill sound of the ringing. Shaking his head in an effort to discover where he was, the dark Latin sat up in the bed and picked up the phone. The sound of the early morning wake-up call stopped immediately.

"Sir, General Brown asked me to invite you to have breakfast with him at zero five thirty. I'll be out front of the BOQ in thirty minutes," the voice on the other end of the phone stated. Esteban had no doubt it belonged to the general's aide who had dropped them off late the night before. Almost as an after thought, the captain who had placed the early morning call added, "Would that be convenient?"

Esteban looked at the clock on the nightstand and then answered, "That will be fine. Please tell the general that we will want a complete briefing at that time."

"Yes, sir."

•   •   •

Michael had been driving for the past two hours. By his watch he figured it was almost 4:30 in the morning. He couldn't quite understand how it was getting light on the eastern horizon. He knew the sun couldn't come up that early, and then he realized that he was in another time zone. Up ahead he could see a sign that said *Missoula 1 Mile*. He moved to the right-hand lane of Interstate 90 and got ready to make the exit. It was only a couple of hours to Kallispel and then across to Big Fork, and Michael didn't want to arrive too early. Grabbing Blake by the shoulder, he woke ManTech's Head of Security. As Blake yawned and stretched his arms, Michael noticed that the former FBI agent's hair was starting to thin. It wasn't a dramatic change, but combined with the slight graying at the edges, it made the forty-eight-year-old investigator seem even older.

"Do you want to stop and get some breakfast?" Blake asked.

"That's what I was thinking. I saw a sign that said there was a Denny's off the next exit. I doubt if anyone is looking for us, but we shouldn't stand out at a place like that."

Blake reached over the back seat and shook Jim, waking him from his sleep. "Wake up. We're going to stop and get some pancakes."

Jim reached down and found the wire rimmed glasses he had dropped on the floor of the car. "Where are we?" he asked.

Michael turned off the interstate and answered, "Missoula. There's Denny's on the right."

As the three men waited for a table, Blake went over and picked up a newspaper that was laying on the brown vinyl bench. The headlines were more of the same - *TERRORISTS EVADE AUTHORITIES OVER NEVADA DESERT*. Blake handed the paper to Michael as the hostess led them to a non-smoking booth against the far window. There were no customers seated at either of the adjoining tables.

After they ordered coffee and breakfast, Michael started reading aloud the main news column of the Missoula morning paper.

"Carson Jeffers, alleged terrorist and front man for La Libertad Occidental, had been pursued by federal authorities. Late yesterday afternoon, Jeffers, accompanied by Nichole Lewis, stole a Cessna Citation jet from the Port Townsend airport, near Seattle, Washington. Reliable government sources have stated that the Citation was last seen heading south into Nevada. It is speculated that Jeffers was heading for Mexico, where he can join up with other leaders of the ruthless terrorist organization, the LLO.

"A high ranking military officer stated that it's possible that the Citation went down in the mountains of southern Oregon or northern Nevada. A full scale search for the fugitives has already begun..."

Blake interrupted Michael before he could finish the newspaper article. The waitress was coming with their coffee. As soon as she left, Michael voiced the question that each of the men were asking themselves. "What do you think? Did he make it?"

Jim reached across the table and took the paper from Michael. "I don't know Carson as well as you two, but I have flown with him a number of times. Unless he was shot down, I don't think he crashed."

Blake put down his coffee on the dark-wood grained formica table. "Jim is right. What we do know is that Carson had a plan to get to Big Fork, and it must have necessitated the theft of the Citation. I'll bet dollars to donuts he'll be at the rendezvous this morning."

Michael sipped his coffee. "I hope so. God, I hope so!"

•   •   •

"That will be all, Ed," General Brown said to his aide as he led the two dark skinned guests into the general's dining room. Captain Edward Mitchell turned and left the formal eating area.

"Robert, this is Ethan Mabry and Carlos Herrera. They are on loan from the CIA and are coordinating the search for Carson Jeffers with Washington, D.C.," the general said as he introduced the two men to his executive officer, Brigadier General Robert Poelman.

Esteban and Ricardo both shook hands with the general officer and sat down at the dining table. General David Brown asked Robert Poelman to review what had transpired during the last six hours.

General Poelman spent almost ten minutes explaining how both ground and aerial searches had begun. "The main problem we have been working with is the sheer size of the area in question. It is possible that the Citation did in fact go down somewhere in Nevada. We haven't called off the search in that area, only scaled it back. At this point in time we believe it more likely that the Citation may have either crashed or landed in the Bitterroot Mountain range in Montana. It is my bet that this Carson Jeffers is probably dead. If he went down in that country, there is little chance that he could walk away from it."

Esteban waited for the general to finish explaining his reasoning before he began his contradiction. "I'm going to have to beg to disagree. Carson Jeffers has been one step ahead of us all along. I find it doubtful that he would crash a plane, one that he was extremely capable of flying. I'm sure that each of you gentlemen have reviewed his service record. His total flight hours in jet aircraft now exceed three thousand hours. And that, gentlemen, is from take-off to touch-down. The Air Force doesn't count flight time like your civilian counterparts, where time is logged whenever the engine is running, on the taxiway or at the gate."

General Brown acknowledged his point and asked, "If he was able to land the Citation, what do you think he is going to try and do?"

"It is my opinion that Carson Jeffers had a specific destination in mind. He's smart enough to know that he might need to refuel and would have anticipated where that fuel would be available. If, somehow, he did run out of fuel, I think you will find the Citation has landed on a road somewhere. I am fully aware of our abilities to interject any intruders entering or leaving U.S. air space. If Carson Jeffers was heading for Mexico, I doubt that he would have crossed the border in that plane."

Everything that Esteban said made sense to the men seated at the table. General Brown turned to his counterpart and asked, "What have you heard from NASA and their satellite surveillance?"

Brigadier General Poelman got up from the breakfast table and turned the map around that was fastened to the easel. "NASA has been photographing all the areas in question. Specific emphasis has been placed in these areas." He pointed to Nevada, Utah, Oregon, Idaho, and Montana.

Captain Ed Mitchel, General Brown's aide, opened the door and crossed the room to the table now flanked by the map of the western United States. "General," he said, handing the paper in his hand to his boss, "NASA has indicated that they may have spotted something in the area near Missoula, Montana."

"Can't they be more specific?" the general asked.

"I placed a call to their main office in Florida, and I was told that any confirmation would have to wait until sometime after 9:30 a.m. Mountain Time."

"Why is that?" asked General Poelman.

"The next satellite won't pass over until just after 9:00 our time. It will take them a few minutes to review and verify the data. As soon as they have something, they will call us here at Hill."

General Brown turned to Esteban and said, "Ethan, I would like you to be ready to join me on the flight line as soon as that call comes in."

Esteban nodded his head in agreement.

•   •   •

Warm shafts of sun and the sounds of morning birds in the woods woke Carson from his sleep. He opened his eyes and rolled over next to Nichole. Sometime in the night she had gotten cold and put the cotton shirt on to protect her shoulders from the night air. Carson reached under the blanket and found her bare waist and pulled her close to him. "We have to get moving," he said as she opened her eyes to the rays of light coming in through the roof.

Not fully awake, she answered, "Going to where?"

He knew she would quickly realize what he had been talking about and didn't answer her question. Instead, he gently pulled her head to his bare shoulder and just held her.

Five minutes later, the two fugitives climbed down from the loft and headed into the woods. Carson still had the duffel bag strapped across his shoulders, while carrying the shotgun in his left arm. Nichole went a little deeper into the forest while Carson crept up to the road to check the traffic. Satisfied there were no search vehicles on the road, he fell back into the green undergrowth.

"I think we're OK. If they had found the plane, by now every road would be packed with military and police traffic. It hasn't happened, and we have a little more time," he said to Nichole as she joined him in the clearing.

"How much time?"

"I'm afraid it is probably not over an hour or two. NASA was recruited several years ago to support anti-terrorist activities, and they will be using all their resources to try and spot our plane. We were able to disguise it, but it is not hidden. My best estimate is that the plane will be found within the next couple of hours."

"Won't they be able to find us right after that?" Nichole asked as she fell in behind him on the narrow path that headed towards Big Fork.

"If they concentrate their search in this area, there is absolutely no doubt. But, I've been thinking. Remember when we were talking about manipulation?"

"Yes. But what does that have to do with the military and their search for us?"

"If you were the government, where would you think we were heading, knowing that the plane was found less than a hundred miles from the northern border of the United States?"

"Canada. You think they will assume that we are taking ourselves out of the game, don't you?"

"It's a better than even bet," Carson answered. "In Las Vegas, even the House wouldn't take your money." They continued marching through the trees, trying to make as little noise as possible. Carson checked his watch and saw that it was almost a quarter to nine.

Nichole touched him on the shoulder, indicating she wanted to ask another question. "What about Michael, Blake, and Jim? Do you think that whoever is chasing us knows they are trying to meet us?"

"They'll probably figure it out in the next little while. When they can't find any of them in the Portland area, the wise guess would be that they are running to join us."

"Then they're not safe either?" she asked as she started walking again.

"I'm afraid no one is safe any longer, Nichole."

She remembered what had happened at Salt Lake, Dallas, and Los Angeles, and knew he was right.

• • •

Blake had been driving ever since they filled up with gas in Missoula, more than two hours before. They had waited in the restaurant, timing their departure so they could arrive in Big Fork as close to

9:00 as possible. Michael was watching for the four-way stop. He almost missed it, but Jim saw that someone had removed the stop sign facing east. Everyone assumed that it had been taken by some kids, just decorating their rooms.

"On the left," Michael said, pointing to the sign that said *Hungry Horse Trading Post*. "It must take its name from the dam," he said.

Blake pulled into the small parking lot on the side of the brown log building and came to a stop. "What now?" asked Michael.

"Why don't you go inside and check if they are there?" Blake answered, pointing to the general store. "I doubt they would chance standing around in a store, but you better check."

Carson had been watching the white sedan as it pulled into the gravel lot. He hoped it was his friends, and when he saw Michael get out of the car, he stood in the woods and followed him across the hardened brown dirt. Nichole was right behind him.

Michael never heard Carson approach and almost fainted when he felt the hand on his shoulder. Jumping and turning at the same time, he smiled when he saw the two of them. "Are you all right? We heard you had crashed somewhere in Nevada." He didn't comment on their new hair styles; he knew Carson would explain it all later.

Carson gripped his friend's arm and said, "Let's hope everyone else thinks the same thing. You remember Nichole?"

"Certainly. I'm glad you two are all right. Let me introduce you to Blake and Jim," he said to Nichole.

By the time that the three of them had reached the car, both of the other men were standing in the gravel. Jim was the first to speak. "I knew you would be here. I'm Jim Tedrow, and I'm also single," he said, grinning at Nichole.

"Blake Terry," the older man stated. "I really am glad to see you. I think we had better get going. It's probably not to smart to be seen standing around here."

All five of them got in the car. Carson and Nichole got in beside Blake, who was still driving. Michael and Jim took the back seat. "All right, where to?" Blake asked Carson.

"You'll have to ask Nichole that question. Her father has a hunting lodge nearby. We are going to go there."

"Actually, it's not as near as you might think. We still have a twenty-five minute trip." Turning to Blake she said, "We need to go back south about eight or ten miles. Then we'll go east until we get near Swan Lake. The lodge is almost hidden in the woods some seven miles off the main road."

Blake turned the car and headed north on Highway 35. The old Indian, who had come out of the trading post, watched the car pull away.

"The lodge is back to the south," Carson said, looking at the puzzled look on Nichole's face.

"My hearing is not bad, Carson." Blake continued to watch the Indian through the rear view mirror. The old man stepped off the porch and walked around the corner of the log building, entering the side door of an adjoining structure. Blake guessed it was the living quarters.

Two minutes later, he pulled the car around and headed south again. "I just didn't think we should advertise the direction we were going," he explained to the other people in the car. "We don't have anyone following us just yet, but unless I miss my bet, we soon will have."

34

Fastening the ear protectors in place, Esteban and Ricardo secured their seat belts in the large Chinook helicopter. Both General Brown and General Poelman had decided to go along on the search. They were, after all, in pursuit of the most cold blooded, ruthless terrorist since Hitler. And Carson Jeffers was definitely a terrorist.

"All set?" yelled the senior general, looking at both Esteban and Ricardo.

Esteban could barely hear what the man had asked, and decided to forgo the yelling exercise. As the twin rotors cut circular paths through the Utah morning air, Esteban raised his right thumb to the sky, indicating he was ready. Ricardo did the same. General Brown said something into the microphone attached to his helmet, and slowly, the green aircraft, painted with a tan camouflage covering, lifted off the ground.

It had only taken seven minutes from the time the call came through from NASA before both helicopters were ready to take off. The first chopper was reserved for the officers, Esteban, Ricardo, and a squad of highly trained and battle tested troops. They were the equivalent of Navy Seals and took the same kind of pride in what they did. The second chopper had two additional squads of men, one was the mirror image of the squad in the general's aircraft, the second were dog handlers. Their dogs were also loaded on the second aircraft.

Esteban was amazed that Ricardo could sleep with the lurching and side to side movement of the giant helicopter. They had only been gone from Hill for fifteen minutes, and his shorter companion in the LLO had closed his eyes and slipped into a peaceful state of near-consciousness. Esteban tightened the band around his dark pony-tail and wondered why he still kept the longer hair. It was a nuisance at times, but he thought it must have been his way of demonstrating his disdain for the organized world in which he lived. The truth of the matter was, he really didn't like the long hair. He decided to try and copy the success of Ricardo. Closing his eyes, he wondered what they were going to find in the mountains of Montana.

General Brown had received the call from NASA at exactly nine twenty in the morning. Two minutes later, The general officers, along with Ethan Mabry and Carlos Herrera, were reviewing the photos that had been faxed from Florida. There were two separate sets of photos. Noting the time code on the first set of pictures, Esteban had determined that the picture was taken at 7:00 p.m. Eastern Time. It was almost too dark to see anything, but there appeared to be some kind of shining coming from a small piece of metal in a field of sage brush. The second set of pictures showed the same pictures, but the shining was now gone.

What was interesting were the circles that had been drawn around certain areas in the second photo. Each area was almost cleared of sage brush. Comparing the two sets of photos, you could see where the brush had been growing the night before, but by morning it was gone. Esteban thought that someone, or some software program, should be complimented for spotting the discrepancy from 17,000 miles away in space. Once the discovery of the missing sage brush was confirmed, it had been relatively easy to spot the tracks that must have been made by a heavy, wide tracked vehicle, or a plane. In the top portion of the photos you could see a larger pile of brush. It must have been covering the plane.

Esteban still couldn't sleep and turned his thoughts to this Carson Jeffers. He had become a formidable opponent, one worth fighting. Why he was involved in *Shortfall*, he couldn't decide. His boy had been killed in Salt Lake, so revenge might have been a reason. But revenge wouldn't have put the man in Los Angeles when the third plane was shot down, or at the hospital when Gunnery Sergeant Baker died. There was no doubt that both Carson Jeffers and the woman, Nichole Lewis, were going to have to die. Esteban hoped, however, that he could question both of them before that happened. He needed to find out how they got involved. If the most important operation of the LLO had somehow been penetrated, Esteban had to know how. Then he would have to do something about it, and hopefully, stop the operation from unraveling.

They had been airborne for almost an hour, and the hull of the chopper had started to heat up. The heavy odor of damp, musty canvas webbing was starting to permeate the cabin area. Esteban could only imagine what the smell must be like in the second chopper, what with the dozen dogs on board. He saw the general motioning to him to look out the open window of the chopper. Below them he could now see the field they had identified in the photos. The pilots of both Chinooks were landing fifty yards apart on the old dirt road. Slowly the metal bird settled onto the road, blowing dust in all directions. Esteban could tell that it hadn't rained in the last few days.

All the soldiers knew what they were supposed to do. The two tactical squads immediately deployed around the helicopters, setting up a defense perimeter, the dogs and their handlers staying close to the helicopters. It was extremely doubtful they would meet any kind of opposition in the high mountain area, but if Carson Jeffers and Nichole Lewis were meeting other members of the LLO, it was better to be safe now than sorry later. General Brown sent out two patrols to reconnoiter the area. Twenty minutes later everyone was satisfied that they were alone in the small valley. One of the squads had located the aircraft, but had not yet opened it.

Esteban was adamant that he be the first one in the plane. Somehow, he knew he had to find out more about this man. What was keeping him going? And, more importantly, what was he thinking? He opened the cabin door with Generals Brown and Poelman close behind him. He motioned for Ricardo to walk around the plane and see what he could find while he went inside.

"What exactly are you looking for?" General Brown asked as he leaned his head in from outside the open door of the Citation jet.

"General, I don't really know for sure," Esteban answered as he climbed into the cockpit. "Carson Jeffers was able to land this plane on a road where most men would have given up and crashed. From what we saw on the road, he started to try to make the sharp turn, and then changed his mind. Even with busted landing gear and a collapsed nose wheel, he managed to maintain some control. The plane should have started cart wheeling as soon as the landing gear came apart."

Ricardo had found the opened tool box near the tail of the plane. At least he had found out what they used to cut the sage brush covering the aircraft.

"General, would you come here?" Esteban yelled back through the cabin of the silver Citation.

Pulling himself into the cockpit, General Brown knelt beside the pony-tailed CIA agent sitting in the left seat of the plane. "What is it?" he asked.

Esteban showed the general the black Jeppeson manual. "Do you know what this is?"

Being a pilot himself, General Brown thought the question a little childish. "It's a Jeppeson manual with approach charts."

"Correct. Now look at this." He opened the manual, using the divider in the approach chart section of the manual. The black binder opened to the chart for Glacier Park Intl. at Kalispell.

"Do you think he was trying to get to Kalispell and just ran out of fuel?" the two star general asked.

"That was my first thought, and then I found this on the floor." Esteban picked up a Low Altitude Enroute Chart with a number 5 in the top right corner. He opened the chart up and spread it out on the right seat of the plane. "Do you see where the chart has been marked in red?"

General Brown nodded and picked up the chart from the seat. "This shows the exact route that Jeffers followed after he passed Strawberry Mountain. The red line goes right through Kalispell and extends up to Cardston, Alberta. You think he might have been heading for Canada after all?"

"It's a possibility."

"What's that pungent smell?" the general asked, looking around the plane.

"I was wondering the same thing. It smells like someone got sick." Esteban opened the seat pocket on the right seat and saw the air sickness bag. He opened it and saw the rag inside. "Unless I miss my bet, Nichole Lewis couldn't take the up and down flying Carson used to evade our radar. She got sick and used this rag to clean herself up."

General Brown grabbed the small plastic-lined bag from Esteban and backed out of the main cabin of the Citation. He called to the dog handler who was keeping his dogs at bay beside the plane. "Get your dogs started. This was used by the woman." The general handed the plastic bag to the airman. "In all likelihood they will be heading for some kind of transportation. The fugitives may be trying to get to Canada."

Airman Richardson took the soiled cloth and went back to his dogs. Five minutes later the dogs were standing on the shore of the creek below the plane. Ricardo had already beaten them there and was explaining to Esteban and the two generals his theory on where the man and woman must have gone.

"It looks like they cleaned up here by the water. See the remains of the sagebrush on the rocks?" Ricardo motioned to the small pieces of sage brush laying beside the smooth boulder. "They must have gotten the brush in their clothes while they were hiding the plane. Anyway, it looks like they headed up that ridge," he said, pointing to the high tree line.

"General, what's in that direction?" Esteban asked.

"The small community of Big Fork and then Kalispell. I just got a call from Hill and was told to pass on some information to you from Washington, D.C. Apparently, three friends of Carson, all employees of ManTech, left the Portland area last night. Do you think they might be trying to meet up with Carson?"

"General, I would bet against all odds that is just what they are doing!" Esteban replied firmly.

• • •

Timing was critical. Carson Jeffers and the woman already had at least a 12 to 16 hour head start on the search party. General Brown decided to divide up his men. Half of the dogs would lead one squad of troops up the ridge and would follow the trail left by Carson and Nichole. The rest of the dogs and men would reboard the choppers and fly to the little community of Big Fork. If Carson was trying to reach transportation, that would be his best bet. He would deploy men and dogs along the road and hopefully find where the two of them came out of the woods. General Poelman would keep one chopper and remain behind with the troops and dogs who would go over the mountain.

• • •

Esteban agreed with the general's tactics. It made sense to try and shorten the lead that Carson had gained. General Brown divided up his remaining men and dogs and had them search in from both directions on Highway 35 leading to Big Fork. Airman Richardson had cut the rag in two and left half with the rest of the dogs on the mountain. He had kept the remaining part to use with the dogs on the Big Fork road. Everyone agreed that the dogs should be able to pick up the scent of either Carson or Nichole. The woman had vomited in the rag, but it had apparently been used on a regular basis to wipe down the windows in the plane. Carson may have used it for the same purpose.

"Ethan, let's go," General Brown stated in an excited voice. "They found where the two of them spent the night. They aren't ahead of us by much."

Esteban followed the general into the helicopter. Three minutes later they were on the road overlooking the old hay barn. Barking and yelping was coming from the building in a wild chorus. Airman Richardson advanced and saluted the general. "Sir, there is no doubt that the two of them were here. We found three cans of soda in the hay loft. It had the scent of the woman. If you will all three come with me, I'd like to show you something," the sergeant said, referring to the general as well as Esteban and Ricardo.

Richardson used a stick to show a moist spot that stood out on the grass. It had a slight ammonia-type odor to it. "The dogs followed the scent to these bushes and started going crazy. It looks like the woman relieved herself here and then joined back up with her partner in that clearing over there," he said, pointing to a break in the woods. "General, I don't think they are more than an hour ahead of us."

"Where does this path lead?" Esteban asked, walking a few steps down the path that was already being used by the dogs.

"We sent two dogs ahead with some of the troops. There is a trading post or general store about a mile and a half down the road."

Esteban and the general were already running back to the chopper on the road. Esteban called back to Ricardo who was starting to follow them. "Stay with the dogs. We'll meet at the general store."

•　　•　　•

"Damn! We lost them," said the airman as the dogs started wandering aimlessly around the parking lot. "They were here, but must have caught a ride. They could be anywhere by now with the head start they still have."

General Brown had radioed his executive officer, and General Poelman was landing in the second chopper in the parking lot next to the road. The troops had stopped traffic in both directions. Only two cars were waiting to get through.

Esteban walked out of the Hungry Horse Trading Post, and while scratching his head, looked up and down the road. "General," he said as the officer approached, "There are two young girls working inside, and they have been there since they opened at 7:30 this morning. No one has shown up that comes close to matching the description of our two fugitives."

"So that's it? Carson Jeffers and Nichole Lewis just walk in and immediately catch a ride? It sounds too coincidental to me," General Brown said.

"I agree," Esteban remarked, scanning the area that surrounded the building. People were starting to gather around the Trading Post, most of them stopping beside one of the two large choppers. It seemed that everyone wanted to find out what the two helicopters were doing in the parking lot. Esteban dismissed the onlookers and noticed a small building that was attached to the main store. Someone was looking through the curtains from the small window facing the parking lot. Suddenly, the curtains closed. "I'll be back in a minute," Esteban told the general.

General Brown had also seen the curtains close and had guessed that Ethan Mabry was going to see if the person behind the curtains had seen anything. He got to the door of the building just behind the pony-tailed CIA agent.

Esteban pounded on the flimsy wooden door. Slowly, the door opened three or four inches. He could see the weathered face of an old Indian, someone who must have seen more than seventy-five Montana winters. With the general standing beside him, Esteban decided not to use intimidation as an interrogation method. At first, the old man acted like he couldn't understand what Esteban wanted. The more frustrated Esteban became, the quieter the Indian became, until finally, General Brown stepped forward and shook the Indian's hand. His uniform must have impressed the weathered man.

"I saw the people," the old man stated, raising his arm towards the morning sun. "Right over there." He pointed to the north side of the parking lot.

"When were they here?" General Brown asked, his eyes searching the area indicated by the man's body language. Esteban had decided to let the general do the questioning.

"About nine o'clock. I just got my coffee from my granddaughter. She works in trading post," he said, using broken English.

"Were they alone?" General Brown asked in a firm voice.

"Just the two, a man and a woman," the Indian answered. "But they met three men in the white car."

"What white car?" broke in Esteban, now refusing to let the general do all the talking.

"Just a white car."

"What did the three men look like?" Esteban asked before General Brown could react to the old man's observation.

"Two looked like white men, and taller man had black skin." The rugged but aged Indian folded his arms across his chest and stared at the two men, indicating he was tired of answering their questions

General Brown stepped forward again and put his hand on the old man's shoulder, a sign of understanding, not intimidation. "Where did they go?"

Accepting the General's gesture of friendship, the ancient warrior finally answered, "All the men and the woman got in car and drove off." He smiled and pointed up the road to the north.

"They went north?" asked the general.

"Yes. I guess men go to Kalispell," the weathered dark skinned man answered, having now come fully outside the door.

General Brown turned to Esteban and said, "It's Canada. They are trying to make it to the border. All five of them. What do you think? Are the other three people the ones your folks lost in Portland?"

"I think so." Esteban saw Ricardo walk up to the porch of the building. He knew that his shorter companion wanted to tell him something.

Esteban listened intently as his companion whispered in his ear. Ricardo made sense. How would Carson's friends have known to meet him here at the trading post? They would have had to be on the road driving when Carson ran out of gas. Ricardo had guessed that the meeting of the five people was set up before Carson ever left Washington state. Nothing else made any sense. Esteban decided not to tell General Brown what they were thinking. Carson and his friends were close, and he would find them.

"Ethan, we have got to get moving," General Brown stated. "If they are heading for Canada, we need to close down the border. And I, for one, believe that is just where they are going. We'll set up a command post at the border crossing at Carway. It is on the way to Cardston. They will have to go through the park. The road is passable, but it's not open to the public yet. Still, I think that's where they are going. I just hope we're not too late."

"General, we would like to stay around Kalispell for a few hours. The three men from Portland may have stayed in the local area last night. Possibly we can find out where and then see if they left any clue as to their future intentions. Could you have one of the choppers drop us off in Kalispell? Someplace where we can rent a car."

"No problem. Come with me. We'll even arrange the rental for you," General Brown said, thinking that he would just as soon drop the civilian CIA men off so that he could do his job. Carson Jeffers and his friends were headed for Canada, and he was going to stop them.

35

Blake kept watching for the *Burma Shave* signs. Nichole had said the turn-off was just after the last sign. She was reasonably sure the red and white markers were still there, as her dad had mentioned the signs when he visited her at Christmas time in Washington.

"On the right. There they are," Nichole said. One at a time the red and white signs passed by. The Montana winters had aged the wood of the signs, but they were still readable.

Blake read each sign as he slowed down.

"YOUR

   FACE

      SHOULD

         NEVER

            BE

               LEFT

               ALONE

            USE

         BURMA SHAVE"

Carson watched for the old road that took off to the left. Blake had seen it first and was already turning into the pine trees. To call the lane a road was probably a miscarriage of justice. It was filled with ruts and holes caused by the snows of the past winter. "Does it get any better?" Carson asked Nichole as she bounced against him in the front seat.

"Not a lot. By mid summer the county will grade the road, but they pretty well leave it alone until after Memorial Day. Everyone figures that it isn't used much until then."

It took them almost twenty minutes to cover the seven miles through the trees. Carson had noticed that there were almost no cabins or buildings after the first few miles. When he asked Nichole why, she explained that most of the land belonged to the National Forest Service. The hunting lodge that her dad and his partners owned was built on one of the few parcels of private land left anywhere near the Hungry Horse Dam. Everyone was quiet as Nichole guided Blake past the few turnoffs that would have left them stranded in the forest, or swimming in Swan Lake itself.

"I would think that your dad would have really appreciated your place on the sound," Carson mentioned to Nichole as they approached the lodge from the west.

"Both he and my mother love it. Everyone in the family has always enjoyed living close to nature." She pointed at the smaller lane that cut off before you got to the lodge. "If you go down that small road for about a quarter of a mile, you will get to the air strip I was telling you about."

"Blake, take the lane," Carson said. "Let's check it out." Looking back at Nichole, he asked, "Are there any out-buildings near the strip where we could hide the car?" He knew that eventually there might be an air search, and a white rental car might just stick out.

"You have to remember that I haven't been here in almost seven years. The last time I was here, Dad was talking about building a maintenance shed or something. I don't really know if he did or not."

Blake bounced with the rest of the passengers as they drove through the trees. "Are you sure there is a landing strip here?" he asked. "It just looks like a lot of trees to me."

Suddenly they broke out of the trees and were into a grassy meadow. The road paralleled a very adequate landing strip. There were a few larger clumps of grass growing on the strip, but it had definitely been maintained. Carson noticed the wind sock that was blowing straight down the runway from the north. Whoever had designed the strip had taken the wind into account. If this was the prevailing direction of the breezes, you could forget about taking off or landing in a cross wind. He guessed the strip was close to four thousand feet in length. Unless it was a hot day, you could count on being able to get out of here. Then he remembered that their transportation was sitting high in a meadow some thirty miles away, hopefully still covered with sage brush.

Nichole tapped Carson on the shoulder and pointed to the wooden structure that was almost hidden under the towering pines to the left. "That building is new. Maybe we can hide the car there."

Michael leaned over the back seat and spoke to Carson. "It looks like a hanger. Any chance there is a plane in there?"

"I doubt it," Carson said as Blake pulled up beside the three thousand square foot building. He opened the door and got out of the car, the rest of the group following closely behind. Carson tried both the hanger doors as well as the side door. Everything was locked. The two windows had shutters closed against them to protect the glass from the January snows. They weren't locked, and he pushed one of the shutters back. Carson broke into a smile when he looked through the glass panes.

"What is it?" Jim asked from the back of the group. He had seen Carson's face light up as the shutter was flung back against the wooden side of the building.

"A plane," Carson answered, talking more to himself than to Jim or anyone else. "It's a small twin. Either a Cessna or a Piper." He picked up a rock and busted a small pane in the window. Reaching inside, he opened the window and then leaped up and crawled through. Less than a minute later he opened the side door of the hanger, and let the others in.

Blake immediately saw that there was plenty of room to park the sedan and asked Jim to open the hanger door while he drove the car inside.

Carson watched as Blake started the white Buick and drove into the safety of the hanger. "Where did he get the car?" he asked Michael.

"Blake rented it from an agency in Portland. He used a fake name and rented it with cash, leaving a large deposit. I gave him the money from the cash I took from the safe."

It was like a game of *Follow The Leader*. Where ever Carson walked, everyone else followed. He took a few minutes to walk around the twin engine aircraft before he spoke. "The Seneca III is a turbo charged aircraft and can carry five passengers plus the pilot with very light fuel. With four fairly heavy men and one woman, I would guess that we could take off with enough fuel to fly four or five hundred miles, maybe more."

"What do you have in mind?" asked Michael.

"To tell you the truth, I don't really know. This plane might be the only way out of here. In the next couple of days we are going to come up with a plan to try and turn this nightmare around, and I can guarantee you that this plane will probably play a part in it. Why do you think it's here, Nichole?"

She had crossed to a metal desk set against the door and was reading some papers fastened to a clipboard. "According to this, Dad and his partners bought the plane so that they could go fishing in Canada or just fly to one of the larger airports. They have had the plane for about 16 months, which is when I would guess they built the hanger."

Carson closed the hanger door and said, "Let's walk up to the lodge and get settled. We'll leave the car where it is for now. Nichole, do you want to lead the way?"

It took them about fifteen minutes to walk back through the trees and up to the mountain cabin. Nichole found a key hidden behind a rock in the fireplace stone. "Dad put this here many years ago, and everyone has always used it whenever they forget their keys."

Michael commented, "I'd say we're pretty lucky it's still there."

To call the lodge a cabin would be a gross understatement. The front door opened onto a split level landing that was twenty feet across. Carson followed Nichole into the tile covered entryway and leaned the shotgun against the wall behind the front door. Nichole explained that the stairs going up to the right of the log structure led to four bedrooms, each with a separate bath. She took them up the stairs and showed the three men where each could sleep. Nothing was said about Carson's sleeping arrangements, but it was understood that he and Nichole would take the last room on the right. Nichole took the group back down to the Great Room that was connected to a library and a large kitchen. The library, kitchen, bathroom, and laundry room were situated under the four sleeping rooms. The Great Room was open to the exposed log rafters. The ceiling must have been twenty feet off the ground. There were three massive windows that looked down on the forest. Three to four miles away you could see Swan Lake. Carson estimated the large room to be more than fifty feet long.

Michael spoke for the group when he asked Nichole, "What does your father do to afford this place? It had to cost way more than a million, and that doesn't count the land and the airstrip."

Nichole smiled at Carson and answered, "Have you heard of Neil Sorenson?"

"The writer?" asked Jim as it suddenly dawned on him who Nichole Lewis was. "Neil Sorenson is your father?"

"One and the same," answered Nichole. She then explained to everyone how her father and his partners came to purchase the lodge and surrounding property. While she talked, Jim and Michael opened the doors to the library and gazed at literally thousands of books. What caught their attention, however, was not the books. They went over to a section of the large room where several computers were sitting on a built-in working station. All the machines, with the exception of the portable lap top, were connected to a surge protector.

"I thought you said that your father and his partners were writers, not software programmers," Jim said.

Nichole led the other two men into the adjoining room and sat down at one of the computers. She looked around for a minute and then turned on one of the machines. "Research is the key to the success of any book, whether it be a historical novel like Dad's, or non-fiction expositions like his partners write." Rapidly, her fingers started moving across the key board, with symbols appearing on the screen in front of her.

Michael came and watched what was appearing on the monitor. After a minute or two he said, "You have accessed the Library of Congress. I take it these systems have modem capability?"

"They do. Now, before you think that I'm extremely smart, forget it. At Christmas time when Dad and Mom came to visit, he explained in detail the system they had installed here at the lodge. He always believed that computers were the key to the future and wanted me to have every opportunity to take advantage of them."

Both Michael and Jim smiled at Carson, indicating their approval of Nichole's newly advertised talents. "Do you mind if I try it?" Jim asked as he sat down at the next station.

"Go ahead," she said.

Less than two minutes later, Jim announced to the group that they were in luck. He was going to be able to access the same data banks he had been using in Portland. "What this means," he said to Nichole and Carson, "is that we are no longer cut off from the outside world. Whatever is going on, we are going to know about it here in Montana."

Carson asked everyone to join him in the larger room. "I think we better bring each other up to date on what has happened to us, and most importantly, what each of us have discovered. Michael, why don't you go first?"

Michael took the next few minutes to brief Carson and Nichole on the shut down of ManTech in Portland. It was amazing to Michael that nothing seemed to get to Carson. He asked a few questions to make sure he understood what had been said, but emotionally, it didn't faze him. When Michael had finished explaining the demise of the Portland company, he opened a small gym bag and gave Carson the remaining portion of the cash he had taken from the safe. "I assume we are going to need this."

Carson then took almost forty-five minutes to bring everyone up to date on what he had seen and experienced. He started with his trip to see Nichole at her cabin on the sound. From time to time he asked Nichole to explain something. She took a minute to regress to how the pictures that seemed to start the whole thing had been taken. She also told more about hiding Carson in the cave. Blake took copious notes of the entire conversation.

Jim asked a question from time to time as Carson told about the two men who had come close to killing him several times. When Carson finally got to how they came to be at the Hungry Horse Trading Post, Jim stood and started speaking. He recounted how he had broken into secure computer systems and data bases across the country. "If we are ever caught, God forbid, I can guarantee you that they could put us away for years just because of my actions." He stopped for a minute and then added, "But, I personally think that is the least of our problems."

Michael then asked Jim if he had found anything new that might tie into what had happened to Carson.

Jim thought for a few minutes and then said, "I came across a couple of things. First, there is a reference to someone called Cleaner, or possibly someone is supposed to clean something up. This came up in both the autopsy report of Gunnery Sergeant Baker/Chapman, as well as in both the NTSB reports from Dallas and Los Angeles. My guess is that there is someone who uses the name Cleaner. Why a code name? I don't know.

"Second, I did some research on possible members of La Libertad Occidental who speak English or have traveled in the United States. There is very little information, and nothing concrete. Two men, however, fit the descriptions that Carson used for the men who tried to kill him at the hospital."

"They also tried in Seattle," Carson added.

Jim continued, as if he hadn't heard Carson's remark. "The man with the pony-tail might be Esteban Moreno, and his partner, in all likelihood, is Ricardo Gutierrez. They have worked together for years. Carson, you may have met, or at least seen, this Esteban fellow. He was in Punta Del Este at the same time you were last year at the trade conference."

"That's who you told me about after the hospital," Nichole said.

"Esteban Moreno has been known to use the name of Ethan Mabry. And you might find it interesting to know that Ethan Mabry was recently issued special CIA credentials."

"Doesn't the CIA know that Mabry is Moreno?" asked Carson.

Blake had been with Jim when he made these discoveries in Kelso, and up until now had remained quiet. He felt that he could explain this discrepancy. "Ethan Mabry has been used for independent, wet work for the agency for several years. We believe that the CIA may in fact know that Mabry is Moreno, but it is highly doubtful that they believe he had anything to do with the recent terrorist attacks. Otherwise, they would never have issued him the highly classified credentials.

"Carson, there's one other thing you should be aware of. I came up with the names of Esteban Moreno and Ricardo Gutierrez using a secure data base belonging to the CIA."

"Is that it?" asked Carson, puzzled why Jim was mentioning the CIA.

"Not quite. There was one other name listed as a leader and potential member of the terrorist organization, someone we all know."

"Who was that?" asked Michael, startled by this last bit of news.

Jim looked at Carson and answered, "Carson's name was the third name. Whoever is setting you up has penetrated the deepest CIA files."

Michael looked relieved. "That's not surprising after the articles in every newspaper and magazine. It all started with *The Wall Street Journal* piece and President Attwilder's news conference."

Jim held up his hand as if to stop Michael from continuing. "These entries that listed Carson as a possible terrorist and member of the LLO go back before the Dallas crash." The impact of what Jim just said now hit each of the people in the room.

"One last thing," Jim said as he sat down on one of the large, over-stuffed, brown leather chairs. Everyone waited for what he was going to say next. After his last revelations, they didn't have any idea of what it might be. "Remember I told you about the reference to the person called *Cleaner*? Anyway, I tried to figure out if any person named Cleaner existed in any of the other data bases. Just possibly, I thought we might get a lead on what was happening by going in this back door."

Michael was intrigued by this approach and asked, "Did you have any luck?"

"I'm not sure. I couldn't find any record of a person using the name of Cleaner who now works for-or has ever worked-for our government or any other intelligence organization." Jim looked at his notes and then went on. "I decided to try and access property tax records, deeds, and real estate transfer documents. It took a long time, but I might have hit on something, especially in light of the fact that Carson recognized this Esteban Moreno in Los Angeles."

The other four people in the room sat up in their chairs and gave the

27 year old computer genius their undivided attention. Carson motioned with a rolling movement of his right hand for Jim to finish his story.

"I found a beach front property on Dana Point, near Capistrano, California, that was owned by a trust called *Cleaner Movements*. By itself, this would not have meant anything, but I checked the utility bills for the property. For the past two years they have been paid by one Ethan Mabry, whom we now believe is Esteban Moreno. Possibly this is the U.S. residence of our pony-tailed assassin."

Michael asked Jim if he could try to confirm the presence of Esteban Moreno at Dana Point in the past few weeks.

"I was working on that when we left Kelso, Washington. With Nichole's permission, I would like to use the computer system to continue that effort."

Nichole nodded and said, "Go right ahead. It all there. Use whatever you want."

36

Nichole and the four men sat around the pine table in the country kitchen of the Montana hunting lodge. It had taken close to four hours before everyone was satisfied they had digested the experiences and discoveries of the others, and Blake had been the first to mention the fact that he was starving. Carson pushed his empty soup bowl away from the edge of the table, moving his chair back as he did so. "Nichole, some day I hope to be able to thank your dad for the use of his lodge, as well as for the food."

"Canned soup is not really a lot to be thankful for," Nichole answered, finishing the remaining portion of her chicken broth. "Still, it really hit the spot."

Blake stood, taking his bowl and putting it in the sink. "Michael, how would you like to take an hour or two and see what the country is like around the house? Whoever is behind this madness is going to be searching this whole area when they find the plane Carson left in that high valley he told us about."

"Sounds like a good idea. What about weapons? Besides the two .38's that you had in the car, what else do we have to defend this place?"

"There is the shotgun we brought with us from Nichole's cabin," Carson said, by now understanding the need of some kind of active defense.

Blake placed one knee on the floor beside Nichole and bent down to ask her a question. In a minute, the two of them went back into the library of the lodge. Pushing on the base of a mounted duck, Nichole opened a hidden room about eight by ten feet. There were rifles and shotguns mounted on three of the walls. The fourth wall was taken up by a large cabinet. Opening the drawers, Nichole showed the group a large selection of ammunition.

"I forgot for a while that this is a hunting lodge. Dad and his friends keep a supply of hunting weapons here. The main reason they chose to build a secret room was for safety in the event that someone broke in. Not just safety for the weapons, but they didn't want to be responsible if the weapons were used unwisely." Carson, Michael, and Jim listened as Nichole explained the purpose of the secret gun closet.

Blake took a 30-30 lever action rifle from the wall and handed it to Michael. He walked over to the built-in pine cabinet and grabbed a box of ammunition for the rifle. "Take this with you, Michael. The shotgun doesn't have enough range, and I want to walk around the perimeter of the entire property to see how prepared we are."

Carson nodded, "Sounds like a good idea, I'm going to go down to the hanger and go over the plane. It is probably in great condition, but I doubt if it has been flown for several months," he said as he picked up his windbreaker, that was now more green and black than white.

"I'll go with you," Nichole offered, more to have something to do than to actually lend any assistance.

Jim had already started walking towards the library. "I think I'll see if I can't find out some more about this Esteban Moreno. Hopefully, we can come up with a more concrete plan by this evening."

•   •   •

"Blake, what do you think is behind this whole business?" Michael asked, as they climbed the hill overlooking the meadow where the landing strip was laid out.

Stopping to take a breath, the ex-FBI agent answered, "If you believe the news reports, it's the LLO. Apparently, they want the United States government to pay a couple of billion dollars to help the oppressed minorities of South America."

"You sound like you don't believe it."

"It's not that I don't believe it, I just think that there is more to this whole thing than a fanatical terrorist action. Don't get me wrong, these bastards know what they are doing. Getting your hands on fifteen Stinger surface-to-air missiles was certainly no easy thing. Then to shoot down three separate domestic airliners without getting caught was another success for the LLO. It just seems that they are getting too much assistance from our own government for this whole thing to only be a mission of the LLO."

"Do you think President Attwilder and the present government will pay the ransom?" asked Michael.

"They can't, at least not publicly. Our country would never stand for being held hostage that way. What we could do about it is anyone's guess. But, yes, they will try to find a way to pay these criminals off. Remember the Iran Contra scandal? Most people forget that we were only trying to buy back innocent civilians. If the government was willing to risk so much to get back less than ten men, what do you think they would do to stop the deaths of thousands? They'll find a way to pay." Michael was impressed by Blake's analysis of the government's position, but then he had worked with the FBI for most of his adult life.

Blake pointed out the heavy tree line to the east. "I seriously doubt that anyone will try and come from that direction. If we are discovered, I think they will probably come in the same way we did. Just to be sure, let's walk up to the hill on the far side of the runway. I think we can see the whole place from there."

Michael changed the rifle from his left arm to his right and fell in behind Blake as he walked through the trees. "I'm still bothered by the objective in all this," he said as they made their way through the trees.

Blake didn't say anything, but he felt the same way. Somehow they had become pawns in a chess game, and he had never seen a game won with only pawns.

• • •

Jim enjoyed the challenge of doing something that was supposed to be impossible. Finding the property on Dana Point had been more luck than skill, but now that he knew about the house, he was determined to try and learn as much about it as possible. The first thing he did was to re-verify the fact that the property was, in fact, owned by a trust called the Cleaner Movement. He backtracked his steps with the utility company and verified that Ethan Mabry had indeed been paying the utility bills. Satisfied that he was still on the right track, he created a computer file and stored the information. Then he reviewed the notes in his notebook, trying to come up with an idea that might reveal who had used the house during the past thirty days. Utility records were not enough to establish who, if anyone, was actually occupying the property at the present time. There had to be something more.

Finally, it dawned on him. He started typing instructions on the keyboard. While the system was searching for his request, he powered up the second computer and fed it a list of instructions and phone numbers to call. There wasn't much he could do while he waited for the search to take place. It might take thirty minutes, or it could take hours.

•   •   •

"What shape is it in?" Nichole asked Carson as he stepped over the flaps and onto the wing.

"From outward appearances, it'll fly. The two biggest problems I see is that it might not start, and we may not have enough fuel to go anywhere. I looked outside and didn't see any fuel tanks, at least above ground." He opened the door on the right side of the plane and crawled into the cockpit. The Piper Seneca is a six seat plane that can cruise at 160 knots. Given a good tail wind, it was possible to do better than 200 miles an hour.

Nichole waited beside the wing while Carson flipped switches and watched the control panel on the plane. "What do you think?" she asked through the door of the aircraft.

"The electrical system is dead. We may have a bad battery," he said, stepping back on the wing. Nichole moved out of his way as he went around to the left side of the aircraft and opened the door to the back four seats.

"We're in luck. The battery was just disconnected," he said, satisfied with his discovery. "I would guess your dad didn't want it to run down when no one was around."

"Did you hook it up?"

"I did. Now let's see what we have." Carson walked around to the front of the plane and took out a fuel tester from the side pocket of the plane. Pressing the tester under the wing, he drained out the water that had settled to the bottom of the tanks. When he was satisfied that the fuel was clean, he got back in the plane and turned on the magnetos. Fifteen seconds later he started the left engine. It ran rough for a few seconds and then purred as smooth as he had hoped. The right engine fired up immediately. Carson held the brakes and let both engines run for several minutes, burning out any carbon residue that might still be left from the last flight.

Nichole had walked away from the plane and was standing in the open door of the hanger. The exhaust from the two piston driven engines clouded up the hanger, but when Carson shut the plane down, it dissipated immediately.

"Now, all we need is a little more fuel. The tanks only have about a quarter tank in each one," Carson said as he unconsciously ran his hand through his now short brown hair.

Nichole knew that her dad would have a tank handy, and in all probability it would be buried. She walked around the side of the large hanger door and found a box set into the wall. Opening the box, she saw a large, black, coiled gas hose. Motioning to Carson, she told him what she had found.

He didn't act surprised, as he had found the switch to turn on the hidden pumps on the opposite side of the wall. "Maybe our luck is starting to change," he said as he pulled out the hose to check its condition.

•   •   •

Blake and Michael were satisfied that any intruders would have to come from the front of the lodge. To get to the back of Neil Sorenson's property, you would have to first cross Hungry Horse Reservoir and then hike 15 miles through the rocks and cliffs of Flathead National Forest.

"I guess we should start back. Nobody is going to try and approach from the rear of the property," Blake said as they looked down from the hill.

"It's possible they could still try and flank us, couldn't they?" Michael asked the more experienced veteran.

"Not only possible, it's almost a certainty. If they discover where we are, they will watch the front and then come in from the side of the property. To tell you the truth, Michael, we had better hope they don't find us. At least not until we want them to!"

"What do you mean *want them to*?"

"We have all had a few hours to think about what is happening to us. Each of us has been brought up to date on what the others have discovered. Now, it's time to put together a plan. Let's hope that Jim has been able to find something out about this Esteban Moreno."

• • •

Carson closed the door to the hanger, shutting off the inside lights as he did so. The afternoon sun was still bright, and even in late spring, the smell of the meadow was already strong. He took Nichole by the hand and started walking down the air strip, away from the lodge. "One last thing. We need to make sure that there are no large rocks or pieces of wood that may have ended up on the strip over the winter. If we see anything, let's just throw it over to the side."

They walked together, stopping from time to time to remove some small obstruction from the grass strip. Carson could tell that the strip might get a little soft right after a rain storm, but all in all it was an excellent piece of work. He stopped and took a heavy stick and dug down in the grass. It was still frozen two or three inches below the surface. "Nichole, have you thought about what you would like to do when this is all over?" Carson waited for her to answer. The main purpose in asking the question was to give her some form of confidence that there might, somehow, be an end to the nightmare.

"Not really. I don't know if I want to fly anymore. It's not that I'm afraid of flying, because I'm not. I just don't know if I could stand dealing with the memories of what has happened to us in the past few weeks. And every time we took off, I know that I would be thinking of Salt Lake and Los Angeles. How about you? What would you like to do?"

Carson hadn't really expected her to reverse the question on him, but as he thought about it, he realized that he didn't have any idea. His son was dead, his business destroyed, everything he had owned or controlled was gone, and he was being hunted by his own government as an international terrorist. Finally, he said, "I don't know. The first thing I need to do is to stop this madness. After that, we'll just have to see."

They had reached the end of the 4,000 foot air strip. The meadow continued on for another half mile before ending in a stand of large pine trees. Pointing to a path that led back through the trees, Nichole kept her other arm wrapped around Carson's. "Let's go back that way," she said. "It's an easy walk, and I'll show you a spring where I used to come and think."

Carson smiled and started walking towards the path. "Nichole, do you ever feel like you're swimming in a river, being rushed out to sea?" he asked.

She was astonished at the insight he had into her thoughts. "It's as if I'm alone in an uncontrollable current, and there is no way to get out of the river," she said.

Taking her hand in his, he stopped and held it to his heart. He whispered gently, as if he didn't want to disturb the air around him, "Nichole, you aren't alone anymore."

Fifteen minutes after entering the dark green pines, they emerged in a clearing covered with the early wild flowers of Montana. It was as if a blanket of colors covered the grass around the pool. "Feel the water," Nichole said.

"It's warm," Carson answered as he put his hand in the pond. "How does that happen?"

"Dad told me that it was caused by geothermal pressure from deep in the earth. Usually, when you have warm geothermal water, it is fairly alkaline, but not this. The water is as pure as you could ever hope. It is just warm. Ice never forms on this pond. Because of the warm water the flowers come earlier and stay longer." Nichole led Carson to some large flat rocks that extended into the seclusion of the warm mountain waters.

Sitting on the rock, Carson took off the timberline oxfords he had been wearing for almost a week. Putting his feet in the warm water, he felt more refreshed than he could remember. Putting both hands behind his neck, he leaned back and looked up at the blue sky. "It doesn't seem possible that everything is coming apart, especially when you have all this around you," he said as he looked at the majesty of the Big Sky Country.

Nichole removed her hiking shoes and laid down beside Carson on the rocks. "Let's go in the water," she said. "It's clean and you already know it's warm."

Carson saw a bull elk cross the meadow and head into the forest. He held Nichole's hand and realized that nothing seemed more important at this moment in time than taking her into the warmth of the pool. He slipped his right arm around her waist and undid the top button of her Levis, pulling her closer to him, almost in the same movement. Using his other hand to unfasten the front of her blouse, Carson felt himself slipping into another world, one where planes were not being shot down and people weren't dying.

Nichole helped Carson remove her pants. While standing on the rocks, she turned her head to his. Their lips touched, and they kissed for what seemed a long time. Carson undid his pants and slipped off his shirt. Together they slid into the warmth of the pond. He found her mouth again, open and inviting, more hungry than before. Wrapping his arms around her, he felt the soft tissue of her breast flatten against his chest, her hardened nipples causing a rippling in his tightened stomach. What had started out as an embrace now seemed like an unquenchable flame. Treading water, Carson felt Nichole wrap her long slender legs around his waist. She dropped her hips further down his body until he was able to enter the center of her total being. Slowly, never rushing, Carson moved in time with the soft current caused by the deep spring erupting from the center of the earth. He felt himself slip into a heaven he had never dreamed existed. Nichole almost stopped moving. Firmly, she pressed her dark pubic hair tighter against his pelvis. Carson felt her shudder, first once, and then again and again. She was crying, her tears disappearing into the waters of the pool.

Carson kissed her gently on the forehead and then on each of her cheeks, holding her securely in his arms. Together they were one. They could hear the whisper of the pines high over their heads. At least for now, they both felt safe.

•   •   •

Jim looked up at the computer, watching the information race down the screen. After several moments, the lines stopped moving, and the screen was still. He read what was listed on the monitor and smiled. "Perhaps, we might have a chance after all," he thought.

Out of habit, he dumped the information into the file he had created. It was labeled Dana Point. The information was saved almost instantaneously. Jim turned on the printer and gave the command to print the contents of the Dana Point file. It was only three sheets, but the information was startling. Clearing the screen, he got ready to exit the program.

"Who's there?" he asked. Startled by the sudden air current coming in from the door of the library, he waited for his friends to enter the book-filled room.

The three white papers from the printer fell onto the shiny pine floor.

37

Ricardo crept around to the back side of the two story log structure. He waited under the landing leading up to the second floor, and once satisfied he hadn't alerted anyone to their presence, he slowly climbed the rough sawn, wooden steps. He took them one at a time, stopping after each step to listen for movement from inside the house.

Esteban gave Ricardo two minutes to work his way round to the back of the building. They had left the four wheel drive jeep a half mile back on the road, hidden in the thick underbrush of the pines. It seemed much longer than six hours since General Brown had dropped them off at the Kalispell Airport. Hertz had come through as promised, and the black jeep was waiting under the name of Ethan Mabry.

Esteban had disliked using the credit card, but with the General literally watching his every move, he didn't have much of a choice. General Brown had selected the jeep in order for Esteban, or Ethan Mabry, to be able to later cross Glacier Park and join them at the border crossing, where the command post would be set up. The general was positive Carson was going to change cars to a four wheel drive. It was the only way he would be able to cross the high road through the park. As Esteban was waiting for his VISA to be approved, he listened to the Air Force general explain how the white car was probably hidden for good by now. There was no doubt in the officer's mind that Carson's friends had arranged a second vehicle and were now heading for Canada.

Esteban hadn't thought so. If Carson was planning on meeting the others in Big Fork, there was little doubt in the mind of the Latin that their true destination was close by. He knew that Carson hadn't planned on landing in the high valley above Big Fork. That had been an accident, a lucky one, but still an accident. As he thought about it, Carson must have been planning on landing somewhere close. Kalispell was too far away from Big Fork. His friends would never have known to meet him at the trading post.

After the general flew off to set up his command post, Esteban and Ricardo had driven back down Highway 35 to the Big Fork area. It was possible that Carson had planned on landing on a road, but Esteban doubted it. Carson was too good a pilot to risk a road landing unless it were an emergency. "No," he thought, "Carson Jeffers was trying to make it to some kind of landing strip." The closest airport with a regular runway was Kalispell, and Esteban had already crossed that out. It had to be a private air strip, probably one used by farmers or rich land owners who only came once or twice a year.

They had started asking for directions to the air strip in the town of Creston, and then moved on to Somers. When people asked what they were talking about, Esteban told them they were meeting five other members of a hunting party. Esteban told them he had arrived early but had forgotten the name of the private strip where they were supposed to meet. Three separate strips that passed for runways were quickly eliminated. Finally, in Swan Lake, an attendant at a filling station told them about the hunting lodge owned by the group of outsiders. It had a landing strip, but he didn't think anyone had been there all winter. Esteban thanked the man and asked for directions. Just before they made the turn off Highway 35, he saw a farmer who had been working on a tractor in a hay field. The old man explained that he was going to till up the entire field but had been broken down for the better part of the day. Yes, he had seen a white sedan with five people in it. They had turned off the road right after the Burma Shave signs.

Esteban knew he had found Carson Jeffers and his friends. Considering what was at stake, he would just as soon leave General

Brown and his troops out of the picture. He decided that they could keep searching for Carson in the national park.

Esteban listened for sounds from the lodge. It was quiet. He guessed that they were all gathered together, trying to decide what evil force had come into their lives. With a calloused smirk on his face, he stepped out of the bushes beside the porch and tried the door. It was unlocked. They must be inside.

As he slipped into the entryway he saw the shotgun leaned against the door. Deciding it was safer to take it with him than leaving it for one of the others, he stepped down into the Great Room. The front door was still open, the air rushing in from outside. He could see Ricardo quietly opening the doors in the hall above him. So far no one had seen them. He wondered where everyone was.

He heard a voice cry out from the open doors off the Great Room. Leaping down the stairs, he pushed the French doors the rest of the way open. Books lined the walls, but his attention was centered on a young man in his twenties, holding some paper he had just removed from a printer.

The man looked at the top page of the papers he was holding, recognition showing on his face. The papers floated to the floor as the man dived towards the stuffed duck on the far wall. Esteban thought he must have a weapon hidden close by. He acted instinctively, raising the shotgun as he moved. The blast from the barrel literally altered the trajectory of Jim's body. He was blown against the wall of books, many of them falling on his now still body. Esteban hadn't wanted to alert anyone, but the man had left him no choice. Ricardo came running down the steps, his pistol in the ready position.

"What happened?" Ricardo asked, surveying the damage from the shotgun. The man's face was almost unrecognizable as being male or female. Seventy-five percent of the blast from the weapon had hit him square in the head and shoulders. Ricardo doubted that he had lived long enough to even know what happened to him.

"I thought he was going for a gun," Esteban said as he looked for the hidden weapon.

Anticipating Esteban's next question, Ricardo said, "The place is empty. The other four are outside somewhere, and they will have certainly heard the shotgun. Any surprise we may have had is gone."

Esteban wasn't listening to what he was saying. He had picked up the papers the young man had been holding. It was evident why the man had recognized him. The top paper was entitled Ethan Mabry and had a picture of himself, the same picture used on his American passport. The rest of the paper had several sections. One of them listed every credit card, VISA, American Express, and Diners Club that had been issued through the Cleaner. The rest of the paper had a list of all the transactions from all of the cards during the past year. During the last 90 days there was only one entry, and it was for a VISA card used that same day at the Hertz Agency in Kalispell.

Esteban picked up the second paper. It was a copy of a temporary registration of a used van purchased from *Rent a Wreck* in San Diego, California. He noticed the date of the registration application had been the day after the crash of flight 1058 in Los Angeles.

The last paper was entitled *Dana Point*. He almost choked when he read those two words. The paper had a listing of fast food restaurants, pizza parlors, and other eating establishments that deliver in the Dana Point area. He read down the list and found that three of them had an address and a date next to the name of their restaurant. The address was the house on Dana Point. The dates were all within the last thirty days.

"We have been compromised!" he yelled at Ricardo. "Let's get out of here."

"What about Jeffers?" Ricardo asked, as he followed Esteban up the steps. He noticed that his pony-tailed companion had dropped the shotgun, and taken the papers with him.

"Apparently they've gone. We didn't see the car when we came in. Whatever the case, we can't sit around waiting for them. I guarantee that we'll get all of them," he said, referring to Carson and the others. "Somehow, they found out about Dana Point. We have to get there, and I mean soon."

Ricardo understood the importance of Dana Point, and ran to catch up to Esteban as they headed down the lane towards their car. Running beside his friend, Ricardo asked, "How are we going to get to California?"

"We'll go back to Kalispell and catch the first flight to Salt Lake, and then on to Southern California."

•   •   •

Carson and Nichole were almost back to the house when they heard the reverberating blast of the shotgun. "Jim," Carson yelled to Nichole as he leapt ahead, running for the house. He already knew that it was too late. There had only been one shot. Still, he kept running, Nichole falling slightly behind him.

Blake and Michael had been running from the opposite direction and met Carson when he reached the porch. Blake spoke first. "I think they're gone. I saw two men running into the woods about two minutes after the shotgun sounded. We were going to chase them, but wanted to check on Jim first."

Carson started to go through the open front door, but Blake pulled him aside, his pistol drawn and held out in front of him, both hands wrapped around the grip. Michael had the 30-30 cocked and held in front of him shoulder high.

"Michael, you check upstairs. Carson and I will go down." Michael started up the stairs, taking the steps two at a time.

Nichole had reached the steps, panting and out of breath. "What happened?" she asked.

"We don't know yet. Wait here," Carson said, as he followed Blake down the steps to the Great Room. Nichole waited two or three seconds, and then followed the men down the steps.

"Oh, God, no!" screamed Carson as he knelt beside Jim. Blood was everywhere. Blake was continuing to search the bottom floor of the lodge, including the kitchen and storage area.

Nichole walked across the room. She leaned over and put her arms around Carson. "When will it stop?" she asked.

Carson looked up at her, his eyes glassy but still focused. "They've gone too far. I will kill them, and if I rot in hell for the act, so be it!"

Nichole stepped back, aware of a side of Carson she must have not recognized before. He wanted revenge. She knew his anger had reached a boiling point. It wasn't that he was that close to Jim, it was just the final straw.

Blake and Michael came into the library together. Michael howled, "Jim!"

38

How long will the layover in Salt Lake be?" Esteban asked the short haired attendant at the Omega desk in the Kalispell Airport.

"With the cutback in flights, I'm afraid you will have to wait for almost an hour and a half. But you will still arrive tonight around 9:00."

"I guess that will have to do," he said, paying for both tickets with cash. The Cleaner had taught him long ago that you should always have at least $5,000 in cash with you whenever you traveled. The lack of money was not a problem to Esteban. He had as much as he could spend. Still, he was always looking for more.

Ricardo came through the doors of the terminal just as Esteban was finishing paying for the tickets. "It's parked in long term parking. If General Brown calls and asks Hertz if we have turned in the jeep, they will tell him no."

Esteban nodded and said, "It's better that way. Our plane leaves in about 35 minutes."

•   •   •

"Why did they just leave so suddenly? It doesn't make any sense. They came here to kill us, but stopped short of completing the job," Blake asked as he covered Jim's body with the blanket Michael had brought down from one of the upstairs bedrooms.

Nichole's emotions were to the numb stage, as she asked, "Did he have a family? I mean was he married? He told me he was single, but I thought he might have been joking."

"No, Nichole, he wasn't married," Michael said as he picked up a few of the books that had fallen on his friend. "At least he wasn't married to a woman. He spent all his spare time on the computer. It wasn't that he didn't like women, he just never seemed to have time to start a relationship."

"How about parents?" she asked.

"They live back east in upper New York somewhere. We'll have to let them know, but right now is not the best time," added Carson. The senior executive was looking at the computers, which were still on. The screens were blank, but they were running. "What had Jim discovered that might have surprised the two killers? Whatever it was, I guarantee you that he wanted us to know it."

Michael moved over to the machines and noticed that the printer was on. "There's nothing in the tray, but it looks like Jim had used the laser printer. Possibly, that might have been what made the two men leave so suddenly."

Nichole walked over to the work station and started using the keyboard. Everyone watched as she worked, confident that she knew what she was doing. Quickly, she started pulling up directories and comparing the last entry times against the time on her watch. Three minutes later, the screen of her monitor started rolling and finally coming to a halt. Turning to check that the printer was still on, she pressed the print command. "Unless I'm mistaken, whatever Jim was working on should be coming off the printer right now."

Carson, Michael, and Blake waited at the printer as the three sheets of paper slid into the paper tray. Carson picked up the first paper, while Michael and Blake took the second and third sheets. Trading papers after a few seconds, they all realized what they had. Nichole already had it figured out.

"We know that Ethan Mabry and Esteban Moreno are one and the same person," Carson said to Nichole as he showed her the photo of Ethan Mabry. "Why he would use a credit card to rent a car here in Kalispell seems odd, but he did. The two men who killed Jim were undoubtedly Esteban Moreno and Ricardo Gutierrez. Esteban had been at this house in Dana Point several times in the past month. The fact that we know about it frightened Esteban into fleeing. Dana Point must hold some secret to this entire operation."

"Then, you think that Esteban is heading for Dana Point?" asked Michael.

Blake answered for him. "He has to. Whatever he thought Jim found out about Dana Point was more important than killing the rest of us, at least for now." Pausing for a second, he added, "Because none of us were in the house, and the car was hidden from view, I would guess that this Moreno thought we might have already started for Dana Point."

"Then you think he'll try again?" asked Nichole as she looked at Jim's body laying on the floor.

"Oh, he'll keep trying until we're dead," Carson said. "Only we're going after him first."

"What do you mean?" asked Michael.

"I'm going to fly to Dana Point and see what is so damned important that it caused him to kill Jim and then leave without trying to finish off the rest of us. Maybe, he thought we were gone, but I think these guys were just impatient enough to put our deaths on the back burner. At least for the moment," he added.

"When do you want to go?" asked Blake, implying that he was planning on going with him.

"It's only 4:00 p.m. in California. I want to leave within the hour." He picked up the shotgun that had been used to kill his friend and set it on the table. "Are you going with me, Blake?"

"Wouldn't miss it. Whoever got Jim will pay. Do you mind if we use some of your weapons in the gun closet?" he asked Nichole, who had become suddenly quiet.

Her response wasn't a direct answer to his question. "You both need to stop and think for a moment. These men have tried to kill Carson on at least three or four separate occasions, and now one of them killed Jim Tedrow. They are undoubtedly responsible for the death of Kelly as well as over a thousand other innocent people. Somehow they have been able to transfer responsibility for all this to Carson and myself. Now you think that you can just waltz down and take them both out with a few shotguns and hunting rifles. Slow down and listen to what you are saying."

"She's got a point," Michael said.

"She's got more than a point," Carson said as he came and stood beside the frightened woman. "Everything she just said is true. I don't think I have a ghost of a chance in killing these two men, but that is exactly what I'm going to try and do. It's not just for Kelly and Jim. But you all need to remember that the LLO has promised to continue this reign of terror. The only way we can possibly stop it is to take out Esteban Moreno and Ricardo Gutierrez, and that may not even be enough to do it."

"What should we do about Jim?" Michael asked.

Nichole looked at the body and then said to the three men, "Come with me. I'll show you something." Just off the laundry and storage room was a door they hadn't opened. Nichole turned on a light and took them to the basement, where there was a giant walk in cooler. "Dad and his friends built this room to store their elk and deer until they could get the meat to a processor. Let's put Jim in here until we can get his body back to his parents."

No one disagreed with the forceful lady. Fifteen minutes later, they had carried the body down the stairs and laid it on the floor of the cooler. The cold of the room must have dried up their tear ducts, as none of them cried. They all just remained silent until the door was shut.

When they came back upstairs, Carson told Blake to gather up what weapons he thought they could use and then to meet him at the hanger. He would go and pre-flight the plane and fill the tanks with gas.

"Michael, you and Nichole stay here. Maybe you can use the computers to feed us more information. As soon as we are finished in Dana Point, we'll meet both of you back here."

"You're sure you don't want me to go with you?" Michael asked.

"No, I think we are going to need you here. See if you can't figure out exactly what Jim was working on." Carson picked up the phone next to the computers and memorized the number, starting with the area code 406. "We'll call you on this number."

Nichole had remained calm while Carson gave instructions to Michael, but now she spoke up. "I am not staying here. Carson, I got involved of my own free will, and now of my own free will, I'm going with you two. I don't know if I can help in California, but anything I could do here, Michael can do without me. Do you see that lap top computer there on the desk?"

Carson didn't answer, not knowing how to stop her from going on.

"That computer has fax and modem capability. It has the fastest processor available on the market. Whatever I could do with that machine in Montana can be done in California. Carson Jeffers, you will not leave me here in Montana never to see you again! I'm going."

Carson knew he was beaten. His only hope had been to keep Nichole out of harm's way, but she was her own boss, and he accepted what she had to say.

"OK, you can go. But will you let us try and take out Esteban Moreno?" he asked as the thunder crackled in the woods nearby. The thunderstorm had come in without anyone noticing. A lightning strike hit in the trees above the house.

"It looks like we'll wait until morning to leave," Carson said, looking out the windows at the towering dark clouds that were moving across the sky. He hadn't survived everything else in the past two weeks just to die in bad weather because he wasn't smart enough to stay on the ground. "We'll try and leave around 6:30 in the morning. We'll have to stop for gas on the way."

"Any problem in doing that?" asked Blake, fully aware of the search that was going on for Carson.

"I think we'll be all right. We'll stop in Tonapah and pay cash for the fuel. Everyone will have quit looking for the Citation by now. Any records that the FBO keeps will list the ID number of a Seneca III that is not wanted for anything. We'll chance it."

Nichole returned from the kitchen with some rags, a broom, and a dustpan. "If you all don't mind, I would like to clean up in here. I'm aware that it is evidence in a crime, but to tell you the truth, I don't really give a damn." She started sweeping as the other three men finished cleaning up the books and broken pieces of wood that had come loose from the shelves with the blast of the shotgun.

•   •   •

Esteban dropped Ricardo off below the house on Dana Point. Ricardo would disarm the elaborate security system until they parked the Lincoln in the garage. Once they were in the house, all the monitors would be turned on again. If anyone was going to follow him and try to gain access to his home, Esteban would know about it.

Five minutes later, Ricardo opened the garage door from inside. Esteban drove the rental car into the garage and hit the garage door opener. He knew that as soon as the door made contact with the small electronic contact, they would be protected from any unannounced intrusion.

"How long are we going to stay this time?" Ricardo asked as he followed his long-time companion into the house. The building was designed by Frank Lloyd Wright and was without question one of the most elaborate buildings he had ever built. It had stood the test of more than fifty years' exposure to the Pacific Ocean and its many storms.

"We will stay until tomorrow night. I have some things that I have to take care of before we leave. In all probability, we may never return. I checked the flight schedule, and even if Carson Jeffers decides to follow us, there is not another plane out of Kalispell until tomorrow afternoon. It would be this time tomorrow night before he could get here. And I seriously doubt that he wants to meet us again. Personally, I think they will try to slip across the border into Canada."

"Will we follow them?" asked Ricardo as he looked out across the lawn that led to the wooden steps that climbed down a hundred feet to the beach below.

"Oh, we'll follow him. We'll follow him and the woman until they are both dead. It's more than a job now. It's personal."

•   •   •

Michael closed the hanger door behind the Seneca. Carson had gotten up early and checked the weather and planned their flight. They were going to be flying VFR or visual flight rules, so they wouldn't have to file an official flight plan. He had filled the wing tanks and checked to make sure that all the deice equipment was functioning.

Several times during the night, Nichole woke him up and asked to just be held. Despite her performance in the library, she was frightened, badly frightened.

Carson taxied the plane to the south end of the grass strip. Turning around he asked Blake if he was all fastened in.

Blake checked to make sure his seat belt was fastened and the cabin door was shut. On the seat beside him there were two shotguns and the 30-30 lever action rifle. His two pistols, along with the lap top computer from the cabin, were underneath the blanket on the opposite seat. Raising his thumb to say yes, Blake closed his eyes.

Carson could tell that the rain had softened the strip, but they should still get off without any problem, even at over 7,000 feet. He wasn't disappointed that the wind was coming out of the north at almost ten knots. It would help create the lift they needed. Stopping at the end of the runway, he looked at Nichole who was sitting beside him, and keyed the mike. He was glad that her father had installed an intercom system in the 1984 Piper aircraft.

"Are you sure you want to go?" he asked as he started to run up the engines, checking the mags as he did so.

"Carson, we went over this during the night. I'm going and that is all there is to it."

He handed her the checklist he had taken from the seat pocket, asking her to read down the list of items as he readied the plane for take off. Her answer had been expected, but he wanted to ask one last time. In his own mind, he didn't give them one chance in a thousand of making it. They were literally making a flight into harm's way.

Carson used the rudders to keep the plane centered down the runway. As soon as he hit 75 knots, he pulled back on the yoke, careful not to stall the engine. He continued to climb as he turned downwind one last time. Michael was still standing by the hanger.

"Will we see him again?" Nichole asked over the intercom.

Carson didn't answer. He didn't know what to say. Slowly, he started to reduce the RPM's and lean out the mixture.

39

THURSDAY MORNING

Vice President Jason Wright arranged his papers on the dark wooden table in the White House subterranean basement. He had asked President Attwilder to have the meeting where absolutely no one would be aware of it. The President had readily agreed. None of the four people waiting at the table had slept for more than three or fours hours a night during the last three days. Less than twelve hours prior to the meeting of the Terrorist Task Force, President Attwilder had declared an Economic State of Emergency. No one was quite sure what it was, since it had never been declared before. The stock markets were closed, banks limited the amount of withdrawals, the prices of commodities and precious metals had gone through the roof, and the international dollar had plunged to record lows. It seemed unbelievable that all of this was taking place because of a terrorist scheme to blackmail the U.S. Government into paying $2 billion.

"I'm sorry you all had to wait, but I was meeting with the White House Cabinet," President Rolland Attwilder said, taking the seat next to Jason. "Everyone wants me to do something, but absolutely no one can tell me what that something is. I hope that you folks have more concrete suggestions than I received from the Secretary of the Treasury. Can you believe it? He actually wanted me to seize all foreign deposits in this country before our trading partners pull the plug on us and take their money and go home."

Hank Grishhold leaned over and spoke quietly to the President. Hank had left the cabinet meeting a few minutes before the President, not wanting any of the political appointees to guess as to where he and the President were going. Even before the meeting upstairs had ended, Hank knew that President Attwilder was being left with very few choices.

"Hank just reminded me that I am scheduled to make another public statement concerning our efforts to apprehend the terrorists from the LLO," the President stated. "The statement will be carried LIVE on all the national networks in less than 50 minutes. So let's get started. Jason, bring me up to speed on the developments of the last few hours."

Jason Wright dimmed the lights in the room, pushing a button that activated the slide projector. "As you can see by these pictures of the New York, Chicago, Atlanta, and Los Angeles airports, the airlines are virtually flying empty. Even the pilots and flight attendants have started an unofficial work stoppage. Not everyone is involved, but the word is that it will continue until the terrorists are apprehended." Moving to the next series of slides, Jason continued, "We are all aware of the disaster on Wall Street. Panic has spread throughout all our financial markets. If the President hadn't closed the stock market for the rest of the week, the loss of equity to investors would have reached more than $100 biilion." Jason continued to show the graphs and charts he had prepared, each one visually depicting the financial disaster sweeping through the American economy.

Switching the screen to a video display, Jason said, "What you see here are demonstrations by students, factory workers, even housewives. The country is at a breaking point. It is time to consider paying the demands of the LLO. I'm afraid we have no other choice."

Both Tom Folger and Seymour Dillan nodded their heads in agreement with what the Vice President was saying. The President's Chief of Staff wasn't quite so quick to agree. "The last missile was used last Friday," Hank said, looking at each of the men around the table. "What is the chance that the terrorists will give it up?"

President Attwilder took off his suit coat and placed it on the empty chair beside him, his lanky frame jutting out over the arm rests. "Hank, there is absolutely none. It's like the saying, 'not a snowball's chance in hell.' They are winning, and they know it. When it comes down to it, they will use the missiles again. They have already proved it. I think the only reason they haven't already taken out another aircraft is because they believe we are trying to raise the money. Speaking of which, Jason, how is Drew coming on the funds?"

Hank knew the President was right; he had only been hoping it wasn't so.

Vice President Wright turned off the slide projector. "I received a call from Drew Matthews in Geneva a little over 24 hours ago. He has set up a special account at the Bank of Switzerland where the funds can be deposited. All $2 billion has been committed. I won't name each of the companies, as it is probably better that we never discuss their names or their officers. The important thing is that the funds can be deposited within 24 hours. I have checked with *USA Today*, and our personal ad can be placed within an hour. Everything is in place. All you have to do is give the final word," he said, looking at the President.

President Attwilder started pacing behind the table. He was wearing burgundy colored ostrich boots. "I will commit to make the decision to pay the money no later than Monday morning. Until that time we are going to make every effort and use every resource available to us to apprehend these people and recover those missiles. And once this whole thing is finished, we are going to do something so that this never can happen again. What those measures will be, I don't know. And how we'll pay for them, Congress is going to have to decide."

Jason waited for the President to finish speaking, and then asked Tom Folger to bring everyone current on the efforts being used to apprehend Carson Jeffers.

Hank remained quiet, still not believing that Carson was a terrorist. But, if he was innocent, why didn't he just turn himself in and straighten out the entire mess. It just didn't make sense.

Tom asked Jason to dim the lights again. Everyone turned to the screen to watch the pictures. Tom first explained the investigative techniques that were being used. No stone was being left unturned. Every available agent had been assigned to this investigation. Now that the true threat of the missiles was known, the investigation was going much faster. "If we had thirty days, I could guarantee that we would recover the missiles," he said as he put up the next picture.

"But you don't have thirty days, Tom," Vice President Wright said, looking at the picture of the Cessna Citation partially covered by sage brush.

"I realize that, Mr. Vice President. We are concentrating our efforts in finding and apprehending Carson Jeffers. I, personally, have come to the conclusion that Jeffers is part of the LLO. This is the aircraft that he stole from the Port Townsend airport. He flew the plane from Washington state to this high valley just outside Glacier National Park. Canada is less than 100 miles away. We have determined that he crash landed the plane in this field and then met at least two or possibly three people who originally worked for his company in Portland." Tom changed the picture to a photo of the Hungry Horse Trading Post. "They met up here and headed north towards the border. General Brown, of Hill Air Force Base, attempted to close the border, but it is entirely possible that they have fled into Canada."

President Attwilder asked, "You said he joined up with two or three people at this place in Montana. Which was it, two or three?"

"At this point, I would guess it was three," he answered. "Another point of interest, originally, we thought there were only two people on the Citation when it left Port Townsend, but now we believe that Carson met the actual shooter of both the Salt Lake and Dallas missiles at the Port Townsend airport."

Scanning the slides he had prepared, Tom put back up the boot print that had been taken from both the crashes. Beside it he put another print. It matched identically. "This boot print was taken at the hanger where the Citation was stolen. We now believe that Carson picked up at least one of the shooters in Washington and then stole the Citation V with Nichole Lewis, heading for Canada."

Even Hank was now beginning to think he might have been mistaken about Carson Jeffers. There was just too much evidence against him.

Tom turned to the director of the CIA and asked him to explain what the CIA was doing in the effort to find Carson Jeffers.

"The FBI and CIA have joined forces in this investigation," Seymour said as he moved to the podium at the front of the table. "We also believe that Carson has escaped into Canada. One of our agents found a chart in the cockpit of the crashed Citation. It was marked up and detailed the flight path the Citation had taken from Port Townsend. The last line went through Kalispell to Cardston, Alberta. The Royal Mounted Police of Canada have virtually surrounded the Montana-Canada border. We feel confident that we will be able to apprehend Carson Jeffers within the next 72 hours."

"I hope so, Seymour," said the President. "That's all the time you have. There's something else you should all be aware of, if you aren't already. A few minutes ago, I said that we had until Monday. There is a reason for this. Hank, would you brief them on the meeting you just set up?"

Hank knew full well what the President was referring to. Early that morning Hank had set up a mini trade summit. It was to be held at President Attwilder's Santa Fe ranch the coming Monday. It was not, in fact, a trade summit of any kind; rather it was a meeting to save the absolute collapse of what was remaining of the United States economy. During the past 24 hours, Japan, Germany, France, China, Mexico, and even Canada had all called the President stating that they were going to liquidate every investment based in dollars. That was what prompted the President to close the stock market. If these trading partners took their investments back across our borders, it would hurt each of them dramatically, but it would destroy the dollar and bring down the final collapse of the stock market. For all intents and purposes, the United States would be destroyed. The country would have lost a war we didn't know we were fighting.

The Chief of Staff spoke in a strong, but deep, voice, "President Attwilder has invited the ranking political figures, prime minister, or president to join him at his ranch in New Mexico on Monday afternoon. Representatives from all our major trading partners will be there. At that time, he has promised to provide proof that this terrorist threat has been ended. If President Attwilder can't deliver, we are finished!" There was nothing further that needed to be said. Everyone at the table now understood the importance of the Monday deadline. Either Carson Jeffers and the LLO were going to be eliminated in the next three days, or the ransom would be paid.

40

Carson dialed in ATIS at 120.15 and listened for the advisory he would need to land at Carlsbad. The weather was clear, and he was making a VFR approach. Using his right hand, he dialed in 108.7 for the ILS approach. He always liked to know exactly where he was, and the instrument approach allowed him to know just that. Five miles east of the field he caught the glide slope and settled into a 500 foot per minute descent. "Is everyone fastened in?" he asked, just prior to again announcing his position to the other pilots in the area.

Nichole tugged on her seat belt and shoulder harness to insure that she was all set. Blake did the same in the rear seat of the plane. "All set back here," Blake yelled up to the front of the plane. "The Seneca is a great plane, but it's a little noisy on the inside."

This was the second landing they had made that morning. When they landed at Tonapah, Carson and Nichole had stayed in the plane. Blake paid for the fuel, using cash provided by Carson. There had been only one person on duty when they landed, and she never appeared the least bit suspicious. Blake told Nichole and Carson there were advisory notices, along with 8 x 10 pictures of both of them on the bulletin board in the office of the FBO. The pictures were no better than those previously printed in the newspaper, and Blake didn't think they would have been recognized if they had been standing right under the photographs.

Carson keyed the mike again. "This is November Papa Lima Four Three Four on a three mile final for 24." Changing to the intercom, he said to Nichole, "When we touch down, we'll do the same thing we did in Tonapah. Let's let Blake refuel the plane and arrange for the tie down. We want the plane fueled so that we can leave when we're finished."

Nichole listened to what he was saying, fully aware that he was trying to sound confident about their future. She wasn't nearly as confident as she would like to be. "Can Blake rent a car at the Carlsbad airport?" she asked.

Carson watched his instruments, making slight corrections to maintain the glide path. Without looking up he said, "They have a Hertz agency." There was a slight screech as the tires greased the runway. Carson used the brakes, turning off the runway, and taxied to the terminal. Taking off his headset, he asked Blake, "You all set?"

"No problem. I'll fuel the plane and then get the rental car. I'll come back to the plane and get the shotguns, rifles, and computer as soon as I've paid for the fuel. You can meet me down the road about a hundred yards."

"Sounds good. Dana Point is about 35 miles up the coast."

●   ●   ●

Esteban had used the car they rented at Los Angeles International and driven up the coast before it was even six o'clock in the morning. He hadn't wanted to leave anything to chance, and was back from his errand to Century City before Ricardo finished his late breakfast or early lunch. Ricardo had offered to go with him, but Esteban said it wasn't necessary.

"Everything go all right?" the shorter Latin asked.

"Fine. Everything's going to work out all right. As soon as I finish on the computer, we can leave. It should only take me an hour or so. I checked this morning, and there is another flight back to Kalispell that leaves Los Angeles at 5:55 this evening. We're going to be on it."

"What should we take with us?" Ricardo asked as he finished cutting the omelet on his plate.

"Take everything that could connect you with this place. As I told you yesterday, we might not be back. Once Shortfall is completed, we will be persona not grata in this country."

Ricardo didn't really care if they came back or not. With the bonus he was promised when the final payment was made, he could live anywhere in the world. It wasn't that he didn't believe in the cause of *La Libertad Occidental,* because he did. He just believed in money more! He picked up his dishes and put them in the sink. Looking out across the lawns to the edge of the cliff, he saw Esteban standing on the redwood deck looking down at the waves of the ocean beating against the rocks a hundred feet below.

●   ●   ●

Blake sat in the front seat with Carson. Nichole didn't mind the back. She was already a little tired of being cramped up. The Seneca had seemed very small after flying in an L-1011. She watched the ocean pass by them on the left, wondering what they would find at Dana Point.

Carson and Blake were quietly discussing the same thing. "I think we should set up some kind of safety point," Blake said, trying not to talk loud enough to alert Nichole. It was a futile effort, but Nichole kept her silence anyway.

"That's a good idea. We can't just drive up to the place and ask these two men to let us in," agreed Carson.

Blake reached in his pocket with his left hand and pulled out part of what was once the yellow pages. "I got this at the FBO in Carlsbad. It is a list of the motels in Dana Point. There is a nice place with quite a few rooms called The Sand Castle. It is just off Highway 1. Shall we go there?"

Carson read the advertisement for the motel and nodded his head yes. Turning around to the back seat, he spoke to Nichole. "I want you to stay at the motel until we find out what we're up against. I promise we won't try and enter the house until all three of us discuss our options."

"That's fine. I've got a few ideas that might help us."

"What are they?" Carson asked.

"Give me an hour or so on the computer, and I'll explain it to you."

Twenty five-minutes later, Blake pulled into the parking lot and went into the motel to register for two adjoining rooms. He paid cash and left a fifty dollar deposit for phone calls. The fewer opportunities they gave someone to recognize Carson and Nichole the better. Returning to the car, he looked over at Carson, realizing he hadn't mentioned the clean clothes that both of them had been wearing when they left Swan Lake. "Where did you get the clothes? I forgot to ask you," Blake said as he closed the car door.

"Dad and Carson are about the same size, and there were a few things in the lodge. I was able to find some clothes I had left there many years ago," Nichole said.

Blake looked at both of them and thought that casual fashions really hadn't changed that much. Carson still had his timberline shoes that looked much like boots but was wearing a faded pair of denim pants along with a button-down cotton plaid shirt. With the Levi jacket, he looked like he belonged back in Montana. Nichole had on jogging shoes, Levis, and a white pullover with a pony embroidered on the pocket. The Polo label never seems to go out of style. She was wearing the same windbreaker she had started out with six days earlier.

"Any problem in getting a room we can check into now? It's not even eleven o'clock California time?" Carson asked as Blake started the blue Ford Taurus.

"They weren't full last night, and we were able to get two rooms on the main floor. Not much of a view, but at least we have rooms."

"Where are the rooms?" Nichole asked, watching the office from her window.

Blake could see what she was thinking. He had thought of the same thing and requested rooms around the L shaped corner from the reception area. It wasn't that Nichole was being paranoid about being recognized, just careful.

"The rooms are around the corner, out of sight of the office and everyone coming and going at the motel," Blake answered, driving the car through the parking lot until he found a space in front of their rooms. Carson used his jacket to wrap up the guns, picking up the computer with his free hand. The rooms were standard twenty-year-old motel rooms. Each one had two queen sized beds, a formica dresser with draw-

ers and a spot for the television, and two chairs next to a lamp. The
phone sat on the edge of the dresser.

Carson opened the connecting door and said to Blake, "These are
fine. Let's take the car and drive out to the end of Dana Point and see
what we're up against. According to the information Jim left, the house
is located right on the cliffs overlooking the ocean." Carson paused for a
second, remembering the man who had provided this information.

Nichole came and stood by Carson. "I'll wait here. And remember
your promise. You're not going in the house until we come up with a
plan."

Carson leaned over and kissed her on the forehead. It was a natural
thing, and none of the three thought the gesture out of place. "I'll
remember. We'll be back in about an hour." Exiting the room, he took
the pistol from Blake's hand and stuffed it in his belt, under the back of
his Levi coat.

•   •   •

It only took Nichole a couple of minutes to figure out how to use the
modem on the computer. She turned on the computer, making sure she
had a connection through the phone jack on the desk. She was glad
Blake had left a deposit for the phone calls. Local calls were seventy five
cents each.

She called up a database her father had shown her. It had access
codes for literally almost anything. The program and data bank had been
developed by a group of college hackers-turned-programmers. So far,
the database was still accessible on the Internet, as long as you knew
where to look. It took her almost forty-five minutes before she was able
to get into the records of the San Diego County Building Department.
With the rash of brush and forest fires in California, she had figured that
older homes would have to be refitted with the new mandatory sprinkler
systems. The county's records were supposedly secure, but her father
had taught her some tricks that can be used to break into most of the
simpler systems.

Once she discovered the password used by most of the employees,
she started to work. As she typed on the keyboard, she thought it ironical

that both businesses and government agencies would install secure computer systems and then give the password to every employee. Usually, the passwords weren't changed, even after an employee was dismissed for poor performance.

Nichole stopped and looked at the screen. She had to use the curser to roll the diagram up and down. There on the screen in front of her were building diagrams for the house on Dana Point. Using the arrow keys on the lap top computer, she started searching the property, completely unobserved by the two men who were trying to kill her.

Carson and Blake had been gone for almost two hours. It was longer than they had planned, but Nichole believed Carson when he told her he would be back. She had been using the pen and paper she found next to the phone to copy the illustration that was still on the computer. At the bottom of the screen, she saw the notation to see another set of blueprints. Changing screens, she saw that the blueprints were for a maintenance shop and underground garage located west of the house. Realizing why the second set of plans had been referenced, she excitedly copied down the information.

•   •   •

Blake stopped the car at the end of the cul-de-sac and turned off the engine. The house on Dana Point was back down the road a quarter of a mile. Not wanting to arouse any suspicion from the men inside, or curiosity from the few neighbors who had estates on the dead end road, they had limited their initial appraisal of the house to three drive-bys. Each of them had been at least twenty minutes apart.

Carson stepped out of the car and looked down at the sandy beach below. "It looks too easy. These guys don't make foolish mistakes, and if they have all the power of the CIA behind them, the house has to be wired."

"That's exactly the way I see it," Blake answered. "Our main problem is that we don't know what type of security system they have and how to disable it. There are bound to be cameras and invisible laser beams that would sound an alarm. Unless we can figure out how to get in unobserved, we will never get out alive."

Carson continued to stare out over the cliff. About a quarter of a mile up the beach he could see a private skeet shooting club. Every few minutes he heard the sound of a shotgun firing at the clay pigeons. The only way down to the beach was a foot path that switched back and forth down a ravine directly at the end of the turn-around in the road. "It's got to be at least a hundred feet up from the beach to the top of the cliff. I don't think that would be the smartest way in. Even if we could climb the cliff without falling, I'm sure they would have any approach from that direction wired with a silent alarm. I don't know, Blake, did we come here for nothing?"

Blake couldn't think of any way to sneak into the house. Finally, he said, "Let's go back to the motel and see if we can't think of something. It's not helping for us to remain here. Eventually, someone is going to get curious as to why we are driving around."

• • •

Carson couldn't believe what Nichole was showing them. When he and Blake returned from the cliffs overlooking the Pacific Ocean, both men were stymied as to what to do next, and then this. Standing directly behind her back, he watched as Nichole showed them the complete floor plans of the Frank Lloyd Wright designed home on Dana Point.

"Go back one screen," Blake told Nichole.

She used the keys on the right side of the key board to bring back the plot plan of the three acre estate. "This one?" she asked.

"Yes, that's it. Apparently there are some buildings on the edge of the cliffs that are part of the property."

Nichole pointed to the same reference information she had seen when first reviewing the plans. "Is this what caught your attention?" she asked.

"What are you two talking about?" Carson asked, a little lost in the conversation. He was still wondering how Nichole had been able to access this information so easily. In a small way, he was learning how an individual's privacy is compromised through the existing computer networks and the power of the Internet.

Nichole called back the plans for the maintenance building, checking her notes as she did so. "Look here," she said, touching the small color screen on the lap top.

Carson immediately saw what she and Blake had gotten excited about. The maintenance shed was accessed from an entrance some two hundred yards before the driveway leading to the house. Neither he nor Blake had noticed this when they drove by the house thirty minutes earlier.

"What about the security system? Are the schematics filed in this data base?" Blake asked, aware of the way they might gain entry into the property.

"Not exactly, but look at this." Nichole changed the screen, pulling up a more complicated set of drawings. "These are the electrical drawings for the maintenance building. Look at the second room, just off the small garage."

Carson could see that there were two breaker boxes, each larger than the one for the entire house. "Why so much electrical power in the building?" he asked.

"That's what I wondered," Nichole said, "so I broke down what the power was to be used for. One of these two breaker boxes controls all the electricity for the building itself." She indicated the smaller of the two. "Electrical power from the second box is used all over the property." Pausing to look at her handwritten notes, she continued, "This power is also tied back into the house itself."

Blake realized what she was saying. "The security system would have to be connected to some exterior power source, and it makes a lot of sense for it to be a source separate from the main house. If the power were to be cut from the main house, Ethan Mabry-or whoever he is-would want the security system to remain intact."

"So if we could somehow cut the power to the second source of electricity, we might be able to disable the security system?" Carson said.

"That's the way I see it," Blake said, smiling at Nichole for what she had been able to do.

Carson knew that both Blake and Nichole were excited about the discovery she had made, but he felt he better remind them of the timing problem. "Esteban Moreno and his friend have probably been back at the house since late last night. I doubt if we have much time before they split, and when they do, it would appear very doubtful that we are going to find out why they left Montana so quickly."

Blake said, "You're right. If we are going to try and get into the house, we had better do it right away." Looking at the computer screen, he asked, "Nichole, can you print us a copy of the last electrical schematic?"

"I could if I had a printer, but I don't." Handing him the detailed drawing she had done by hand, she said, "This is the best I can do."

Blake took the paper. "This will do just fine."

It only took the three of them ten minutes to come up with a rough plan. Nichole would drive the car, dropping the two men off below the maintenance shed. From there, they would try to break into the outbuilding, or cut the electricity to the security system. Nichole would drive the car past the house and park in the cul-de-sac overlooking the beach. She would wait for ten minutes and then drive down the road and park opposite the driveway, hopefully to pick up Blake and Carson. Blake suggested that he and Carson each take a pistol. Carson would also take one of Nichole's dad's shotguns while Blake kept a 30-30. Nichole would keep the shotgun that had been used to kill Jim.

• • •

Blake told Carson to wait in the thick underbrush while he checked out the building built into the cliff. It was possible that he was being observed even as he crawled along the side of the building, but it was a chance he was going to have to take. There were no electrical wires running into the building. Checking the small, but detailed, drawing that Nichole had made, he found the hidden box where the electric meter was found. Blake used the end of the 30-30 to bust off the top of the green cover. It only took him a second to trip the master breaker. The secondary power was off. Now if the people in the house just didn't notice it.

• • •

Ricardo had finished packing a small bag with a few clothes and personal items. He was ready to go as soon as Esteban finished on the computer. He wasn't sure just what his friend had been doing for almost two hours, but he knew that it was important. Fifteen minutes earlier, Ricardo had gone into Esteban's office next to the living room. Esteban was still working at the computer. He told Ricardo he would be done in twenty or thirty minutes; he just had to double check everything.

Walking into the kitchen, Ricardo passed the massive bank of electrical monitors connected to the security system. The monitors were all functioning, but the screens were blank. He knew that something was wrong. He tried flipping the control switches. Nothing happened. Seconds later he verified that the entire security system was down. Running back into Esteban's office, he yelled, "The security system's down. I think we have a problem."

"Throw the bags in the Lincoln in the garage, then do a check around the house. And, be careful," Esteban answered. "I've just got to copy this information." Esteban took a three-and-a-half inch computer disc out of a box and inserted it into the powerful machine.

• • •

Nichole turned the car around in the street, facing down the hill. She was nervous and scared. The shotgun on the seat was loaded, but in her present state of mind, she doubted that she could even use it. When she dropped Carson and Blake off below the house, she had a feeling that something terrible was going to happen. It was a feeling that wouldn't go away. She tried to convince herself it was just nerves, but in her heart she knew it was something else. Looking at her watch, she continued to wait. Three more minutes and she would move the car.

• • •

No alarms had sounded. Carson thought there might have been dogs, but then someone would have to take care of the animals when Esteban was not there. They hadn't tried to break into the maintenance shed itself. Once the men in the house discovered that the system was down, any element of surprise would be gone. Surprise was the only hope they had of getting to the killers.

Blake tapped him on the shoulder and whispered, "I'll come in through that sliding glass door on the redwood deck." He pointed to the glass door. "You go around to the front. When you hear breaking glass, go in the front door. If it's locked, use the shotgun and blow your way in. Stay low and watch yourself."

Carson nodded. "Good luck," he said. There really wasn't much else to say. Checking that the safety was not on the 12 gauge, he crawled off to the left heading for the row of trees running alongside the home.

Blake worked his way to the deck. There was a portable barbecue next to the door. He inched his way towards the black metal object.

• • •

Everything seemed to happen at once. Ricardo had just closed the back door of the Lincoln and come back past the video monitors. Glass came flying across the room, several large pieces hitting him in the head. Blood rushed down from his forehead. He knew he was hurt, but not badly. Acting instinctively, he dropped to his knees and rolled under the kitchen table, barely missing the black barbecue grill now lying in the kitchen. He had hit the floor when he heard the blast of a shotgun from the front of the house. What had happened? Grabbing his .44 caliber pistol from the holster on his back, he saw the man step through the broken door.

Blake never knew what hit him. Ricardo fired three times in less than a second. The first shot caught Blake square in the head. The second and third shots opened his chest, knocking him back through the door, onto the weather stained deck. His life was finished before he hit the ground.

Ricardo didn't take time to check if the man was dead. He had to get to the front of the house. Whoever fired the shotgun was still alive.

Esteban had just removed the disk from the computer when the front door exploded from the blast. Seconds later he heard the sound of Ricardo's pistol. He had heard it enough times to identify the weapon. Clutching the disk in his hand, he shut off the computer and grabbed his pistol with his other hand. Ricardo crawled through the door, keeping low to the ground.

"How many are there?" asked Esteban.

Ricardo shook his head, indicating that he didn't know.

"Let's get out of here. Get to the car." Esteban said, trying to keep his voice low.

•   •   •

Nichole heard first the shotgun blast and then the three pistol shots. The noise was loud but was soon lost in the sounds of the ocean. She was starting to panic, but knew she needed to be at the end of the driveway. The wheels on the rental car squealed as she sped back towards the house.

•   •   •

Carson heard the pistol shots, hoping they had come from Blake's pistol, afraid they hadn't. Working his way along the wall of the open beamed entryway, he headed towards the back of the house. He kept the shotgun ready, a shell chambered.

Entering the kitchen, he saw the blood on the side of the broken door. As soon as he made sure the room was empty, he ran for the door that was now completely demolished. Carson cried out as he looked through the broken glass. Any reference to deity was gone, instead he yelled, "Damn it to hell! Blake, I'm sorry." He quickly felt what was left of his friend's neck and backed into the kitchen once more. If the door hadn't been shattered, he might not have recognized the reflection that would have been staring back at him. The crease above his brow was tighter, his eyebrows flatter, his eyes colder and tense, his mouth determined. He would have seen the anger of a world destroyed.

Esteban and Ricardo heard the movements coming from the kitchen. "I'll see if I can finish it," Ricardo said, crawling towards the sounds. "I'll kill Carson. And I mean now!"

Still holding the computer disc in his hand, Esteban asked, "It wasn't Jeffers you shot in the kitchen?"

"No. But it's got to be him making the noise."

"Leave him. It's more important right now that I get this disk to somewhere safe. We'll get the man!"

Ricardo followed Esteban out of the office and into the kitchen. Neither man noticed that the video monitor was still on, despite Esteban having turned off the CPU.

Conscious that the two men in the house must be armed, Carson took each step slowly, trying to move as fast as he could. He recognized the sound of the garage door opener. It was starting to lift the wooden panels behind the Lincoln. Running through the house, he reached the door just as the Lincoln cleared the double wide doorway. Still moving, Carson raised the shotgun to his shoulder and fired three quick times directly into the retreating car. The windshield on the passenger side buckled and then collapsed inside the car.

Esteban hit the brakes hard and then pushed the gas pedal to the floor. The Lincoln flipped around, sliding onto the grass and then careening down the driveway.

Carson couldn't catch them, running as fast as he could in a futile effort.

• • •

Nichole knew she should probably have parked across from the driveway, but she somehow wanted to be as close as possible so that Carson and Blake would have a shorter distance to the car as they ran from the house. Now she was parked directly in front of the driveway, waiting for the men to emerge down the curved lane.

The white Lincoln came roaring down the driveway. As it rounded the last turn, before leaving the property, the driver must have seen her car. Nichole saw him at the same time. She didn't have time to put the car into gear. Diving across the seat, she tried to get out of the way of the large mass of metal. It was too late. The moving vehicle tried to avoid hitting her, driving across the lawn instead, and the tactic almost worked. The left front bumper hit the right fender of Nichole's car. Almost instantaneously, a piece of the firewall over the tire dropped down and sheared a piece of rubber out of the tire. Nichole heard the second explosion as the rest of the tire burst from the pressure. Instinctively, she looked over the dashboard to see the rental car driving down the street. She could see two men in the car. The passenger looked like he was wet. She didn't know it was blood.

"Nichole, are you all right?"

She jerked her head back in the direction of the driveway, looking for the face behind the voice.

41

Esteban used the pistol in his right hand to knock out the remaining portion of the windshield. Turning the corner towards 101, whatever was left of the tinted glass slid from the car and crashed onto the pavement. "Are you hit bad?" he asked Ricardo, seeing the blood coming from his head and right shoulder.

Ricardo lapsed into his native language without thinking. "No es mucho. El vidrio me corto la cabeza, y el hijo de puta me pego en el brazo. Pero mas que nada es mucho sangre. No te preocupes en mi."

Esteban was glad to hear that the blood was caused by the broken window, and the blood on his arm was a flesh wound from Jeffers shotgun. He had told The Cleaner that he would kill Carson and the woman, but now he knew that he would complete the job even if the sanction were somehow removed. Jeffers was either very good or just extremely lucky, and he was convinced it was more of the latter.

"We'll leave the car in Mission Viejo and catch a cab to a hotel by the airport. Are you going to be all right?"

Ricardo had already started wiping up the blood with a piece of his shirt. It didn't matter if he ruined his clothes; there were more in the trunk. "I'm fine. Did you get the disk?" Ricardo didn't know for sure what was on it, but he knew it must have been extremely important.

Esteban patted his shirt pocket where he had placed the valuable computer storage device. "I've got it. We're going to find a place to spend the night, and then I've got a plane to catch."

"What about Jeffers and the woman?"

"Trust me, we'll get them!"

• • •

The adrenaline in Carson's body had not subsided, and he was still operating on a level almost void of emotion. When Nichole fell into his arms, he started to realize what had happened to them. Esteban Moreno could have killed both of them, but he didn't. Then he remembered Blake lying on the back deck of the house.

Surprisingly, no one had come and investigated the shotgun blasts or the gun shots from Ricardo's pistol. Then he recalled the skeet range just to the north of the property. Undoubtedly, most of the people in the neighborhood already accepted the sounds of gunfire as a natural occurrence in the area. Carson wondered if that might have been one of the reasons that Esteban had chosen this particular house. Then he realized that was just too much of a coincidence. Or was it?

Holding Nichole an arm's length away from his body, he quickly looked to see if she had been shot or was bleeding.

"I'm all right, just scared and shook up. I'm sorry I didn't park across the street like you asked me." Noticing for the first time that Carson was alone, she asked, "Where is Blake?"

Carson pulled Nichole close to him again. "I'm sorry, Nichole. Blake didn't make it. He didn't stand a chance."

Nichole began to cry, unaware of the tears now running down her face. "When is it going to end? Carson, we have to run. We don't have a chance against these men." She stared into Carson's face. "Not a chance in hell!"

Her pleading had no effect on Carson. Walking over to the car, he immediately saw that it was undrivable in its present condition. The front tire was ruined, and the fender was smashed into the wheel. There was a tire in the trunk, and he knew he could fix it in a matter of moments, using the tire iron to pull out the fender. It would have to wait for a few minutes. The rented Ford Taurus was still parked near the side of the road, and would probably not draw any attention from a car driving into the area. Taking Nichole by the arm, he led her back into the house. Somehow they had to take care of Blake.

Nichole stayed by the door of the kitchen, not wanting to go out on the patio. She had learned to like Blake a great deal in just over twenty-four hours, but looking death in the face wasn't helping her. Carson understood, and lifted Blake's body in his arms. He brought it into the kitchen, placing Blake on the floor under the cabinets.

"What are we going to do with his body?" she asked as Carson tried to cover it with some towels he found in a drawer.

For the last several minutes, Carson had been asking himself that exact same question. He didn't like the answer any better than Nichole was going to. "I'm afraid that we don't have much choice. We can't take him with us. Hopefully, in a few days, we can let someone know he's here. In the meantime, we'll turn the air conditioning as low as possible. Even with the broken sliding glass door, the place should stay fairly cool. The heavy, hot summer weather is still more than a month away."

Nichole was surprised by the callous attitude of Carson. Speaking up, she said, "We could take his body with us on the plane. When we get to Montana, we'll bury Blake, and then get Michael and go to Canada."

"Nichole, we're not going back to Montana, at least not yet. And we are definitely not running to Canada. Esteban Moreno and Ricardo Gutierrez are not going to stop until they kill us. They weren't running because they were afraid of us. They took something with them, and I want to know what it was. Maybe we shouldn't have tried to get in the house, but we did. Now Blake is dead along with Jim and my son Kelly. I will not rest until I know why they all had to die."

She knew he was right; it was just that she was extremely scared. When Carson became emphatic, she understood they had no choice. None whatsoever. "What about Blake's family?"

"He was divorced. His wife never accepted the fact that he left a secure paycheck and a long term retirement to go into business for himself. They haven't spoken for years." Guessing what she was about to ask, he added, "They didn't have any children. Maybe that was part of the problem."

Nichole was defeated, but she had to do something. If she was not going to run, she might as well try and help. "What do you think they came back to get?"

"I don't know, but they were both in the front office when I found Blake." Needing to start somewhere, he got up from the kneeling position he had maintained beside his dead friend and walked into the office. Nichole turned and followed him down the hall.

After five minutes, neither Carson or Nichole had found anything that seemed out of place in the office. They had emptied the desk, moved the books on the shelves, and looked for notebooks or scratch pads. There was nothing. Nichole had found a box of computer software. There was a copy of the most current release of WordPerfect along with several windows applications. Nothing seemed out of the ordinary. She also found a few disks which had no labels. Guessing, she thought they must be blank.

"Find anything?" Carson asked, still searching through the remaining file drawer in the desk.

Nichole didn't answer. She just realized that the video monitor was turned on. A screen saving device had blackened the monitor, but it was on. The CPU, or main central processing unit, had been turned off. Flipping the switch behind the main computer box, she saw the screen light up.

Carson saw that she was doing something on the computer. "What is it?"

"Do you think that one of the men might have been working on the computer when Blake broke the glass door?"

"I wouldn't bet against it. What are you thinking? The computer was turned off."

Nichole loaded up WordPerfect and issued several commands. In less than a minute, she was convinced that one of the men had been using the computer and, in fact, was working in the word processing program. "When I turned on the computer, I was told that there was still a remaining back up file. The computer had been shut off without properly exiting the program. By using this command, I was able to restore the last document that had been viewed on the computer." She showed Carson what she had done.

Carson looked at the list of numbers, names, and encrypted instructions. None of it made any sense, but it might be the missing piece to the puzzle. "What is it?"

"I don't know, but I'm going to save it and take it with us." She grabbed a disk and checked to make sure that it was formatted and empty. It was both. Seconds later, she had copied the entire file to the three-and-one-half inch black disk. Nichole then deleted the active file and shut down the machine. "If this is what was so important, then I fixed it so no one else can get a copy."

Carson checked his watch and saw that they had now been in the house for almost fifteen minutes since Blake's death. "We better get out of here. I'll prop the front door shut with a chair and then leave through the garage. I'll meet you at the car."

"I don't think it's drivable."

"It will be in a few minutes," he said, already propping the chair against what was left of the door handle. He checked to make sure that he still had the pistol and the shotgun Blake had given him. Nichole's weapon was still in the car.

•   •   •

Michael listened quietly as Carson explained what had happened since they left Swan Lake. "When are you coming back?" He was thinking along the same lines as Nichole had earlier.

"We don't know. These men are not going to quit. Somehow we have to find out what the computer file has to do with it," Carson said over the phone. "Nichole is trying to decipher the information, but it doesn't make any sense."

"Why don't you ship me a copy and let me see what I can do?" Michael asked.

It sounded like a good idea, and Nichole already had demonstrated the modem capability of her computer. "Just a minute, Michael." Tapping Nichole on the shoulder, he asked, "Did you say you can fax with this computer?"

"Yes, as long as the file is in the computer." Not having heard

Michael's suggestion, she immediately understood why Carson was asking about the fax capability of her lap top. "Do you want me to send the file to Michael?"

"As soon as you can."

"Tell Michael that I will send the file as soon as you hang up. I need the phone line to do it."

Carson told Michael what they were going to do and then came back to Blake. "We had to leave his body at the house."

"Do you want me to alert the police anonymously?" Michael asked.

"Not yet. If that file doesn't answer our questions, we may need to go back there. But believe me, that is not our first choice. And, Michael, be careful. It's possible that these guys think we're headed back to Montana. If they do, you aren't going to be safe for very long."

"I understand."

"We thought about trying to find another place to stay but didn't want to take the chance of being recognized. Don't call us here unless it is a matter of life and death! It's probably better not to go through the switchboard unless you have to. I'll check in with you first thing in the morning. See what you can come up with on the computer disk."

42

FRIDAY MORNING

E steban walked across the grass bordering the Mississippi River and found a seat on one of the green metal benches under the giant arch. The St. Louis monument was built to symbolize the connecting of two sides of the country, East and West. Esteban had suggested a meeting spot that was convenient for the two of them, but it was almost ironic that they were meeting under a monument built to connect two worlds. At ten o'clock in the morning, Esteban waited for The Cleaner to appear. There was no doubt in the Latin's mind that The Cleaner could not be trusted-that is unless he was left with no other alternative. This morning Esteban was about to remove all the remaining options.

Across the park, a gray haired gentleman stepped out of a limousine. The Cleaner looked from left to right, as if to assure himself that it wasn't a trap. Satisfied that Esteban was alone, he strode confidently to the agreed-upon meeting place.

"All right, why the demand for a meeting halfway across the country? Surely we could have discussed everything on the phone. The lines would have been kept clean." The Cleaner demanded a response, knowing full well that Esteban would tell him what he wanted to know.

Thursday night Esteban had decided to only tell The Cleaner that the house on Dana Point had been compromised. Until he could speak to the man face-to-face, he wasn't going to tell him about Carson Jeffers and Nichole Lewis. "As I told you on the phone, Dana Point has been compromised."

Interrupting the taller Latin, the distinguished executive of the LLO broke in. "You told me that last night. How did it happen?"

"Carson Jeffers, Nichole Lewis, and another man, whom I assume was one of the missing ManTech employees, broke into the house after disabling the security system."

This information was as startling to the man from the limousine as it had been to Esteban, but he tried to remain calm. What was happening? How did Jeffers always seem to be just a step ahead of them? "Carson Jeffers was in your home? I understood he had escaped to Canada, or was at least trying to."

Esteban thought that he probably should have alerted The Cleaner as to the events that transpired in Montana, but he hadn't. "I killed one of Carson Jeffers' employees outside of Kalispell. Before the man died, he showed me proof that Carson had knowledge of my home in Dana Point. I felt it best to return to California and evaluate the position. Besides, I knew where he was hiding in Montana." Esteban wasn't quite ready to tell the older man why he was so concerned about Dana Point. Not yet.

"You knew where he was hiding, but you didn't tell me. Can I ask why you failed to keep me informed?" the older man asked.

"We both know you had issued a sanction order on Carson Jeffers and Nichole Lewis, and I had not yet completed their termination. As soon as they were killed, you would have been told."

The Cleaner kept looking at his watch, as if he were trying to hurry Esteban into revealing the true reason for this meeting in St. Louis. In reality, he wanted to distance himself from the man as much as possible. Once Shortfall was completed, he wanted to forget Esteban Moreno had ever been born.

"What do you want, Esteban?" He decided to ask the reason for the meeting.

"First of all, I would like to know what Carson Jeffers has to do with this entire operation. From the beginning he has been one step ahead of me. He was in Los Angeles when Flight 1058 was shot down; he was in the hospital room with Adrian Baker when the termination was in process; he escaped from Ricardo north of Seattle; he alluded every military and civilian authority while fleeing to Montana; and then he broke into the house at Dana Point."

The Cleaner noticed that Esteban did not claim ownership to the home originally designed by Frank Lloyd Wright. The truth was the home was purchased by a trust, of which The Cleaner was the trustee. It had been the exclusive residence of Esteban when he was in the United States for almost five years, but it didn't belong to him. Still, Esteban had a valid question. How were Carson Jeffers and Nichole Lewis involved? And most importantly, who were they working for?

"Second, and most importantly, I'm getting out when Shortfall is completed." Looking at the Cleaner, as if peering into the depths of his mind, he continued. "We both know that when my usefulness is served, I am expendable. Don't try and deny it. It is something that I've taken for granted from the first day I met you, some fifteen years ago. And from that day forward, I have been preparing an insurance policy, one with a lifetime retirement system." Esteban took out a small three-and-a-half inch computer disk and showed it to The Cleaner. "It is only a copy, so don't worry about trying to take it."

"What is it? And what do you mean it is your insurance policy?

"If this were the only copy of this information, which it is not, you would quickly discover what I mean by *insurance policy*. You could take this disk and call up every operation we have been involved in, from the revolt in Chile to the sanction at Punta Del Este. You would also find a list of account numbers containing your profits from operations in the past, as well as from Shortfall."

The Cleaner acted as if he were going to speak, but then checked himself and remained quiet.

"Now as to Shortfall, I would suggest that you contact one Tony Batista in National City, California. The remaining missiles from El Toro have all been moved. I figured that you might try and short-circuit the end goal and return the missiles. That is no longer a possibility. The eleven remaining missiles are solely under my control." Holding up the disk in his hand, he went on, "On this disk there is a list of cities. Each of the eleven missiles will be used to destroy an airliner, everything happening almost simultaneously at eleven separate locations in the United

States. It will be the final blow by La Libertad Occidental, one that, with
this disk, will be fully attributable to yourself. If you ever think of turning me over, I have arranged for the release of this information. When
that happens, there is not a place on the planet where you would be
safe."

"And yourself, you couldn't hide either?"

"My fellow compatriot, I'm well aware that I would be a dead man
if you decided to make this public, but you can rest assured your life
would be terminated immediately after any such disclosure."

The Cleaner was visibly shaken by this turn of events. Perspiration
beads were now forming on the brow of his forehead. "You can't be serious about shooting down that many planes. You'll never get away with
it."

"Oh, It's far more than a plan!. The missiles are going to be delivered to a cell of *La Libertad Occidental,* one which knows nothing about
me. Each of the shooters are willing to give their life for the cause. A
cause that you and I both know is a lot of bullshit."

All of a sudden, The Cleaner knew he had underestimated this pony-
tailed Latin American. Still, The Cleaner could collect his profits from
Shortfall, and he, too, would be able to retire with more money than
even he had dreamed possible. But he also knew that he could never live
with the threat of exposure hanging over his head. Somehow, he would
have to do something about Esteban. He couldn't be allowed to complete
this final act of madness.

Changing his strategy, pretending to go along with Esteban, he said,
"All right, but you have to finish the sanction on Carson Jeffers and
Nichole Lewis. There is a slight chance that someone would believe
them if they went to the authorities. That must never happen!"

This was one thing that Esteban and The Cleaner agreed on one hundred percent. "You can consider them dead. When I'm done there won't
be enough of them left to identify, even from dental records."

"I hope you're right."

"Oh, I'm right. And by the way, there is one more little thing."
Esteban handed The Cleaner a 3 x 5 card with a series of numbers. "That
is an account located in the Caiman Islands. You are to deposit an addi-

tional $50,000,000 into that account no later than Monday morning. I don't have to spell out what might happen if you don't."

"You're not serious? You have already received an advance payment of $5 million for Shortfall. Another $10 million is to be paid when the final payment to the LLO is received."

"Count on it. I'm serious. And, just so there is no misunderstanding, the $50 million is in addition to the $10 million you so graciously reminded me of."

• • •

Nichole was sitting at the desk next to the television, manipulating the information on the disk. She was still dressed in just the pullover cotton blouse she had put on in the middle of the night. Her body temperature must be lower than Carson's. He had held her most of the night, but she couldn't seem to get warm, even with his muscular body keeping her close. As she thought about it, she decided that her fear of the future was affecting her physically.

"Do you have it figured out yet?" Carson sat on the end of the bed, his Levis pulled on, but unbuttoned. Together, the two of them had tried to break the code on the disk. They didn't have much doubt that the numbers were some kind of account information. But where, or to what, they didn't know.

"Nothing. We're still at the same place we were a couple of hours ago."

Carson looked at his watch and decided to call Michael in Swan Lake. Maybe he was having more luck than they were. Picking up the phone, he dialed the number direct.

Michael answered on the second ring. "Thank God you called. I was going to call you in the next 30 minutes, even if you didn't call. Do you have any idea of what you are mixed up in?"

Carson instantly realized that Michael must have gotten much further than the two of them. He motioned for Nichole to stop what she was doing and listen to what Michael was about to explain. She put her head right next to Carson's so as to be able to hear Michael's voice.

"What are you saying?" Carson asked. "Were you able to figure out what the information on the disk means?

"Most of it. I'm still working on some of it. Let me tell you what I now know, or in some cases, just believe."

"Go ahead," Carson said, indicating to Nichole she should use the pencil and paper she had picked up to take notes.

"The first list of numbers are account numbers in a Swiss bank. I used an access code and verified the amount in those accounts."

"How much is it?"

"I'll get to that in a minute. There's more. I was able to break the code using a computer program our CIA data bank so kindly furnished." The CIA had no idea that Michael had broken into their computer network. "There is a list of eleven cities, all major airports, along with specific flight numbers. Next to each airport is the code name of an individual, whom I would guess would be a member of the terrorist organization. All of the flight numbers are to depart Monday morning between 9:00 a.m. and 11:00 a.m. Eastern Time."

"My God, Carson," Nichole said, loud enough for Michael to hear on the other end of the line. "Someone is planning on shooting down almost a dozen planes all across the country! Can they be stopped?"

Michael answered for Carson. "Nichole, I think the only way to stop this nightmare is to get the missiles and destroy them. I don't think you can go to the authorities. They wouldn't believe you're not terrorists yourselves, and then there is the list of phone numbers that I found in the file."

Carson had a number of questions, but settled on one, "What phone numbers?"

Michael answered, "The next to last section of information on the file had a list of eight numbers. I started to call the numbers on the list, but stopped after the first call."

"Why?" asked Nichole.

"The first number was a private number that was answered, *Washington, D.C.* I had no doubt that the voice on the other end was a government official. When I didn't say anything, the voice asked for my authorization code. Someone pretty high up is involved, right up to their neck. I thought that the line might be traced and so I hung up immediately."

"A wise decision," remarked Carson, thinking of the many times that the U.S. government had been involved over that past two weeks. "Leave the other numbers alone, at least for now. I wish there was something we could do."

"Maybe there is," Michael said. "The last section of information listed the address of a long term auto storage facility, along with a number, which I believe to be a license plate. The same address showed up in the section with the eleven cities. It's my guess that the missiles might be stored in that garage. And, Carson, there is a date beside the address of the garage. It's my guess the missiles are about to be moved."

"What's the date?" Carson asked, motioning for Nichole to write it down.

"Saturday. That's tomorrow. Whatever they're planning is going to happen soon!"

Carson was already thinking of a plan. If he could get to the missiles, just maybe he could find a way to stop the insanity. "Where is the garage, Michael?"

"It's called *Secure Parking*, and is located near the Los Angeles airport." Michael gave Carson the address of the garage, along with the supposed license plate number: RWC1834. Nichole wrote the information down on the pad of paper.

After Michael explained how he had been able to put all of this together, Carson asked him about the money. "How much money is in the accounts?"

"I hope you are sitting down. I've checked three times, and the total amount has been increasing each hour. Right now there is almost 12 billion dollars. Carson, that is B for billion."

"I don't get it. What is the money for? And where is it coming from?"

"I don't know, but I'll keep trying to figure it out. There is another program that I'm going to try. I'm sure that I will need some kind of authorization, but I've got a few ideas."

"Keep on it," Carson said. "We are going to try and check out the garage."

"Be careful," Michael said as he hung up the phone.

• • •

"Are you all right, sir?" The limo driver didn't know who the man in the back seat was, but he could tell that something was wrong. Whatever had happened under the monument had affected him greatly. He looked in the rear view mirror and saw the man rubbing his temples vigorously with his thumbs. It was as if he was trying to stop a giant headache, one that kept increasing with each second.

Realizing that the man had spoken to him, The Cleaner said, "I'm fine. Just get me back to the airport. And make it fast; I've got a plane to catch."

As the car sped away from the parking lot, he thought there must be a way out of this mess. Slowly he started developing a plan, one that would eliminate Esteban Moreno for good. By the time the stretch limo reached the St. Louis airport, the driver noticed that the man was no longer rubbing his head. His gray haired passenger almost seemed asleep. His eyes were closed, and he was leaning back against the leather head rest. Something had changed.

43

The Cleaner met his pilot, Phill Underman, in the new General Aviation Lounge of the St. Louis terminal. The Lear jet was a great aircraft for travel within the United States, and the silver haired executive used it often. They had left Kennedy Airport four and one half hours earlier. By the time his boss returned from the monument on the river, Phill had already filed a flight plan for the return trip to New York.

"Phill, I want you to change your flight plan. We are going to San Diego."

"When do you want to leave?" the pilot of the Lear jet asked.

"Just as soon as you can get clearance. If it helps, take off VFR and then get IFR clearance in the air."

"That will help. I've topped off the fuel, and we should be able to leave within the next 30 minutes."

While Phill made the last-minute preparations for departure, The Cleaner placed a call to Tony Batista. There was no answer at the warehouse. Finally, he called a cellular phone that was always monitored.

"Steve Hacking, West Coast Imports. What can I do for you?" West Coast Imports was a business that specialized in electronic shipments from Asia. At least 90 percent of its business was legitimate, the remaining 10 percent accounted for 90 percent of its profits. As The Cleaner thought about the political support he provided for the import business, he knew why Tony Batista was willing to pay him five percent of the gross sales from all phases of the business. The Cleaner had the contacts to make sure that Tony's international shipments reached the proper hands.

"I need to speak to Tony at once," the man in St. Louis answered.

"I'm afraid that won't be possible. Tony's not here and is not expected back. May I help you?"

The Cleaner could sense from Steve's choice of words that there was a major problem. He had met Steve Hacking at least three times when dealing with Tony. Steve was Tony's second in command, not only at West Coast Imports, but in other *family business* as well. There was only one reason why Tony was not expected back at West Coast Imports. "Steve, this is The Cleaner. I will be landing at San Diego in just over two-and-a-half hours. Can you meet me?"

Steve Hacking was well aware of the importance of the man called The Cleaner. He knew the only way he was going to be able to stay in business was to get this man's blessing. "Absolutely. I'll meet you at the general aviation terminal. Will you be in the Lear?" One thing that Steve had learned from Tony was to know as much about the people you deal with as they knew about you. He knew that the Cleaner owned a new Lear jet.

"Yes, we'll be in the Lear. We'll see you in a couple of hours," The Cleaner said. He would like to have asked Steve about Tony but knew that wasn't safe. If Tony was dead, as he believed, he would know it in a matter of a couple of hours.

•   •   •

Steve sat across from The Cleaner in the back seat of the long Lincoln Limousine. The partition was raised behind the front seat, the driver not hearing a word that was being said. They drove south on Interstate 5, exiting at National City. Twenty-five minutes after picking up the gray haired man in the five thousand dollar suit, the driver got out and opened the rear door of the limousine.

The Cleaner regretted not letting anyone else in on the special storage instructions he and Tony Batista had worked out three weeks earlier. At the time, they both believed that there was added security in secrecy.

If Steve would have known about the storage container mixed in with the Korean stereo speakers, there was no doubt in The Cleaner's mind that Esteban would have never gotten away with the removal of the balance of the missiles. Each time that the Latin had needed a missile, Tony had accompanied him to the warehouse. Tony had never asked what was in the cases; he really didn't care. The Cleaner had already paid him $500,000 for advance storage of the fifteen crates. He had been promised an equal payment when all the cases were removed.

"How long has Tony been missing?" The Cleaner asked Steve.

"To the best of anyone's knowledge, he was last seen on Sunday afternoon. Since that time, no one has seen or heard from him. Do you think he's dead?"

"Unless I miss my guess, I think we will find Tony in the warehouse."

Steve removed a set of keys and then shut off the security system for the building. After he opened the doors, he was surprised that neither of the black Dobermans came running to greet him. The only people the dogs would let in the building alone were Steve Hacking and Tony Batista. Steve turned and saw both dogs laying on the concrete floor inside the door. They had been shot several times each. "Where did you put the container?" Steve asked the older gentleman, ignoring the dead animals.

The Cleaner pointed to a metal container two aisles away. The words *Matson Shipping* were stenciled on the side. "There."

Steve examined the lock on the container and found it to be in excellent shape. "If he's in there, he would have had to lock himself in."

"He's in there, and I guarantee you he didn't lock himself in."

Using the master key that unlocked all the containers, Steve removed the lock. He and Tony had the only keys to the container locks. After he opened the door, the silver haired man stood in the doorway looking at the body of Tony Batista. Except for the body of the forty year old Italian, the container was empty-that is, except for a note laying on Tony's chest.

The Cleaner had to give Esteban credit. He was covering his bases. There was no doubt that the Cleaner had underestimated the Latin.

Picking up the note on the body, he saw the neat holes over the heart. Tony had died quickly. In the large warehouse, no one would have heard the shots, especially on Sunday, if that was when Tony was killed.

"My fellow compatriot,

When you find this body, you will already know about the missiles. I found it necessary to take out a little added insurance. Tony was kind enough to open the storage container when I told him you would be meeting him here. I just forgot to tell him that it wouldn't be for another week. Trust me when I tell you that the weapons are safe. Soon they will be destroyed, bringing destruction with them. I hope that you will follow the instructions you will by now have received. Failure to do so will certainly merit prompt action on my part. Have a good day.

"E. M."

The Cleaner noticed that Steve had been reading the note along with him. "I won't explain everything at this time, but I want the contents of this storage container returned. If you help me and we are successful, I will personally pay you the sum of five million U.S. dollars."

Steve knew better than to ask too many questions, but he had to have a little more information to go on. "What was in the container?"

The Cleaner realized he had to give him some information and said, "Some weapons in green plastic cases. For now that is all you need to know. Can you help me?"

By the time The Cleaner finished speaking, Steve was already walking away from the container. He went into the office and checked the security system. It was all functioning, with the exception of the video taping system that kept track of who went in and out of the storage area. The taping device was broken and the tape removed from the machine.

The Cleaner had followed Steve into the office and quickly saw what he was looking for. Esteban must have driven some kind of vehicle into the warehouse with Tony. The videotaping system would have a visual record of what happened. Looking at the smashed system, The Cleaner said, "Whoever killed Tony must have known that the encounter was being taped. We aren't going to have much luck in finding anything out from this."

Steve was already opening a small section of a stereo speaker box mounted on the wall in the office. When the cover was removed, he checked a mounted camera.

"What is that?" The Cleaner asked.

"Tony and I figured that if we were ever robbed, the thieves would be smart enough to either take the tapes out of the storage area and the office, or just smash the machines. As you can see they did both. What they didn't know is that we had a second video surveillance system installed that was motion and sound activated. This small camera would automatically record from the time a sound was heard in the warehouse or motion of any kind was detected in the office. It was set to record for 15 minutes after the sound or motion stopped."

"Do you have to change tapes?" The Cleaner asked.

"Only after 20 hours of actual recording. It is a compressed digital super 8 system, and it only records during non-business hours."

Noticing how the camera was pointed, the Cleaner asked, "How will this help us if the camera was just aimed in one direction? It will show us the man that busted the monitors, but I need to know what vehicle he used to transport the cases."

Steve took the tape from the hidden camera and placed it in a video player he found on a work bench. Turning it on, the two men watched Esteban smashing the video equipment. "Is that your man?" he asked.

The Cleaner nodded as Steve rewound the tape a little further. When Steve turned it back on, The Cleaner saw why the hidden camera was so important. When Esteban drove into the warehouse, his blue van had activated the taping equipment. The monitors captured the entire episode filmed by the cameras in the warehouse area. The hidden camera was fixed on the monitors viewing the warehouse area. Up until the time the monitors were destroyed, the smaller camera had seen everything, as it was fixed on the monitors. "Stop it right there!" the older gray haired man said.

Steve did as he was instructed. There on the small screen was a picture of the monitor, showing Esteban and Tony getting out of the blue van.

"Can you zoom in with this?" The Cleaner asked.

Steve nodded and tightened up the picture. In front of them was the license number on the van. It was a temporary California registration - number RWC1834.

"Find that van in the next three hours and I'll pay an additional $3 million. $2 million if you find it in six hours and $1 million if you find it after that," The Cleaner said. "And I don't want the van opened until I get there or there is no payment at all."

"I understand," Steve said, already starting to make some telephone calls. He was promising one third of the reward money to the person or persons who find the van. With that kind of incentive, he felt confident that if the van was in Southern California, it would soon show up. In a matter of moments, he was guaranteed that no fewer than five thousand people would be looking for the van within the next thirty minutes.

The Cleaner waited while Steve made the calls. "What will we do now?"

"Wait," Steve answered. "Is there someplace I can reach you?"

"I'll be at the Marriott Marina on Harbor Drive."

• • •

The Cleaner was out an additional three million dollars, eight million dollars altogether.. It had taken Steve less than two hours before he found the old van. A Los Angeles youth gang had found the van parked in a long term auto storage facility just off the LAX property. They knew better than to look inside the van, considering who was paying the reward. Besides, they got a cool one million for just finding the van. Steve picked him up at the Marriott and drove immediately to the airport where Phill Underman was waiting to fly them to Los Angeles.

As soon as they landed, Steve had a car waiting to take them to the long term parking garage. It had only one entrance, obviously for security reasons. There was only one way in and one way out, and you had to pass right under the sign that said *Secure Parking.*

Steve paid the attendant three hundred dollars, and the young black man pointed up the ramp and said, "The car's on the third level."

Steve had thought about bringing another person with them to the van, but when he suggested it, The Cleaner had said no. On the way up from San Diego, the two men had talked about how they wanted to handle the van. The Cleaner convinced Steve that if the cases were in the van, it would certainly be booby trapped and rigged for explosion. Steve understood that the man paying the reward wanted the van to remain where it was found.

The first thing The Cleaner saw was that the van had a flat right front tire. He didn't doubt that the air had just been let out of the tire and could be refilled with a flat tire *fix it* can in seconds. Undoubtedly, Esteban had flattened the tire to stop a would be thief from even considering stealing the car. After all, who would steal an old beat up van, especially one with a flat tire!

"Are you sure you know what to do?" The Cleaner asked Steve as he crawled under the van.

One of the reasons why West Coast Imports was able to make a profit on the legal side of its business was because of Steve's electronic abilities. He knew quality equipment, and had been trained in electronic repairs. Now, he was about to get to test his abilities. After crawling under the van, Steve found that the van was wired with more than ten pounds of C4 explosive. It appeared to be rigged to go off if the tires rolled more than twelve inches or any of the doors were opened. Steve knew that there would have to be some kind of shut-off or disabling device on the van. After twenty minutes, he found it hidden up inside the front right wheel well. It was almost invisible with the front tire flattened. Thirty seconds later the bomb was temporarily disabled. Steve crawled out from under the car and used a flat slender shaped tool to open the door of the blue vehicle.

The Cleaner looked inside and verified that all eleven cases were there. He opened the top case to make sure that the contents hadn't been removed. They hadn't!

"Go ahead and reset the security system, including the bomb," he told Steve. "My people will take it from here."

While Steve was resetting the security measures Esteban had placed on the vehicle, the Cleaner removed a small cellular phone from his coat pocket. Looking around to insure he couldn't be heard, he dialed two numbers. The first was to Washington, D.C., and the second was to his accounting department at the brownstone on Madison Avenue in New York City.

When he finished the calls, he asked Steve to drop him at the Bonaventure Hotel on Wilshire. He had no reason to go back to San Diego. Smiling to himself, he knew that he was back in control. Washington, D.C., was on top of the Esteban situation, and even more importantly, he was now more than $12 Billion richer.

44

"Is this what you wanted?" Nichole asked as she handed Carson the sack imprinted with the name of the store - *Radio Shack.*

Carson opened the plastic bag and examined the small electronic motion detector. The device itself was about two inches square, with a remote sensing receiver that was advertised to have a reception range of a quarter mile. "It's perfect."

Nichole had made two trips into the Capistrano Beach electronics store. The first time, all she did was to pick up a catalogue listing all the Radio Shack products.

Carson had considered trying to change cars but decided there was too great a risk of being recognized. Besides, in Southern California a fairly new Ford Taurus with a smashed fender did not seem out of place. "And the other item?" he asked Nichole.

Nichole took out a long barbecue spatula and handed it across the seat to Carson. "Why you want a motion detector and a barbecue spatula is beyond me."

"Trust me, you'll understand. Let's get on the freeway. It's still at least an hour and a half to Los Angeles."

●   ●   ●

"Two weeks will be $88 in advance," the young black boy told Carson as he waited at the entrance to *Secure Parking.*

Taking out five twenty dollar bills from his Levi jacket, Carson handed the boy the money. It was evident the kid didn't like his job; he was far more interested in listening to the deep bass sounds coming from the boom box on the counter of the cashier's booth.

After the parking attendant punched in the vehicle information on the computer terminal, Carson and Nichole still had to wait almost a minute before a light blue receipt was printed. "Put this in the window of your car. You can come and go as much as you like during the next two weeks. Take space C-12 on the third level." Almost as an afterthought the boy added, "If you decide to leave the car after the two week time period expires, you need to pay in advance or the car will be barreled."

Carson tipped the bill of his baseball hat and drove up the ramp, not surprised that the boy hadn't recognized either of them. Exiting on the second level, he quickly determined that there was no vehicle with the license plate number RWC1834.

"If the missiles are still here, we're probably looking for some kind of truck," Nichole commented as Carson started driving down the aisles of the third level.

"Over there," Carson said, pointing to an old blue van. "Look at the license plate."

Nichole read it out loud. "RWC1834. It must be the car."

Carson pulled into the empty space beside the van. If the vehicle still contained the missiles, there was no doubt that the owner had also rented the spaces on either side of the van. Nichole was the first one out of the Taurus. "Don't touch anything," Carson said as he stood beside her on the dirty gray asphalt.

"How will you know if it is wired or has some type of security system?" she asked.

"It won't have a regular security system. If the alarm went off, everyone would come looking around. That definitely wouldn't do for Mr. Esteban Moreno. No, I think he would have wired the van so that it would be destroyed if anybody tried to break in."

Nichole noticed the right tire was flat on the front side. "Why would he leave the van with a flat tire?"

"In all likelihood, I would guess our killer let the air out himself."

"Why?" she asked.

"No one would suspect a van with a flat tire."

"Maybe so," she said as Carson started to look under the van for some kind of destruction device or bomb.

Nichole leaned over the windshield and read the expiration date on the parking sticker. "Carson, the van's parking permit expires tomorrow." Both of them realized that Esteban was going to move the vehicle within the next 24 hours.

"There's C4 explosive of some kind wired to a detonation device," he said, inspecting the vehicle's undercarriage. "It looks to me like this van would take out a major section of this building if someone were to accidentally set it off."

"What are we going to do now?" Nichole asked as she walked around the van and knelt beside Carson, who was still laying under the car.

He didn't answer immediately. Instead, he slowly pushed himself behind the flattened tire. Gently, he raised his arm up into the wheel well, careful not to touch the car. "Go stand behind that pillar," he said. "It looks like there is a disarming device hidden behind the tire. I'm going to flip it and see what happens."

Nichole knew it wouldn't do any good to argue with the man and did as he had asked.

Waiting until Nichole was clear, Carson touched the aluminum colored box and pulled the toggle switch back towards the tire. Nothing happened, at least nothing loud. Carson heard a slight click, and then silence. It must have worked.

Just as Carson pulled himself out from under the van, a VW bus drove by, the driver thinking that Carson was trying to fix the tire. He didn't stop.

"Is it safe?" Nichole asked.

"As safe as we can hope for. Now, where is that barbecue spatula?"

Nichole opened the door of the Taurus and handed him the aluminum instrument. It had a flat blade at least 18 inches long. She still was not sure what Carson was going to do.

Carson took the spatula and walked over to one of the cement pillars supporting the structure. Without saying a word, he started rubbing the edge of the cooking surface against the corner of the concrete. Five minutes later, the spatula had a hook on one side of the blade. Carson walked back to the van. "Behold, our key," he said as he slipped the blade of the spatula down beside the front window and quickly pulled the instrument diagonally across the door. The lock released and Carson opened the van.

Sliding a dark curtain open that was hanging between the two bucket seats, Carson saw that the back was filled with green cases marked with a series of numbers and the letters, USMC. He had no doubt they had found the missing Stinger missiles.

Nichole looked over his shoulder and immediately understood what they had located. "Are we going to try and steal the van?" she asked, thinking they had to get the missiles out of the building.

"No. We have to have Esteban Moreno and the missiles together. All we have right now are the missiles, but I want Moreno!" Carson crawled over the top of the cases and opened the rear door of the van. "Open the trunk of the rental car," he said as he pulled the top five cases from the van.

Nichole popped the trunk and came back to see what Carson was doing. He opened one of the cases and took out one of the deadly missiles, placing it in the trunk of the Ford Taurus.

"Hand me the motion detector," he instructed Nichole.

She handed him the small electronic sensor and watched him set it and then place it in the empty case that had held the Stinger missile, now in the trunk of the Ford.

Placing the empty case almost at the bottom of the pile of green boxes in the van, he continued replacing the cases in the van. When he was finished, he locked both doors of the van and then crawled under the front of the car. Seconds later, he reset the detonation device.

Checking to make sure that the light on the motion sensor was on, Carson said, "Let's get out of here." As they drove down the ramp to the single entrance of the building, they saw the young black boy talking to two men in a white van with darkened windows. He was motioning them to go to the third parking level.

Carson never saw the driver of the van put his government identification back in his pocket. And then, neither did the CIA surveillance team see Carson and Nichole drive out of the concrete parking structure.

45

Carson turned right down the one-way street leading to the entrance of the 405 freeway. One week had passed since the crash of Flight 1058, and Friday afternoon traffic was as bad as ever. Local commuters were inching their way towards the newly opened San Diego Freeway. One block from the entrance to *Secure Parking*, Carson pulled into an alley that emptied into a parallel street running north. Waiting for the young girl, who appeared to be a dental or medical assistant, to start her car and leave, Carson prepared to park the Ford Taurus in her space next to the *Airport Inn Motel*.

"Are you sure you want to stay here?" asked Nichole as she watched the homeless *wino* wander down the alley. "It doesn't look too safe."

Carson picked up the receiver for the motion detector, assuring himself that the green light was still on. Flipping a switch, he listened to a steady hum from the audio section of the receiver. Everything was working perfectly. "This will do nicely. Let's get checked in. I hate to send you in alone, but let's not take any chances."

Nichole opened the door and went around front to the reception area of the thirty-five year old motel. The name, *Airport Inn*, was undoubtedly the ninth or tenth name the place had been known by. Carson had told her to request a room facing the street. As she went in the building, she saw that all of the front rooms in the two story building had small patios enclosed with a metal railing. None of them were large enough for anything other than two small folding chairs. Glancing up the street, she saw an old pick-up truck looking for long-term parking go into *Secure Parking*.

Five minutes after Nichole walked into the Airport Inn, she emerged from a side door of the building carrying a blanket. "We are in room number 216. The room is actually quite clean," she said as she handed Carson the blanket.

Carson took the blanket and wrapped it around the Stinger missile. He put the shotgun under the mat in the trunk and closed the lid. "Do we have to go through the lobby?" he asked as he gathered up the receiver for the motion detector.

"No. There's a stairway just to the left of the side door," she answered, picking up what few clothes and personal possessions they had with them.

•   •   •

The Cleaner looked down on the lobby of the Bonaventure Hotel and considered his next move. As the elevator rose through the open atrium of the building, he mentally went through a checklist. He had been assured that President Attwilder would capitulate and authorize the $2 billion pay-off before the end of the weekend. The money would be deposited in a Swiss bank, with instructions in place to disburse the funds to separate banks and accounts immediately.

There were two remaining loose ends. First, Carson Jeffers and Nichole Lewis. As long as they remained alive, they could destroy everything. Esteban had promised to eliminate the two of them. But now, The Cleaner knew that other arrangements would have to be made. After tonight, Esteban Moreno and his Chilean companion would be dead. They were the second loose end, and it would be tied up within 24 hours. It was never the Cleaner's intention to turn the world into total chaos. He had always planned to just bring the United States into submission and then to turn the whole thing around. When the actual shooter of the missiles was killed, along with the destruction of the remaining missiles, everyone would step back from the abyss, thankful for the intelligence services of the United States. As he thought about public opinion, he knew that President Rolland Attwilder would always shoulder the blame for the terrorist plot.

• • •

Special Agent John Feather of the FBI put his coffee mug on the counter top of the Fleetwood motor home and listened to Warren Alexander, Deputy Director of the CIA, review the details of the surveillance operation.

"No one can move the van without alerting our team that is in the parking garage. The van must turn right after exiting the building, and our trap is set to be sprung just before the first intersection." Warren Alexander was referring to the joint FBI/CIA operation to capture the terrorists and the missiles.

"And if the shooter decides to go the wrong way on a one-way street?" Agent Feather commented.

"We doubt that will happen, but in the event that we're wrong, we have a second tactical squad ready to stop the van if it goes north."

Agent Feather couldn't find fault with the plan. When the van was moved, it would be stopped and the missiles destroyed or recovered. He had originally wanted to apprehend both the shooter and the missiles together in the garage, but Washington had vetoed that idea and come up with this instead. It wasn't that he didn't appreciate the assistance of the CIA, but he felt that the FBI could handle this on their own. John Feather was a professional, and if Washington wanted the CIA involved, so be it.

For the next hour, John Feather and Warren Alexander double-checked each step of the operation. Both of them realized that they were not to take any prisoners. Washington wanted the whole mess ended neatly, and that meant no long trials. With armor-piercing bullets and rocket propelled missiles, each man knew there wouldn't be enough left of the terrorists to identify, especially when the Stinger missiles started going off. Hopefully, there wouldn't be many civilian casualties, but they both realized that was something they couldn't control.

• • •

Pizza was not Carson's favorite food, but they do deliver to hotels in the airport area. He took another bite of the pepperoni and cheese dish, aware that Nichole had hardly touched a thing. "Nichole, you really need to eat something," he said.

Something new was bothering Nichole. With everything that had happened to them in the past two weeks, it would be impossible for any normal person not to be affected. This was something different. From the time that Carson put the missile in front of the window leading to the tiny patio, he had felt a chasm open between them. She became almost sullen, refusing to answer anything but the most simple questions. He needed to know what was going on. "Speak to me, Nichole. Tell me what you're thinking," he said, putting his pizza back in the Domino's box.

She waited for thirty or forty seconds and then asked, "You are really going to kill this man without giving him a chance to even surrender?"

This was it. She couldn't accept what Carson knew he had to do. "Nichole, I'm not going to try and lie to you. In a matter of a few hours, I'm going to take this missile and coldly fire it at the terrorist who killed my son, my friends, and thousands of other people. Am I acting like judge, jury, and executioner? The answer is yes! In my mind, I'm not going to even try and justify my actions. If I do what I know I must, then many thousands of people will live, and we may have a chance to go on with our lives. As long as Esteban Moreno and Ricardo Gutierrez live, we will never be free. I don't have any real hope that we'll ever be free again, but this much I do know: Esteban Moreno will die! I will see to it."

Nichole listened to this man, a man who she knew loved her. His speech was not what she had hoped for. She felt that Carson was almost becoming like the man he was hunting. Still, she knew that he was probably right. And for better or worse, she was going to stand by him. "I'm all right," she said. "I just want this to end."

Carson rolled across the bed and took her in his arms. He wanted to tell her it really would be all right, but anymore, he just didn't know. Esteban Moreno would die in the next few hours, he would see to it. But, he wondered, who was behind this whole thing, and would he and Nichole ever be the same again? He felt Nichole sobbing softly, the tears slowly creeping down the soft skin of her face.

• • •

Esteban and Ricardo left their new rental car parked two and a half blocks from *Secure Parking*. Ricardo had picked Esteban up as soon as the plane from St. Louis landed at the airport. Not surprisingly, there were less than twelve people on the entire flight from the Midwest. All the way back on the plane, Esteban thought that the Cleaner had given in too easily. Putting himself in the Cleaner's place, he would have tried to work out a better compromise.

"Was it really necessary to wait until 1:00 in the morning?" Ricardo asked as they worked their way to the front of the long term storage facility.

"We are moving the missiles to Las Vegas, where they will be picked up later this morning and driven to eleven airports within a radius of 1,000 miles. I wanted to have the least amount of traffic possible. The last thing we need is a traffic accident with a van full of stolen Stinger missiles."

The older Hispanic attendant was reading a Spanish magazine when the two men slipped by him unobserved and walked up the ramp to the third level. "Wait," whispered Esteban, putting a hand on Ricardo's shoulder.

Ricardo looked around and instantly saw what had drawn Esteban's attention. A man had just got out of a white van with darkened windows. He left the side door of the vehicle partially open while he took a leak against a concrete post. Inside the van, they could see a second man sitting behind the steering wheel, staring at the blue van. He had a set of earphones on, as if he were listening to someone.

Esteban knew instantly that the Cleaner had given in too easily. At that minute, Esteban changed his plans. He knew that the missiles would never be used to shoot down another plane. He had hoped for the remaining $60 million, but, then, he had enough money to live comfortably for the rest of his life-that is, if he didn't have to share it with anyone, including Ricardo.

"Someone is watching the van," he said. "It might be some of Carson Jeffers' people." Esteban knew this couldn't be true, but he didn't want Ricardo to guess what was waiting outside.

"I saw them," Ricardo answered. "How do you want to handle them?"

"Do you still have the silencer on your .44 magnum?"

Ricardo nodded that he did.

"One man is sitting in the drivers' seat and the other in the right passenger seat. We'll slip up beside the van, and when I give the word, you come from the left and I'll take the right. Fire at least four or five shots into your man. We don't want either of them to alert Carson."

Slowly the two Latins worked their way up to the van, using the parked cars and concrete pillars as hiding places. When the two men had both got in position, Esteban raised his hand giving the signal. They stood and fired point blank into the dark tinted glass of the windshield. The only sounds that could be heard was the popping of glass as the silent bullets whipped through the windshield, splattering blood everywhere. Esteban quickly opened the door and checked to make sure that each man was dead. He felt a slight pulse from the driver, and fired two shots straight into his right eye.

"Let's get out of here," Ricardo said, as he jogged across the lot to the parked blue van. Esteban was right behind him.

Ricardo waited while his companion disarmed the bomb under the van.

"Use the can of pressurized tire *fix it* on the floor in the front seat, and fill the tire. I'll check the missiles," Esteban said as he walked around behind the van. Instantly, he knew that someone had been in the van. He had placed a thin piece of thread on the bottom of the door over the bumper when he parked the truck. It was gone. He doubted that the missiles had been touched or that the hit was to take place in the garage.

The two men in the white van were only lookouts. Opening the rear door he pulled the top case out of the truck and placed it behind the concrete post, unobserved by Ricardo.

"Everything OK?" asked Ricardo, as he came around the van, just as Esteban was closing the door.

"I think so. Let's make sure there are no other watchdogs when we leave. I'll stay behind and check to see that you aren't followed out of the building. You know where the rental car is parked. Meet me there in five or ten minutes. Let's just be safe about this," Esteban said.

"Five minutes then, at the car," Ricardo said as he got into the van and took the keys from Esteban.

46

SATURDAY MORNING

T he buzzing of the audio alarm on the motion detector woke Carson from his light sleep almost instantly. "Wake up," he said, shaking Nichole. Neither Carson nor Nichole had gone to bed. Everything had been packed for a speedy departure when they laid down on top of the queen sized comforter. Carson had explained that when the time came they would only have two minutes at the most. The motion detector would alert them the minute the front tire was being filled.

Nichole picked up her bag and opened the door to the hall. Pausing momentarily, she was about to ask if Carson was sure what he was doing. When she saw him open the sliding glass door and put the missile on his shoulder, she knew better than to ask. Instead, she said, "Be careful. I'll be in the car."

"Go!" Carson said over his shoulder. Sighting in on the entrance of the garage, he waited for the van to appear. He would wait for the man to make the corner and then lock onto the heat source from the exhaust. Before he laid down, he practiced locking on to the exhaust from passing cars. He knew he would have no problem. Almost two minutes had passed since the signal had sounded. The motion detector was flashing bright red.

•   •   •

"John, we may have a problem. I can't reach the two men in the parking structure," Alex said, referring to the CIA lookouts previously positioned on the upper floor of the concrete building.

"Did you check the radio? Is it working?" John asked, knowing that his counterpart in the CIA would have done so before alerting him. Not waiting for Alexander Warren to answer his first question, Agent John Feather exclaimed, "They've got to be moving. Alert your team. It's got to be going down." Both men by now had deduced that the men in the building had been taken out, or they would have checked in.

Alex was already calling the special joint tactical commanders out on the street. They were about to put a finish to the worst terrorist attack ever perpetrated against the United States.

Agent Feather had special night vision binoculars up to his eyes, watching the exit from the *Secure Parking* structure three blocks to the north. Without warning, he saw a blue van exit the garage and then turn south down the four lane road. "Get set," he yelled to the other men in the motor home. "Make sure he's almost in the intersection." The last instruction was unnecessary. All the agents were set to provide crossing fields of fire. Fortunately, the only structures on the opposite side of the intersection were two warehouses. The owners would be compensated later.

• • •

Carson locked on to the heat from the van's exhaust as soon as it made the turn. When he heard the steady hum from over his right shoulder, he pulled the trigger. Surprisingly, he felt nothing. It didn't release the demons in his mind, but neither did it cause him any remorse. He did what needed to be done and nothing more. Carson knew that he needed to leave, but he wanted to see the missile actually destroy his nemesis. It had to be over.

One moment the van was traveling down the street, the next instant there was a wall of flame and smoke fighting to escape in all directions. The noise of the explosion was greater than he could ever have imagined. Microseconds after the first explosion, the remaining portion of the van exploded, again and again and again. By the time the last Stinger of the missiles ignited, the repercussion of the first explosion had reached the *Airport Inn*. The blast of air knocked Carson back across the room, blowing him into the bathroom that was now on fire, a result of the back blast of the first missile leaving Carson's shoulder. The Stinger hull slid across the motel room floor. Dazed but awake, Carson crawled to the window a second time to see a 4,000 degree wall of flame consuming parked cars on both sides of the street. Running down the stairs, he bumped into several guests trying to escape the building. Fire alarms were sounding everywhere. He jumped into the passenger side of the previously damaged rental car as Nichole sped down the alley.

"Are you all right?" she asked, focusing on the alley exit straight ahead.

Carson looked back over his shoulder, still unable to fathom the destruction left in the wake of his missile. At least the man Esteban Moreno was dead. It didn't seem enough, but it was a start.

•   •   •

"God, what happened?" asked John Feather as he picked himself up from the floor. The motor home was still upright, but it almost seemed like a miracle, considering the blast that just shook the metal structure.

Jumping from the control center, Alexander Warren ran to see if any of his men were hurt. It appeared there were several with some second degree burns, and three men had been hit by flying metal, none seriously. It was amazing nobody had died. Screaming at the top of his voice, he yelled, "I said not to fire until they got to the intersection!"

His second in command ran to his side from the opposite side of the street. "Sir, we never fired at all. The van just exploded. It looked like there might have been some kind of projectile fired at the rear of the van."

John Feather had just emerged from the motor home when he heard what the CIA agent was saying. Pulling Warren apart, Agent Feather asked, "Was there a backup operation in place that neither of us were aware of?"

The CIA operative nodded his head and answered, "I wouldn't bet against it. Whatever happened, I can assure you that we better make the best of the situation."

Agent John Feather agreed. Both men ran towards what was left of the blue van.

• • •

Esteban stood in the shadows next to the entrance of the *Secure Parking* structure. He had been walking down the ramp to the first level when the initial explosion took place. Secondary explosions shook even the concrete parking garage. Electrical power was out everywhere. The Hispanic who had been sitting in the booth was gone, either to see what had happened or just running from fear.

Putting the green case on his shoulder, Esteban slipped into the darkness. He only had to walk two and a half blocks. It was plenty of time to begin planning how to extract revenge. After all, he still had one missile. In his mind he knew that he would kill both The Cleaner and the Butterfly. He had already forgotten about Carson Jeffers. He was no longer important.

47

W e'll take the Pacific Coast Highway for three or four miles, and then try and catch the 405," Carson said as Nichole turned south on Sepulveda. Off to the east, they heard the sounds of fire trucks and emergency vehicles responding to the explosions and fires on the feeder road leading to the interstate.

"Do you think anyone died?" Nichole asked, visually recalling what Carson had just done.

"Esteban Moreno is history. I'm assuming that he and his companion from *La Libertad Occidental* were driving the van. I doubt that enough of their bodies will be left to identify, but I personally watched the van explode. They're dead."

"How about people in the surrounding area? The sound of the explosion and the fire was horrible," She asked as she went through an empty intersection heading south.

"Nichole, I hope that no one was hurt, but I can't promise you they weren't," Carson said, watching the road. He didn't say anything else, knowing that Nichole was still thinking about the innocent people who may have been hurt on the road near the parking structure.

Twenty minutes later, Nichole turned south onto the 405 and headed towards the Carlsbad airport.

• • •

"It's on the second floor next to the pool," Nichole said as she told Carson where the room at the Best Western Oceanside Inn was located.

"Did the clerk act like he recognized you?"

"No. He was just anxious to get back to studying some text book. I gathered from the papers on the counter that he was a student who had taken the night job as a way to earn money and study at the same time."

Carson was already removing the shotgun from the trunk as Nichole finished speaking. It was almost three in the morning, but both Carson and Nichole were wide awake. Nichole closed the door leading from the hallway, noticing for the first time that Carson was bleeding from his right arm again. In the light of the room, she saw that his recently dyed dark brown hair was almost black. She hoped it was just dirt, and that it hadn't been burned. It was both. "Are you all right?" she asked, putting down her bag on the bed and taking his arm in hers.

Carson hadn't felt any pain from either the minor burns in his hair or the opening of the week old wound on his arm. "It's all right. Just let me clean up, and I'll feel a lot better." Kissing her on the forehead, he turned and walked into the bathroom.

Nichole turned on the television and listened to a local newscast. The broadcaster said that initial reports confirmed that federal authorities had destroyed the remaining missiles originally stolen from Marine Corps Air Station, El Toro. She was about to turn off the set when Special Agent John Feather of the FBI began to speak into the microphone.

"We are pleased to announce that a van carrying Stinger surface to air missiles has been completely destroyed, along with terrorists of the radical organization, La Libertad Occidental. The operation was conducted as part of a joint FBI/CIA Terrorist Task Force, under the special direction of the Vice President of the United States - Jason Wright..."

Carson was too tired to pay attention to the television sounds coming in through the open bathroom door. He heard what was being said, but his own thoughts were focused on the problem still at hand. He knew someone high up in the government had been feeding Esteban Moreno and his Latin companion false information about himself and Nichole.

Somehow, he had to neutralize this threat and get back a normal life. Right now, he doubted that this was possible.

"Are you awake?" Nichole asked, standing in the door looking at Carson soaking in the tub with his eyes closed.

Without opening his eyes, he answered, "Barely."

Nichole suddenly realized just how deeply she felt for this 44 year old man. He had entered her life in the midst of tragedy, and she had been praying in her soul that he wouldn't exit in the same way. Silently, she pulled off her blouse and removed her pants, and then stepped into the tub. She felt him move back to give her room to sit in front of him. As she leaned back, she felt Carson's chest through the warm water of the tub. Without saying a word, he wrapped his arms around her, cupping her breasts in his hands. Nothing more needed to be said. She leaned her head back on his neck as he kissed her cheek. Everything else could wait until morning.

•   •   •

Carson had a towel wrapped around his waist and was just finishing shaving. Five hours had passed since they checked into The Best Western Inn in Oceanside. After a warm shower that ended with purposely cold water, he was refreshed. Nichole was still lying on the bed, naked except for the sheet that was draped over her body. He had let her continue to sleep, hoping to sort out the remaining questions. Over the sound of the running water in the sink, he almost didn't hear her speak.

"How long have you been up?" Nichole asked as she came and wrapped her arms around him.

"Not long. Are you sure you don't want to sleep some more?"

"No, I'm fine. I think we need to talk. It's not over, is it?" she asked, holding him from behind.

He turned and looked down at her pleading eyes, fully aware that she had been trying to answer some of the same questions he had. "Nichole, someone besides Esteban Moreno and Ricardo Gutierrez is involved in this terrorist action. All along, this person has been feeding information to the press, manipulating government agencies, and providing Esteban and his companion with vital intelligence. We are still a deep threat to this person, whoever he is. There is no doubt in my mind that we have to find out who he or she is and then somehow put a stop to the rest of the operation. For the past hour, I have tried to figure out who we are dealing with, and absolutely no one makes sense."

"You don't have any idea?"

"None that even I would believe," he said, leading her back into the bedroom. "Let's call Michael in Swan Lake and see if he has had any more luck in deciphering the rest of the information we took off Esteban's computer." Nichole slipped back under the sheet on the king sized bed as Carson picked up the phone and began dialing Montana.

"Carson, I'm glad you called. The *Today Show* had a special on about the destruction of the Stinger missiles and the deaths of the terrorists. I kept hoping you weren't involved."

"Michael, we were there in Los Angeles. In fact I fired the missile that destroyed the van and killed Esteban Moreno and his friend."

"Where are you now?" Michael asked, wanting to make sure that Carson hadn't somehow been apprehended.

"In Oceanside, California, at a Best Western Inn."

"Carson, you and Nichole are still in deep trouble. On the news it was announced that you are still being sought in connection with the terrorist threat."

Carson sat on the wooden chair at the desk and listened to Michael relate what had been said on the *Today Show*. Nichole listened to half the conversation, realizing that Michael was an hour ahead of them. She turned the television on low to the same program that Michael had been talking about. Turning the volume down, so as not to disturb Carson, she tried to listen to both Carson and the television newscaster.

After relating what had been said on the *Today Show*, Michael got back to the computer information. "Several things have happened in the past few hours. First of all, I was able to access the individual overseas accounts. The $12 billion that was spread throughout the numbered accounts is no longer there."

"It's not?" exclaimed Carson loudly.

Nichole turned down the volume on the television set, startled by his outcry.

Carson could almost see Michael grinning as he listened to his best friend continue. "Let me back up. Remember when we found reference to someone known as The Cleaner?"

"Yes," Carson answered. "What about this Cleaner?"

"At first I thought that Esteban Moreno might have been the Cleaner, but it just didn't make sense. It appears that this Cleaner fellow has been feeding Esteban information. He is also the person with withdrawal authorization on all the accounts."

"The accounts that are now empty?" Carson questioned.

"The same. Anyway, I have been up all night trying to figure out the authorization codes to access these accounts. The simplest codes are usually tied to specific dates, like birthdays, deaths, etc. In the case of this Cleaner, we didn't have any such information, and I seriously doubted that he would have used something so simple. So I started manipulating letters and numbers related to the word Cleaner itself."

"Did you have any luck?" asked Carson, hoping that somehow they might find out who this Cleaner was.

"If you mean, do I know who the Cleaner is? The answer is no. But I did finally break the authorization code for the accounts, and it was always the same."

"You what?"

"I broke the authorization codes for the accounts. I assigned numbers to the letters for the word Cleaner. C was number 3, L was 12 and so forth." Trying to go slow so that Carson could take notes, he finished, "The numbers were then 3, 12, 5, 1, 14, 5, and 18. After I had the numbers, I multiplied them all together and came up with the number 226,800. I used this as the authorization code, and it worked."

"But the money was gone?" Carson added.

"Well, not at first. I hope you are sitting down," Michael said. "I personally transferred all of the money from the individual accounts to a separate off-shore account, and then retransferred all of the money to another account. Carson, all of the money is now in an account you still have in the Caimans. Over $12 billion three hundred seventy million dollars."

Carson couldn't believe what he was hearing. "How did you do that? I thought all of our accounts were seized by the government."

"Six years ago we set up a small account to pay for licensing fees in connection with the drilling rights in the North Sea. The account was still in existence on the Island of Man, even though it has been dormant for more than five years. Before this morning there was a total of $458 in U.S. funds in the account. It was only a custodial account, and no one in the States ever knew about it. Anyway, I transferred all the money into that account, and then retransferred the money to a similar custodial account that ManTech had in the Caimans. The United States Government does not know about either of these accounts. In a nutshell, the money belonging to this Cleaner has vanished."

Carson took a minute to answer, not really knowing what to say. Finally, he asked, "Is that all?" He could feel the tone of the conversation change immediately.

"No, Carson it's not. Remember the list of phone numbers in the file?"

"Yes."

"I ran a computer trace on all of the numbers. All but one of the numbers were businesses, which I suspect are fronts for the CIA, or some intelligence operation. Each of the companies deals in overseas shipments of goods or services."

"And the last number?" Carson asked, bewildered as to where Michael was going.

"We knew it rang in Washington, D.C., but I was able to narrow that down a lot more. Carson, it rings straight through to the office of the Vice President of the United States."

Carson didn't answer.

"I rang the number and said the call was from the Cleaner. The person who answered the phone immediately put me through to Jason Wright. I hung up before the call could be traced."

• • •

The Cleaner laid in the tub, listening to the news broadcast detail the destruction of the missiles and the killing of the terrorists in the van outside the Los Angeles Airport. The job was a little messy, but at least Esteban Moreno and Ricardo Gutierrez were out of the picture. Now all he had to do was to finish off Carson Jeffers and Nichole Lewis. With the full power of the United States government at his disposal, he had no doubt that the two would soon be found. A basic plan of action was already forming in his mind when the phone on the wall by the tub rang.

"Yes," he answered.

"Is that you?" the familiar voice asked on the phone.

"Jason, are you crazy? Why are you calling me here? You know the risks."

"The risk in not calling you is even greater. You've seen the news this morning, I take it?"

"If you are asking for a compliment, then you have my congratulations," The Cleaner said.

"Congratulations are not in order. The missiles in the blue van were not destroyed by either the CIA or the FBI. It appears that a separate Stinger missile was fired from a hotel room across from the parking garage. The room was rented by a blond, who closely resembled Nichole Lewis. It looks like our friend Carson Jeffers destroyed the missiles. If he found out about the missiles, he may have found out a lot more."

"Get rid of him and the woman. They must be terminated immediately."

"It'll be done." stated the Vice President emphatically over the phone.

"Let me know when it is!" ordered the Cleaner, hanging up the phone. It amazed the silver haired man in the tub how true power doesn't rest in the office holder but, rather, the person who put the elected official in office. This was certainly true of the Vice President of the United States. No sooner had he replaced the phone in its cradle when it rang again. He wondered who it was this time, still content that everything was working out better than planned.

"Sir, I hate to call you like this, but I knew you needed to hear what happened," the voice said.

"Chris, is that you?" asked The Cleaner, recognizing the voice of his chief accountant.

"Yes, sir."

"Go on, Chris, tell me why you called so upset."

Not knowing how else to say it, the accountant just blurted out what he had to say. "It's gone, all gone, every last dime!"

"What's gone?" asked the Cleaner, already infected by the distress in Chris' voice.

"The $12 billion dollars, sir. It's all gone."

The Cleaner pulled himself out of the tub, grabbing a towel and yelling at the same time, "What are you saying? It can't be gone."

"I'm afraid it is, sir. This morning I went to check the balances of the separate accounts and found that all the money had been transferred to an account on the Island of Man at just past five o'clock your time in California."

"Get it back!" ordered the Cleaner to the frightened accountant three thousands miles away.

"That's not possible, sir. It was transferred to a numbered account, and in all likelihood has been moved again in the past couple of hours. It could be anywhere in the world. The money's gone sir," Chris said, waiting for The Cleaner to answer.

The Cleaner hung up the phone without saying another word to his accountant. He had to think this through. Somehow, Esteban was able to access the funds. After all, only Esteban, Chris, his accountant, and himself knew about all the accounts. And only his accountant and himself knew the authorization code to transfer the money. How Esteban got the authorization code was unknown. Suddenly, it dawned on him. Esteban was already dead when the transfer took place at five in the morning.

Pacing the floor of the hotel room, he kept saying, "How? How? How?"

Stopping in front of the large window looking west to the ocean, he knew who had taken the money: Carson Jeffers! He couldn't figure out how he did it, but there was no doubt that if Carson knew about the missiles, he must have known about the money. Picking up the phone on the desk, he dialed the private number of Jason Wright. "Jason, at the peril of your own life, Carson Jeffers and the Lewis woman are to be brought to me alive! If they die, you die! Do you understand?"

The Vice President said that he did, and then asked what all this was about. Jason didn't say a word as The Cleaner explained what had happened in the past few hours.

• • •

"Michael transferred over $12 billion of someone else's money to you?" Nichole asked as Carson finished explaining what Michael had said on the telephone.

"That's about the size of it," he answered, turning up the volume on the television set as the graphics advertising a special news announcement flashed across the screen.

"It's coming from the White House," Nichole said, referring to the news conference that was about to start on television.

Carson and Nichole watched as President Rolland Attwilder and Vice President Jason Wright stood on the raised platform ready to speak to the American people. President Attwilder stepped forward to the microphone, the glare of the lights accenting his ruddy complexion.

"My fellow Americans. It is with a great deal of satisfaction that Vice President Jason Wright and myself stand before you this morning, only hours after the worst terrorist threat in our country's history has been eliminated. I won't attempt to detail all the resources used to destroy the Stinger missiles early this morning in Los Angeles. Instead, I want to compliment the overall supervisor of this successful operation, one that does this country proud. Join me in thanking Vice President Jason Wright, who was responsible for giving our country back to the people."

Carson and Nichole watched as President Rolland Attwilder took Jason Wright by the hand and raised their arms in a victory celebration.

Following President Attwilder's remarks, Jason Wright gave a more detailed speech outlining the success of the joint FBI\CIA Terrorist Task Force. Jason Wright then took questions from the Press Corps.

Vice President Wright pointed to Tom Sanders of the *Washington Post*. "Mr. Vice President. Were the terrorists, Carson Jeffers and Nichole Lewis, apprehended or killed in this operation?"

When Carson heard his name, he sat forward to listen, prompting Nichole to do the same.

"Neither Carson Jeffers nor Nichole Lewis were killed or apprehended. They are still at large and are wanted for questioning in this terrorist threat, as well as additional attacks against other democratic nations. It is believed that both of these people possess certain vital information that can eliminate many terrorist organizations around the globe. It is imperative that they be taken alive. Under no circumstances should anyone try to apprehend them. Instead, call the nearest FBI office."

"What was that all about?" Nichole asked, referring to the fact that they must be taken alive.

"Unless I miss my bet, someone has just discovered that they are missing $12 billion, and they told the Vice President of the United States that they want it back!"

48

"Is the boss in?" Hank Grishhold asked Sandra Kennard. Deep furrows on Hank's forehead seemed to aggravate the lingering questions he had refused to confront.

"Go right in. He's been expecting you," the President's personal secretary answered, looking up from the stack of papers on her desk.

"Take a seat, Hank," President Attwilder said, motioning to the chair by his desk. "It looks like this whole thing is just about over."

"Yes, sir. Just about." Hank knew what the President was getting to. Carson Jeffers and Nichole Lewis had still not been apprehended, and at this point there appeared to be little doubt that Carson was a member of *La Libertad Occidental.*

"I'm sorry it has come down to this, but we both have to face facts. There is just too much evidence to ignore. If your friend was not guilty, why hasn't he come forward and given himself up?"

Hank wanted to tell the President that with the press and media coverage concerning Carson there was virtually no way he could ever get a fair trial if he were even taken alive. Instead, he said, "It looks pretty bad, but somehow I feel that if he has the chance, he will be able to explain everything."

"Vice President Wright has assured me that he will do everything possible to bring both Carson and Nichole Lewis in alive. After that, we'll just have to see. But, I must tell you, Hank, I personally believe that Carson Jeffers is as guilty as sin," President Attwilder said, while looking at the piece of paper he had been writing on when Hank entered.

"I hope you're wrong, sir."

The tall statesman from New Mexico nodded and then went on. "Hank, we're not out of the woods yet. We have destroyed the missiles and killed at least some of the terrorists, but until we bring in Carson Jeffers, public opinion is still going to be against us."

Hank knew that the President was getting to something else. "What do you want to do about it?" asked Hank, referring to some plan that the President must have to get the best public image possible.

"In the next couple of days, we have to restore the market economy of the United States. Somehow, we have to revitalize confidence in the stock market and everything that goes with it. The mini trade summit is supposed to take place at my Santa Fe ranch on Monday. We both know that the summit was really called in order that we could put some kind of pressure on our trading partners to leave their U.S. investments in our debt and equity markets."

"With the destruction of the missiles, I think that this will take place as planned," Hank said, still not sure what the President had in mind.

"Hank, we need something much stronger than a status quo from countries like Japan and Germany. If, together with these nations, we could somehow manipulate public opinion in such a way as to turn the market around immediately, then our trading partners would be able to recover the value of their U.S. dollar investments that was lost in the last two weeks. The domino effect of this would be to restore the lost equity in everything from mutual funds to certificates of deposit for every American investor, large and small."

The President's Chief of Staff could see what the President wanted to do, but he didn't have the slightest idea of how to do it. "What can we possibly do that will restore such overwhelming confidence in the stock market, literally overnight?"

President Attwilder rose from his chair and started to pace the room, a little unsure of exactly how to say what he had been thinking. Finally, he stopped by the fireplace and turned to Hank. "I want to literally use a form of insider trading to prop up the market." Knowing that he had Hank's undivided attention, President Attwilder went on. "Drew Matthews arranged for $2 billion to pay the ransom demands of the

LLO. This money was coming from eleven of the top Fortune Five Hundred companies in America. This money will not have to be paid, now that the missiles have been destroyed."

As the President hesitated a second time, Hank asked, "And?"

"Hank, I want these eleven companies to use this money to get our country out of this mess."

"What can they do now that the missile threat is destroyed?" Hank asked, still unsure of what President Attwilder was asking.

"Hank, what I am about to ask you to do is in all likelihood illegal, but I firmly believe it is in the best interests of the companies in question, of our trading partners, and of the American people. I want these eleven companies to use this money to start buying back the stock in their own companies at the market price as of Thursday two weeks ago. This was one day before the crash of Flight 421 in Salt Lake City. Then I want to put as much political pressure on the remaining public companies to do the same thing. Come Monday morning, I am going to ask each of our major trading partners to start investing along the exact same lines. Everything will happen simultaneously before the opening of the stock market on Tuesday morning."

Hank got up from his chair and walked over to the fireplace where President Attwilder was still standing. As he looked up at his boss, Hank smiled and said, "By God, it will work. Once the investors see the confidence of the major companies, as well as that demonstrated by our overseas investors, the market will turn around overnight. But you're right. It is certainly illegal. What do you want me to do?"

"Vice President Wright has been coordinating all communication with Drew Matthews, and normally I would ask him to run interference with Drew on this matter. But, if it all goes down the toilet, I think we better keep at least one of our country's top two executives clean. I want you to get hold of Drew Matthews as soon as this meeting is over and explain exactly what I've told you. Invite him to attend the trade summit in Santa Fe with us on Monday. Ask him to make contact with the eleven parties who were willing to put up the money for the ransom payment, and find out if they are willing to go along with me. You can stress the point that we are still willing to cut taxes and give them the other incentives they asked for. I'm confident that Drew can pull this off. Then arrange for him to meet privately with you and me in Santa Fe tomorrow morning, a day ahead of the summit."

"What about Vice President Wright? Won't he think it funny that Drew Matthews is invited to the summit, and he isn't?"

"Don't worry about that. I've already arranged for Vice President Wright to be in Santa Fe by this evening."

•   •   •

"Nichole, somehow we have got to explain to President Rolland Attwilder that Vice President Wright is involved in this terrorist threat," Carson said as they watched the early afternoon news on CNN.

"You've seen the news," she said. "Vice President Wright is being given total credit for bringing an end to the madness. Why will the President listen to us? We're the terrorists most people still believe are at least partially responsible for the deaths of thousands."

Carson got up from the bottom of the bed in the Best Western Oceanside Inn and walked over to the window, where he could see the surf crashing into the rocks two hundred yards away. "President Attwilder is not going to listen to us if we are captured. If Vice President Wright is still supervising the operation, we need to accept the fact that we will die before we have a chance to talk to President Attwilder or anyone else who could blow the whistle."

"Then what do you propose to do?" she asked, still lying on the bed with her head propped up between her hands.

"We have to meet with the President, or at the very least get a private conversation with him on the phone."

"How do you propose to do that?"

"You remember Hank Grishhold, my air force buddy, who is now the Chief of Staff for the President?"

"The same fellow who refused to help you when you called from Portland? Why would he have changed his mind now?" She rolled onto her side, so as to talk face to face with Carson, who was still standing across the room.

Turning away from the window and walking to the phone, Carson said, "He won't have changed his mind. This time, I'm not going to give him a chance to turn me down." He picked up the phone and dialed a number in Alexandria, Virginia.

The phone rang three times and then was answered by a woman with a pleasant western accent. "Hello."

"Nina, is Hank there?"

"No, he's not. May I take a message?" she answered, not recognizing Carson's voice.

Pausing just for a second, Carson answered, "When do you expect him?"

Knowing that the number was unlisted, Nina Grishhold assumed that the caller was a friend of her husband. "Hank should be home within the next half hour. Can I tell him who this is?"

"Just tell him Jughead called."

"Jughead?" she asked, puzzled by the name.

"He'll understand," he said, hanging up the phone.

Nichole had been listening to the conversation, and asked, "What did you mean by the name Jughead?"

"Back in Vietnam my call sign on the radio was Jughead. I already told you that Hank and I remained close after Vietnam, and one of the biggest reasons for this was because I saved his neck when we were flying over Hanoi. If I hadn't arrived when I did, Hank would be dead, or at the least would have spent several years in a prisoner of war camp. When I used the name, Jughead, I was reminding him of the debt that he still owes me."

"Will he remember?" Nichole questioned.

"Oh, he'll remember. Whether he will help us or not remains to be seen."

Thirty minutes later, Carson put a call through to Hank's home. He decided there was probably less risk in making the call from the hotel room than in wandering around town looking for a secure phone. If they traced the call to Oceanside, Carson knew that they wouldn't have a prayer of escaping anyway.

"Hank, this is Jughead," Carson said, waiting for some type of response on the other end. If the response seemed forced, Carson was already planning on hanging up.

Hank knew that he should never have taken the call without getting a trace on the line, but he also understood the significance of the name Jughead. "Carson, you need to give yourself up immediately. It's your only hope, and it's also the only hope that your lady friend has."

Nichole was sitting next to Carson on the bed, with the phone positioned between their two heads, so as to listen to both sides of the conversation. It was working.

"Hank, I can't do that. But I can tell you that the reports that you hear on television are not true."

"Did you shoot the missile that took out the van in Los Angeles?" Hank asked.

"I did, but it's not what you think. Hank, I need to talk personally to President Attwilder."

"Carson, you know that's not possible. President Attwilder has turned the supervision of the terrorist operation over to Vice President Wright. Turn yourself in, and I can assure you that the Vice President will meet with you immediately."

Carson didn't want to divulge the Vice President's role in the terrorist action until he knew who else was involved. "Hank, that won't do. I insist that you set up a meeting with the President." Hesitating, he added, "Hank, you owe me!"

Hank understood that his career in public service had probably just ended, but Carson was right, he did owe him. He owed him his life. There really was no option. "All right. I'll do it, but you had better make it good. The President is already on his way to the Western White House for a trade summit to be held on Monday."

"In Santa Fe?" asked Carson, wanting to make sure that Hank was referring to President Attwilder's New Mexico ranch.

"Correct. I'm leaving myself later this afternoon. I'm going to give you a secure phone number that rings straight through to the President's office. Call this number tomorrow morning about eleven o'clock. I'll make sure that you get the ear of the President, but I can't do any more than that. After that, you are on your own." The President's Chief of

Staff then gave Carson the unlisted number, known to less than a dozen people in the world.

• • •

Esteban closed the door to the used 1990 King Cab Ford pick-up and walked around to make sure the metal top covering the bed of the truck was also locked. He had purchased the white pick-up earlier that morning in Riverside, California, and then driven back to the Ontario Airport Hilton. Using a blanket from his room, he had wrapped the missile and then placed it in the back of the truck along with the wooden two by fours. Taking the package of electronics parts and hardware supplies he had purchased thirty minutes earlier, he walked into the hotel, ready to begin his final act of revenge.

After he opened the door to his room, he turned on the television to CNN. There was virtually no other news other than the destruction of the missiles in Los Angeles. As he listened to the announcer tell about the hunt for Carson Jeffers, he decided that before he was finished, he would still finish the termination on Jeffers and the Lewis lady. It had become personal. Just before the half hour, the CNN reporter explained that President Attwilder and Vice President Wright would be attending a trade summit in Santa Fe on Monday. Both the President and Vice President were already on their way to New Mexico.

Esteban used the remote control and muted the volume on the television, saying out loud, "Perfect. I'll take care of Jason Wright, and before he dies, he will tell me where to find The Cleaner."

49

SUNDAY MORNING

I t only took Carson twenty minutes to drive from the Best Western Inn to the Carlsbad airport, and at five in the morning there was virtually no traffic. He had originally planned to wait in Oceanside and then call the President at 11:00, but then decided that somehow he must meet face to face with President Attwilder. That could only happen in Santa Fe.

"Will anyone stop us from taking the Seneca?" asked Nichole as they drove the rental car up to the Carlsbad Airport FBO.

"No one will arrive at the FBO office until around six or six thirty. As long as we have the key to the door of the plane, we'll be fine. That's the reason Blake fueled the plane when we landed." Carson's voice got a little softer as he remembered how Blake had literally given his life trying to find an answer to why all of this was happening.

"And the rental car?" Nichole said, wondering what they should do with the vehicle.

"We'll leave it parked in the public parking area. Hertz will not be looking for the car until it's overdue, and that won't be for five more days. We need to park it so that the damaged fender is not visible from the road. Hopefully, no one will stop to check it out."

It was still dark, and Carson turned off the lights on the Ford Taurus belonging to Hertz. "I'll pre-flight the plane while you find an inconspicuous place to leave the car," he said, walking around to the trunk to get the shotgun. He wasn't sure why he kept taking the gun, but it somehow gave him a sense of security. In his mind, he knew that it would be of virtually no help at all. If, somehow, they could get in to see President Attwilder, he knew they couldn't bring the shotgun with them.

He walked out to the plane parked near the wire fence and found it was still tied down with safety chains. Sometimes, the FBO finds it necessary to move a plane, but apparently Carlsbad is not too busy, and no one had touched it. By the time Nichole got back to the plane, he had checked the fuel for water condensation and completed his walk around.

The front right door of the plane was open. Nichole stepped up onto the wing, insuring that she missed the flaps. "How soon before we can get out of here?" she asked as she leaned over and crawled in the co-pilot's seat.

"Five minutes, no more," Carson answered, while listening to the radio for wind and weather conditions.

"I'm glad. Dawn is starting to appear on the eastern horizon, and I'm concerned that someone will come and ask questions as to our being here."

Carson nodded without answering and continued reading the *Before Taxi Checklist*.

•   •   •

"Mr. President, Drew Matthews just arrived," Hank stated.

"Show him in. Let's find out how much success he has had in the last twenty-four hours," President Attwilder said, wiping his mouth with the breakfast napkin he picked up from the southwest table in his Santa Fe kitchen.

"Mr. President, I'm glad we are meeting under the present scenario instead of the one that was originally planned," the distinguished business leader stated.

"So am I, Drew. I assume Hank briefed you on the plan for turning around public opinion concerning the stock market?"

"Completely, and I want to add that I think it will work."

The truth of the matter was that Drew had considered the plan and all of its ramifications and firmly believed that it was in fact, brilliant. Eventually, the market would recover on its own, but it might destroy many good and excellent companies along the way. True, there would be a few people who would profit greatly from the increased stock prices from Monday to Tuesday, but overall, the effect would be positive.

The President motioned to the empty seat at the old pine table. "Take a seat, and join Hank and myself for a true Western Omelet."

"I've already eaten. But I would like some coffee."

President Attwilder pressed a buzzer beside his plate and a steward appeared almost immediately. "How do you want it, Drew?" he said, referring to the coffee.

"Black will be fine, Mr. President."

As soon as the steward poured the coffee and left the room, the President continued. "OK, you agree with our plan. I'm not going to insult you by explaining the potential legal problems which could result by our discussion becoming public. But I would like to know what success you have had in getting our eleven financial backers to agree."

Drew took out a piece of paper that contained eleven names. Staring at the paper for a moment, he handed it to the President. "During the last twelve hours I have personally talked to or met with each of the people on that list. Beside the name of the person is an amount they were previously willing to put up on behalf of their companies to make the payment to the LLO."

"Why did you give me this list?" questioned the President. "Is it really wise for me to know who these people are?"

Hank wasn't aware that Drew was going to make this move, but he understood why Drew thought it necessary. If the plan to manipulate the stock market ever became known, Drew and the people on that list could state that everything they did was done with the full knowledge and consent of the President of the United States. "Drew, I don't think that the President needs to have the list."

Drew ignored Hank, put down his coffee cup on the weathered table, and looked directly at the tall lanky cowboy dressed in a cotton denim shirt, Levis and boots. "Mr. President, the list is a form of security for the eleven people we are talking about. As far as anyone else knows, neither this conversation nor my previous discussions with these gentleman will ever become public knowledge." Keeping his hands on the wooden table, so as not to have to take back the eleven names, Drew went on. "Each of those individuals have agreed to back your plan one hundred percent. By Tuesday morning, the entire $2 billion will have been committed in the stock market. For all practical purposes, this money will remain unavailable to these companies for the foreseeable future. There is not a problem with this as long at your administration fulfills its commitment to back a corporate tax rollback, along with the elimination or substantial reduction of the capital gains tax. These two moves will open up the equity market in such a way that the companies can recover this money."

President Attwilder looked at the list of names in his hand and knew that he really had no choice but to go along. He didn't appreciate the implied threat from the chief executives of the eleven companies, but he really couldn't blame them. In their position, he probably would not have done any different. Putting the small, but crucial, piece of paper in his shirt pocket, he asked, "What do you need to do to put the operation into effect?"

"Nothing. As long as I don't personally contact each of these people, the stock market will open higher on Tuesday morning. I told each of them that the only reason I would be contacting them would be to put a halt to the plan. But you do realize, Mr. President, that this amount of buying will not be enough to support the market in its entirety. You are going to have to get some additional support."

President Attwilder looked across the table at Hank and then said, "Drew, I want you to spend both today and tomorrow here at the ranch. Hank will make sure you are comfortable. I can assure you that by this time Monday afternoon you will be able to personally see the additional support we have solicited to help in this effort."

"Whatever you say, Mr. President. But could I ask why the Vice President is not here this morning?"

"He'll join us later this afternoon. I would ask that you not relate any of this conversation to him. I personally believe that the fewer details he has of this plan, the better off he will be. And he is still very involved in winding up the operational side of this LLO threat."

• • •

Esteban had to show his CIA credential to two separate Secret
Service agents as he turned off state Highway 76. He explained that he
was to see Vice President Wright, and they passed him through, reminding him to check in with the agents at the front gate of President
Attwilder's ranch. If they had called and asked to speak to Vice President
Wright, Esteban had no doubt that Jason Wright would have passed him
through, but Esteban's plans would have changed a great deal.

Two miles before he would have arrived at the Western White
House, Esteban turned east away from the presidential property. It took
him almost a half hour and six miles of steep terrain before he parked the
white pick-up with the covered top. Getting out of the truck, he could
see the President's ranch house several thousand feet below him. The
house was surrounded by tall pines that in their own way guarded the
President every bit as much as the one hundred Secret Service agents
who were gathered on the property. Taking out the powerful binoculars
that had been resting on the front seat under his leather jacket, he sighted
in on the property. He could read the government license plates parked
around the compound.

"It couldn't be better," he commented to himself as he got back in
the truck and backed it into the pines nestled against the hill on the edge
of the Santa Fe National Forest. He had purchased a topographical map
of the area, and was confident that he wouldn't be disturbed. In the event
that he was wrong, any intruder would quickly become a permanent resident of the national forest. Taking the sniper rifle and his .44 magnum
pistol, he spent the next 45 minutes insuring that his map had been correct. It was, and he was alone.

• • •

There had been a slight tail wind from the coast, and the total flying
time had been just over three hours and forty-five minutes. Nichole listened quietly as Carson alerted the neighboring aircraft that he would be

taking a long final for Runway 22. Carson had chosen to land at
Coronado Airport to minimize any chance of recognition. The smaller
general aviation landing strip was five hundred feet higher in elevation
than Albuquerque International and was located some twelve miles to
the north.

Carson dialed in 110.0 on Nav 1 for the Instrument Landing
Approach. It was only 9:30 a.m. in Oceanside, but with the hour time
change, he only had thirty minutes until he was supposed to make the
call to the number in Santa Fe. Weather conditions were good and winds
favored Runway 22.

"How are we going to get a car?" Nichole asked as they began their
final descent.

"We're not. We'll make the call to the President as agreed. If some-
things wrong, I hope I'll be able to sense it when I get Hank on the
phone. We have enough fuel to make it to Durango, Colorado, and if we
have to, we'll take off immediately. But that is only the optional plan."

"What do you mean 'optional plan'?"

Carson continued his approach for landing on 22 and answered
Nichole at the same time as he lowered the landing gear on the Seneca
II. "If things go as I hope they will, Hank will come and pick us up to
meet with the President. And they will, if I can convince the President to
trust us enough to meet with us."

It was an eggshell landing, and Nichole was becoming more
impressed with Carson's flying skills with every touch down. The one in
the mountains of Montana didn't really count. As she thought about it,
Carson had done an extremely good job to even land the Citation. Five
minutes after landing, Carson put on a baseball cap and walked away
from the plane to a phone booth located beside the FBO. Nichole held
his arm. Normally the phone was used by pilots when they landed after
the FBO was shut down. This morning, he was going to call the
President of the United States.

• • •

It was almost eleven o'clock, and Hank had just finished briefing

President Attwilder on the upcoming telephone call. President Attwilder had been furious when he found out that Hank had had a conversation with Carson Jeffers, and then kept that information secret. After he calmed down, he agreed that he would take the call on the condition that Carson agreed to turn himself in. Hank had stated that was Carson's intention, not knowing if it were true or not.

"Where is he calling from?" the President demanded in an angry voice.

"I don't know, Mr. President. I just told him to call at eleven o'clock sharp. To the best of my knowledge, he's still in California."

"Hank, I want this call traced. I am not going to do anything about apprehending him until after he calls, but it is imperative that we know where he is. Do you have a problem with this?"

"No, sir."

"Then set it up. I assume we are still equipped to do this?"

"We are, Mr. President. In fact, every call placed to the ranch is automatically identified by number. I'll make sure that we have the location of the call before you finish talking."

Hank left the room to make the arrangements and returned two minutes later. The phone on the President's roll top western style desk rang just as he entered the room. As President Attwilder motioned for Hank to take the call, Vice President Wright stepped through the door. Hank had given Jason a preliminary briefing as to what was happening when he met the Vice President in the hallway.

"Take a seat, Jason. We are about to talk to Carson Jeffers." President Attwilder motioned for Jason to find a chair.

Vice President Wright was flabbergasted by the turn of events taking place at the ranch. First, he had come down for breakfast and found Drew Matthews in the kitchen speaking with President Attwilder and Hank Grishhold. He had done all the coordinating with Drew about the payment of the $2 billion to the LLO, and if the President wanted the man invited to the trade summit, he should have been the one to issue the invitation, not the Chief of Staff.

And now he had been left completely in the dark about this development concerning Carson Jeffers. There wasn't anything he could do until the call was completed, but he had to make sure that Jeffers never spoke to the President alone. Jason wondered if anyone suspected what his true involvement in the terrorist action really was. He doubted it.

When Hank picked up the phone, the call was already being traced. Seconds later, the Secret Service had identified the location of the phone booth at the Coronado General Aviation Airport. Having received instructions just to establish the location, no agents would be dispatched until the Chief of Staff, Hank Grishhold, so instructed.

"President Attwilder's office," Hank answered into the mouthpiece.

"Hank, is that you?" Carson asked from the phone booth located next to the small terminal at Coronado.

"It is. You better make this good. I only told the President about this call a few minutes ago, and he was extremely reluctant to even talk to you. I'll put him on."

President Rolland Attwilder took the phone from his Chief of Staff, and then answered in an authoritative voice, "This is the President. Carson, I demand that you turn yourself in. Whatever it is that you want to discuss with me can wait until we talk face to face."

This was exactly what Carson had hoped for. He had considered telling President Attwilder about his suspicions concerning the Vice President, but he doubted that they would be believed when they were being made from some out of the way phone booth. "Mr. President, that is exactly what I would like to do. I would be more than happy to turn myself in." He paused noticeably, and then added, "On one condition."

President Attwilder was losing his patience. "And what condition would that be?"

Carson glanced at Nichole standing beside him in the phone booth and thought he should have consulted her before he agreed to give themselves up. But the decision was made, for better or worse. In a level tone of voice, he answered, "We will turn ourselves in to whoever you appoint as long as Hank Grishhold comes along."

President Attwilder realized that this was not an abnormal request. In the event that Carson was in fact innocent of the allegations that had been leveled at him, which the President firmly doubted, then he would have some assurance that he would in fact be brought to see the

President himself. If, on the other hand, he and the Lewis woman were guilty, then he would want the same measure of protection. "I agree," the President answered.

Neither Hank nor the Vice President had heard the other side of the conversation.

"Carson, I'll put Hank back on the phone, and you can let him know where to pick you up. By the way, where are you?"

"Coronado Airport in Albuquerque, Mr. President."

"Carson, did I understand you to say that you are turning yourself in?" Hank asked.

"You did, on the condition that you pick us up. Will you do it?"

"Tell me where you are."

Carson repeated what he had just told the President of the United States.

Turning to the President to get approval for what he was offering, he said, "I'll get the President's helicopter and be there in a matter of minutes."

President Attwilder nodded his approval of the arrangements.

"Hank," Carson said, "This LLO affair is not over. Be careful. There are people around you that can't be trusted."

"What are you talking about?" the Chief of Staff asked.

"I'll explain everything after you land," he said and then hung up the phone.

Turning to Nichole, Carson said, "We have to turn ourselves in. I used to think we could just find out the answers to what was happening and then start over. It's not possible. Remember when we decided to choose the third option -the *D&R Selection?*"

"What you explained before we left Washington?" she asked.

"In order for us to use this option, we must first discover who is pulling the strings, and then reverse the roles. The only chance we have of doing this is to turn ourselves in to the President."

"You'll get no objection from me."

• • •

"What is going on?" the Vice President asked as Hank hung up the phone.

Turning to face the Vice President, Hank said, "Carson Jeffers and Nichole Lewis are going to turn themselves in. I'm arranging to pick them up in just a few minutes."

Vice President Wright suddenly realized things couldn't have transpired any better. "I'll take care of it. Where are they at?"

Hank suddenly noted that the Vice President was planning on taking over the apprehension. "There is one condition that Carson demanded and the President agreed to."

"Which is?" asked Vice President Wright.

"Carson Jeffers and Nichole Lewis will only turn themselves into me. I'm going with you when you pick them up."

"That won't be necessary, Hank. I can handle it."

President Attwilder had been quiet during the exchange but now interrupted, "I gave the man my word. Hank is going. We'll see what he has to say when we get him back here. Jason, take Hank with you in the chopper. It's part of the deal."

Vice President Wright knew that he was left with no alternative, but he was already plotting how to either destroy Carson Jeffers himself or at the least destroy his credibility.

•   •   •

A cool breeze had now turned into a cold gale on the mountain overlooking the President's ranch. Esteban zipped up his coat and focused the field glasses on the compound. The coming storm had lowered the temperature all over the area. There was smoke now coming from the fireplace at the ranch. Scanning the windows of the President's ranch house, Esteban noticed a few lights going on as the sky darkened. Suddenly, he noticed a group of people running for the chopper parked on the helipad behind the house.

Focusing the glasses tighter on the group, Esteban swore in Spanish, "Hijo de Puta, a donde va nuestro Vice Presidente ahora?"

50

Exactly twenty-eight minutes passed from the time Carson hung up the phone until he heard the flutter from the rotors on the Presidential helicopter. Everything seemed to happen at once. The moment the chopper sat down on the taxiway of Coronado Airport, a dozen Secret Service agents ran from the side door. Some of the men were carrying shotguns while others had high caliber pistols. Carson and Nichole stood by the phone booth as the troops surrounded them. Not sure why he was thinking about Nichole's shotgun, Carson almost wished he had picked up the weapon from the rear seat of the Seneca. Carson wrapped his arms around Nichole, trying to protect her from the wind caused by the helicopter blades. Rain was starting to fall, and the sky was getting darker by the minute. Suddenly, Vice President Jason Wright and Hank Grishhold stepped down from the helicopter. Carson heard the Vice President say something to Hank.

"Stay here, Hank. Carson sees you, but we don't want to take any chances. I'll handle it now," Vice President Wright said, moving down the steps in front of the Chief of Staff.

Hank felt something was wrong, but he couldn't put his finger on what it was. He had received an order from the Vice President to stay where he was. He paused momentarily in the doorway of the giant green helicopter and then rushed forward to catch up to Jason Wright.

With the sound of the whirling rotors and the falling rain, Jason Wright hadn't heard Hank running across the tarmac. From his pocket, Jason pulled out a small snub nosed .38 caliber pistol, oftentimes referred to as a Saturday Night Special. Jason Wright was now less than twenty feet from the phone booth. Yelling in the wind, the Vice President started to raise the pistol while yelling, "He's got a gun!"

Carson moved his right hand in an unconscious gesture, pushing the brown hair of his head back across his head. His left arm remained tight around Nichole's shoulder.

Hank saw Carson move and recognized the movement for what it was. He had seen his friend brush his hair back literally thousands of times in the past twenty years. There was no gun. Leaping through the air, Hank hit the Vice President's arm at the same time as the pistol exploded.

Nichole screamed as she saw the Vice President of the United States fire his weapon in the wind.

Carson recognized what Jason Wright was doing and pulled Nichole to the ground with his left arm, just as Hank hit the Vice President from the rear. None of the Secret Service agents had spotted the gun that Vice President Wright had supposedly seen. Their weapons were aimed and ready to fire. The glass of the phone booth exploded at the same time as Carson and Nichole hit the ground.

"Mr. Vice President, what in God's name were you doing?" Hank said as he helped the man to his feet.

"Hank, Carson was pulling a gun from behind his head. He almost killed someone else."

"Mr. Vice President, there's no gun. Carson was just brushing his hand through his hair." Assured that the immediate danger had passed, the Chief of Staff ran over to Carson and Nichole. "Are you two all right?"

"We're OK," Carson answered, helping Nichole back to her feet. "Why is the Vice President here?"

Hank didn't answer him; instead he turned to the agents who were now less than a few feet from the two fugitives. "It's all right. They're not armed."

Vice President Wright had hoped that he could kill Carson and the woman while claiming they were trying to escape. When he saw Carson move his hand, he actually thought for a moment that there might have been a gun. "If only Hank hadn't been here, they would both be dead by now," he thought.

"Come with me," Hank said, pulling Carson and Nichole along beside him toward the helicopter."

Carson did as he was instructed, maintaining eye contact with the Vice President until they had both boarded the aircraft.

Under instructions from the Vice President, a government agent started to cuff Carson and Nichole but was waved off by Hank. "I'll take full responsibility for the two of them. They are not armed." Turning to Carson and Nichole, he said, "I'm sorry about what just happened. It was a mistake, almost a tragic one, but a mistake, nevertheless."

Both Carson and Nichole knew otherwise. Any doubts either of them had about Jason Wright's involvement in the LLO had just been erased. Carson wasn't going to try to explain it all to Hank now. It would all become clear when they met with President Attwilder. Keeping a close surveillance on the actions of the Vice President who was seated across the aisle, Carson leaned closer to Nichole and asked, "Do you still have the computer disk?"

Nichole gave a feeble attempt at a smile and whispered, "It's in my coat pocket. Do you think it will help?"

"It's all we've got. Let's hope it's enough," Carson answered as he pulled her close to him.

• • •

Esteban heard the wind starting to howl through the thin camper shell that covered the back of the pick-up. Placing the missile in the bracket he had fastened in the back of the truck, he fastened down the clamps. It had been relatively easy to construct a simple system to hold the missile in place. Using 2 x 4's bolted to each side of the five foot bed, he had then secured the housing of the missile across the three planks. The Stinger missile was now pointed, right through the front windshield of the truck, aiming straight over the hood. Tugging on the missile and the planks to insure they wouldn't rattle loose on the journey down the mountain, he felt confident of the construction.

"Only one more thing to check," he thought to himself. Silently he pulled out the electronic device no larger than a remote control for a television, which in fact it was. Pressing the power button, he saw the small red light on the side of the missile turn red. No problem. He pushed the power button on the device a second time, and the light went out.

Before climbing out of the confined space, he placed several empty boxes around the missile and then covered everything with light blankets. On top of the blankets, he threw some clothes, a back pack, and a bag of potato chips. To the casual observer, the back of the truck was filled with camping equipment. They couldn't have been more wrong.

The sky was getting darker by the minute, and the intermittent rain had become steady. Standing beside the truck, he knew he would have to soon start down the mountain. He hoped that the Vice President returned soon. After the helicopter left, he realized that none of the people he saw get on the helicopter had any bags or briefcases. Wherever the helicopter was going, it was certain to be a short trip.

He thought he saw something out of the corner of his eye and quickly raised the binoculars to his face. There it was. The helicopter was landing on the helipad again. Concentrating on the aircraft, he watched the side door open. Four people led the group off the aircraft. He recognized three of them. Vice President Jason Wright was the first one off, followed by a man and a woman, Carson Jeffers and Nichole Lewis. The fourth person was familiar, but he couldn't put a name to the face. He had seen him in the news several times.

Swearing silently to himself, he now understood what had happened. It had been a set-up from the very beginning. Carson Jeffers and Nichole Lewis were working for the government. Why else would they just be walking off a presidential helicopter with the Vice President. Jason Wright must have been supplying them with information. Jeffers and the woman were always just far enough ahead of him to keep the hunt real, but in fact, Esteban now understood that Carson had never been the target, but rather the hunter.

Getting into the cab of the truck, he wished The Cleaner were here and he could finish everything with one quick push of the finger. He would take care of him later. Putting the remote control housing in his coat pocket, Esteban checked to see that the CIA credentials of Ethan Mabrey, along with the specially encrypted Presidential Seal, were on the seat of the truck. They were.

•   •   •

Hank had wanted to ask Carson what was going on, but had decided to wait until they got back to the ranch. After seeing his friend, he knew he was not a terrorist. How he got involved in this bizarre operation was beyond his comprehension. Remembering Vice President Wright's actions at the small Albuquerque airport, Hank considered Carson and Nichole lucky to still be alive. A near mistake on the part of Jason Wright, and this meeting would never be taking place.

President Attwilder motioned for the two Secret Service agents, who had followed the group into the house to wait in the foyer. When Hank and the others returned to the ranch, the President had been speaking privately with Drew Matthews concerning the upcoming trade summit. The more he thought about it, the more President Attwilder thought that Drew should be apprised of the total plan.

"Do you want me to leave, Mr. President?" Drew asked as the group of three men and one woman entered the large western study.

"I don't think that's necessary, Drew," the President said as he dropped another log in the fireplace. "Whatever Mr. Jeffers has to say concerns all of us, and that includes you."

Jason Wright looked at the distinguished business leader and wondered what they had been discussing in his absence. Whatever happened in the next few minutes, he knew that he had to destroy the credibility of Carson Jeffers and Nichole Lewis. As he thought about it, his actions at the airport might not even be mentioned.

Hank moved in front of the large glass windows facing the freestanding fireplace. President Attwilder had a small library on the back side of the rock fireplace, but now everyone was in the study itself. Carson and Nichole were still standing by the large conference table, facing the rest of the group.

President Attwilder spoke, while at the same time using his hand to indicate that they could take a seat at the table. Neither of them did so. "Carson, I have wanted to believe from the beginning that you weren't part of this insidious plot to destroy our country, but I have to admit that I find it harder and harder to do so."

Carson knew that he was not going to have much of a chance to convince the President that he was innocent before the Chief Executive lost patience, and locked up both himself and Nichole. He wondered what Drew Matthews was doing at the ranch. They had never personally met, but Carson was well aware of his involvement in American business and that he was, in fact, the chairman of the American Alliance. Nichole deferred any explanation to Carson.

"Mr. President, let me start by saying that everything is not as you have been led to believe. Neither myself nor Miss Lewis are members of the LLO, nor have we ever been such. In the past two weeks we have inadvertently become entwined in a plot to destroy the United States, a plot so twisted that it wasn't until early this morning that we understood what was happening."

The Vice President interrupted. "This is not getting us anywhere, Mr. President. Let me take these two and get a statement, after which we'll see if what they say is true."

President Attwilder knew that it would take some time to debrief the two of them, but he wanted to hear what Carson was getting to. Holding up his hand to quiet the Vice President, he said, "Go on. You have my attention, and, I'm sure, that of everyone else in the room."

Jason was losing control, and unless he could get Jeffers and the woman separated, everything was going to come apart. Glancing across the room at Drew Matthews, he saw that the executive was listening intently to what Carson was saying.

Nichole reached in her coat pocket and removed the small three-and-a-half inch computer disk and handed it to Carson.

Taking the disk, Carson started speaking again, "Mr. President, just over two weeks ago I was returning from a ski trip to Park City with my son. Minutes after take-off the plane crashed, and, as you are well aware, most of the crew and passengers were killed, my son among them. Miss Lewis and myself were two of the survivors."

President Attwilder nodded. "Go on."

"Everything started with an unexpected interrogation by two FBI agents in the Omega hanger."

"Carson, we are all aware of the separate plane crashes and the use of the Stinger missiles by the LLO. Please get to the point of how you became involved," The President demanded.

Carson could see that he wasn't going to have time to explain everything that had happened during the past two weeks, and he wasn't sure that he could do so anyway. He decided that he had to get to the computer disk and the information that it contained. Holding up the disk that Nichole had just handed him, he said, "This computer disk contains crucial information taken from the computer of one Ethan Mabry, better known as Esteban Moreno. Esteban Moreno was, in fact, the terrorist that fired at least two of the Stinger missiles. We followed him to a home on Dana Point in California, where you will find the body of a close friend of mine, Blake Terry. Before Esteban Moreno escaped from the house, he was using a computer." Turning to Nichole, Carson continued, "Nichole was able to recover the data that Esteban had been working on."

Everyone in the room was paying attention to what Carson was saying, including Drew Matthews.

"With the help of Michael Randall, a trusted friend, we found out what was so important about this file. It contains a list of overseas accounts that originally had in excess of $12 billion. In addition, the disk contains information detailing planned terrorist attacks on twelve additional U.S. cities. These attacks were to take place tomorrow morning."

"The missiles have all been destroyed," interrupted the Vice President. "None of this information is new. The man is just trying to find a way out for himself and the woman."

Hank knew he was out of place but said, "Let him finish."

"Go on," President Attwilder said, agreeing with his Chief of Staff.

"The Vice President is correct," Carson said. "The night before last, the remaining missiles were destroyed outside the Los Angeles Airport. I was there, and, in fact, used one of the Stinger missiles to destroy a blue van driven by the terrorists as they exited a long term parking structure."

"All of this was in the papers," shouted the Vice President.

"Jason, I'll tell you only one more time. Let the man finish!" President Attwilder said, raising his voice to reprimand his second in command.

"Back to what's contained on this disk, and what I firmly believe has taken place. The $12 billion is money that was deposited in the accounts within the past two weeks. At first, I didn't have any idea where the money was coming from, and then early this morning I called Michael Randall and had him access the accounts and check where the deposits originated from. I won't explain how he did this, but trust me, my information is accurate. Each and every deposit made into the accounts were made from international brokerage houses. The first deposits were made when the terrorist attacks were made public."

Carson looked at Drew Matthews, and thought that he understood what had happened, but he needed to explain it to both Hank and the President. "Someone was running a stock manipulation plan that netted over $12 billion in profits. Whoever was behind this scheme knew that by destroying the American airline industry, it would have a domino effect in the stock market. They then shorted stocks across the board, concentrating on those hit hardest and first, the airline stocks. I'm sure you understand that when you short a stock, you are betting that the price will go down, and the farther it drops, the more you make. That is just what happened here."

President Attwilder was astonished. Carson might just be telling the truth. "If what you say is true, then why the ransom demand for $2 billion?"

"If you agreed to pay the money, the perpetrators of this plan would collect that money, too, but the ransom was really immaterial to the whole plan. I also believe, Mr. President, that Esteban Moreno got out of control. The proposed attacks on the other 11 planes were really not part of the original plan. If I could put myself in the place of these economic terrorists, which is what they really are, I doubt they ever planned on shooting down another plane. They wanted the stock market to rebound, and then they could use an option strategy and make money when the stocks increased in value."

"Could this really be true?" asked President Attwilder.

Drew had been following the explanation and realized that Carson Jeffers had figured out the entire operation. "It would work just the way he said," remarked the business leader.

"What about the money?" asked the President, speaking to Carson. "You said it used to be in the accounts. Where is it now?"

"I took it. Right now, I won't try to explain how, but rest assured that I have it. And Mr. President, there is a list of phone numbers on the disk. All but one of these numbers belong to international business operations."

"And the one number that doesn't?" asked the President.

Carson turned to the Vice President of the United States and said, "The number rings straight through to the office of Vice President Wright!"

•   •   •

The rain drops sounded like a chorus of drummers on the top of the truck as Esteban pulled up to the sentry at the gate of the Presidential Compound. Rolling down the window, Esteban handed the secret service agent his CIA credentials along with the Presidential Seal. "The President is expecting me."

"Just a minute, sir. I'll need to verify this authorization." Looking Esteban clearly in the face to insure that he could remember his face, he walked into the sentry shack. He had only seen a Presidential Seal a couple of times, but he had been trained on the procedure. Using the computer, he punched in the authorization code on the seal and waited for the computer to give him final instructions. Seconds later, Esteban's picture flashed on the screen, along with the needed authorization.

"Sorry, you had to wait, Mr. Mabry. But I'm sure you understand the need to check everything out," the agent said. "Been camping?"

"Just for a few days, but the weather hasn't been too accommodating," Esteban answered, realizing that the man had looked in the back of the truck.

"You can park your truck anywhere in the compound. Just check in with either of the agents at the ranch house."

"Is it all right if I park under those trees over there?" Esteban asked, pointing to a stand of pines across the compound from the ranch house.

"That'll be fine, Mr. Mabry."

Esteban drove into the yard and then backed under the trees, the hood of the truck pointed directly at the window where the group of men were speaking. Through the rain, he couldn't see who was who, but he had no doubt that it was the Vice President and guests. By the animation of their body language, he could tell that some of the people were raising their voices.

Before stepping out of the truck into the rain, he checked the remote device and pushed the *power* button. Sliding open the rear window of the cab, he could see the red light appear under the blanket. He pushed the *channel up* button, and a second red light appeared. Listening quietly, he knew that the missile was locked onto the flames in the fireplace across the compound. All he had to do now was to punch the *enter* button.

"Can I help you, sir?" the agent at the desk asked as Esteban shook off the rain from his coat.

Esteban handed him the same CIA credentials he had shown the man at the front gate. He had known the authorization would still be in the computer. After all, why would the Vice President have erased it when Esteban Moreno was supposedly killed in an exploding van? As the agent entered the data, he saw the second agent standing by the closed door leading to the room with the fireplace. Removing his jacket, he took hold of the end of the silenced .44 magnum pistol and fired twice through the fabric. The agent by the door slumped to the ground as the second bullet entered the head of the agent at the computer. Esteban walked over to the door and shot the man a second time through the side of the head, and then repeated the action for the man slumped over the computer. When he left the ranch he would use one of the cars parked in the yard. He had wired the remote so that it would send from the other side of the gate.

Opening the door to the President's office, he stepped into the room and suddenly realized it would all be finished when he drove away.

Pointing his gun at the group, he said, "Everyone stay where you are. No one move!"

"Esteban! What are you doing here?" Drew asked.

"You know this man?" asked the President.

It all suddenly made sense to Carson. He had been trying to figure out who The Cleaner was and kept coming up with a blank. Then he understood who could have masterminded this entire operation. It wasn't the Vice President, and it certainly wasn't Esteban Moreno. The person driving the van must have been Ricardo Gutierrez. Esteban hadn't died in Los Angeles.

"Everyone shut up." Calling The Cleaner by his given name, Esteban said, "Drew, you should never have tried to double cross me. You know I would have let you live, but that is impossible now." Esteban knew that he needed to get the attention of the group. Aiming his pistol at Drew's right knee, he fired. Drew cried out and slumped to the floor.

Carson had stepped closer to Nichole, who was shaking uncontrollably. After everything they had gone through together, it was going to end in her death after all. He had his right hand in his Levi pocket and was fingering a small red knife that had the name Neil printed on it. Apparently, Nichole's father had gotten the knife in Switzerland and had left the one and one half inch item in the coat pocket. It wouldn't do any good now.

President Attwilder realized that everything that Carson had been telling them was true, and most importantly he understood how foolish he had been to surround himself with people like Jason Wright and Drew Matthews.

"Mr. President, I'm sure you're wondering what is really going on," Esteban said. "Before you all die, you will have the chance to ask your good Vice President how he was able to finance his campaigns. You'll find that Drew, here, has bankrolled him for almost fifteen years. I'm sorry to have to inform you, but your Vice President has never been Jason Wright. Drew Matthews has pulled the strings from the beginning." Walking over to the bleeding man on the floor, he said, "Drew, I want you to know that the money was never as important to me as it was to you."

Jason Wright had slowly been moving toward the door. He had left his small .38 caliber pistol in the coat pocket of his wet raincoat still hanging on the coat tree. If he could make it to the coat, he might have a chance.

Esteban pointed the gun directly at Jason's heart and said, "Move one more step, Jason, and the next bullet will put an abrupt end to your breathing. Now, let's see how we are going to handle this."

Removing a small roll of gray duct tape from his coat pocket, he tossed it to the Vice President. "Everyone please sit at the chairs around the table. Jason, would you be so kind as to pull The Cleaner up to the table?"

The Vice President did as he was instructed.

"Tape their hands together, and then tape everyone back to back so the chairs can't go anywhere. And you can start with Carson Jeffers and the woman."

Jason did as he was told, beginning with Carson and Nichole. As soon as he was finished, he taped the President and Hank together. Finally, he pulled the whimpering Drew Matthews up to the table and taped him to a chair. "Maybe I'll leave with Esteban," he thought.

Such was not to be the case. "Sit in that chair." Esteban ordered.

Jason knew better than to argue. He had seen what had just happened to Drew. Less than a minute later Esteban finished taping Drew and the Vice President together. "I would like to stay and chat, but I'm sure you will all understand the necessity of my leaving. But, just so that you won't wonder what is about to happen to you, let me be brief." Taking the remote control device from his pocket, he explained, "Parked on the opposite side of the ranch yard is a white pick-up truck. Go ahead and look out the window. I'm sure you can all see it. Before Mr. Jeffers so callously attempted to end my life in the parking structure, I removed a single Stinger missile. It is now mounted in a special bracket in the back of that truck. This little device has been rewired to perform three functions. The first two have already been completed. The power to the missile is on, and is now locked on to the heat from the fireplace that President Attwilder so kindly furnished."

"You will never get away with this!" exclaimed the President.

"Oh, but I will. You see I am not going to fire the missile until I have exited the gate in one of your cars. When I press this *enter* button, the explosion will center all attention on the house, and for all practical purposes I died in Los Angeles. You see, I will get away with it, and there will be no one left to dispute the fact."

Carson had been using the small Swiss army knife to cut through the tape that was binding him to the chair. He was almost finished. All he could hope for was that Esteban kept talking.

"Enjoy the rest of your afternoon, I'm sure I will," Esteban said as he closed the door to the study.

He had forgotten to find the keys to one of the cars. Stopping at the first dead agent who was leaning against the bottom of the wall in the foyer, Esteban carefully searched his pockets. Nothing. The other agent must have kept the keys.

Carson cut through the last strand of tape holding his hands together. Rushing, he quickly cut the gray strap still binding Nichole to the chair. "Get the President and Hank. I'm going after Esteban," he told her in as quiet of voice as he could. "Take this knife."

Nichole ran down the room and crossed to the other side of the table. Quickly, she started slicing through the tape holding the President of the United States and his Chief of Staff.

Esteban heard the door open just as he was taking the car keys labeled with a government license plate number from the right pants pocket of the dead man who had bled on the computer. He had placed the .44 caliber pistol on the desk. The remote control device was still in his hand.

Carson ran across the room leaping in the air some six feet before he reached the computer. The brunt of the force was absorbed by the dead man, but it knocked the gun to the floor behind the desk. Carson used his left arm to grab Esteban by the neck while hitting him across the jaw with his right elbow. Esteban's head seemed to jerk momentarily, and then the pony-tailed Latin pulled Carson to the floor in front of the desk.

Both men struggled to gain control of the other. Esteban searched for the pistol, keeping the remote in his left hand.

Carson saw the silencer sticking out behind the wood paneling and gave the desk a kick. The pistol went flying across the room as Carson tried to grab the remote device from Esteban's hand.

Pulling himself halfway to his feet, Esteban tried to work his way to the pistol now laying ten feet away.

Using all the energy he could gather, Carson pulled the man back towards the desk. With a movement of his foot, he kicked the Latin in the right shin with the toe of his hiking boot. Together the two men slammed into the desk, knocking the computer to the floor. The noise had alerted two Secret Service men who were in the yard, and they came through the door just as Carson fell to the floor, Esteban landing on top of him.

"You should never have gotten involved, Jeffers!" Esteban snarled, while catching the movement of the two agents coming across the room. Raising the remote above his head, he said, "I'll see you in hell."

Esteban pushed the *enter* button on the remote, while still staring at Carson lying on the floor. The explosion seemed to happen almost simultaneously, even though it took almost a second for the missile to enter the window of the study. It exploded just in front of the fireplace, sending rock and debris flying in all directions. A piece of flying shrapnel caught Esteban just above the neck, severing his head from his torso, blood streaming in all directions. The two Secret Service agents were killed instantly, one caught with a piece of the rock fireplace, and the other had his head smashed against the wall.

"I can't be alive," Carson thought, wiping his eyes clear. He moved the desk from his body and saw what remained of Esteban Moreno. The force of the blast had tipped the desk over on top of Carson, protecting him from the rest of the flying debris. Bloody and bruised, he got up from the floor and walked into where the study had been. Surveying the carnage, he saw what remained of two bodies still taped together, after having been blown all the way across the room. Walking closer he tried to recognize who they were. It wasn't the President and Hank, as the

President had been wearing boots, and neither of the two men had boots on their feet.

"I'm sorry, Nichole," he cried, looking for what he knew could only be her body. Slowly, he turned his head to a sound coming from the back side of what remained of the rock fireplace. Rushing across the rock and rubble, he started moving boards and furniture.

"Down here," he heard. It sounded like Hank's voice. Carson worked harder, throwing smaller pieces of wood everywhere. From his back, he heard several people coming to help in the rescue effort.

Tears streamed down Carson's face as he saw the three bodies lying next to the base of the fireplace. President Attwilder was the first to stand, followed by Hank, and then Nichole stood and looked at Carson.

He rushed to her side and took her head in his wet hands. "Thank God you're alive," he said.

"God had something to do with it, but President Attwilder definitely helped," she answered, kissing his cheek. "He pulled both Hank and I to the floor as you left the room."

President Attwilder spoke for the first time. "I thought it more prudent to get out of harm's way than to release those two," he said, pointing to the two bodies Carson had first seen when he entered the room.

EPILOGUE

SWAN LAKE

On the deck of the hunting lodge, the breeze coming off the Swan range felt cool and refreshing. Michael had gone back to Portland earlier that morning, and Carson and Nichole now had the place to themselves.

"It's the same story in all the papers," Carson said as Nichole put down the copy of the *USA Today* they had picked up when they dropped Michael off at the Kalispell airport.

Nichole laid the paper on top of *The Wall Street Journal* and *The Los Angeles Times* and smiled at Carson. "Is it really finished?" she asked.

Carson got up from his chair on the deck and walked over to the small stack of newspapers. Glancing down at the papers, he looked out over the Montana landscape. Before answering, he thought of how remarkable the speed of the economic recovery of the country was. It was only Thursday morning, and the stock market was only down less than one hundred points from where it had been less than three weeks ago. Someday he would try and figure that one out, but now it just didn't seem important. Turning to Nichole, he said, "Yes, it's over."

Nichole came and stood next to Carson as he leaned against the log rail. "Will the country buy it?" she asked referring to the headline on *USA Today*?

Picking up the paper, he read, "VICE PRESIDENT WRIGHT DIES IN FINAL TERRORIST ATTACK." Scanning the first part of the article, he answered, "The country will believe it because they want to."

"Vice President Jason Wright was killed in a thwarted terrorist

attack at President Attwilder's ranch in Santa Fe, New Mexico. The Vice President was to attend a trade summit being held at the President's ranch on Monday. An investigation has revealed that the terrorist, Esteban Moreno, had not died in Los Angeles as earlier reported. In a final act of revenge, Esteban Moreno used a Stinger missile in an attempt to kill both the President and the Vice President of the United States. The Vice President sacrificed his life trying to apprehend the terrorist, Esteban Moreno. Both men died when the missile exploded. The distinguished chairman of the American Alliance, Drew Matthews, had just arrived to attend the trade summit, and was killed in the same explosion.

"As a note of interest: President Attwilder has revealed that Carson Jeffers and Nichole Lewis were responsible for the success of the operation. They had been working undercover for the Vice President..."

Nichole handed Carson the letter she had been reading along with the newspapers. "I guess it really is over."

Carson reread the final paragraph of the letter:

"The 12 billion dollars has been used as restitution for the victims and to make your company whole again. I hope that the amounts we have remitted will, at least in a small way, help make up for your losses and suffering. You have my personal thanks, as well as the gratitude of the American people. I trust that we can remain friends. Again my heart-felt wishes for your happiness."

Sincerely,

Rolland Attwilder
President of the United States of America